I0689699

SONG OF THE SHIELDMAIDEN

ASHLEY HAGOOD

ARROW HEART PRESS

Song of the Shieldmaiden by Ashley Hagood

Copyright © 2023 Ashley Hagood

All rights reserved. No portion of this book may be reproduced in any form without permission from the author.

PUBLISHER'S NOTE: This is a work of fiction. Any references to historical people, events, places, organizations, and establishments are the product of the author's imagination or are used fictitiously. Any resemblance to living persons is purely coincidental.

Cover art by Ashley Hagood

Published by Arrow Heart Press

https://www.ashleyhagood.com

Created with Vellum

For my husband, mi vida, who makes all my dreams possible

PART I

CHAPTER 1

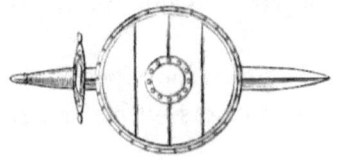

SVANHILD

S vanhild swung the sword, hitting the practice pell right above its straw thigh. She cursed. It was not where she wanted the blow to land.

Sweat plastered her dark blonde hair to her forehead. As the night grew colder, her breath came out in clouds. Her body steamed like water vapor from a hot kettle, yet still she battled on.

Across the yard, a door was open to the longhouse. Light streamed out from the grand hearth within. Svanhild heard a cacophony of familiar sounds inside—the voices of her family, the sloshing of ale horns, the friendly taunts and laughter of the warriors just home from their latest journey across the sea.

It was the end of summer, a time of celebration.

The smell of roasted meat and fresh bread made Svanhild's stomach growl. But she could not stop now. She still could not land a hard blow against the pell after spinning.

Knowing that someday she would feel the surprise of an enemy behind her, she wanted to master this move.

She had to be prepared for anything if she was to be a shieldmaiden. She needed to prove herself. If she succeeded, skalds would sing songs of her bravery, and when it was her time to leave this realm, Odin would welcome her into Valhalla.

This time next summer, she hoped to go raiding with her father and his loyal warriors—if her family allowed her, of course.

She let out a battle cry, spinning with her sword outstretched. The edge of it lodged into the straw practice pell, but it was not enough force to stir many needles.

"Hold the sword tight to your body, until you are ready to strike."

The familiar voice made her stop. She turned to see her father, Jarl Tove, standing between her and the longhouse, a horn of mead in one hand. He wore his best fur-trimmed cape tonight, his long brown beard knotted and adorned with silver rings. He made a formidable shadow against the light from within the hall behind him.

Even in the darkness, Svanhild saw his twinkling eyes. She smiled. Whatever revelries he had been enjoying with their family and his warriors inside, he was taking time to come and watch her train. As he always did.

"Show me," Svanhild said, thrusting the sword hilt out to him.

They exchanged mead for training sword. Svanhild took a sip from the horn while her father got into position. The mead was sweet tonight, like berries and honey. As she watched Father swing the sword at the straw man, she took another gulp from the horn. She had not realized how thirsty she was until now.

"Do you see?" Jarl Tove asked. He demonstrated the move

again, holding his sword upright before him as he whirled around to face the practice pell. Then, just as swiftly, he jabbed the sword directly into the stomach of the straw man. "Swords are made for slicing, not stabbing, but that is how we take the enemy by surprise."

Though Svanhild would have enjoyed more mead, her fingers itched for the sword again. "Let me try," she said, hurrying to return her father's ale horn to him.

Once the sword was back in her grasp, she faced away from the training pell. She tried to mimic her father's move, holding the sword flat in front of her face. Then, she twirled as fast as she could. The moonlit world of the training yard swirled around her.

"Hold the momentum inside your core," Father said.

She held her breath as she spun. As soon as the straw man swam into her vision, she slammed her boot into the ground and lunged forward, sword pointing out from her waist. The tip of the blade dug into the straw with a satisfying crunch.

Her father whistled his approval. The sound made Svanhild glow inside.

"What are you two doing out here?" came another voice.

"Hello, Mother," they both said at the same time, then laughed.

Svanhild's mother, Helga, stood in the light of the longhouse door. She wore an embroidered red dress, her thick golden hair braided and swept over one shoulder so it hung in front of her. Despite her status as the jarl's wife, she wore only a simple necklace set with a delicate green stone—not nearly as much as she could be wearing, given the treasure the men had brought back from their travels.

"Come in from the cold," she called to her husband. "Your people dislike getting drunk without your example."

Tove returned to her, giving her a kiss on the cheek. He

stroked her braid, probably a little drunk already. "Whatever you say, my shieldmaiden."

Helga laughed, shaking her head at him. "It's been too many winters since I last held a shield."

"You will always be a shieldmaiden to me." The jarl kissed his wife again, this time on her long neck.

Svanhild made a face at them to get them to stop, though she didn't really mind. Her parents were always particularly affectionate after her father returned from his summer travels.

As her parents headed back to the feast, Helga called over her shoulder, "You're coming too, Svanhild."

Sighing, Svanhild lay her training sword next to the pell and followed them into the building.

Inside the sprawling main hall, the air was thick with smoke and the smell of roasted meat. Wooden tables ran the length of the room, with benches and stools where men and women sat together, flirting and sipping their mead. Everyone feasted on plates of goat meat, roasted vegetables, and bread twisted into the shape of elaborate knots.

At the center of the festivities, a fire roared in the hearth, making faces flush and sweat form on the brows of those who had drunk the most. The smoke drifted into the rafters, disappearing out smoke holes in the roof. Svanhild glimpsed moonlight there. As happy as she was to be with her family now, she wished she could be out in the fresh air, sword in hand.

Shaking off the thought, she joined her family at the jarl's table. Positioned at the end of the hall, it faced the rest of the longhouse so they could look upon their people. Jarl Tove and Helga sat together in large chairs at the center of the table. They were already flanked by their two other daughters, Svanhild's younger sisters.

"How fast can you eat?" Svanhild teased Brynja, the youngest of the brood, whose plate was already empty.

Her sister peered at her through her curtain of shimmering brown hair. "It's only my first plate," she insisted, smiling a little. Though she was easily the most beautiful of the three sisters, Brynja hid her gaze behind her lashes and seemed overly occupied with her food.

Nearby, a group of warriors eyed Brynja, nudging each other as if to see who would dare approach her. Svanhild wasn't surprised. Half the men in the village had been waiting for Brynja Tovesdotter to reach marrying age. Yet now that she had, no one seemed to have the courage to approach her—especially as she sat right beside her father, the king of the land.

"You have admirers," she pointed out.

Brynja blushed and stuck her tongue out at Svanhild, making them both laugh.

Svanhild moved around the far side of the table to sit beside Haldis, the middle sister. Tonight, Haldis wore a hood to hide her all-white eye and red rash from company, even though everyone in the village had seen these features at some point. Her long, straight hair streamed out the sides of the hood, pale as moonlight. With her seeing eye she scanned the room, watching everyone, observing everything.

"How is the feast so far?" Svanhild asked.

Her sister glanced at her from beneath her hood. "I see you wore your best dress to sword practice."

Svanhild laughed. Though Haldis's high-pitched voice always sounded lost in dreams, Svanhild had learned to read when her sister was teasing her. The voice only made it more comedic to Svanhild.

"I always train in dresses," she said. "This way, I'm prepared for anything."

"In case you are attacked at a feast?" Haldis said.

7

"Are you still teasing me? Now I can't tell."

Svanhild saw the flash of a smile beneath Haldis's hood. She returned the expression. Then, feeling flushed from her training, she lifted her dress at the shoulders and waved the fabric a few times, generating a breeze beneath the layers of wool and linen. The gown closest to her skin was stuck to her back and sides.

"Perhaps I should have changed into something lighter," she admitted. At least tomorrow she was due for her weekly bath.

A thrall brought her a plate of goat meat, vegetables, and a knot of seasoned bread. She bit into the meat with relish, famished after her training session. When the thrall returned with a horn filled with mead, she gulped it down as quickly as she could, without a thought for what the strong drink might do to her head in a few moments.

Haldis watched her. "Are you trying to pass out as an excuse to go to bed early?"

"That's not a bad idea. If you see a thrall, let's ask for another round."

Haldis laughed. The sound was light as a feather drifting in the breeze—so different than the growl and crackle of the last village völva, who had died last year of old age. But that was what Haldis was training to become: someone who would commune with the gods, cast lots, and tell fortunes. Such work was of special benefit to a jarl, who needed to consult with the gods to lead his people well. But Haldis would also share her gifts with anyone in the village who sought to know the plans of the Norns, the female deities who wove everyone's fate.

Svanhild downed another horn of mead. The sweet flavor was catching up to her, making her even thirstier than before. Still, the drink dulled the aches in her body where training had challenged her. Watching her father's warriors celebrating, sharing stories of their bravery with their wives and children, she felt a pleasant tingling throughout her body.

This was true happiness. Family, friends, warriors home from battle.

And someday, she would be with those men, telling stories of her own.

A man's voice interrupted her peace. "Good lady, may I share this drink with you?"

Svanhild looked over to see a man standing at her end of the table, ale horn raised to toast with her. He had a long red beard, ruffled and unkempt. On his wrist was a bracelet, a chunk clearly missing where he must have paid someone with the silver.

"What makes you approach the daughter of the jarl?" she asked. She was used to invitations from men who wished to woo her, but only during these festivities each summer— after weeks of travel and an abundance of ale—did men approach her quite this drunk and disheveled.

The man swayed a little. His cheeks were almost as red as his hair. "It would honor me to drink with the jarl's daughter. And it would honor me to drink with a woman so beautiful as..." He lifted his horn even higher, raising his voice. "The great... fierce... Svanhild of Kaldvik!"

She heard a few chuckles from a nearby table, where several other warriors were watching this exchange. She wondered why this poor man had chosen to approach her over her sister Brynja. At least Brynja would have turned him away with a blush and a shy smile.

"If you wish to drink with me, you'll need to entertain me," Svanhild said. "Tell me, what is the most difficult battle you have faced so far? If it is grander than *my* greatest battle, I will drink with you."

The man chugged from his horn before answering. "Well,

once I faced..." His eyes seemed to go out of focus for a moment as he thought. "I faced a great black bear, in the forest beyond this village!" He sounded quite proud that he had thought of this story. "I know it was a test from the gods, for it sought me out while I was hunting..."

Svanhild lifted a hand to stop him. "If the hardest battle you've fought is a bear, then I am afraid we must part ways for the night."

Haldis giggled beside her. She felt the eyes of her parents watching this interaction now, too.

"You fought something bigger than a bear?" the man said incredulously.

"Oh, I faced a far greater battle," Svanhild said, "when I was forced, against my will, to weave the tapestry that hangs on that wall." She pointed to a large tapestry nearby, taller than the man and draped across a large part of the wall. It depicted the god Odin leading the Wild Hunt, his horse Sleipnir proudly paving the way through a dark forest; above them, the sky was speckled with stars, and the shadows of two ravens could be seen soaring over the raiders' heads. Svanhild shuddered to remember the weeks of torturous sewing, while their seamstress Ursula hovered over her and rapped her knuckles at every tiny mistake.

The man studied the fabric for a moment, then guffawed so loudly Svanhild nearly dropped her ale horn in surprise. Several people nearby turned toward the noise, and the men who had been watching all laughed along.

"I suppose I will have to try again another night, then," the man said, bowing at the waist to Svanhild. The gesture seemed to unsteady him, for he staggered a step backwards, still chuckling to himself.

Svanhild inclined her head to the man as he took his leave.

Helga clucked her tongue at her daughter. "That was not

your cruelest rejection. You must be in a good mood tonight."

"It was not your cleverest either," Haldis said.

Svanhild shrugged. "I am not trying to best Loki. At least it got rid of him. And look, he's still laughing."

"I think he's too drunk to let anything bother him tonight," said Haldis.

Svanhild nodded in agreement. "Everyone here is happy to be alive. That is what they say battle does. It brings pure joy that cannot be had with a simpler, less courageous life."

Jarl Tove leaned forward to meet his daughter's gaze. "We do not travel just to fight, Svanhild." His amber eyes seemed to shift and flicker in the firelight. Svanhild, knowing this signaled the gods' wisdom working in him, listened more carefully as her father continued, "We fight to protect one another and what is ours. That is the call of a warrior. But with cleverness, we can avoid most fights and gain a new treasure in the process."

Svanhild took her father's bait. "What treasure is that?"

"Respect," said Tove.

Svanhild frowned. Though she had heard this wisdom from Father before, it rankled something inside her. Rather than thinking on it, she said, "It's good I have many years before I become a jarl, then. Perhaps I could be a bodyguard. The more dangerous the post, the better."

"That you would do well," Father laughed.

Rising to his feet then, he called for attention in the hall. His deep voice resonated against the timbers of the long-house, as though he was so much a part of this place, he was inside the walls. The chatter died down as everyone turned to listen. Tove took a moment to look over the crowd, a soft smile on his lips.

Finally, he said, "Nothing brings such a smile to my face

as seeing all of you here in my hall. You are the reason I make this beautiful land my home."

Several men and women lifted their ale horns to toast his words.

"When the gods first brought us to this land, it was cold and barren," Tove continued. "But Kaldvik is a place with a secret magic. The All-Father's ravens make their nests in these forests. Since we arrived here, Freyr has blessed this land with bountiful harvests year after year, for generations. Like me, you have all believed that the gods have a plan for Kaldvik. It is that belief, along with your loyalty and hard work, that has made our lives so rich."

Several people cheered at that. Tove took his wife's hand in his and lifted it in a show of unity. Helga watched him with bright eyes, a smile playing at the corners of her lips. When they lowered their hands back to their sides, Svanhild noticed they kept them linked.

"As many of you know, I met my wife on the battlefield," Tove said. "I saw she had the swiftness of a raven, and I knew she would make a fine wife." He glanced at Helga, smiling. "I was not wrong."

Helga nodded demurely, but Svanhild caught the smile in her mother's eyes at his compliment. Several people in the hall raised their horns and cups to toast the couple, for they knew their jarl had married in a love match and were happy for it.

"Now, I sense the same stirring in my daughter Svanhild. Many of you have seen how she trains with a wooden sword… and scares away marriage proposals."

The people laughed, and Svanhild joined in, for it was true.

"My wish is that my daughter never has to wet her blade with blood, but I cannot ignore the whispers of the gods."

Svanhild's breath caught in her throat. Where was he going with this?

"The goddess Freyja has first pick of fallen warriors on the battlefield," her father said. "As you know, the chosen ones will join her in Fólkvangr, while the remaining half join Odin in Valhalla."

He turned to Svanhild then, his eyes dancing. She raised an eyebrow at him in question, her heart racing as she sensed where this was headed.

"I have no desire for myself or my family to meet the gods yet," Tove admitted, eliciting a few chuckles from the crowd, "but I would rest happy to know that someday, far in the future, my daughter will join Freyja in her hall. That is why, with a father's pride, I announce that my eldest daughter will join us on next summer's journey."

A warmth spread through Svanhild's blood as all eyes turned to her. This was what she had dreamed of, the moment her father would finally invite her to join him on his travels. She smiled at him, unable to keep the excitement from her face.

Jarl Tove lifted his ale horn. "This year will be a year of training for Svanhild. I expect all of you to help me with that. And should the day come when an enemy lifts his blade against my daughter, I trust that every warrior here will protect her, as you have protected me, and as I have protected you."

Svanhild's smile flickered. When a warrior pledged himself to his jarl, he swore to protect him with his life, knowing his jarl would do the same for him. She imagined it would be the same when she was a warrior, yet the way her father worded it, he clearly wanted to shield her from the bloodshed the men experienced.

Haldis leaned toward her and whispered, "Do not worry, sister. Every father is overprotective of his daughters."

Svanhild nodded, keeping the smile on her face as the warriors raised their horns to make their pledge. Many watched her as they did so, smiling warmly. They had seen her grow up. They would protect her on the battlefield, too. Though she did not want any special treatment, she sensed their care for her—and for tonight, that would be enough.

"To Svanhild!" Tove shouted, beaming at his daughter. "May Thor grant you strength and Tyr guide your blade."

Voices shouted, "Skol!" as men and women lifted their ale horns to toast the announcement.

Svanhild lifted her own horn to her lips and drank deeply. In the heat of the hall, filling herself with mead, she was starting to feel dizzy. Part of her longed for fresh air, but now she did not want to leave the feast. Not during such a happy celebration. Not when her dreams of being a shield-maiden finally felt in reach. Not when her heart felt so full.

"Soon we shall have a song from our skald Valí," Father continued, "but first, let us hear a song from our future shieldmaiden."

Svanhild stood as several people whistled in anticipation. Ever since she was a child, she had been singing at these feasts. If she had not dreamed of being a shieldmaiden, she would have wanted to be a skald, for the gods had blessed her with the gift of song.

"Any requests?" she asked.

"I trust your taste," her father replied.

Svanhild had memorized several songs, taught to her by their house's skald. During a celebration like this, she would normally choose a tale of Thor's bravery or a hero's saga. But tonight, something else came to her: a song of the Valkyries, who flew over battlefields to send brave warriors to Fólk-vangr and Valhalla.

"For those who have fallen in battle," she said, and then began to sing.

The hall hushed to silence as her voice wafted into the rafters, the crackling hearthfire her only accompaniment. As she sang, her eyes drifted shut, her mind picturing the scenes as though they were happening in front of her. After a time, she no longer heard her own voice. The words simply flowed through her, a gift from the god Bragi.

Someday, skalds would sing such songs about her, as they would her father before her.

The game was that they had to die first.

CHAPTER 2

HALDIS

$\mathcal{A}$s the celebration wore on, Haldis watched. While men drank mead and kissed thralls—some in full view of their wives—Haldis watched. While women flirted and cuddled close to their warriors, Haldis watched. While her older sister sang a song of the Valkyries, Haldis watched. While her younger sister hid her shy smile from several men who filled her ale horn, Haldis watched.

As a future seer, this was her duty. Yet at some point during her seventeen years of life, the people of Kaldvik had stopped seeing her. They did not want to look on a girl with only one seeing eye.

This invisibility made it easier for her to watch everyone else.

On one side of her face, she was a beauty: soft pale skin, with a brown eye so dark it was nearly black and shone like a polished gemstone. But the other side of her face looked like it had been burned in the fires of Muspell. Some called it the sign of a curse. A deep red rash ran down the left side of her face, where a white orb took the place of a normal eye. This all-white eye was supposed to connect her to the gods, allowing her to see their realm where others could not.

But she had never seen the gods. She was a stranger to Asgard, and she always would be. That, she believed, was her true curse.

Svanhild stirred beside her. Ever since their father's announcement that she would join him on next summer's travels, Svanhild had been flushed like a cat who just lapped up some buttermilk. "How are you enjoying the feast?" Svanhild asked her.

Haldis frowned. She wanted to congratulate her sister, but something caught her tongue. Was it fear? She needed to talk to Svanhild outside, away from the chaos of the hall.

"The smoke is making me dizzy," she said. To prove her point, she issued a light cough into her fist.

Svanhild laughed. "Let me finish my bread and I'll pretend to feel unwell too."

Haldis glanced down the table and waved to capture Brynja's attention. Her younger sister looked over, her face pink and dewy from all the rounds of mead. Haldis made a gesture—a fist to her mouth, feigning a cough—and raised her eyebrows. In response, Brynja grinned and nodded.

They would go together then, the three sisters. This was a game they played at almost every feast—escape the long-house—though they had to be selective about when to complain of the smoke. Of the three, Svanhild was the one who most enjoyed these celebrations, but she took any excuse to be out under the open sky. And Brynja, the lady of them who always enjoyed seeing friends at such feasts, was secretly as free-spirited as her sisters; Haldis imagined that her little sister must be even more excited about their game tonight, if it meant she could evade the attention of all the young men staring at her. Haldis would make sure no one followed them out.

After finishing swigs of mead and bites of bread, the three of them stood and slipped out the side door of the hall. Tove and Helga cast them sidelong glances but did not stop them.

Haldis followed Svanhild into the training yard, Brynja trailing behind. When a drunk young warrior staggered toward the doorway, Haldis raised a palm to warn him away. It was enough; the man hiccuped and returned to his friends. Haldis found a gesture from a völva was always enough, even if she didn't feel any magic in her fingers.

Passing through the doorway was like leaving a sauna. A refreshing breeze blew through Haldis's hair. The moonlight cast long shadows behind the training pells, the weapons rack, and the wood fence that swept around the yard in a semi-circle.

Svanhild strode to a training pell and picked up the wooden sword there. "Can you believe I'll be fighting with Father's warriors this time next year?" she breathed, smiling.

"I am happy for you," said Brynja. "Maybe you'll find yourself a warrior to wed while you're out on the battlefield, just like Mother and Father."

"Be careful teasing me like that," Svanhild replied. "If I wed, that means you're next."

Haldis listened to the two of them banter, a strange chill running over her skin. She knew she should be happy for her sister, but the thought of Svanhild in battle frightened her. She could almost taste the blood in Svanhild's future, like cold metal in her mouth.

When her sisters grew quiet, Haldis said to Svanhild, "You should not go looking for battles, sister. Men who search for fights end up dead before their time."

"I don't intend to die," Svanhild said. "I intend to win my battles."

"That is not your choice. It's the will of the gods."

Beside them, Brynja hugged herself, shuddering in the cool night air. Or perhaps it was Haldis's words that chilled her. Haldis would be glad if they did. More people should worry for Svanhild, if Svanhild refused to worry about herself.

"You *should* be careful, Svanhild," Brynja finally agreed. "Remember what Father said about respect."

Svanhild studied the wood training sword as though imagining it transforming into Hrafnblód, their father's rune-covered blade. Her eyes glittered in the moonlight like pools of starlit water. "I will earn respect with my prowess in battle. That is what all good warriors do." Then she turned to Haldis, her expression darkening. "Have the gods shown you my future? Will something happen to me?"

Haldis shook her head. "I have seen nothing from the gods. I only worry about you, sister. Brynja's fate seems clear to me. She'll marry a kind man, bake bread, and have children."

She glanced at Brynja, whose cheeks grew red.

"If she can ever pick a husband," Svanhild teased, nudging her little sister with her elbow. "Or perhaps you already have."

"What do you mean?" Brynja exclaimed.

"The son of Torven and Ragnilde is growing very handsome, if you like dimples and that little dip in his chin," Svanhild said.

"That would be like marrying my brother!" Brynja's nose wrinkled in an expression of disgust that made Haldis and Svanhild burst into laughter. But their littlest sister stood her ground. "Do you really not understand our friendship after all these years? That makes me sad."

Haldis placed a hand on Brynja's shoulder. "Do not let

Svanhild's teasing bother you. I admire your friendship with Erik. It's something I've never had."

"You have us, though," said Brynja.

Haldis smiled sadly at her younger sister, but before she could thank her, Svanhild tutted at them.

"You enjoy feeling sorry for yourself, Haldis," she said. "But you could be so powerful, so revered, if you only embraced your gifts."

Haldis wanted to snap back at her sister, but she took a breath to think through her next words. She had never shared her memories with her sisters—that night by the lake, abandoned as an infant—for she did not want to turn them against her father. But by now, they knew she did not wish to be a völva. So why did Svanhild always push her toward that path?

"You must let me find my way, sister," Haldis said at last. "You may run recklessly toward your destiny, but I am not like you."

"Father will protect me. I will travel with him, raid with him if he wills it. That is all."

Haldis didn't answer. Absently, she reached for the pendant that hung around her neck.

"What is that?" Brynja asked. Her green eyes grew bright with curiosity.

Haldis opened her palm to reveal a small silver coin stamped with the image of a raven. In the middle of the coin was a tiny hole so it could hang from a thin chain around her neck.

"You and your ravens," Brynja said, grinning. "What is your obsession with them, anyway?"

Haldis tucked the coin into the front of her dress. "Thought and Memory, the ravens of Odin. They keep appearing in my dreams."

Svanhild stared at her. "Do you think the gods are trying to tell you something?"

"Don't believe everything you hear about me, sister. There is a reason I am alive right now, and it's *not* because of any gift from the gods."

Frowning, Svanhild lay down her sword and took Haldis's hands in her own. Where Haldis's hands were like ice, her older sister's palms were warm as coals. "You shouldn't speak like that, Haldis. I know it wasn't your idea to be trained as a völva, but it's a life of adventure. Communing with the gods, reading runes for important men..." Her eyes, a mixture of their mother's green and father's brown, danced as she spoke. "It's an exciting life. And it's clear the gods will this path for you."

Haldis glanced at Brynja almost without meaning to, but she knew the reason her gaze betrayed her. Where Svanhild longed to see the gods, Brynja hid her face from them. That is why whenever Haldis needed someone to complain to, Brynja was the one who understood, who didn't pester her for rune readings, who didn't care if Haldis just wanted to sit and eat cloudberries and pretend Asgard didn't even exist.

Before either of them could say anything, a rustling in the nearby trees drew their attention. Svanhild dropped Haldis's hands, leaving them cold again. Beyond the training yard, a figure emerged from the forest. The shadows made it impossible to discern who it was, but from the heft of his cloak, he was an important man.

"He is surprisingly steady on his feet, for a feast," Haldis said.

"Why was he in the forest?" Brynja asked.

Svanhild cocked her head. "Why do you think?"

They all laughed. Home from their voyage, half of the men inside were so thrilled to be reunited with their wives, they would have trouble waiting until they were home later to be alone with them. And the other half of the men—married or not—were already making eyes at the thralls who served their mead and meat.

"I do not envy the slave women tonight," Brynja remarked.

Haldis agreed. She shuddered at the thought of having to warm a strange man's bed. But her father's warriors knew better than to grab at any thrall they liked anytime. The jarl only allowed his men to take his thralls to bed during celebrations like this—and he made it clear the women should be returned whole and unmarked in the morning.

A raven cawed overhead, swooping across the training yard to show off its majestic black wings. But something in the sound made Haldis shiver.

"Why is a raven here now?" she said.

A rustling sounded in the trees nearby, and a twig snapped. But no one emerged from the forest; instead, a contrived silence followed, as if whatever—or whoever—had made the noise was now being still on purpose.

Haldis froze. When she caught her sisters' gazes, she put a finger to her lips. The three of them ducked into the shadows of the longhouse, watching the treeline for any sign of movement. If a forbidden couple was trying to hide their presence, Haldis would expect to hear a moan or giggle. Instead, there was an eerie silence. The only noise was the hoot of an owl and pine branches blowing in the breeze.

Perhaps she imagined the noise. Just as she was about to say this to her sisters, their father's voice drifted from inside. "Where are my daughters?" He spoke loudly enough that wherever his daughters were, they would hear him.

Haldis exchanged looks with her sisters, and by silent agreement they returned to the feast.

As Haldis passed her father to sit down again, he caught

her wrist. "Daughter," he said, his voice low, "I have a strange feeling in my heart tonight. Will you read the runes for me?"

Haldis nodded. She wasn't surprised; her father called her for readings every time some concern crossed his mind, no matter how small. Once, he had asked her to cast lots for him over a stomachache from foul fish. And though she did not enjoy it, this is what she had been trained for all her life: reading runes, telling fortunes, communing with the gods on others' behalf. A jarl would make good use of a völva like her. It was this connection with the gods that spared her life when she was barely born.

If only it were not a lie.

Jarl Tove led her through a small doorway behind their table, to the family quarters. This part of the longhouse was partitioned off from the rest of the hall by a thatch wall. Just behind the wall, a great bearskin rug lay across the dirt floor, with two benches making an L shape. Feather-filled pillows and rugs were thrown on the benches, adding warmth and comfort to the small space.

This was the jarl's meeting room. During any gathering, having this area so close to the throne and family table made it easy for Tove to invite a guest here for private conversation.

On the wall behind the benches hung a large tapestry depicting Odin hanging upside-down from the sacred tree Yggdrasil. The jarl studied it for a moment, lines of worry etched across his forehead.

"I am glad to have you with me tonight," he said at last. "The All-Father sacrificed himself when he hung from the sacred tree. He wanted to prove his worth, and in doing so, he finally learned the secret knowledge of runes. I keep this picture here as a reminder to seek wisdom above all else." He looked at Haldis then. "You are the knowing one in our family. The gods have chosen to speak through you, and for that, I am grateful."

The words struck Haldis like stones, but she did not argue. Her father expressed his gratitude for her whenever he needed her, but it was not the same thing as love. He had never looked at her the way he looked at Svanhild, his chest swelling with pride when he announced his eldest daughter would join him on his travels. He would not ask the entire hall of warriors to protect *her* life with their own, the way he did for Svanhild. No, Haldis was more seer to him than daughter, and most days she felt like just another member of the jarl's household staff.

He sat on a bench, leaning forward to rest his forearms on his knees. Haldis kneeled before him on the bearskin rug. She plucked her small leather bag of runes from around her neck, where they always hung.

"Why do you ask for a reading now, Father?" she asked. Sometimes understanding the other person's concerns helped her complete an accurate reading, or at least leave the person satisfied.

The jarl stared at the thin wall separating them from the rest of the party. Hoots of laughter and boasting voices filled the hall outside. Following his gaze, Haldis peeked through the wall's slats at the backs of her mother and sisters where they sat at the family table.

"I sense something tonight," Tove said simply. "A taste in the air. Like blood."

"You fear an accident? An injury?"

He looked at her then, his amber eyes darkening. "Or war."

Haldis shuddered at the way he said it. "Why do you fear this tonight?"

"For weeks, I have been having strange dreams," he admitted. His voice was lower now, and Haldis got the impression he had not shared this with anyone else—perhaps not even her mother. "They started when we were making our voyage home. I thought we would be ambushed. During our trip, a band of warriors came to steal the treasures we had fairly traded, so I worried they had sent for reinforcements and now followed us up the river."

Haldis frowned. "But nothing happened?"

"Nothing. Yet I had such a nightmare last night."

"What happened in the dream?"

As he ran a hand over his face, his gaze grew misty. Haldis thought he would begin to tell the story, but instead he shook his head as though flinging the memories from his mind. Steadying his gaze on her, he said, "I won't trouble you with my dreams. Tell me what the gods know."

From their leather pouch, Haldis spilled her set of wooden runes onto the floor between them. Someday, she would ingest potions that would help her see the gods, but for now she simply used these rudimentary carvings as divination tools and hoped no one would wonder too much at her connection to Odin, Thor, and Freyja. Each piece of wood was carved with a runic symbol. She took a moment to set her hands upon them, closing her eyes and praying that the gods would be with her, despite her doubts that they heard her at all.

Thor, Odin, and Freyja, she prayed, *guide this reading. Guide my words. Speak to my father through me.*

She picked up the handful of wood chips and cast them on the ground again, letting them fall where they may. Tove leaned forward to study them.

Looking up at the ceiling of the longhouse, she imagined she could see the sky above the rafters, where the gods watched her. Keeping her gaze lifted, she felt around and picked up the first wood chip her fingers touched.

"Thurs," she said, reading the rune without looking at the chips still on the floor, "a giant."

Tove frowned. "What does it mean?"

She ignored the question to reach for a second piece of wood. "Fé, wealth."

"A giant seeking wealth," her father guessed.

She pulled a third chip from the pile, which would complete the reading. "Naudr," she read.

Her father's face darkened, for it was not the first time Haldis had read this rune for him—and it never signaled anything good. Some would interpret it to mean *need*, but it could also indicate a threat.

"So we will face an emergency." Her father wiped his hand over his face, a habit when he was worried. "Perhaps someone will come to steal from us. Or perhaps we should take care with our greed the next time we travel."

Haldis nodded. "The gods clearly wish to warn you of something."

"Can you hear them? Ask them what we must look out for."

She decided honesty was best. She had read the signs as best she could, and perhaps the gods had spoken through her after all. Perhaps she wasn't meant to feel anything as she performed her duties—just trust that she had picked up the chips the gods had intended her to read.

"I cannot tell you more detail now," she admitted. "The gods have shared what they can with you tonight."

As she palmed the last wood chip, the sound of flapping wings drew her attention. A breeze stirred her hair as a raven, black as night, swooped above her and landed in the rafters. It seemed content to stay there, watching her.

"A sign from the gods?" the jarl asked.

Haldis nodded. "An omen." As the words left her mouth, she shivered. The hairs on her arms stood up.

Perhaps her father was right. There *was* something in the air tonight.

CHAPTER 3

BRYNJA

*a*s she sat at her father's table watching the celebrations, Brynja could not remember a time she had felt so happy.

After just two cups of mead and three dances around the fire, her body felt like it was packed with hot coals. Sweat beaded on her forehead and trickled down her back, but she didn't mind. This was how the hall always felt after people had been feasting, drinking, and dancing for long enough. She associated it with her father's return every summer, a night she always looked forward to.

The hall was noisy, the sound of voices mingling with the song Valí strummed on his lyre. Tables had been deconstructed to make room for dancing. Even the people sitting on the sidelines banged silverware or stomped their boots to the beat, making the hall vibrate in rhythm.

In the midst of the crowd of revelers were Brynja's parents, dancing with their people. Earlier, Father had disappeared to his meeting room with Haldis—no doubt for a rune reading—but when he emerged, she watched him cast the darkness from his eyes as he smiled at his people. He always put on a brave face for Kaldvik. And the first thing he did was ask Valí to start a song so he could dance with his wife.

A voice sounded nearby, startling Brynja. "You look like you could use fresh air," said the young warrior, grinning at her from where he stood against the nearest pillar. "Care to join me for a stroll outside?"

Another time, the man might have looked friendly enough, but tonight Brynja trusted no man with an empty ale horn in his hand. Her mother had taught her such caution, especially now that she was of marrying age. A man could find a thrall if he truly desired someone to spend the night with.

Shaking her head, she tried to find the most polite way to decline the invitation. "I am waiting for someone," she lied, "but I appreciate the offer."

The warrior shrugged. "You are missing a great battle story, one that would rival even the exploits of Thor. Find me later if you want to hear the tale."

He stood straighter then, broadening his shoulders. Brynja could see the muscles moving beneath his blue tunic, but this type of display didn't interest her. She had yet to find any man who intrigued her in that way. In fact, most of the time she wished she could hide from all the lustful warriors behind her curtain of long brown hair.

"You might look more cheerful if you had a sewing needle in your hand," came a familiar voice.

Brynja smiled as her childhood friend Erik Torvenson approached—the one boy she liked to be around. His wavy blond hair hung freely, skimming his shoulders. His skin had the sheen of so many others tonight—from drinking and dancing and sitting too close to the fire—making him look wilder than usual. Some would call him handsome, but to her, Erik was like the brother she never had.

"Well then, what do you say we get out of this stuffy room and sit by the fjord?" he asked.

Brynja clucked her tongue at him. "You know I love going to the water, but not tonight. We should enjoy the feast. I haven't seen my father in almost three moons." Seeing Erik's pretend pout, she added, "I heard the cooks are heating more goat meat."

His eyes brightened at that. Brynja's mother had once told her that while a man won a woman with his sword, a woman won a man with her cauldron. And though Brynja had no intention of winning Erik in that way, she could see now how right her mother was.

"Did I really look so glum?" she asked, thinking back to his first words to her.

"You look like you always do, pretty and perfect." Erik jerked his chin toward a pair of warriors nearby. "They looked like they were about to come over and ask you to dance, so I thought I'd save you."

"Well, it's true I've danced enough for tonight," Brynja said.

She had chosen the safety of dancing with Svanhild, then her parents, and finally an older warrior she knew to be married. Now, she was happy to have a moment alone to catch her breath.

Erik slid into an empty seat next to her.

"You are bold to sit at the jarl's table uninvited," she joked.

Erik shrugged. "I never liked waiting around for invitations."

Brynja shook her head at him, laughing. Erik had not changed much since they were children. They had grown up together, picking berries in the forest, playing with wooden swords, swimming in the lake, sitting on the pier under the moonlight to gossip about everything and nothing. Though Brynja's parents sometimes frowned to see their daughter spend so much time with a boy instead of other girls, in time they grew to enjoy Erik's dimples and jokes. He had even slept in a spare room in the longhouse, on those nights he and Brynja stayed up too late playing for him to safely walk home to his farm.

Now Tove and Helga returned from the dance, their faces flushed from exertion. Both were smiling, casting glances at each other that made them look like they were Brynja's age again. She wondered how they must have acted when they first met. Of course, her mother had been more like Svanhild then—a shieldmaiden unafraid of battle. Still, she could picture her parents' youthful romance.

She wondered why she had never craved such a flirtation herself.

Jarl Tove studied Erik for a moment with narrowed eyes, but Brynja caught the grin at the corner of her father's mouth.

Erik looked innocently back at him.

Finally, Tove said, "I could have sworn I had only daughters. Who is this new addition to the family?"

Erik laughed like bubbling water. Brynja smiled to hear the familiar sound. Even as everything about Erik aged—his voice deepening, his hair growing longer, his shoulders expanding—his laugh remained the one truly boyish part of him.

The tension broken, Tove asked, "Will you be joining me on my travels next summer, Erik? You're old enough." He slapped Erik's shoulders as though testing their strength. "Big enough, too."

But Erik shook his head. "You know my family. We're

farmers, and there's nothing I enjoy more than working the land."

The jarl smiled. "A good answer. Kaldvik needs good farmers like you and your father. I hear your mother lends a strong hand, too."

"Some think she would have made a good shieldmaiden," Erik remarked with a laugh. "But I think her tongue is sharper than any sword."

Brynja giggled at that. His mother, Ragnilde, was known for her brutal honesty. During one feast, her harsh words had even made a warrior cry—albeit a very drunk warrior.

Standing, Erik inclined his head to Jarl Tove, then Helga. "I should go," he said, "but don't be afraid to send a thrall my way when the goat meat is ready." As he strode from the table, he glanced back and shot Brynja one last grin.

Rather than taking his seat, Brynja's father remained standing and lifted his ale horn to call for attention in the hall. Valí stopped strumming his lyre, and the stomping of boots thinned out until everyone was quiet.

When Tove began his speech, his voice carried without effort, as naturally as water rushes down a river. Brynja listened in awe, as she always did when her father spoke. He commanded attention without trying, a respect that was earned.

"I am happy to see you all so full of joy tonight," he said. "You honor the gods with your appreciation of life's treasures."

Several people picked up cups and horns to toast the gods.

Father continued, "Tonight, we celebrate the success of our summer travels. Forty of us, men and women, sailed across a savage sea to the kingdom of the Franks." He nodded to several of his warriors, including a scarred woman wearing a shield across her back. "We saw foreign lands and met foreign men. They admired our craftsmanship, our curiosity to travel so far, and the strength of our will." He named several of the village's craftsmen, including the black-smith Balder and the tailor Revna. He even called the name of their household seamstress Ursula, a thrall. "They paid us for your goods, and they now see the skill and stature of our people." He smiled then, giving a nod to his housecarl Alf. "And they paid us in gold."

Alf, who stood along a nearby wall, pushed open a chest to reveal a pile of gold coins and ingots inside. Brynja gasped at the sight, as did several others in the hall. It was like opening a door to pure sunlight.

"With this gold, we will adorn our homes, create beautiful jewelry, and continue our trade when we travel each summer," Tove went on. "And this year, we brought back many foreign-made treasures."

On cue, Alf opened a smaller box and pulled out a few items one at a time, holding them up for everyone to admire. As Father's right hand, he had the honor of briefly explaining what each one was, eliciting excited chatter from those in the hall. First was a comb carved in the shape of a creature called an elephant, which was made from the animal's tusk. Next was a shimmering fabric called silk. There was ornate pottery, sparkling jewelry, and glassware in shapes Brynja had never seen before.

Finally, Alf approached the jarl's table and extended the box toward Helga.

"Please, choose something for yourself," Tove said, his voice quieter now, so it only reached his family's ears.

Helga held a hand to her chest for a moment, as though her heart were beating too fast. Only after Tove nodded encouragement did she reach into the box and pull the ivory comb from the pile. Brynja hid a smile at this; it was just like her mother to choose something with a practical purpose.

"Thank you, husband," she said, inclining her head to Tove. Then, she combed a few strands of her hair in an exaggerated manner, as though showing how it worked. Several people laughed, cheered, or whistled.

"And for my daughters," Tove said.

Brynja watched her sisters choose their items first. Svanhild paused for a long moment, biting her lip. Brynja sensed her sister's hesitation at choosing such a luxury for herself, not out of any humility but out of a preference for battle. If her father had presented Svanhild with a sword, she would have grabbed it out of his hands. Finally, Svanhild plucked an amber pendant on a gold chain from the box and put it on.

"One of Freyja's tears, which I will keep close to my heart."

Cheers filled the hall at her words. Brynja caught her sister's eye and smiled. Of course Svanhild would find something that connected her to the gods.

Next, Haldis chose a black gemstone, roughly shaped and almost as big as her fist. Brynja thought it an odd choice, until her mother said, "The perfect adornment for your staff someday. May it garner the gods' attention."

When Alf finally brought the box to her, Brynja held her breath. She tried not to appear too eager as she leaned forward to peer at the treasures inside. They were a jumble of sparkling gemstones, necklaces, rings, combs, beads, and bits of silk and leather. She wanted to wade through them so she could be sure to make the right choice.

Gingerly, she placed her fingers into the box and began sorting through the items. After digging for a moment, she heard a few chuckles. Looking up, she saw her father grinning down at her.

"Can you tell which of my daughters most enjoys these luxuries?" he teased, drawing more laughter from the crowd.

Brynja's cheeks grew hot, but she smiled. It was true.

Sometimes she wondered why she seemed to be the only one of her sisters who acted like a lady. Not that she didn't enjoy playing with swords like Svanhild and running through the forest like Haldis—but she enjoyed finer things, too. There were benefits to being a jarl's daughter, and this was one of them.

Not wanting to take too much more time sorting through the goods, she spotted a thin gold band set with an emerald in the center, which reminded her of the gem hanging from her mother's neck tonight. She pulled it from the box and studied it a moment, trying to decide if it was an arm ring or a neck ring.

"It is for your head," Father said, tapping his brow.

She placed the ring on her head. Her mother reached over to adjust it for her, until it nestled into her hair at the edges of her forehead.

"Tonight, my youngest daughter is a Frankish queen," said Tove, making a few people whistle.

Brynja blushed. Now she realized she had chosen a tiara. She tried to explain, "The gem is like Mother's," and pointed to Helga's necklace.

Mother smiled. Touching her necklace, she explained more loudly to the crowd, "My daughter has chosen a gem that matches my own." Turning to Brynja, her green eyes dancing, she said, "Now we are linked."

Brynja smiled back at her mother. She had always pictured her future much like Helga's, and she especially admired the way her mother ran the hall. Helga commanded servants with the perfect blend of authority and generosity, her set of housekeys jangling on her waist, a sign of her authority. She placed loving hands on the shoulders of the thralls who served her, making them feel at home while accepting only their best work. She foresaw problems and planned for them, as if the gods had granted her visions of the future. She practiced womanly arts such as cooking and weaving, yet she enjoyed walks in the forest and time spent by the fjord just as much. This was how Brynja hoped to be one day, running her own home with the unique grace of a Norsewoman.

Of course, she would have to be married first. If only she could find someone she desired.

"You have seen that my family has good taste," Tove said with a chuckle. "Now, allow me to bestow these gifts on all of you. For those who joined me in battle, an arm ring to mark your bravery and your loyalty. For those who joined me in these journeys, a jewel to honor your curiosity. And for those who stayed home..." He eyed several of the community's most well-loved farmers, craftsmen, and elders. "For you, only pure gold can honor the work you do to make our village a success."

The longhouse erupted in cheers. Voices shouted, "Skol!" as men and women lifted their ale horns to toast their jarl.

A few thralls emerged from the back of the longhouse then, carrying glass jugs of red liquid. They began pouring the drink into empty cups around the hall. Several people emptied their horns and extended them to the thralls to try the strange drink, their brows furrowed and eyes bright with interest.

"This is Frankish wine," Father explained to the crowd. "It is a sweet, pungent drink the nobles enjoy."

A few people tasted the wine. Brynja giggled at the mixed reactions. A man nearby wrinkled his nose at the flavor, while others sipped and smiled politely. Meanwhile, a red-haired warrior—the same one who had tried to share a drink with Svanhild earlier—downed the wine in a single gulp before calling to the thralls for more.

One of the servants came around to fill Brynja's cup. Her stomach flipped at the idea of drinking more tonight. Her head was already spinning. "Is it strong?" she asked her father.

He smiled gently. "A little."

She made a gesture for the thrall to serve her only a small amount. Once her cup was half-filled, she took a sip. The rich berry flavor made her pucker at first, but as she swallowed, it settled on her tongue like fresh soil. She sniffed the liquid, enjoying the dark scent, before taking a deeper drink.

"Do you like it?" Father asked.

"Very much," she said, smiling. "It's not as sweet as mead, but it makes me feel like a woman."

This comment made both her parents laugh.

Her father turned back to the crowd then and announced, "Tonight, we drink like Frankish kings."

A round of cheers rose to the rafters, and Brynja asked for her cup to be filled with more.

BY THE TIME the moon had shifted to the other side of the night sky, Brynja had a sewing needle in her hands.

Most of the revelers had gone home for the night, leaving the hall strangely quiet as the last flames sputtered in the hearth. Aside from Brynja and the small group now gathered around the fire, the only people who remained in the hall were a few particularly drunk men who had passed out and now snored where they lay.

As a servant added fresh wood to the central fire, Brynja watched the flames spit and spark as they accepted the new kindling. She sat on the packed earth floor, leaning her back against Svanhild's legs. Her oldest sister sat behind her on a stool, gently braiding her hair, untangling it, and then re-braiding it. Brynja enjoyed the tension and tingling of her scalp as Svanhild worked her hair. In every gesture, she sensed her sister's excitement over the night's events; now that she would travel as a shieldmaiden with her father next summer, she could not sit still.

Meanwhile, Haldis sat on the floor beside Brynja while their mother braided her hair. On Helga's other side sat their father, then their housecarl Alf, then an elderly couple who sold eggs in the village market, and finally Erik, carving shapes into a block of wood with a pocket knife.

The red wine left Brynja feeling long and loose, like thread unraveled from a loom. A fine-spun fabric was stretched across her lap, dyed the pale blue color of the summer sky. She knew it was her mother's favorite shade. Though she had not told anyone yet, she sewed this dress for her mother, stitching a swirling pattern in yellow thread around the hem. The minute movements of her bone needle soothed her as she listened to her father's deep voice. He had regaled them with tales of his travels, and now he spoke of the gods.

"Just as Odin sought wisdom, the goddess Freyja sought beautiful things. She appreciated luxury, and she knew quality when she saw it." He winked at Brynja. "We have someone like Freyja in our midst tonight."

Everyone laughed. Brynja stopped sewing to lift a hand to her tiara, which still rested on her head—albeit lopsided from Svanhild mussing her hair. "I don't mind being compared to Freyja," she admitted with a shrug, making everyone chuckle again.

"Tonight we will hear a story of how Freyja sought a necklace, not unlike the one Svanhild now wears," Tove continued, nodding to his eldest daughter. "As you know, the dwarves are the finest craftsmen in all nine realms, and so Freyja found herself drawn to their forges. There, she saw the dwarves creating the most beautiful golden necklace she had ever seen. Naturally, she wanted it for herself."

"Not *naturally*," their mother jumped in. "Freyja gets into trouble over her greed."

"Come now, when we married you promised you would let me tell the stories," Tove teased.

They all laughed as Helga mimed stitching her lips shut. Everyone knew the story by heart anyway.

The jarl continued, "Seeing this beautiful necklace, Freyja offered the dwarves all of the silver and gold she had in exchange for the jewelry. But they had another form of payment in mind, for Freyja was the most beautiful goddess in existence. Do you know the secret desire each of those four dwarves held in their hearts?"

"I don't think the desire was in their hearts," Svanhild said. "They wanted to take her to bed. And they called *her* the greedy one."

Everyone laughed.

"Perhaps," Father said with a shrug, "but Freyja agreed to spend a night with each of them. At the end of those four nights, she got what she wanted: the beautiful necklace called Brísingamen. Everyone was happy, you see." His eyes sparked like fire as he glanced around at each of them for their reactions. "Of course, she intended to keep this a secret, as she was Odin's lover and did not wish to upset him."

"She was not even his wife," Svanhild argued. "Why would he care if she slept with another man?"

"Or four?" Haldis added.

Brynja giggled. "Or dwarves?"

Chuckling, their father continued, "The trouble was, Loki had followed Freyja and witnessed the whole scene. He knew her secret. And you know Loki…"

"The god of mischief," Haldis said softly.

Tove nodded. "To cause mayhem, he went and told Odin everything he had seen. Odin was outraged. He ordered Loki to steal the necklace Brísingamen from Freyja."

"That seems cruel," Brynja said, mulling it over. "He should have confronted her about her betrayal, but stealing the necklace helps nothing."

Beside her, Erik grinned. She interpreted the smile as him patronizing her, so she stuck out her tongue at him.

"I believe the necklace held magic," Haldis said. "Perhaps that is why she slept with the four dwarves, to imbue the necklace with some special power."

"A fine idea," Father said.

But Brynja didn't like that. She had never been one to pray to the gods anyway, and imagining a goddess not only stealing a necklace, but stealing a *magic* necklace just went too far. But she bit her tongue. Between Haldis who trained as a völva and Svanhild who prayed to Odin as often as she drew breath, there was no point in debating about the gods with them.

Instead, she continued sewing, enjoying the sound of her family's voices as they shared their interpretations of the story. She focused her own attention on the pattern she was stitching. The yellow swirls were growing larger, which she had not intended. Perhaps if she let them grow from one side to the other in an even manner, to make it appear purposeful...

A thud sounded behind her, and a gust of cold wind blew into the hall. Her father's voice stopped. Everyone froze. Brynja looked up in time to see her mother's eyes shoot open, staring at something behind Brynja.

"Girls, run," she said. Her voice was strangely low and still.

There was a growling behind Brynja, followed by the clatter of metal. The sound was unmistakable.

Weapons.

"Brynja, hurry!" Svanhild shouted.

She grabbed Brynja's wrist and yanked her toward the back of the hall.

Brynja's heart pounded in her chest. She forced her feet to move, but she could barely think.

Her father stood and pulled his sword from its sheath. His eyes were set on whomever was invading the hall.

Suddenly Svanhild threw her hands over Brynja's back and pushed her down. Brynja nearly knocked her chin against the floor. She heard a swoosh and felt a breeze stir her hair as a massive axe swung over her head.

Then she was up again, running with Svanhild for the back of the hall. Haldis was already there.

She had no idea where Erik was, or the elderly couple who had been with them, or their housecarl. There was no time to think about all that.

She had to keep moving.

Her feet moved without conscious thought.

Once they had made it to the back of the hall, Svanhild shoved her into their father's meeting room. Haldis was already crouched there behind the wall.

"Stay here," Svanhild snapped. "And stay quiet."

Svanhild ran back into the main hall, taking position behind the head table beside their mother.

Brynja tried to control her breathing, but it was no use. Her heart thumped too hard in her chest, nearly drowning out the sound of clashing blades in the hall.

And so she stayed there with Haldis, watching the battle through slats in the wall.

There was Svanhild, standing behind the head table, a knife in her hands. She looked unsure of what to do, but Brynja knew her sister would not hide from something like this.

There was her mother, standing guard in front of the table, sword in hand. Even in her red dress, she looked poised for battle. Though she did not join the fray, Brynja thought she looked like a bear guarding the entrance to her cave. Helga would not let anyone come near her daughters.

But where was Erik? Brynja looked around until she spotted him standing with the elderly couple. They huddled together in the shadows behind a pillar, Erik with a battle axe in his hands. She had never seen him with a weapon before. In his thin tunic, he did not look like a warrior. But there was no time to worry about him now.

A drunken warrior had awoken and stood at the ready beside him, blinking the sleep from his eyes.

There was her father's housecarl Alf, rushing into the fight, his sword flailing in the air.

Then she laid eyes on the enemy. A man like a great bear led the charge. In a blur of fur and heavy axes, he let out a roaring battle cry and dove straight for her father.

Tove flew to meet him with the swiftness of a raven. In his hands, he raised his silver sword Hrafnblód. It glittered like a jewel in the dimming light.

Brynja stifled a gasp. She reached for Haldis's hand, seeking comfort. Her sister's fingers were smooth and icy to the touch, but they gripped hers and squeezed.

She watched the ensuing fight through the slats. The small openings gave her an odd view, like watching a shadow show playing against a firelit wall.

Behind the leader who charged in like a bear were several other enemy warriors. Like the bear, they wore heavy furs. Wielding a mix of axes, swords, and short spears, they clashed with the warriors remaining in her father's hall.

But there were far too many of them. She counted nine bears.

On her father's side were Erik who stood helplessly with an axe, the drunken warrior still waking up, the housecarl Alf, and the elderly couple. The old man's hands shook as he clung to his heavy sword with both hands; his wife stood defiantly beside him, glaring at the intruders though she held no weapon.

That made five against nine, and those five were too old, too young, too inexperienced, or too drunk to be of much use.

They would all be in Valhalla soon. Too soon.

The intruders lunged at them, slicing through the old man and woman with their swords like knives through butter. Brynja's heart beat so fast, she had to shut her eyes and lower her head to keep from fainting.

She felt cowardly, hiding here behind a wall. But what could she do? She was no warrior. She was still a girl.

Haldis's grip on her hand tightened. At least they were together.

When she opened her eyes again, she spotted Erik shrinking into the shadows behind a pillar. Two enemy warriors approached him like wolves circling prey.

Standing nearby, the drunken warrior howled and waved his sword like a wild creature. The oncoming warriors halted and dodged awkwardly to avoid his weapon.

After a moment of chaos, one of the enemy warriors plunged his blade into the drunken warrior's stomach. Brynja winced as he crumpled to the ground.

The two warriors ignored Erik then, turning to watch the main fight. Brynja was thankful they saw he was still just a boy and no threat to them.

She watched her father battle the bear in the center of the hall. They danced around the hearth, barely avoiding the fire. When they accidentally knocked the kindling, the flames roared in anger.

Her father spun, faster than lightning. As he came to a halt facing the enemy, he swiped his sword using only his wrist, quick as a bee sting.

ASHLEY HAGOOD

It should have at least nicked the man's side. But he missed.

Brynja could barely watch. She felt sick with terror.

The enemy was much bigger than her father, and his axe looked heavier. Every move he made was like a great boulder rolling toward the jarl.

But there was a reason their family's symbol was the raven. It was why Brynja and her sisters had escaped the bear's axe just now.

They did not just run. They did not just fight.

They flew.

Again and again, Jarl Tove dodged the enemy's axe. He was swift. At times, the enemy had to stop, looking for where the jarl had dropped or slid.

The others in the hall had stopped fighting to watch too. This was no longer a battle of warring clans, but a holmgang between two great men. As in any duel, only one would come out alive.

Brynja held her breath. She was sure that at any moment, her father would slide into the bear's weak point to deliver the killing blow.

The enemy moved to one side of the fire, Father at the other side. The enemy's axe hung low in his hand, as though he were resting. His shoulders pulsed with his heavy breathing.

He was tired. That was good.

Her father circled the fire. With the tip of his sword he nudged the wood, sparking fresh flames.

His opponent growled at the distraction.

As Father came around to the bear's side of the fire, he raised his sword to prepare for a heavy blow. But before he could deliver it, the bear sliced his axe straight up into the jarl's abdomen.

Brynja shut her eyes against the sight.

CHAPTER 4

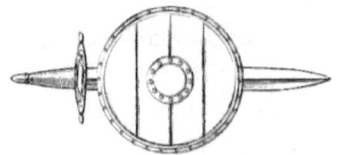

SVANHILD

The aftermath of the battle felt like a dream. Svanhild was sure the usurper would slaughter their family. Though she held a dagger in her hand to defend herself, she felt frozen. It was not so much fear that overpowered her now. Instead, she felt detached as she watched her fate unfold.

Is this what the gods wanted?

Her father's form lay on the ground before their table. Blood pooled around his body.

Tears stung her eyes, but she blinked them away. This was no time to cry.

Draped in heavy furs, the beast who had killed her father looked like a monster from the sagas. He approached the table now, stepping over Tove's body, splashing the blood.

Svanhild glared at him. If he was going to kill her, she would spit at him first. Maybe she could try to stab him. It might not be enough for Valhalla, but she would be as much of a shieldmaiden as she could in this final moment of her life.

She should have fought with her father. She should have defended her family. Why had she frozen in fear?

Svanhild heard movement behind the partition to the jarl's meeting room, where her sisters hid. She prayed they would stay quiet. Perhaps they could escape...

But it was too late. Ulrik put a hand behind his ear. "I heard Tove was cursed with too many daughters. Let's all spend this moment together." He beckoned with his hand.

There was a long silence as Svanhild held her breath, as did everyone else.

Ulrik narrowed his eyes then, a dark brown with a flash of gray like lightning in the night. Svanhild's sisters must have noticed the anger there, for they emerged from behind the wall and stood beside her.

Ulrik gave them an ugly wave of greeting, then set his sights on their mother. "You must be Helga." His voice was a low growl that suited such a beast. "I would apologize for murdering your husband, but you must know this is the fate of many jarls."

Helga dropped her sword. It clanged against the stone floor. Standing so close to her, Svanhild noticed her mother's hands shaking—but her face was still, emotionless. She lifted her chin at the man.

"I am Helga," she confirmed. "Who are you?"

The man bowed to her at the waist, a dramatic gesture. Svanhild could not tell if he was mocking them or not.

"My name is Ulrik, son of Otso, jarl of Mosfell."

Svanhild recognized the name Otso. Her father had traveled to his village many times over the years, had dealings with him, exchanged goods. Though Jarl Otso must be old now, he had long been a respected leader, both in Mosfell and neighboring jarldoms.

"If you are the son of Otso, you must know of the agreement my husband has with him," Helga said. Despite her trembling hands, her voice was sharp and steady. "And if you know of their alliance, you must be here without your father's blessing, for Otso would never break an oath."

Ulrik waved his hand to dismiss her words. "My father is old. He can continue to rule Mosfell for now. My brother will take over after him. I seek my own land."

"And you chose ours," Helga stated.

"And I chose yours." Ulrik grinned again. His teeth were yellow, his lips thin. It was a menacing expression. "Get your little one to stand up straighter," he barked.

Brynja straightened her shoulders, but Svanhild saw how they shook. She understood her sister's fear. Brynja, only 15 years old, was born with a soft heart. It was her best feature —but in moments like this, it could also be her greatest weakness.

"No need to fear us, as you will soon see," Ulrik said to her.

Brynja's face was pale. She didn't respond.

"Now, we have a problem," Ulrik continued, addressing Helga again. "Tove was a respected leader here in Kaldvik, that much I know. If it were up to me, I would slaughter you all where you stand, but it is not so easy when your family is so well-loved. If I kill you tonight…"

He lifted his axe and ran a finger along the bloodied edge, then licked the blood from his finger.

Svanhild inhaled sharply. That blood belonged to her father.

"If I kill you tonight," Ulrik went on, "I may have berserkers shouting Tove's name at my door tomorrow morning."

"Tonight, they are drunk," Helga said. "Tomorrow, they will seek their revenge."

"That may be, but tonight they have no idea I'm here," Ulrik replied. "I may be large, but I can find my way in the dark better than most."

He motioned for one of his men to come forward then. A young warrior in a light gray fur cloak stepped up to his side. He was just as tall as Ulrik with a strong, thin frame beneath his cape. His hair, tied back from his face, was the shade of polished bronze in the firelight.

Immediately, his gray eyes landed on Svanhild.

"My son Andor," said Ulrik, "may help us solve this problem."

Svanhild's stomach clenched as she sensed where this was going. As the eldest daughter, she would be the first in line to marry.

Andor must have known who she was, for his eyes studied her now. He had not even cast a fleeting glance at Brynja, who everyone knew was the prettiest of the three sisters.

Helga stiffened at Svanhild's side. "No," she spat.

Ulrik chuckled, and a few of the men behind him laughed along. "You have not even heard my offer."

"An offer?" Helga laughed bitterly. Svanhild had never heard her like this before. "You hope to buy the favor of our family with a marriage."

"Oh no, you have it wrongly framed," said Ulrik. "I hope to buy the favor of your *people* with a marriage. And you will be buying your lives."

Helga stared at him for a long moment. Svanhild could almost hear her thoughts whirring in her head.

Her own heart beat fast now, like the flapping of a raven's wings. She was already 18 years old—older than most women when they married. She had scared off suitor after suitor, determined to devote her life to the sword. To marry now would be to kill that dream. To marry the enemy would make her a traitor.

Andor continued to watch her, as though curious about her reaction.

Svanhild felt her mother moving beside her. It was only a twitch, but she sensed what was in her mother's mind.

Helga was reaching for her sword. She was ready to defend Svanhild with her life.

Svanhild pictured it all then.

There was blood everywhere. The bodies of her mother, her sisters, were splayed on the floor of the longhouse. A raven circled overhead, cawing in grief to the gods.

In the doorway of the longhouse, a gigantic bear plodded in to take the throne. With large paws, he snatched the raven from the air and ate it.

Jarl Tove's family was dead. They had no one to carry on their name or their bloodline.

The raven house was no more.

"I will do it!" Svanhild shouted.

The sound of her own voice surprised her, but she had to say it before her mother's hand reached her sword. She shivered then, her body chilled to ice from her vision. All eyes snapped to her.

"I will marry him," she said.

Mother's face deflated, while Ulrik's gaze sharpened in suspicion. Only Andor seemed not to react, but Svanhild caught a flex of his jaw. He never pulled his gaze from her.

Now, she had to convince them.

"I will marry Andor, but only when winter turns to spring," Svanhild said. "It is a tradition in our family to marry after the last of winter's snow melts. The village knows it brings luck from the gods. If you announce the wedding for the spring, they will trust you all the more."

It was true that her parents, and her grandparents before them, had married here in this very hall in the springtime.

One could argue that it was a tradition to wed during the spring blót, a time of sacrifices to the gods. Why not pretend that such timing brought luck from the gods? The lie would buy Svanhild time.

She sensed Loki, the trickster god himself, had given her the right words to say.

Svanhild kept her eyes on Ulrik now, her chin lifted. Whether he would see it as confidence or defiance, she could not say.

Ulrik rubbed his beard for a moment, reflecting. His eyes were still narrowed as he studied Svanhild.

Finally, he nodded his approval. "Very well." Turning to Helga, he reached across the table to take her hand in a show of unity. Svanhild noticed her mother flinch at the touch, but she did not pull away. "Andor and Svanhild will marry in spring," he said, "when the snow melts and the first wild-flowers bloom."

Svanhild let all her breath leave her then. Only now did she realize how she had been holding it in.

Their family would survive. Her sisters were safe.

At least for now.

CHAPTER 5

HALDIS

$\mathcal{I}$t took hours for the thralls to clean up all of the blood.

Haldis stayed in the loft that ran the length of the main hall, overlooking the banquet tables and hearth. Her sisters joined her. They huddled close together on the single bench there, a large blanket draped over their shoulders. A nearby smoke hole made the high space colder than the room below, but Haldis was glad for the fresh air.

The raven—the same one that had flown in while she was casting lots for her father, another creature who had witnessed the battle—remained on a beam beside her, watching the scene below.

Haldis watched, too. Jarl Tove's slaves joined Ulrik's to drag the bodies from the room, the two houses working together during this strange time. When they removed the bodies of an elderly couple, their shoulders touching in death, Brynja began to cry.

Haldis hugged her little sister as she shook with sobs. "They must be entering Valhalla now."

"They were farmers," Brynja said. "They never hurt anyone. They were just here to celebrate with us..." Her voice trailed off as fresh tears streamed down her face.

They watched as the thralls scrubbed the blood. Through the smoke hole overhead, the sky changed from the purple of night to the pink of sunrise.

Once Brynja had stopped crying, she looked at Svanhild. "Are you really going to marry that monster?" she asked, gesturing to the jarl's table below, where Ulrik and his son Andor now stood talking in low voices.

Svanhild shook her head. "Of course not."

"You're not?" Brynja perked up in surprise. "How will you avoid it?"

"I don't know yet. I believe Loki has a plan."

Haldis looked at her older sister. *Svanhild.* The name meant "swan warrior," and it suited her. She had inherited their mother's long, graceful neck and golden tresses. Yet she was fierce, too. Her nose was sharp, her jaw wide, her mouth an angry rune scratch above her chin. If only she didn't say such things, Haldis would not have to worry about her so much.

"You favor Loki too much," Haldis warned her sister. "Someday he will get you into trouble."

Svanhild cast her a sideways glance. "At least he is smart. He'll scheme something for us, I know it."

"In the meantime, may Odin protect us all," came their mother's voice.

Her face appeared at the top of the ladder to the loft. Her eyes were red from crying. Though she gave them all a sad smile, she remained on the ladder rather than joining them.

"Ulrik has provided a room for us to sleep," she said. "I

just met with Alf. He will need to find someplace else to stay now, for Ulrik has his own housecarl."

That made sense, for what new jarl would want the former jarl's right hand lurking about? Yet Haldis worried, not only for Alf but for all of their household servants and thralls. If Ulrik cast them all out at once, they would have trouble finding new work.

Feeling Brynja sagging beside her, she sensed this was not the time to bring up such problems. For now, they just needed to find Alf a new place to stay.

"Siggy might take him in," she suggested, referencing the village's healer woman. Siggy had taught Haldis how to craft potions from herbs collected in the forest—poisons too—and promised to concoct the mixture that Haldis would one day drink to truly see the gods. Though such things frightened Haldis, she trusted Siggy. "She will house him just as she houses the sick, until he finds a place of his own."

"A good idea," Helga agreed. Her voice was gentle. "Will you come sleep now? You must be exhausted after last night."

Haldis shook her head. "I'm not tired." She wanted the words to be true, but her reed-like voice was weak as dying grass in the wind, ready to snap. Knowing her mother would not believe her, she gestured to the raven in the rafters and added, "I will stay as long as Odin does."

Referencing the gods was enough. Helga nodded, turning her attention to Brynja who had been weeping silently for a long time now. "Brynja, come with me," Helga said. "I need rest, and I do not wish to sleep alone."

Brynja shook with a soft sob, then slid out of the blanket and tucked it over Haldis's shoulder. With a quiet good night, she followed Helga down the ladder and retreated to their family quarters—or, the jarl's quarters.

"Strange, to think those chambers no longer belong to us," Svanhild said.

"You read my thoughts."

"Someday, they will be ours again."

Haldis studied her sister's profile. Svanhild spoke a single sentence with more certainty than Haldis had ever felt in her life. "Did the gods tell you that?" she asked.

"I thought *you* were the one who communed with the gods."

Below, Ulrik retreated to the jarl's quarters, leaving his son behind for a moment. Having removed his fur cloak, Andor now wore a simple blue tunic and dark trousers. His gaze wandered up to the loft and found Svanhild. He gave her a small nod.

Svanhild tensed. Suddenly she turned and grabbed Haldis's hands, looking at her with wild eyes. "Let us leave this place," she said. "Let's go to the lake. I want you to cast lots for me. I need to hear from the gods, to learn what I must do next."

Just then, the raven stirred from its spot. Its wings created a cool breeze as it soared from the loft and flew out the front doors of the longhouse, into the new day.

Whether it was truly a sign or not, Haldis decided it was time to take her leave of this place too. There was too much death here. She needed to breathe the free air again.

"Let us go," she agreed.

THE AIR OUTSIDE was warm today, but a cool breeze coming in from the fjord signaled the end of summer.

Haldis didn't mind. She looked forward to winter every year, when the lake froze over and few people bothered to take the long walk from the village to visit it. In winter, it felt like the lake belonged to her.

Today, she would share it with her sister.

She sat facing Svanhild in a patch of clean dirt, the lake just a stone's toss away. The gentle sound of water lapping against the shore calmed her spirit. It was the perfect place for a casting.

"What is your question for the gods?" she asked. She hoped for some insight into what Svanhild wanted the answer to be. That would make the reading go more easily.

"I want to know…" Svanhild bit her lip, thinking. "I want to know how to kill Ulrik."

Though Haldis knew better than to be surprised at her sister's boldness, still her eyebrows shot up. "Is that a real question?"

Svanhild nodded with more determination now. "Do you not wish to kill the man who murdered our father?"

Haldis didn't answer. Her sister had a very different relationship with Jarl Tove than she did. And though she held no love for Ulrik after his murdering spree and threats to their family, she did not have revenge on her mind yet—only survival.

"I do," she said slowly, "but action is useless without thought."

"That sounds like something Father would say." Svanhild's eyes looked wet, and she blinked hard. "That's why I consult the gods. What do they recommend?"

Spilling the wood chips from her pouch, Haldis did her duty and read three runic symbols for Svanhild: man, danger, and rain. But when Svanhild asked for their hidden meaning, Haldis blanched.

"I don't know if I can do this," she admitted, staring at the wood chips. She knew their meanings, but personalizing an interpretation just felt like lying.

She felt blind in both eyes now.

"Forget the runes, then," Svanhild said. "What do you *see*?"

Restraining a sigh, Haldis shifted her legs to relieve the numbness building up in them. She did not want to pretend a connection with the gods again—the performance tired her —but for her sister, she would try.

Taking a deep breath, she strained her mind upwards, outwards, searching for the rainbow bridge that would take her to the gods in Asgard. Where were they? Why did they not answer when she sought them out? How would she ever know if they heard her?

She pictured something then: Svanhild, her golden hair longer than it was now, caught in a tangled braid. There was dirt on her face, a smudge of blood across her brow. She held a massive sword in both hands, the blade glowing with runes. Haldis recognized it at once: their father's sword.

"I see you with blood on your face," Haldis said, "a glowing sword in your hand."

Svanhild wriggled closer to her, leaning in as if she might see the vision too, from the right angle. "What else do you see?"

Haldis's vision blurred. It was as though she saw two things at once, two worlds overlapping. In one, there was Svanhild, cross-legged on the ground before her. In the other swam a different Svanhild, farther away, on her knees...

Haldis shut her eyes, and the second dream took over.

Svanhild was inside the longhouse, crying, begging. Haldis sensed why without knowing the exact reason. The idea just came to her, and her skin prickled as it did when she heard a song or story she knew was true.

"Your heart..." she breathed. "Your heart will surprise you. You will learn to forgive, for you, too, will need a second chance one day."

She opened her eyes to find Svanhild frowning at her. "What do you mean, a second chance? What happens?"

The vision was gone. Haldis wasn't even sure where the words had come from. "I don't know."

"What did you see?"

"You were on your knees, asking forgiveness for something that makes you weep. I did not see what it was, but I sensed the pain in your heart."

Svanhild nodded, her mouth forming a resolute line. She seemed to accept the reading, even if it bothered her. "And what should I do next? About Ulrik? About the marriage to his son?"

"The gods are not ready to tell you yet," Haldis said.

It was true that she had not seen an answer there, and she wasn't sure she ever would. Perhaps her sister would come up with a solution before long, and Haldis could do another reading to confirm whatever Svanhild had already planned, instilling her with courage. As a false seer, that was the best she could do.

Svanhild seemed to read her mind, as she so often did. Clasping her sister's hands in hers, she said, "You are a true völva, Haldis. Believe in your abilities. You saw a vision of me, right? I know you weren't lying to me."

"I did see something, but how can I know it comes from the gods? It could be my own mind's creation."

"That is how the gods speak to you," Svanhild insisted. "They speak to me too. Give me visions. It doesn't happen often, but I saw it last night. I had a vision of what would happen if I did not agree to marry Andor. I saw our bodies…" Her gaze drifted toward the lake, and she stared as though picturing the scene there all over again. Then she shuddered. "So much blood." Turning back to Haldis, she said, "It was the gods showing me a path I should not take. Loki gave me the words to say. He's planning some trick, I just know it."

Haldis did not doubt her sister's vision or her faith. She

57

believed in the gods' power, too. It was her *own* power she struggled to accept.

Svanhild leaned in to hug her. "Thank you for doing this," she said. "There are still many questions, but I feel better now."

"You are not scared for the future?"

Svanhild shook her head. "Of course not. Trust that the All-Father has a plan for us. We are his ravens, are we not?"

HALDIS STAYED BEHIND after Svanhild returned to the village. Her sister knew better than to insist she accompany her back, for Haldis had always loved to spend time alone at the lake. It gave her a rest from the curious eyes of the villagers. Though they were accustomed to seeing her at feasts and events, she preferred to hide in the longhouse most of the time, avoiding the rest of the world. She did not want everyone staring at the rash that ran along the side of her face, or her all-white eye through which she could not see. She did not want everyone asking her to cast lots for them and read their futures.

She wanted to disappear.

She lay on her back beside the lake, staring up at the bright blue sky. The sun was not yet overhead, making it comfortable to gaze up. The lake was surrounded on all sides by trees. This created a beautiful circle of greenery around the periphery of her vision, like the frame of a tapestry, with the sky at the center of the picture.

She closed her eyes and inhaled the fresh scent of the pine trees. The sounds of nature kept her company: water stirring in the lake, birds cooing in the trees, a wolf howling in the distance.

If only she could live here all the time.

She wondered at her affinity for this place. It was as if her spirit lived here even when she was not physically present.

Perhaps that's because her father had once left her here to die.

The memory of it came to her with the cawing of one of Odin's ravens. She recognized the bird as Muninn. *Memory*. It overpowered her. The memory played in her mind like she was experiencing it all again, her infant-self retrieved, the smells of the forest so new to her...

She lay on her back, still a newborn infant. Though she knew no words, she saw her father's face as he patted her belly one last time. She saw no tears in his eyes. His jaw was firm, his mouth set.

"You belong to Odin now," he said. "A sacrifice for the gods." Turning his face up to the sky, he said, "May you be pleased."

He looked at her one last time with his gold-flecked eyes, then rose to his feet and strode away into the woods.

Now she was alone. Abandoned.

Haldis's eyes shot open. The sky above was just as blue as before. The forest was peaceful. She breathed in and out, trying to calm her racing heart. She did not want to remember this, but Muninn was insistent today. Perhaps it was a reaction to Tove's death. Perhaps Odin wanted her to remember her father today, even if the memory pained her.

She closed her eyes again. The smell of pine, the lapping of the water... Then she was lost to memory again.

Her mother's face, peering down at her. Green eyes watching her, wet with tears. Above her mother's head, a raven circled, then lowered. The bird dropped onto her belly. She felt herself giggle. It might have been her first laugh.

Her mother's face widened in surprise. Tears filled her eyes. Then, a smile.

"Come, my raven daughter," she said. "Now I know how to save you."

Haldis opened her eyes again. Her mother had concocted the story about her. She claimed Odin's ravens had led her to the forest, led her back to her baby. Since Tove had been the one to leave her by the lake, there was no way Helga could have known where to go without the gods' help. Such was her story. The ravens landed on little Haldis, and she laughed. A newborn should not be able to laugh. It was a sign from the gods.

Since then, Haldis had been trained as a seer. Everyone believed she had a special connection with Asgard. It had been clear from her birth, her markings a tattoo of the gods. Even Jarl Tove had seemed to believe in her powers. In recent years, he had started inquiring after her for readings, wanting to know what was on the horizon. Plagued by nightmares, he knew something was coming.

How right you were, Father, Haldis thought now.

Yet she had never sensed anything too dark—other than the ravens who sometimes seemed to watch her with their dark eyes. Were they trying to warn her all this time? Had she been ignoring them, not taking them seriously enough?

She sat up and clutched the coin that hung around her neck, carved with the image of a raven. The seeress who had trained her, a woman named Asta, had given her the gift before leaving on a journey to the gods. Haldis had been too young to understand what that meant, but she treasured the coin, praying it would connect her to the gods as she so desired.

"Do I have a gift," she whispered into the wind, "or is it all just a story my own mother invented?"

She listened for an answer, but nothing came.

Then, a flutter of wings sounded near her ear. To her surprise, a raven perched at her feet, gazing up at her with its knowing black eyes. Somehow she sensed this was the same raven that had appeared in the longhouse last night, when she was casting lots for her father... the same raven who had spent the morning with her and her sisters.

"Are you here to keep me company?" she asked. "I hope you are not always a bad omen."

If only she could *truly* speak to the raven...

Just then, she heard an otherworldly voice in her head, as though from deep underwater. The raven tilted its head, and somehow Haldis knew it was the source of the words.

Your spirit understands. Trust in the gods, and trust in yourself.

CHAPTER 6

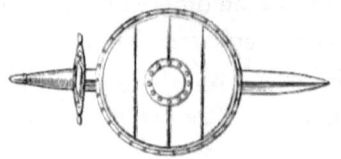

SVANHILD

"Ulrik is a two-faced trickster. He's not a man of his word."

Svanhild listened to talk like this as she strode through the village. Word had spread of last night's attack. As warriors and women awoke, suffering headaches from too much ale, they learned from Tove's housecarl Alf that Ulrik had attacked in the night, killed her father, and taken the high seat of Kaldvik.

"He's the son of Jarl Otso, who has long been a loyal friend of Jarl Tove," the man went on. A fisherman who went by the nickname Fish-Nose, he stood outside his house, speaking with the village's healer woman, Siggy, and black-smith, Balder. "Ulrik went against his own father to attack an ally of his own people." He spit on the ground in disgust.

"He chose the night he knew we would be at our weakest," said the blacksmith. "He must have been watching us. He knew about the feast."

"At least he waited until we were back from our travels," Fish-Nose said bitterly.

Siggy glanced up when Svanhild passed and waved for her to approach. Svanhild made her way across the crushed pine boughs that marked the road. The fisherman's house reeked of fish, onions, and leeks from whatever leftovers he was heating inside for his morning meal.

As Svanhild drew close, Siggy put an arm around her. "We all mourn the death of your father," she said. "I only wish we had seen some vision of this coming."

"My father often had bad dreams," Svanhild admitted. "He sensed something, but this…"

"It is too terrible a tragedy to comprehend," Siggy agreed.

Balder's jaw twitched. "I wish we had been there last night. I would have gladly followed your father to Valhalla."

Svanhild's heart beat faster at the thought. If they still expressed their loyalty to her father, would they follow *her* into battle? She had yet to prove herself as a warrior, but hearing their anger at the usurper Ulrik gave her hope. Perhaps they would band together with her, and they could be rid of Ulrik before he even had time to settle into a bed here.

Still, the idea of leading men into battle made her skin go cold and clammy. She longed for it and feared it at the same time.

Lifting her chin as her mother did when she needed confidence, she said, "I will not allow Ulrik to sit long in my father's hall."

She expected nods of agreement, perhaps a cheer of support.

Instead, Balder chuckled. "You are truly your father's daughter. He would be proud of you, little one."

Little one? She was old enough to marry, old enough to fight.

"You should go rest, Svanhild," said Siggy.

Fish-Nose simply stared out at the fjord, as if she was not even important enough to listen to.

Svanhild bit her tongue to keep from lashing out at them. At this point, it was her mouth that got her into more trouble than any sword she wielded. She imagined what her father would say in a moment like this: *Quiet your voice and you will hear the people. Stay still and you might hear the gods.*

Forcing her tone to remain steady, she said, "If you would truly stand with my father, then stand with me now. With enough supporters, we can seek vengeance against Ulrik."

"If we rush into the hall today, Ulrik will murder us on the spot," said Fish-Nose, turning to them at last.

Svanhild raised her eyebrows at him. "So you *were* listening."

"I have ears and eyes like Heimdall," he replied, referencing the watchman of the gods. "If it's supporters you need, I'll look out for them."

Balder nodded his agreement, his jaw tightening with resolve. "We need to formulate a plan before we rush into battle."

Svanhild would smile if she could, but her heart felt like it had been burned to ash. How long would it take for her to find her revenge? She wanted to burst into the hall now, but she knew these men were right to be cautious. And her sister's vision this morning had felt like a warning. Why would she be on her knees begging forgiveness?

She shook off the thoughts that swirled in her head. It was too much to process, for both her mind and her heart.

"We will set our plans then," she said. "Find as many men and women as you can, people willing to take up arms against Ulrik on my command. I won't put my family at risk. We fight when we know we will win."

"May the gods find favor in this plan," Siggy said.

Balder studied Svanhild. She tried not to squirm under his gaze. "Are you sure you're ready for this, little one?" he asked.

She fixed him with a fiery gaze. "I appreciate your concern for me," she bit out, "but you heard my father last night. I was to join you all next summer, sword in hand. Now, I intend to lead you. Will you stand with me?" She hoped the words sounded strong enough, for despite her nerves, her resolve felt forged in fire.

Balder nodded. Though he said nothing, it would have to be enough for now.

To Frode Fish-Nose, she said, "I will find you again to see what you discover."

Fish-Nose nodded without looking at her. Siggy gave her arm a squeeze, and it was done. They exchanged farewells, until happier days.

Svanhild turned to follow the main road back to the long-house. The path ran alongside the fjord, with small shops and houses on one side and the docks on the other. Her father's longships, still decorated with their red and white shields, bobbed in the water.

She looked beyond the village to the mountains, their peaks always white with snow. Kaldvik was a northern town —so far north, it was the only town for days, for outsiders feared frost giants here. But nestled between mountains on the edge of the fjord, Kaldvik had forests full of game and fertile soil where people built farms among the trees. It was a beautiful cove, blessed by the gods.

Svanhild would fight for it.

After she had walked several paces, she heard Balder's voice, lower now. "She would have made a fierce warrior, were she born a man. Such a shame Jarl Tove had only daughters."

The words struck Svanhild like a slap across her face. She

had never regretted being born a girl; her family never made her feel as though she was lacking.

Now she saw the truth. Perhaps it was not a curse to be born a girl, but she would have to cross a stonier path if she were to lead men now. Though her father usually led at least one or two shieldmaidens among his warriors each summer, Kaldvik's skald did not sing songs of *their* bravery or strength, for they were never known as the bravest or strongest. Still, Svanhild had always admired them, always pictured herself as one of them. But would the other warriors ever follow a shieldmaiden? Fresh doubts now flickered in her mind.

As she passed some of the houses that lined the road, the smell of fresh porridge and leftover stew wafted from a nearby roof as it was heated for dagmal, the first meal of the day. Svanhild wondered if she would have to share a meal with Ulrik this morning. The thought made her stomach churn.

Through an open door, she overheard a conversation from within one of these houses. Though she could not see who was inside, she halted along the outer wall to listen, careful that no one saw her.

"There is no one here who can lead us against Ulrik."

"What of Helga? She was a shieldmaiden once."

The sound of laughter filled the room. It sounded like at least three or four men.

"Not for eighteen years or more, since before her eldest was born. And she was never a leader of warriors."

"I've seen Svanhild train with her father. She may not have Thor's thunder, but she is quick as lightning."

"Are you suggesting we follow a girl?"

The men chuckled again.

"We need someone strong and experienced to lead us. And we need more men. Too many here support Ulrik."

"We should have been more prepared for this fight."

Svanhild bit her lip. The way these men spoke, it was as if this attack were not entirely a surprise. If Ulrik had supporters here, it would explain how he knew the precise moment to attack. The thought turned her blood cold.

Just then, she heard a voice from the street shout, "Everyone gather at the longhouse! Your new jarl wishes to address his people and put any fears to rest."

Svanhild watched the man make his way down the road, repeating his announcement as the people of her village began to stream from their homes and shops. She joined the throng as they headed to the longhouse, perched on a slope at the end of the road.

"Svanhild, take heart," said Revna, a raven-haired woman in town known for dying fabrics and weaving durable clothes. She caught up with Svanhild to stride beside her for a moment. "Your father died a warrior. He will be in Valhalla now, feasting with the gods."

Tears stung Svanhild's eyes, and she felt a ball forming in her throat. If she stayed in the crowd hearing people's condolences, she would burst into tears before them all. Such behavior did not befit a shieldmaiden—at least not one who wished to earn the trust of warriors when still unproven in battle.

Thanking Revna, she slipped away from the gathering and found a spot to stand in a small grove of trees. Though she was still close enough to see and hear everything happening at the longhouse, the shadows would hide her.

Once most of the village had gathered, Ulrik strode from the door of the great hall. He wore the same fur cape he'd had on during last night's battle. In the light of day, Svanhild saw streaks of blood running across it.

Her father's blood.

A tear slipped down her cheek. She did not bother to

brush it away. Safe in the trees, she let the hot tears roll down her face, making no noise. It was not a burst of emotion, but a slow release of grief as the reality of what had happened finally hit her.

All those years her father had spent training her, teasing her, taking her hunting in the forest, telling her tales of his battles and listening to her sing songs from the great sagas… It was all over. She would not see him again in this realm, in this life. He was off to meet the gods, and she was still here. Without him.

She felt a hole inside her at the idea of him not being there at the morning meal today. He always split his bread so the two of them could share it. But not today.

Not ever again.

At least, not until she joined him in Valhalla one day.

She clenched her teeth, glaring at Ulrik where he stood in front of the longhouse. That hall belonged to her family. It was her home. Grief would do her no good, unless she could shape it into an arrow of revenge. She would have her home back. And if men hesitated to follow her, she would find her father's rune-covered sword and lead them with the strength of a Valkyrie.

Ulrik's voice rose above the crowd. Other voices hushed to listen. Leaves stirred in the branches of the tree above her, as if even they were settling in to hear what this usurper had to say.

"People of Kaldvik, I come to you today with the hope of a new beginning. I am Ulrik, son of Otso of Mosfell. Like any warrior, I have come to make a name for myself. And like any jarl, I have come with the desire and intention to lead."

A few people in the crowd whispered to each other. Svanhild sensed their discontent.

Ulrik made a hand gesture over his shoulder then, and Helga appeared at his side. "As most of you know, I have slain the jarl to claim this house as my own, but I have spared the family of your beloved Jarl Tove. I know how much you respected his leadership. His family is safe with me."

He turned to Helga, taking her hand in his and lifting it in the air. Standing together like this, they looked completely united. But Svanhild noticed how her mother's hand was limp as a doll's. Her green eyes held a blank, dreamy expression. Had she ingested something, or was she simply delirious with exhaustion?

Whatever the truth was, Svanhild knew none of this was her mother's idea.

She winced to herself. The tears were already drying on her face, and now she realized how terrible this looked. If she wanted to convince the people of Kaldvik to join her family in an uprising against Ulrik, this show of support was not helping. It looked like one of two things: weakness or betrayal. Svanhild did not know which was worse.

Dropping Helga's hand, Ulrik continued, "The gods have already divined a plan to unite our people. First, as you know, we practice many trades in Mosfell that you do not yet know here in Kaldvik. Our craftsmen will come and share with you both their knowledge and their goods."

Svanhild laughed bitterly. He spoke as if her people had no skills, when Kaldvik's trade every summer was dependant on the people's incredible craftsmanship.

"Mosfell will serve as a place of commerce," he went on, "a point of contact between you and the Eastern and Saxon traders who are so far from here. Through this connection, Kaldvik will no longer be the cold cove in the north, but a flourishing town. " He paused, scanning the audience with his dark eyes. Silence hung like thick smoke in the air. Then he added, "This means you will all be far richer than you have ever been before."

"What of raids?" came a shout from the crowd.

Svanhild frowned. With songs of sea-kings making their way through the land, several men of the village had begun dreaming of raids. Though Kaldvik was very far north of any raid-worthy places, their fjord provided perfect access—and Skarde, their shipbuilder, was one of the best in the north. But Tove had never been eager to join in the new raiding tradition. Though he battled with the ferocity of a berserker when the need arose, he preferred trading expeditions and spent his summers making friendly connections with other Norse villages, merchants from the East, and trading towns that sprouted up where rivers converged. Kaldvik's would-be raiders grumbled, but they respected his decisions—or so Svanhild had always thought.

Now, Ulrik's eyes danced at the question. Even from this great distance, Svanhild recognized the bloodlust in his expression. "Of course we will raid!" he roared. "This reminds me of something I saw when I went raiding in the land of the Rus. The people there had a strange tradition of chaining wild bears, of trying to tame them. They would play games with these bears, the ferocious creatures held captive with collars. It was unnatural for such predators to be treated this way.

"Now, I know of your bravery in battle, and I believe you have been strangled in the same way as those bears, unable to show your true courage." Now his dark eyes glinted like shards of glass. "But you will be chained no more! With your skill in battle, Kaldvik will grow richer and gain more respect than ever before."

Several men cheered their approval. Svanhild wanted to note their faces, in case these were the traitors who had helped install Ulrik here, but their backs were turned to her. Other people shifted in response, speaking in low voices to each other. Did they agree with his plans, or were they expressing their concern?

Whatever they said, Svanhild sensed the mood changing, and she didn't like it.

Ulrik went on to detail several of his successful raids over the years. It sounded like he spent his summers raiding while his father stayed behind to rule in his old age.

"I also know you are skilled farmers," Ulrik went on, changing tone. "Your knowledge of how to make seeds flower and turn soil into food is well-known across this land. I look forward to learning from you and continuing to grow in abundance."

Svanhild shook her head. There was that word again: abundance. As if they did not already have everything they needed here in Kaldvik. She knew Ulrik's town was flourishing, but that was all based on raiding. Mosfell's land was rotten, its soil barren. Its inhabitants could not grow their own food, and this reliance on theft made them weak.

Now she saw why Ulrik wanted to expand here. Perhaps his father had sent him after all. With their houses united—one a southern town wealthy from raids and flourishing through commerce, the other a rich northern farmland with many skilled laborers—they would be doubly successful.

But Kaldvik's farmers did not need Ulrik—not the way Ulrik needed Kaldvik's farmers.

"And the gods have shown us another way forward. I have seen this in my dreams for so long, and now the time is here." Ulrik looked around the crowd as though searching for something. "Where is Tove's daughter Svanhild?"

Her stomach dropped. She cursed under her breath.

Behind Ulrik, Andor stepped into the light. His gray eyes were like a storm. She wondered if he was as unhappy with this arrangement as she was.

To her surprise, his gaze went directly to her hiding place among the trees. She tensed, but it was too late. There would be no more hiding today.

Rising, she strode into the sunlight. Heads turned to look at her as she passed. Though she heard more whispers, she could not make out what anyone was saying as she went to join Ulrik, Andor, and her mother in front of the gathering.

A fleeting thought passed through her mind then. If she shouted a battle cry now, would the mob descend on Ulrik? She imagined them tearing him apart with their bare hands —an ugly thought, but not unsatisfying.

But no, such a thing would invoke chaos. From what she had gathered this morning, the villagers saw her as too young and inexperienced to lead them. They did not even believe in Helga, who had once been a shieldmaiden. It was a part of her mother's history she rarely spoke of, too far in the past.

Standing beside Andor, Svanhild faced the people of Kaldvik. She knew almost every face staring back at her. Today, she saw too many frowns and furrowed brows, questions on people's lips and tears in their eyes. It was as if she saw their hearts breaking in front of her.

To them, this looked like betrayal. Maybe it was.

Svanhild thought back to last night. Maybe she had been weak. Her mother had been ready to wield a sword against Ulrik, knowing they would all die. Why had Svanhild given in?

She could have let Ulrik kill her. She had been ready for it. But the thought of her mother and sisters being slaughtered was too much for her. The idea that her father's bloodline would die with them was too hard to bear.

When Ulrik announced the marriage between Andor and Svanhild, audible gasps shot out from the crowd. This was the stitch that completed the tapestry. A new day dawned, whether they liked it or not.

At the back of the crowd, she caught the blacksmith Balder's eye. His mouth was stitched in a frown. What must he think, seeing her beside the enemy's son moments after pledging her vengeance? She held his gaze, hoping he would see through this.

Odin, guide me, she prayed. *Let the people know we are not traitors.* She looked up at the blue sky, hoping the gods would hear her.

Haldis had seen her in a vision this morning, on her knees and crying for forgiveness. Was this betrothal to Andor the betrayal she wanted to be forgiven for? Or was worse coming?

She tried to shake the stubborn doubts from her mind. The gods must have a plan for her. Loki had put those words in her mouth, after all. And in her vision, Haldis saw her wielding a glowing sword.

She would be a shieldmaiden yet.

CHAPTER 7

BRYNJA

B rynja awoke to the sound of shouting outside her
door.

Sitting up, she took in her surroundings, confused for a
moment about where she was. Instead of her usual fur-
covered bed, she was on a single tapestry covering the hard
earth floor. Feeling a lump digging into her hip, she reached
under the tapestry and removed a pebble.

"And where is your cursed sister with that ugly,
unseeing eye?" came the man's voice again, just outside the
door.

She tensed, remembering the bear of a man who had
burst into their hall two nights ago. It was his voice that
bellowed outside the door now.

Her mother lay on the ground next to her. Brynja saw her
eyes flutter open, a sad look crossing her face as she, too,
realized where they were.

The nightmare was reality.

Outside the door, Svanhild's voice answered. "My sister's eye sees more than you know."

"Remember where you are," the man growled. "This is no longer your father's house, girl. You will not come and go without consulting me first."

"Are we to be captives in our own home, then?"

"Like any good Norseman, you must earn the trust of your king," he replied. "Now, get inside and change for breakfast. You reek of fear and the forest."

The wooden door swung open and Svanhild was shoved inside. Brynja saw a flash of dark fur in the doorway—the usurper. She shuddered as memories of that night flooded her, bringing tears to her eyes again.

Once the door was shut, Svanhild collapsed onto the floor in a sighing heap. "Did you hear him?" she said. "*We* must earn the trust of our king? First, he's not a king. And that entire statement should be reversed. Father always said a jarl must earn the respect of his people, not the other way around."

Helga lay a hand on Svanhild's arm. "Quiet, or he'll hear you."

Svanhild's hazel eyes flashed like a lightning storm in a forest. Brynja studied her sister, who had their mother's golden locks and their father's sharp features—a combination that made her look both beautiful and fierce. Brynja shivered at the wildness in her sister's eyes now. She would not want to face that look in battle.

"How can you not fight him?" Svanhild said. "I saw how he took your hand in front of all those people just now. *Our* people. He made it look as though you two were united."

"And you stood beside Andor, your future husband," Helga said calmly. "This is the way it must be for now."

"You mean we must look like traitors *for now*," Svanhild spat.

But Brynja understood her mother. They needed time to come up with a plan. "We are four women alone," she said. "We should not poke the bear, especially when he's still in his battle rage."

Mother nodded her agreement. "Once he is happy here, fat and well-fed…"

Brynja finished for her. "Then we can put poison in his honey."

"We'll anger Thor if all we do is poison his honey," Svanhild said, "and I doubt Odin would be eager to welcome us to Valhalla for such a trick." Then she tilted her head, considering. "Maybe Loki would visit us in Hel, though."

Brynja surprised herself by laughing. She didn't think she could do that, with the pain still twisting her stomach into knots. But having the company of her mother and older sister made her feel that despite everything, at least she was home.

The door squeaked open then, and Haldis slipped inside, shutting the door behind her. Her presence brought a new peace to the room. Though Brynja had never put much stock in the gods, she sensed something special in her sister, a glow that set her apart. Brynja had often wondered if they truly shared the same parents or if Haldis had been born in another realm, a child of elves or giants or the gods themselves.

"Our new jarl is in a foul mood," Haldis remarked, sitting on the floor with them and crossing her legs at the ankles. She pushed down her hood, revealing the moonlight strands of her long, straight hair. "I just passed my old bed. Someone else is sleeping in it, a dark-haired girl. She must be Ulrik's daughter."

Helga's jaw tensed. "We will have our revenge, daughters. Trust that Odin has a plan for his ravens."

"I spoke to a few people yesterday," Svanhild said. "The

blacksmith Balder and Frode Fish-Nose are upset about what happened. They are looking for more supporters now. When we have enough, I will lead them in battle against Ulrik." She pursed her lips in thought. "I am not sure everyone will be eager to follow a woman into battle, but I will prove myself to them."

Brynja could picture her sister leading men into battle, their family's raven shield in one arm and their father's sword in the other. With her blonde hair waving behind her, Svanhild would rush into the fray like the beautiful Valkyrie Brunhilde.

Yet as Brynja imagined the fight, memories flooded her—of the great bear entering the hall, of his wild battle cry, of his axe slicing through her father...

Tears stung her eyes. She could not lose Svanhild the way she had lost her father. She didn't want to say goodbye to anyone else from her family.

"It's too dangerous, Svanhild," she said. "You're not ready."

Her sister's hazel eyes burned through her. "I am tired of people telling me I'm not ready." As a tear slipped down Brynja's cheek, Svanhild's gaze softened. "Brynja, I'm sorry. I know it is dangerous, but this is my destiny."

"Then why did you agree to marry Andor?" Brynja asked.

"I wish I hadn't. They are all monsters. But I saw a vision of what would happen if I did not agree to the engagement, and then Loki gave me the words..." Svanhild's voice trailed off, and she chewed on her lower lip as she remembered.

Helga put a hand on Svanhild's leg. "You did what you could to defend your family," she said softly. "You may not have used a sword, but you were brave all the same."

Svanhild shook her head but said nothing.

Haldis's dream-like voice drifted in like smoke. "Ulrik knew the precise moment to strike, after the hall had cleared out and everyone was drunk and asleep. He must have had help from people here in Kaldvik."

"I hate to think it, but it would not be unusual for a usurper to have supporters," said Helga. "How else would he be able to steal the throne from a jarl so beloved?"

Brynja's eyes widened. "Do you remember the voices we heard in the forest, when we left the feast for fresh air?"

The idea of traitors in their village clawed at her stomach. Who in Kaldvik would betray their family? She went for frequent walks with her father through town, visiting people in the marketplace and checking on farms. The people had always greeted Tove with a smile, offered him ale, happily discussed their work with him like children eager to please a parent. As far as Brynja had seen, her father had been loved by all.

"Even if some have betrayed us," she thought aloud, "we must still have many supporters. Our family has been ruling here for generations."

That word "generations" reminded her of a story her father had told her once, after he attended the annual assembly where jarls and free men gathered to discuss laws and settle disputes...

"Father once told me of a raider," she began, "who returned home after weeks at sea, only to find another man living in his home. This man had laid claim to the raider's farm." She squinted at the circle of floor between them, trying in vain to recall the details. "I don't remember all the reasons why, something to do with marriage."

She returned her gaze to her family. Her mother stared at her with rapt attention, while her sisters leaned forward on their knees to listen.

"But the raider insisted that the farm belonged to him, because it had been in his family more than six generations. And he won his case."

Haldis's dark eye gleamed. "Our family has lived here for more than six generations, right?"

Brynja nodded, flushing with satisfaction as her idea found purchase in their minds. "Which, by law, makes this hall ours and ours alone."

Helga's eyes were bright now, and her words spilled out in a rush of excitement. "You are right, Brynja. It is not unheard of for jarls to steal titles from other jarls, but we could make such a case for our home. It would be a start."

But Svanhild scowled. "We cannot wait for the law. We have a right to seek revenge. Ulrik stole his title from Father without honor."

"And what would you do, sister?" said Haldis. "Would you invite Ulrik to a duel?"

"Would that be such a terrible thing? It is what brave men do…"

"Brave *men*." Haldis sighed. "We all admire your resolve, sister, but to rush into battle is to rush into death. You are a woman. You have never led anyone before, and you have never seen battle. You need more training."

"You're saying you do not believe in me?" Svanhild lifted her chin, but Brynja saw her eyes clouding with doubts.

Their mother was the one to answer Svanhild, her voice gentle. "Your sister is right. We must take care with our actions now. We need a good plan. Brynja has a clever idea, for the law will be on our side."

Brynja swallowed in a dry throat. She knew how to win this argument. "You know what Father would say about all this."

All eyes turned to her.

Realizing they did not understand, Brynja explained, "Father would want us to resolve this without bloodshed. At least we should try."

Svanhild took a shaky breath, as though releasing all the

tension inside her. Then she nodded. Brynja sensed she did not like the plan, but the mention of their father's wisdom was enough to quiet her for now, just as Brynja had hoped.

"When does the assembly next meet?" Haldis asked.

"In late spring, before the summer raids," said Brynja. "But only men may attend."

Svanhild groaned. "Of course that is the way."

"All we need is a man to represent us," Haldis said. "Perhaps Alf. He is our housecarl, and he always accompanied Father before."

Brynja considered. "As a free man, he could attend. But would his status be enough to represent the case of an earldom?" She remembered her father telling her about the important men who attended the annual assembly, many of them jarls and wealthy landowners. "Someone who is family would be more appropriate, but we have no male family here."

Their mother hummed in thought, then said, "We may not have family here in Kaldvik, but your father has a brother."

"Our uncle Asmund," Brynja smiled.

They had not seen their uncle in years. His first wife, here in Kaldvik, had died in childbirth when Brynja was seven years old. She still remembered the screams as Haldis helped the priestess carve runes into their aunt's palms, the metallic scent of blood poisoning the air.

And in the end, it was all for nothing.

The next summer, Asmund never returned from the annual raids, for he had met and married another woman in the great city at Uppsala. It was at least a fortnight's trip down the fjord, making it difficult for them to visit each other. Brynja had not seen him since.

"I thought he did not wish to return here," Brynja said. "For him, this place is too haunted by dead spirits."

"He will come for this," said Helga. "I know Asmund well. He may be wounded by his past, but he loved your father greatly. I believe he would do anything for this family."

"What if he wants to rule?" Svanhild asked.

Their mother shook her head. "He is within his rights to take the high-seat, but he never sought power. I believe he will defer to whatever we wish in these matters."

Svanhild frowned. "We should not need a man to help us."

"Perhaps not, but the truth is that we may need him," said Haldis. "It is wise to seek support, especially from our own family."

Ignoring Svanhild's disgruntled look, Helga said, "Uppsala is far. If someone left at the full moon, they would not return until the next, or likely several days after. And that is only if they make good time in a longship."

Brynja smiled at the thought of the four of them taking off in a longship together. As a girl, she had spent many days in ships with her sisters, playing raiders as the boats bobbed against the wooden docks, still tied to their posts.

"Perhaps we can all travel together," she said. "I will fish, Haldis can read runes, and Svanhild and Mother will be the shieldmaidens."

Mother gave her a sharp look. "This is not an adventure from the sagas, daughters. We need to stay here and look after our people, keep an eye on Ulrik, appease him. Svanhild, remember you are set to marry Andor. We must not let anyone know of our intentions here."

Svanhild glared at the floor. Brynja had the impression her sister would rather be scowling at their mother, but she did not dare. After all, Helga made sense. Even if none of them liked the idea of playing nice with Ulrik and his family, it was the smartest way to stay safe until they had the support they needed.

"Who do we send, then?" asked Haldis.

"It should be Alf," Mother replied. "There is no doubt he is loyal to our family, and he is a good rider. We'll send him on horseback to deliver the message to Asmund in Uppsala."

"On horseback?" Svanhild puffed out an incredulous laugh. "That would take weeks, in both directions."

"Then we wait," Helga said sharply.

Brynja looked around the dim room. Her hips were sore from sleeping on the floor, and the air tasted damp like something was rotting. As far as she could tell, this was an empty storeroom. She longed for fresh air.

"How do we ask Alf to undertake this mission?" she asked, thinking of the force with which the new jarl flung Svanhild into this room and slammed the door behind her. "It sounds like Ulrik intends for us to be prisoners here."

Svanhild lifted her chin. "I will sneak out."

But Mother put a hand on Svanhild's knee to quiet her. "We cannot arouse suspicion so early. Remember what Ulrik just said. We must earn his trust."

Svanhild scoffed. "I don't intend to do any such thing with that monster. *He* is the one who should earn *our* trust…"

As Svanhild ranted and Helga attempted to hush her, Brynja's mind darkened with images of that night. There she was, cowering behind the thatched wall, while her father's blood splattered across the floor of the hall. The memories were like a cold gale washing over her, making her shiver. Perhaps this hall was haunted now.

Watching the anger flash in Svanhild's eyes, Brynja knitted her brow. Why wasn't she courageous like her sister? Why was it that, every time she thought of what happened that night, it was not rage that welled up in her chest, but a sadness so overwhelming she felt she would be washed out to sea? She longed for even a flicker of Svanhild's indignation to light her heart on fire. But all she felt was cold, scared, tired…

"I will tell Alf," she said suddenly, interrupting her sister. The air in the room went quiet as everyone stared at her in surprise. "Remember how I used to sneak out of the hall to find Erik? Yet you never saw me leave. I know how to walk unnoticed." She swallowed the lump in her throat. "It is the least I can do, after all that has happened."

Mother's eyes were wet with tears. "We are all brave in our own ways," she said, giving Brynja's arm a loving squeeze.

"Where can I find him?" Brynja asked. She didn't want to sit and debate it, or spend too much time planning. Better to get out of this stuffy room and finish the job, before she could feel too many emotions—especially before any fear set in.

"He is likely at Siggy's," said Haldis. She watched Brynja with her seeing eye, so dark it seemed like an endless hole through which Brynja could see the gods, if only she had more faith. "Take the back door, sister. And don't let anyone see you."

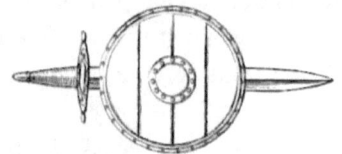

CHAPTER 8

SVANHILD

"*A*ndor, my son, take your betrothed for a stroll around the village," Ulrik barked, as they finished their morning meal. "People in town are bound to discuss the news of our takeover this morning. I want them to see you two together as soon as possible. It will put their minds at ease. A smooth transition of power."

Svanhild felt sick. So she was to be just another playing piece in Ulrik's game of power.

When she sat up to complain, her mother shot her a warning look from across the table, and she snapped her mouth shut. She had promised her mother she would behave to avoid arousing any suspicion.

But she was not convinced their plan was strong. In her heart, she believed having their uncle attend the annual assembly for them was a cowardly path. Her father would have wanted them to stay safe, but he was also a man of courage. After years of training with wooden swords at

Father's side, she saw the warrior in him. If he were alive now, he would kill Ulrik for trying to steal his home from him. She could not picture him hiding behind the mumblings of law men. Not when steel rang louder.

Ignoring her upset stomach, she shoveled one last bite of porridge into her mouth. She knew she needed to eat to keep her strength.

"Yes, Father," Andor agreed.

All morning, he had cast glances at Svanhild, questions in his eyes. Now, he looked at her again.

She glared back at him. The last thing she wanted was attention from this man. Whatever she had promised, she would not marry him. She just needed time to come up with a plan.

Odin, tell me what to do, she prayed.

Seated beside Helga, a girl about Brynja's age sat up straighter. "Father, may I take Helga and Haldis for a walk around the village?" she asked in a sweet voice. "Perhaps they could introduce me to some of the people here. I would love to see what these famed farms are like." Her hair was nearly the same chestnut shade as Brynja's, but curly where Brynja's was straight.

Ulrik grunted as he swallowed a hefty bite of food. Once his throat was cleared, he said, "I don't trust them to leave the longhouse. Talk to them here, if you must." He turned to Helga. "Where is your other girl, the pretty one with the dark hair?"

Svanhild tensed. Brynja had slipped out just before their meal to find Alf and send him to Uppsala. Even if she found their housecarl at Siggy's house soon, it would take some time to make her way back to the hall.

"Her name is Brynja," said her mother. "She must have gone for a walk."

Ulrik's gaze darkened. "She left the hall?"

85

Svanhild barely noticed her mother's hesitation before she said, "My family is accustomed to morning walks." Her tone was light, as though she had not sensed the threat in Ulrik's voice.

Snarling, Ulrik waved to a pair of guards at the front doors of the hall. "Go look for her," he called to them. "When you find her, don't be too gentle in bringing her back. She should learn not to leave without permission."

Svanhild glared at him. "Are you afraid of what a fifteen-year-old girl will do?"

Ulrik's gaze swiveled to her like a ballista seeking its target. Though her heart thumped harder, she kept her eyes locked with his, refusing to back down.

Helga's voice jumped in before either of them could exchange more words. "We would be happy to accompany you on a walk when your father feels it is safe, Kindra," she said to the girl who had spoken before. Svanhild had no idea how her mother had already learned the names of Ulrik's family members. "For now, I'm sure Svanhild will enjoy time with her future husband." She caught Svanhild's gaze then, a warning flash in her eyes.

Svanhild bit her tongue to keep from arguing. She hated the way her mother agreed to Ulrik's commands, the way she diffused tension, the way Ulrik ordered them all around. He treated them like dolls who were supposed to put on a good show so he could win the favor of Kaldvik's people. Her father would have found Ulrik's behavior weak and pathetic.

But if they played along, they would be safe. Her family would survive.

Everyone waited for Ulrik to rise from the table first. As soon as he did, Andor stood and extended his hand to Svanhild.

This was another of the enemy's performances. Where

Ulrik made demands, it seemed his son would try to trick them with kindness.

She forced her hand into Andor's. His fingers closed around hers in a warm, sturdy grip. Though she needed no assistance, she let him help her to her feet.

"Thank you," she said through gritted teeth.

Andor inclined his head to her. He had spoken little at breakfast. *A man of few words is a man of many thoughts*, her father had always said. Sometimes, such a man possessed true intelligence, weighing things in his head before speaking so that every word had true meaning. Such a man could make a strong ally. But other times—too many times—it meant the man was scheming, untrustworthy. *Trouble.*

Andor dropped Svanhild's hand. With a word of farewell to the others present, he led her out the front doors of the hall.

Outside, the sun shone brightly, the air a warm kiss on Svanhild's skin. Summer was showing off one last time.

"It is a beautiful day," Andor said, as they strode down the slope toward the rest of the village.

Svanhild glared at him. No one else was nearby now, and despite her mother's warnings to play along with Ulrik, she did not see why she needed to be so nice to the beast's son. Perhaps she could test his temper now.

"It seems the sky has yet to hear about the tragedy that has befallen Kaldvik," she said.

Andor remained silent. The only sounds were birds singing in the trees and the crunching of their own footsteps in the dirt. Just as Svanhild wondered if he would ignore her comment, he said, "Everything happens as the gods will it."

"A diplomatic answer," Svanhild said. "Will you be jarl after your father?"

"That is his plan for me," Andor replied.

Imagining Andor as jarl of Kaldvik—two generations

ruling this land that was her home—made her stomach tighten. She clenched her fists at her sides, her nails biting into her palms.

Why was she even out here with Andor now? She wanted to be away from him, away from his whole family. This walk could not be over soon enough.

They made their way onto the main road that ran along the fjord, stretching from the longhouse to the farmland. A few voices called from houses and shops, but it was too early for the market. The people of Kaldvik were still attending to morning chores and enjoying dagmal.

She turned her attention to the fjord. Almost every day she enjoyed this scene, the sparkling waters of the fjord taking on the colors of the sky and forest.

On the docks she spotted the shipbuilder Skarde, his back hunched and his long red hair flung back over his shoulders, hammering wood to form the sloping sides of a longship. But today a strange ship bobbed in the water at the edge of the northern woods. Even from this distance, she saw the front of the ship was carved to resemble a dragon's head, while the back of the ship was shaped like a tail pointed toward the sky.

Andor must have followed her gaze, for he said, "My father's ship. It carried us to these shores."

"Made to look like a dragon?" Svanhild pursed her lips, studying it. "Dragons are greedy creatures, are they not?"

"One could argue that." Andor parried her jab. "But they are also fierce, intelligent, and feared among men."

"The fierce and feared may be fitting," Svanhild said, "but let's not go too far." She glanced at Andor to catch his reaction. Was that a twitch in his jaw?

From the docks, Skarde looked up from his work and waved at them. "Good morning, Svanhild!"

Though his eyes darted to Andor, he did not greet him.

Was he waiting for an introduction? Svanhild did not want to be the diplomat, but there was no way around it. Andor would learn everyone's name in time, whether she helped him or not.

"This is Andor, son of Ulrik," she said. She introduced Andor to Skarde in turn. Turning to the shipbuilder then, she asked, "I thought you built your ships in your private inlet?" Usually new ships were built away from the harbor, closer to Skarde's house where he could easily source materials from the forest.

"I do," he replied, "but I'm meeting a few others here for work today. I could use the company."

"Did you hear Ulrik's speech yesterday?" She hoped he might give some hint about where his loyalty lay, for a ship-maker would make a useful ally.

"I slept overlong yesterday." Skarde's shoulders hunched, and he ran a hand through his tangle of red hair. "When I awoke, my head felt like it had endured a good pounding from Thor's hammer."

Svanhild laughed. "You are not the only one, I'm sure. How are you feeling today?"

"Not much better."

"You should ask Siggy for a tonic."

"Fresh air is all I need," he replied. His eyes scanned the blue sky overhead, and he smiled. "Freyr is with us today."

Svanhild frowned. If the gods were angry at what had happened here, the skies should be storming. So why did the god Freyr bless them with sun today?

Taking one last stab at learning where Skarde stood, she said, "Perhaps he is giving the people of Kaldvik some small happiness in the midst of our grief."

"It certainly does sweeten it," Skarde replied.

She studied him for a moment, wishing she understood him better. But to ask him outright if he was upset about what happened, with Andor standing right beside her, might be taking things too far. As much as she hated being with the son of her enemy right now, she knew better than to anger him too much. First, she needed to see what kind of man he was—and if he was the same form of beast as his father.

After bidding Skarde farewell, she and Andor continued on the path through the village. Opposite the fjord was a row of wooden buildings, the shops and homes of laborers and craftsmen who worked in town rather than farming their own land. She breathed in the familiar chatter of her people as they began their day's work. If only Andor were not beside her, she could almost pretend everything was the same as it had always been.

"Can you tell me who is important here?" Andor asked.

Svanhild gave him a sharp look. "Everyone is important here. These are my people."

"You know I meant no offense."

"You will not bite back, then?" Svanhild observed. In her young lifetime, she had met many jarls and sons of jarls. All had thought themselves gods, and many made themselves even less attractive with their short tempers. Perhaps Andor was of a different build.

"I will not take the bait," Andor corrected her.

She looked to find his gray eyes dancing, a smile playing on his lips.

"Oh, so you think you know me," she said. "You think I'm testing you."

"Do you deny it?" Andor didn't wait for an answer. "Over the years, I have met many daughters of jarls. All of them are spoiled in their own ways… and some are too clever for their own good."

Svanhild scowled. Here was a young man unafraid to insult his future wife. Perhaps she had been right about him after all—he *was* a self-centered jarl's son.

"You realize I am not happy to be here with you," she said.

"Yet you agreed to my father's idea of marrying me."

It took everything in her not to tell him why she had done it—that it was only to save her family, that she had no intention of going through with it, that she wanted nothing to do with his terrible family.

"I can point people out," she said begrudgingly, "but I won't introduce you to everyone."

Andor inclined his head, accepting the offer without argument. She hated him more for that. Why was this son of Ulrik so calm?

As they passed people, she felt eyes on her. On *them*. She did not want any of them thinking this stroll with the enemy was her idea, so she added, "I won't be smiling, either."

Andor surprised her by chuckling. "I would not expect anyone to lie about the feelings of their heart. Especially not someone like you."

Svanhild wanted to ask what he meant by that, but she bit her tongue. If he refused to argue with her, it was better not to engage him in a conversation. She wanted to finish this walk as quickly as she could and return to her family.

They passed the home of Siggy, the town's healer. A table ran along the side of the house, shaded by an awning. Siggy normally sat working at this table, but today she was nowhere in sight. Svanhild noticed several tiny pouches labeled with the rune ⁎, which she inscribed on her health poultices; they were the tonic people sought after a night of excess. Herbs were scattered across the table, as though Siggy had just left them there.

"That is the home of our healer woman, Siggy Larsdotter," Svanhild explained to Andor. "She is well-respected throughout the village."

"Is she a völva?"

"No, but you see the concoctions on her table? Some say

she imbues them with magic. She does not practice seidr, but it's clear she has a connection with the gods."

Just then, Siggy appeared at the back of her house. Her eyes met Svanhild's, wide with worry. Svanhild's hair stood on end as she realized the secret message in the healer woman's expression. Her sister must be there with Alf.

She grabbed Andor's arm without thinking, turning toward the fjord so her back was to Siggy's house. Andor's eyebrows shot up, but he turned the same direction.

"Do you see the treeline there?" She pointed to the left side of the fjord, fighting for something to say that would distract Andor for the moment. "That is where the ship-builder lives, just around that bend in the fjord. He builds his ships there. It's a beautiful spot."

Though Andor eyed her with curiosity, she kept her gaze on the water until he looked there too. Then she gestured to a place down the road, keeping herself pointed away from Siggy's house.

"That's where we have the market," she said, ushering Andor along.

They continued on past the row of small buildings. Svanhild breathed in relief when their backs were to Siggy's. She prayed her sister had been successful in her quest.

As they made their way through the village, Svanhild pointed out the blacksmith Balder, who was polishing swords; the tapestry-weaver Revna, who sat mending a red raven banner of Jarl Tove's family as though nothing had changed; and several farmers who had come to town to sell chicken eggs, fresh vegetables, and pastries made with berries.

"You care for these people," Andor said. "I can hear it in your voice."

They wove around the back of the village now, returning through the pine trees. Svanhild was glad to be away from prying eyes. On the slope ahead of them, the massive long-house sat with smoke from the hearth curling out its rooftop. Her home, now held hostage by these usurpers.

"My father loved these people," she said. "My family has been ruling here since Kaldvik was founded more than six generations ago. We are farmers who love the land."

"I know this must be painful for you."

She laughed bitterly. "Don't pretend to apologize–"

"I wasn't going to," he said quickly, surprising her.

As they came to the last patch of trees before the clearing to the longhouse, Andor stopped. Svanhild halted to face him. He studied her for a moment, his gray eyes like an over-cast sky in winter. Was that the way of his spirit, then?

"I am loyal to my father, as you were to yours," Andor explained. "I cannot pretend I would have done all of this the same way my father did, waiting for the cover of darkness, conquering in the shadows while the enemy's best warriors slept." He shook his head, his jaw twitching. "But I will stand by my father until the end. And I can promise you, he is not such a terrible man."

Svanhild wanted to argue. Ulrik was a beast. Whether he wore his bear fur or not, she had seen the cruelty in his eyes when he licked her father's blood from his axe.

Tove had been a brave, wise leader, worthy of his family's loyalty. Ulrik was not.

Now, she offered Andor the only truth she had in this moment. "I understand loyalty."

Andor nodded. "And that is why I understand that you will always be loyal to your family, even after our marriage. I promise I will take care of you when that day comes. In the meantime, anything I can do for your family–"

Svanhild raised a hand to stop him. "I don't want your promises. Not now. Just…"

She sighed, not knowing what she wanted. She hated

seeing the honor in this man, for what she truly wanted was to hate him. But some part of her resolve there was crumbling now, like a leaf crushed and swept away in pieces on the wind.

"It's best if we don't spend much time together," she said at last. "There is no need for us to be friends, or to pretend such. Let us go about our business and take care of our families, as our hearts tell us."

Andor opened his mouth to say something, then snapped it shut. With a nod of cold agreement, he turned to walk back to the hall.

Svanhild followed, sneaking a glance at him in an attempt to read his thoughts. But his face remained stoic, his mouth firm. Whatever cool calm he had exhibited before was turned to ice.

She smiled in relief, for his coldness was far easier to stomach than his kindness.

CHAPTER 9

BRYNJA

*B*rynja moved in shadows, soft and swift as a deer in a forest clearing.

She had sneaked through the village like this many times before, usually to meet Erik in secret—though sometimes all she needed was an escape from a feast where she drew too much attention.

As a child, she had received compliments on her sweet demeanor and her bright green eyes. But people forgot about her as soon as she retreated behind her parents' legs. Only recently had her mother started insisting that, as a lady of the hall, she braid her hair more often and line her eyes with kohl. That is when she noticed men's gazes landing on her like moths drawn to lamplight, and sneaking in shadows became more challenging in the same measure it grew more desirable.

If only she could don *tarnkappe*, the legendary cloak of invisibility.

But there was no time to fret about that now. She had to focus if she was going to make it to Siggy's house unnoticed.

The healer lived in a small wooden home perched on the main road that ran through the village, the fjord right across from her front door. There was no way Brynja would make it if she aimed for that door—too many people milled about the main road, setting up for market or working on the docks. Better to weave her way through the forest that ran behind the buildings, where sunlight had to work hard to break through the canopy of pine trees.

Here, Brynja could remain in shadow, as long as she was careful.

She darted through the trees, keeping her movements quick, in part because this instilled lightness to her body. Each time her boots crunched on a pine bough underfoot, she sucked in her breath. Then she set her gaze on the path forward, searching for the shade, forcing other thoughts from her mind. She would not grow fearful. Not anymore.

Once she was out of the shadow of the longhouse, she slowed her pace, breathing easier. Ulrik was unlikely to have guards this far from the main hall. And there, just beyond a small clearing, was the long table that ran along the side of Siggy's house.

As she approached the place, a rattling sound erupted from the shade of a nearby tree. She froze. Looking toward the noise, she spotted a man curled up beneath his wool cloak, his eyes shut. Another snore shook through him. Brynja exhaled in relief. Tip-toeing past him so as not to wake him, she continued to Siggy's house.

The healer sat at the wooden table beside her home, an awning overhead shading her from the morning sun. A branch snapped beneath Brynja's foot. Siggy's gaze shot to her like an arrow, but the alarm faded when she recognized the source of the noise.

"Brynja dear," she said, "what are you doing here?" She kept her voice low, as though she understood that Brynja should not be out. Though Siggy claimed no direct connection to the gods, Brynja had always sensed a strange wisdom about her, for she grasped things by instinct that others would not.

Brynja glanced around to see if anyone else was nearby.

"We are alone," Siggy said. She finished tying a piece of twine around a pouch of healing herbs, then patted the wooden bench next to her. "Come sit, dear. I heard what happened to your father..."

Brynja shook her head, a snapping gesture to indicate her hurry.

"Or we can go inside," Siggy suggested.

Brynja wanted to be done with this, fast. Though she was not looking forward to being back in the longhouse where Ulrik roamed like a bear scenting a new cave, she preferred that to being discovered outside the hall.

"He doesn't know I'm gone," she explained. "I am looking for Alf."

Siggy nodded, then quickly stood and led her to the back of the house. Opening a small door here, Brynja stepped into the one-room home, where a humble hearthfire flickered in the center of the room. The smell of herbs and hearth smoke made her throat itch. She blinked as her eyes adjusted to the dim lighting, for the house had no windows. It was no wonder Siggy preferred working at her outdoor table.

When the healer called Alf's name, the housecarl appeared from behind a wooden partition as though conjured from the smoke. His red hair, normally well-combed, was ruffled like a bunch of bird feathers. As he drew near, Brynja noticed a splatter of blood on his fur-trimmed cloak.

She remembered the sight of him rushing into the battle

97

against Ulrik, sword in hand. Where was that sword now? How had he escaped?

Another time, she would have discussed the horror with him, but she did not wish to relive it now.

He inclined his head to her, affording her the respect he always had. Just two days ago, he had been the most esteemed servant in their hall. Now, he hid here like an animal from a hunter.

"Forgive me for not being with your family during this difficult time," he said.

"There is nothing to forgive," she said. "I am relieved you are safe. But I come now with a favor to ask of you."

"Anything," Alf promised.

In the flickering hearth light, his blue eyes shone with reverence. Haldis had once told Brynja that this was a man who believed the gods had called him to their household, who performed every task as though he were serving the All-Father himself. Brynja realized now what she was asking him to do—realized he would never refuse her—and her heart ached.

"My family wishes to call on my uncle Asmund," she explained. "We need his aid to regain our home from this usurper."

"A wise plan. What do you need me to do?"

"Deliver the request to Asmund. He is living in Uppsala with his new wife, though we have not heard from him in many months. Tell him we need his aid as soon as he is able to come. We would prefer it if he makes the journey back with you."

Alf stroked his beard for a moment, toying with one of the silver rings that held a braid in place. "If he asks what is required of him when he arrives, what should I tell him?"

A good question. Brynja knew her uncle did not wish to return to this place, where his first wife rested in her burial mound. As much as she believed Asmund loved his brother—loved their whole family—it would take a strong argument to convince him to make the journey back to Kaldvik.

"Tell him we hope to bring our case to the ting," she said, referring to the assembly. "I can't speak for my sister Svanhild, but I *think* my family wishes to avoid bloodshed."

A smile crossed Alf's face at her small joke, but his eyes were still sad. "Your sister may yet have her chance to be a shieldmaiden, though I have no desire to see more bloodshed in your family's hall."

Brynja thanked him for that. "Do you need anything? If you require another place to stay…"

"He is welcome here for as long as he needs," Siggy jumped in.

"I will be fine," Alf said. "And I will undertake this task with haste. Perhaps it is wise to wait until nightfall to leave."

Siggy nodded in agreement. "The new jarl won't like to see anyone sneaking out of town, especially if he recognizes your face from that night. I saw you joined in the fighting."

Alf nodded. "This usurper did not see fit to cut me down, once Tove was dead. I do not believe I am destined for Valhalla."

Brynja placed a hand on his arm, letting her instincts guide her. Though she had never formally learned how to behave as a jarl's daughter, she had watched her mother enough to catch which gestures indicated compassion. In this moment, she wished she could bring Alf back to the longhouse with her, where he could be a familiar face, his gentle voice filling their hall again…

But she shook away the thought. In just a single night, their entire world had changed.

"I feel as though I am seeing the world upside-down," she said.

Alf placed his hand atop hers where it rested on his arm. "Like Odin hanging from the sacred tree."

Brynja gave him a sad smile.

Patting both of their arms, Siggy said, "Let us hope it brings new wisdom, then."

Brynja wished them both well and took her leave. Siggy helped as lookout, making her wait a moment as someone passed by. Only when the healer woman motioned that it was safe did Brynja dart back into the shadows of the forest.

The trip back to the hall was quicker, her heart light as she realized her quest was a success. Alf would deliver their message to Asmund. Now all they had to do was wait.

As she approached the longhouse, leaves rustled near her shoulder.

Holding her breath, she slipped behind a tree to hide. But it was too late.

A hand shot out and grabbed her arm, the grip so tight she gasped.

"There you are," said a gruff voice. Brynja didn't recognize the man, but she spied a ring in his beard marked with the symbol of a dragon. If he were from Kaldvik, he would wear the mark of the raven.

"Who are you?" she asked.

He ignored her question, pulling her along toward the longhouse. "Jarl's been looking for you. You missed dagmal."

Brynja forced herself to breathe, though each breath shook as the man violently dragged her toward the hall. With each step, he pulled her forward before she could fully catch her footing. Every time she tripped, his grip on her arm only tightened and he yanked her harder.

She had seen thralls treated this way in other households, when they were weak and underperforming. Now she knew how terrible it felt.

When they finally made it to the hall, he released her with

a shove toward the jarl's table, where several people now sat finishing the morning meal. She barely had time to spot her mother and Haldis at the end of the table before Ulrik was on her.

"Where have you been?" he demanded. His huge form loomed over her, casting a shadow that made her feel more exposed than being in a sunlit clearing.

She felt the eyes of everyone at the table staring.

"I was taking a walk," she said. She hated how her voice quavered, revealing her fear for all to hear.

"You are not to leave whenever you like," Ulrik said. "As I told your sister earlier, you and the rest of your household must earn my trust."

She nodded, forcing herself to stand straight even as every muscle in her twitched with the desire to cower. "I understand."

"Good." Ulrik nodded to the man who had brought Brynja in, thanking him for his work. Then he grabbed Brynja's arm in the same spot the guard had. She winced at the bruising pain. "Get to the table," he barked, launching her toward the onlookers.

She jolted from the shove, relieved only that her arm was free again. Without thinking, she clutched at the place that ached. A couple of the women at the table, whom Brynja did not recognize, looked away as though embarrassed for her. Though she wanted to rub the pain from her arm, she stopped herself, realizing that would look weak.

She took a seat beside her mother, glad to be far from where Ulrik sat at the table.

"Are you all right?" Mother whispered.

Brynja understood the hidden question there. "Yes." She nodded too, a confirmation that her duty was done.

Despite her bruises, Alf was on his way to Uppsala.

CHAPTER 10

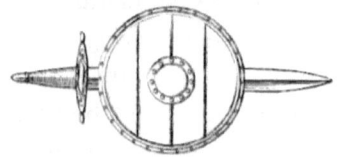

SVANHILD

*A*s preparations began for Jarl Tove's funeral, Svanhild felt on edge. A strange quiet filled the longhouse, making her restless. She longed to be out in the wild air of the forest, free from the daily duties of sewing her father's funerary clothes. She needed something to distract her from worries about Alf on the road to Uppsala.

And though she knew it was a fair plan—seeking rights to this land by law—she felt nobody would respect them for it. The people respected warriors, strong men who fought for everything they had, people willing to die for it.

Only through bloodshed could her family gain respect here. Even as women.

Svanhild liked to think she was not afraid to die for her land, her family, her people, her home. But in truth, she trembled every time she thought of fighting Ulrik.

And so she armored herself with her father's words: Fear is the egg that hatches courage, for one cannot be brave without first being afraid.

If only she had a way to prove her skill with the sword. That would be the first step in leading warriors to seek revenge.

While Haldis was busy studying with their gothi, preparing to lead the funeral procession, she and Brynja moved their massive loom into the main hall so they could sew Father's funeral outfit. But the work of stitching was not enough for Svanhild. The longhouse, her home all her life, now felt like a prison.

They sat by the light of the hall's side door, so the sun could guide their hands on the loom. Several times, Brynja had to nudge Svanhild to pay attention to her labor, for she kept gazing out the door, imagining her father there with Alf, surveying the fields and forest, discussing the year's harvest and trade. She would never see her father out there again.

So much loss for a single moon cycle. As the tears burned her eyes, that same heat seared a fire in her heart.

She would have her revenge.

Guide Alf's path. Bring us our uncle, she prayed. And then, clutching the teardrop pendant around her neck, she added, *Guide my sword when I seek vengeance.*

One afternoon, after Svanhild had pricked her finger with her bone needle for the fifth time, Brynja offered to take over the sewing herself. Svanhild thanked her. Brynja was the only skilled seamstress in the family anyway, and Svanhild could tell the repetitive work soothed her younger sister's mind. Since they had stood at the loom or sat with fabric in their laps, Brynja had not cried even once. Svanhild hoped it was a good sign.

This was Svanhild's chance to escape. No more wasting time on chores; she needed to be out in the village, finding supporters. Every day that passed with Ulrik seated in the jarl's chair was a day wasted, and she feared he would garner support sown from seeds of apathy over time.

She just needed an excuse to be out of the longhouse.

Announcing to the guards in the main hall that she would help with the animals, she went to the back of the longhouse, on the opposite side from the family quarters. Here, the kitchens smelled of savory onions, leeks, and fish as the thralls prepared stew for the evening meal. As she moved past the servants' quarters, her nose tickled as new, musty smells mingled with the cooking. The back door of the longhouse was open to the sunshine outside, and she was greeted with the bleating of goats, snorting of pigs, and trembling mew of sheep. She smiled as she walked out of the building and into the animal pens, separated and enclosed by short wood fences. With an animal at her side, perhaps she could sneak into town and pretend she was on an errand, should anyone under Ulrik's command stop her.

Jumping over a fence to the sheep pen, she grabbed a rope hanging on the fence and used it to tether two sheep together.

"Hello, smelly creatures," she said.

One of the sheep let out a high-pitched *baaa* in response. The other merely stared her down with his tiny black eyes, like two beads on a doll's face.

"You are cute, for a wild thing," she said. She wondered if that's how people saw her when she wielded a training sword. The thought made her laugh at first, then scowl. If only she could prove her skill with a blade...

Holding the rope at the other end, she led the two sheep out of the pen. The quiet one stubbornly stood his ground for a moment, but with a gentle *coo* she was finally able to convince him to follow. She led them around the other pens to the edge of the forest, where a makeshift path snaked through the trees, running parallel to the main road of the village. Here, she would tread a quieter path away from prying eyes.

Breathing in the scent of pine, she sent up a silent prayer to the gods, thanking them for this freedom and asking them to guide her path now.

She headed toward the home of Frode Fish-Nose first. Though only a few days had passed since she'd spoken with him, she hoped it was enough time for him to keep his promise. As a fish-seller, he would have had plenty of conversations with other villagers. He probably sent fish to local farms, too—and he could have packed a note in them, a piece of wood carved with runes, seeking support for Tove's family.

It was a dangerous game, but one they had to play.

As she neared the back of Fish-Nose's house, a few shouts and cheers drew her attention. She followed the noise to a small clearing in the forest, popular as a dueling spot. Here, a group of about thirty people were gathered in a group, their backs to Svanhild. She approached, urging the frightened sheep with her. As she pushed her way into the crowd, she saw what they had gathered around: a pair of men, sparring with daggers. They had removed their shirts; sweat gleamed on their backs as they circled each other, taking turns lunging and jabbing. The crowd cheered them on, whistling or wailing when one or the other delivered a nick deep enough to draw blood.

"What's going on?" Svanhild asked an older man standing at the back of the crowd.

He grinned at her, revealing a missing tooth. She wondered if he'd lost it in battle or from an accident. "The lads are practicing their form. Thorbjorn and Hafdan, warriors from your father's pack."

She watched the two men in their battle dance. They were hardly lads, but young warriors at least a year or two older than she was. If they had battled with her father, they probably had several years of experience already—experience she wished she had been afforded.

One of the men, with wild blond hair and eyes as blue as a summer lake, struck with the quickness of a snake. He hissed and howled as he leapt around his opponent, grinning in enjoyment of the bloody game. A silver pendant depicting Thor's hammer Mjolnir bounced against his bare chest.

"Who's that, with the light hair?" she asked.

"That's Thorbjorn," replied the man, "the crazy one. He may wear that pendant in honor of his namesake, but he has Loki's mischief in him."

Svanhild stifled a laugh at the description. She understood the feeling of being blessed—or perhaps cursed—by Loki's spirit. Her father had said the same about her when she used to wave her wooden sword as a child, claiming she was a girl who would never be tamed.

She watched Thorbjorn's opponent then, a dark-haired man with a neck so thick with muscle, it reminded her of knotted rope. His steps were slower, steadier, and he stared at Thorbjorn like a watchful wolf.

"That one seems the smarter one, with the dark hair," she said. "I can almost hear his thoughts."

"Hafdan is new to Kaldvik, but your father trusted him greatly this summer. He proved himself a wise warrior, but..." The man stopped talking, his eyes widening as Thorbjorn jumped forward and unleashed a flurry of dagger attacks, slicing Hafdan's arms several times. The old man whistled through his teeth at the spectacle. "But Thorbjorn is the better warrior," he finally went on. "All the men here know it."

To Svanhild's surprise, Thorbjorn refused to let up in his attack. She admired his unrelenting energy. How would such energy translate off the battlefield? Watching the sweat glisten on Thorbjorn's strong back, it was not hard to picture his passion in other places, too. But thinking of such things made her blush. She shook the fantasies from her head, focusing on the battle again.

Hafdan tried to parry and dodge Thorbjorn's continuous slicing, but it was too late—Thorbjorn had his knife at Hafdan's throat.

"Yield," Thorbjorn said, panting like a dog in the sun.

Hafdan took a long breath, then exhaled, his shoulders slumping in defeat. "I yield."

The crowd cheered. Thorbjorn grinned as he removed his dagger from Hafdan's throat. Then he grabbed the man's hand in his and lifted it in the air, turning to the crowd.

"Let the gods see that on this day, I have bested Jarl Tove's greatest warrior!" he shouted. Then, still smiling, he added, "And let it be known that Hafdan is probably still the better warrior, but I will take what victories Thor grants me."

Everyone chuckled, and Hafdan slapped him on the back in thanks. The men parted as friends, a respectable end to the performance.

"Is he humble, too?" Svanhild wondered aloud.

The man shook his head, chuckling. "Everyone knows Thorbjorn is the better warrior. He says things like that to win more favor, is all." Winking at Svanhild, he added, "Honeyed lies, just like Loki."

As the crowd began to break up to talk in smaller groups or return to the day's duties, Svanhild noticed Thorbjorn eyeing her. Figuring he needed her acknowledgement, she inclined her head to him. But instead of returning the gesture, he approached her, as though taking up some unspoken invitation. As he neared, she smelled sweat and dirt on him, the musk of a man doing what the gods intended for him.

"You fought well," she said, flushing at his nearness. He drew too close to her, as if he already knew her. Perhaps she could use this quiet moment to win his support, if he was so well-known among her father's warriors. "Thank you for speaking my father's name here today. Did you respect him?"

"I respect him still," Thorbjorn said. "You're his little warrior daughter, aren't you?"

A heat rose in her at the word *little*. "My path is one of a shieldmaiden," she confirmed, lifting her chin.

Thorbjorn backed away from her then, spreading his arms as another of his devilish grins warmed his face. Loudly, he said, "Did you all hear that? Jarl Tove's daughter walks the path of a shieldmaiden, yet I have never seen her in battle." He eyed the sheep behind her. "It looks like you have important women's duties to do instead of fighting."

The words stung like a slap. It was bold, to insult a jarl's daughter. But Svanhild supposed she was no longer a jarl's daughter.

She studied him for a moment, trying to collect herself so she wouldn't simply snap at him. Yes, Thorbjorn was insulting her, but from the dancing light in his blue eyes, she could tell he wanted her to react in front of all these people. It was another performance—a bit of flyting, where two warriors insulted each other with brags about their own battle prowess—and she could be a part of it if she took the bait.

Perhaps the gods had guided her to this moment, to this crowd, to this man fresh from a fight.

Her heart racing, she shot him her sweetest smile. She would take the bait. "Is this second-best warrior trying to challenge me?"

"Ah, I never said I was second best, but I take your meaning." Thorbjorn's tongue played at the corner of his mouth as he thought for a moment. He was clearly enjoying the attention as people began turning to watch what would happen next. "Why is it up to me whether I challenge you? Does this daughter of a jarl let others decide her fate?"

Svanhild glared at him. If she let him get away with this, nobody would ever follow her to seek vengeance for her father.

"I challenge you, Thorbjorn," she said.

The crowd hooted in surprise, and several women in particular cheered. As a breeze stirred the pine branches around them, Svanhild closed her eyes for a moment, sensing the gods watching. They *had* guided her here. This was her chance to show her skill with a weapon, in front of so many people of Kaldvik. Perhaps then she could persuade them to follow her.

"Name your terms," Thorbjorn said.

She thought for a moment. Her own training had prepared her to wield a sword or an axe, and from what she had just witnessed, Thorbjorn relied on his swiftness. He did well with a tiny dagger, but how would he do with a heavier weapon? Though he was not the biggest warrior she had seen, he was still bigger than she was. If she could call on the swiftness of the raven, she could beat him.

"Swords and shields," she said. Then, thinking it best to keep the battle short and relatively bloodless, she added, "We fight until first blood is drawn." It was not as fierce as battling until someone yielded, the way Thorbjorn and Hafdan had just fought, but it would suit.

Thorbjorn agreed. People gathered around them to watch as a nearby warrior handed them each a simple sword and an unpainted shield. A woman took the ropes of the sheep from her, her eyes alight with excitement at the performance she was about to witness. It was not every day a woman challenged a man to a battle.

Svanhild took a moment to familiarize herself with her weapon, feeling the leather grip of the hilt and weighing the blade. She was used to training swords, which were made of lighter metal or wood. This weapon would require more of her strength.

In her right hand, she gripped her shield.

Feeling the crowd surrounding her, she realized she was now in the battle arena, watched by dozens of pairs of eyes. Her mouth went dry. Her heart beat like a drum in her chest. She imagined her father in the crowd, his amber eyes watching her form and technique. She just needed to remember everything she'd learned…

"We start at the clap," said the warrior who had handed them the weapons.

Thorbjorn nodded to him; Svanhild mimicked his gesture, trying to recall what warriors did before these show battles. Though she had seen them before, she had never studied their intricacies.

When Thorbjorn lowered into a half-seated stance, like a cat about to pounce, she bent her knees too. She bounced a few times, feeling the supple give of her knees, the strength of her thighs, the lightness of her feet. She wished she were not wearing a dress, but at least the fabric was lightweight.

She remembered her father's training. Wield your weapon like another limb. It is part of you.

Everything went quiet. No one spoke. Svanhild forced herself to breathe, the only small sound she could hear now.

The warrior clapped. The snapping sound stirred birds from nearby trees.

And then Thorbjorn was on her.

He swung his sword at her waist. She leapt backwards, avoiding the blow just in time. He swung again. Dodging, she gasped, realizing he was hitting her on her unprotected side. Her shield was in her right hand, her weapon in her left—opposite to most. Her father had told her to train with whichever hand felt natural for her to hold her blade.

But she had never fought against someone like this. Not where they could draw blood.

Gritting her teeth, she focused on *his* unprotected side—the same side where her own sword was now raised.

She swung her blade toward his shoulder, taking care to attack without hitting him too hard. He jumped back to avoid the blow easily. Still, his blue eyes gleamed when she came at him again in the same way. This time, he parried with his sword, knocking her left arm back. Pain shot up from her wrist. Seeing her stagger, Thorbjorn grinned.

She glared and lunged at him again, aiming straight forward this time. He blocked the jab with his shield and countered with a stab of his own; she blocked too.

They danced like this for a time, jabbing and blocking, until sweat began trickling down Svanhild's back. She saw why the warriors had removed their shirts and wished she could do the same. The thought almost made her laugh.

Thorbjorn's blade hit her shoulder—the one that held her shield. She thanked the gods there was no searing pain, so no cut. But that was lazy. She needed to focus.

The cheers of the crowd rang in her ears as she circled Thorbjorn, keeping her weight low, waiting for an opening. Her father would have wanted her to think through the battle—but how?

Thorbjorn held his shield as protection against the left side of his body, while his sword rested comfortably in his right hand. He watched her with the same careful expression in his eyes, only he was smiling.

Then he bowed low, like cattle, and with a bellow that

echoed through the forest, he slammed his entire body toward her.

She blocked his sword with her shield, but the blow still knocked her backwards. She winced as she hit the ground, hard. The wind blew out of her all at once. To inhale again was another battle.

As she scramble to her knees, she realized her shield was gone, flung a meter to her right.

The flash of a blade drew her eyes. She rolled to avoid the blow. Barely.

A smile crossed her face as she saw her opportunity. If she took time to grab her shield, he would nick her. If she hit him on his left, he would block. If she hit him on his right, he would parry. But if she could distract him...

As she leapt to her feet, her fingers skimmed the ground to grab a handful of dirt.

She flung the dirt in his face.

Thorbjorn blinked, fast and hard. This was her chance.

She spun out of his reach for a moment. She readied her sword to jab him.

But as she planted her foot to stop her spin, she felt a searing pain on her left arm, saw the glint of metal.

She didn't even have time to lunge forward.

Looking down at her arm, she saw her sleeve was torn, revealing a red gash across her skin.

First blood. The battle was over.

She had lost.

Thorbjorn threw his head back and howled like a wolf at his victory. The crowd cheered, though a few mumbled as though disappointed at the predictable outcome. Svanhild imagined nobody was surprised. How could she, a girl who had never seen battle, best her father's most respected warrior?

She glowered as Thorbjorn celebrated, leaping about like

a drunk man around a fire. Perhaps he *was* the best warrior in Kaldvik, but he acted like a boy rather than a man. She knew he was a respected warrior, but his behavior now only made her defeat sting worse.

Thorbjorn surprised her then when he grabbed her wrist, causing her to drop her sword onto the forest floor. Lifting her hand in the air, just as he had done with Hafdan, he said to the crowd, "I cannot take great pride in besting a woman in battle, but I have given her an honest fight, without holding back."

Svanhild knew she should thank him for that, but all she could do now was scowl. She had failed. She deserved to fail. All her life she had dreamed of being a shieldmaiden, and now—when the gods gave her this opportunity to prove herself—she had shown nothing but weakness.

The crowd finished their cheering and began to trickle back to the village, returning to their duties. This left Svanhild and Thorbjorn alone in the clearing. Thorbjorn turned to her, still grinning. His face was flushed from exertion, the smell of sweat wafting from his bare skin even stronger than before.

"Did you have fun, princess?" he asked.

"Did I have fun being defeated and humiliated?" She hated how bitter she sounded, but the words flew from her lips before she could stop them.

Thorbjorn showed her his own arm, which was covered in marks, some fresh and some scarred. "The life of a warrior. If you're going to be a shieldmaiden, you'd best get used to it."

He left her there then, chewing over his words. At least he had not discounted her. But after her poor display in battle, he would be the only one to call her a shieldmaiden. She wondered if he only did it in jest anyway.

Branches stirred behind her. Turning, she was surprised

to see Andor walking toward her. What was he doing here? He wore only a simple blue tunic today—no fur cloak—and his bronze hair was combed back and tied behind his head. She was surprised at how fresh and handsome he looked. Or perhaps in her defeat, she was just tired of being around sweating warriors right now.

"Did you see the fight?" she said.

She hoped he hadn't. But why did she care what he thought? Perhaps it was better to appear weak to him, so his family would underestimate her. Yet for some reason, she hated the idea of Andor—specifically *him*, this calm, steady man who thought he would marry her one day—seeing her fail.

He cleared his throat. "My father is looking for you. He is not happy you're missing from the longhouse."

"I'll bet he's not," she muttered. The only thing to make this day worse was a lecture from Andor and a reprimand from Ulrik later.

Andor drew closer to her, bringing with him the rich smell of cedarwood and something sweeter, like honey. It was an intoxicating scent. He surprised her then by ripping the trim of his shirt and reaching toward her upper arm, which was still bleeding lightly.

"What are you doing?" She flinched away from him out of instinct.

"You should cover that wound."

She relaxed enough to let him wrap the torn piece of fabric around her upper arm. Her dress today was yellow, and the blue fabric from Andor's tunic complemented it. She almost made a comment about it but bit her tongue in time. There was no need to befriend this man just because he wrapped her arm in some cloth. He was here to retrieve her on his father's orders, after all.

Still, she was glad it was him and not one of Ulrik's

guards who had found her. After seeing the bruises on Brynja's arms, she did not want to be handled by any of Ulrik's other men. For some reason, she trusted Andor not to harm her.

She felt a wave of exhaustion then. If only she could collapse right here on the forest floor. She longed to be away from Andor, away from the crowd, away from everyone. She had come out here seeking supporters, and now she walked away in dishonor.

What did the gods think of her now? What would her father think if he saw this? She hoped he was not watching from Valhalla.

"I did not see the battle," Andor said, answering her question at last, "but I am sure you fought well."

She glared at him. "I wish that were true, but no. I've humiliated myself in front of the people who swore to follow and protect my father. That was my chance to…" She stopped, realizing she was saying too much. "Just take me to your father, and I'll endure whatever punishment he has for me. I want to go home. If I can still call it that."

Andor studied her for a moment, his gray eyes softening. "I'll tell him you were out picking mushrooms. You don't even have to see him. You should rest."

"I hardly have a bed anymore."

"That has already been remedied."

She narrowed her eyes at him. "What do you mean?"

He didn't answer, but turned to lead her back to the longhouse. His calm demeanor made her itch to test him, just as she had on their walk a few days before. But now was not the time. She hardly had the energy left to open her mouth, let alone argue with Andor.

Suddenly remembering the sheep, she looked around for the creatures. She spotted the woman who had been holding them for her, partially hidden in shadows where she stood between two forest trees, waiting.

Svanhild cursed to herself. This woman had seen her exchange with Andor and heard her speak of her humiliation. She thought she had hit her limit for embarrassment already, but clearly she was wrong.

Forcing a smile and thanking the woman for her help, she took the ropes of the sheep and began leading them back toward the longhouse. Andor strode alongside her. They walked in silence for a moment, the only sounds birds overhead and twigs snapping beneath their feet. Then she noticed the corners of Andor's lips twitching, as if he were laughing.

"Is something funny?" she snapped.

"I just..." A chuckle escaped him. "I don't understand the sheep."

She shook her head. The nerves of the battle hit her all at once then, and when she let out her breath, she laughed. Perhaps it *was* ridiculous to be leading a pair of sheep through the forest right now, after everything that had happened. The laughter lightened the load on her heart, and she breathed in the fresh air with a small smile.

"This day could not get any worse," she moaned, then laughed again.

Andor smiled at her. "I swear the day will get better. I will take care of my father for you, and you can take one of those naps you are so fond of."

She gave him a sidelong glance, sure he was teasing her. She *did* enjoy sleeping during the day when she could. "Thank you," she said, feeling strangely more cheerful at his side. And she had to say it. In this moment, no matter how much she wanted to hate this son of her enemy, she was grateful for his help.

Now she just needed to recover from her humiliation. There was no time to even look for Frode the fisherman anymore, or seek anyone else to fight with her. She was almost afraid to ask anyone now. Who would follow her after seeing her failure?

Looking up at the canopy of pine trees overhead, she issued another prayer to the gods.

I have failed you, Odin. Help me recover from this.

It was the only prayer she could think of.

CHAPTER 11

HALDIS

*H*aldis was in a back room, tracing runes onto a twisted wooden staff, when Svanhild's head peeked into the doorway. "Haldis," she whispered, "I need to talk to you."

Haldis glanced at the gothi Gorm, who had been watching her and correcting the symbols over her shoulder for what felt like half the day now. Her eyes burned from the incense wafting through the room, the earthy scent making her head spin. Gorm, their household priest and Haldis's instructor for the past several years, claimed the herbs would help her connect to the gods. If that is what this clouded feeling in her head meant, she wasn't sure she wanted to.

Gorm said, "Svanhild, your sister is at work today." This is what he always said when Haldis had a long day ahead of her.

"It's important," Svanhild said, still keeping her voice down. Then, glancing around her as though to make sure she was alone, she added, "Sorry, Gorm."

The gothi narrowed his kohl-rimmed eyes at Svanhild, then turned to Haldis. At nearly sixty years old, his face was covered in wrinkles, which seemed to swirl and blend with the runes Haldis had just drawn on his forehead and cheeks earlier to practice the art. Someday, she would draw such runes on the jarl's skin—the jarl who was not her father. Or so Gorm claimed, but Haldis had yet to find any evidence that Ulrik even knew she was alive in the longhouse. Though glad to hide from the new jarl, she worried that all his attention went to her mother and her poor sisters. Brynja still had bruises from being handled so roughly a few days ago...

"Hurry, before someone finds me," Svanhild hissed, ignoring any judgment from Gorm. "Andor is talking to his father for me, but I don't know how long it's safe to be out here."

Haldis gave Gorm a small nod. "Thank you for your lessons," she said, standing. "We will continue tomorrow?"

Gorm nodded, saying nothing. Perhaps the greatest lesson Haldis had learned from him was the power of communicating through silence. As she slipped from the room, she shuddered to feel him watching her, wondering what he must think of her. But still he treated her like a jarl's daughter, and without her father to command her, she was able to do as she pleased. She only chose to study with Gorm these days because it kept her out of the main hall and away from Ulrik's gaze.

Besides, in just a few days, she would help lead her father's funeral. She needed to prepare.

Now, she followed Svanhild down the lamplit corridor to the room where they had been sleeping. Opening the door, they found four straw pellets covered in wool blankets and pillows. It no longer looked like a cold storeroom, but a cozy bed chamber—only a little crowded with the four beds.

Haldis and Svanhild exchanged glances.

"It is true," came Brynja's voice behind them. "Someone has prepared our chambers for us."

The three of them slipped into the room and shut the door behind them. Brynja held a candle, which she used to light three wall sconces. Haldis could almost swear they were new too.

"Well, I'm not complaining," Svanhild said, flopping down on one of the beds. "But I had a terrible day. That's why I needed to talk to you, Haldis."

Sitting on the bed across from her, Haldis folded her hands in her lap to listen. Though the room smelled damp, she was glad to be away from Gorm's incense. Already her head felt clearer.

"I went out today," Svanhild explained, "intending to seek out Frode Fish-Nose who is supposed to be finding supporters for us. On the way, I discovered two men fighting in a clearing. They were Father's warriors."

"Who were they?" Brynja asked, sitting beside Haldis.

"Their names were Thorbjorn and Hafdan."

Brynja nodded. "Two of Father's best warriors. Hafdan just arrived in Kaldvik two summers ago, after his wife's father left them his house here. And Thorbjorn's axe is nicknamed Blood-Drinker. They say he's killed more than a thousand enemies, but I'm sure that's an exaggeration."

Svanhild raised her eyebrows. "Do you know everything about everyone in Kaldvik?"

"I used to walk through the village with Father every month," Brynja replied with a shrug. "I got to know people."

Haldis hid a smile at Svanhild's reaction. Sometimes her older sister was so absorbed in her own world, she failed to notice the merits of those around her.

"I knew their names, but I had never seen them in battle before," Svanhild went on. "After they fought, Thorbjorn came over–"

"Who won?" Brynja interrupted.

"Thorbjorn." Svanhild waved her hand to brush away any other questions Brynja might have. She clearly had a story to tell. "He insulted me. He was taunting me. So I challenged him to a fight."

Haldis closed her eyes, grimacing as she imagined the scene. As skilled as Svanhild was with a training sword, to pit herself against Thorbjorn—the greatest warrior of her father's pack—was foolish, not to mention dangerous.

"I hoped to gain favor with our people, if they saw me fight," Svanhild said, then bit her lip. "But I lost. Terribly. I was humiliated."

Haldis shook her head. "Did you believe you could win the fight?"

"Of course," Svanhild said.

Haldis took a deep breath to find her inner patience. Allowing no judgment to enter her voice, she asked, "And what made you think you could best our father's greatest warrior?"

Svanhild leaned forward on her knees. "The gods led me there, Haldis. If the people here are going to follow me to avenge Father, then I have to prove myself–"

"Stop being so impulsive." The words snapped out of Haldis before she could catch them. Svanhild's eyes widened as though she had been struck. Taking another deep breath to steady her voice, Haldis continued, "If you try to fight every man who challenges you, your life will be too short for your revenge."

"Our goal should be to win back our home," Brynja added. Her brown eyes flashed in the dim light of the room, surprising Haldis. Her little sister did not usually get upset. "That's bigger than your pride, Svanhild."

Haldis watched as Svanhild chewed on her lower lip for a moment, then buried her face in her hands. She almost thought her older sister might be crying, but her shoulders stayed still and no sound escaped her. When Svanhild finally emerged from the shell of her hands, her face was pink and her eyes pleading.

"What do I do?" she said, looking pointedly at Haldis. "Ask the gods. Tell me what to do to recover from this."

Haldis felt for her sister. She had never heard Svanhild—her brash older sister—sound so unsure of herself. The lost battle must have broken something inside her.

"I have told you what I saw," she said softly. "You will fight with Father's sword, and your hair is not much longer than it is today. That is all I know." Thinking back to the vision, Haldis considered another meaning she had not seen before. "*If* the vision is a sign that you will fight Ulrik, let us hope it does not show you seeking revenge before you are ready."

"What do you mean?" Svanhild frowned.

"Remember the other part of my vision. You were begging forgiveness for something. We must be careful, sister."

"That's why I was trying to win support by fighting…"

Haldis lifted a hand, quieting her sister. "I know you are eager for vengeance, but your skill in battle is not what will win support. You have never even *seen* battle, sister. Be honest with yourself and your limitations."

Svanhild set her mouth in a firm line, but she did not argue.

Haldis continued, "The people of Kaldvik fought for our father, even when he did not seek battles. They will follow you, too. But I believe you need to find another reason for them to."

"Like what?" Svanhild asked.

Haldis had no answer for that. Svanhild's gaze darted to Brynja, who shrugged. They all stared at each other a moment, reflecting.

"We wait for our uncle Asmund," Brynja said softly, interrupting the thought-filled hush in the room. "We can win this without bloodshed, remember?"

Haldis nodded in agreement, but she caught Svanhild biting her lip again.

If her vision of Svanhild as a shieldmaiden was true, they would not win through words alone.

CHAPTER 12

BRYNJA

*P*reparations for Tove's funeral kept Brynja's fingers busy for several days, but her mind was not so fortunate. She was tasked with helping their household's seamstress weave funeral clothes for Tove, every stitch a reminder of who she had lost.

When memories of her father's death did not cloud her thoughts, she worried for Alf. Each day she and her sisters marked how far he must be on his journey to Uppsala. When there was no word of him for five days in a row, Brynja finally began breathing normally again, knowing he must have made it out of reach of any spies Ulrik might have planted around Kaldvik. Yet still she wondered how her uncle would react to their plans. Would he be willing to come and help them, or had he put his life in Kaldvik behind him forever?

"Watch your stitching," said Ursula, the thrall who had

been seamstress in her family's household since before she was born.

Brynja blinked back to the present moment. It was not the first time she had lost her way in the forest of her thoughts.

"Sorry," she said, redirecting her attention to the intricate stitchwork before her. The wool, dyed in their family's signature red color, was rough beneath her fingertips as she sewed a raven design into the tunic's chest. "I wish this were a softer fabric."

"Funerary clothes don't need to be soft."

The words made Brynja frown, but she did not argue. Ursula was the one who had taught Brynja to sew and work a loom, and she was relieved the elderly thrall had been kept on as part of Ulrik's household staff this week. Most of their servants had not been so fortunate.

Brynja continued her work in silence for a moment, letting the breeze from the open doorway cool her. Though Ulrik insisted she stay in the longhouse, she needed light for her needlework—a good excuse to sit near the door, letting the last rays of the summer sun touch her skin. Yet the breeze today was cold, a reminder that winter was on the way.

She closed her eyes for a moment, embracing the chill. Losing herself in her thoughts again. Remembering what it was like, just a few short days before, to be free with her family around her.

"Watch your fingers," Ursula warned. Though her voice quivered like a feather about to blow away in the wind, her tone was sharp as ever.

Brynja opened her eyes, smiling despite herself. In her years studying stitchwork under Ursula's care, there were many times the old seamstress almost made her cry. But not anymore. Now, Brynja took pride in sitting beside her instructor, the only one of her sisters still sewing of her own volition. As melancholy as the task of making her father's funeral clothes was, she knew it was an honor, too.

"Your sisters lack talent with the needle and the loom," Ursula said, as though reading her thoughts. "But Haldis is more careful than you are, and Svanhild is quicker. You retain too many sloppy habits to make a great seamstress."

Brynja shrugged off Ursula's scolding, as she often did now that she was older and accustomed to the old woman's bite. "At least I'm here," she said.

Ursula eyed her with a misty look, which Brynja knew was another sign of her age. Her eyes had once been clear blue; now she looked like half of her was already seeing the halls of the gods. Her olive skin was wrinkled with age, and her hands shook as she sewed the trousers Tove would wear on his journey to Valhalla.

Now that Brynja was confined to the longhouse, she wondered at the thrall's life. Her family had never been possessive of their servants or slaves, trusting them to complete their work each day before returning to families or enjoying their own meals in privacy. While some served at feasts, Tove had always made sure they took turns and had opportunities to partake in the revelries—or retreat to private quarters, if that was their preference. Brynja had never paid much mind to what it must feel like to be a servant with such duties. Now, watching Ursula weave, she imagined life as a thrall was a cursed fate, especially if one was under the command of someone like Ulrik.

"I hope he keeps you here," she said softly. The only other people present were a pair of Ulrik's warriors sitting on the other side of the hall, talking and drinking cider. Though they ignored Brynja and Ursula, still Brynja was careful not to be overheard. "You are part of our family, Ursula."

The old woman eyed her, questions fogging in her eyes. Finally, she said, "The Norns decide our fate the day we are born. They knew your father would die on the night of the full moon. They know the day I'll die, too." She jerked her chin to the half-finished tunic in Brynja's lap. "Until then, I weave."

Brynja took the hint and returned to her work. Ursula often spoke such mysterious words, a woman guided by the gods. Perhaps faith in the Norns' plan was what provided a slave peace at the end of the day.

Brynja wasn't sure she had such faith. Although she believed her life was fated like everyone else did, she did not bother with prayer or offerings the way her sisters did. She had better things to do.

After a long silence, Ursula glanced at Brynja's work and said, "You have a steady hand."

A rare compliment. Brynja grinned to herself.

Hearing a mewing sound near her ankle, she looked down to see Ursula's cat—a fat, fluffy creature with brown and gray fur—weaving between their legs. She bent down to scratch the creature behind the ears.

"Good morning, Mouse-Hunter."

Mouse-Hunter—who had never hunted a mouse in her life, as far as Brynja could tell—purred in response.

"She's still happy after dagmal," Ursula said, "but it won't be long before she's begging us for her next meal."

"Have you ever let her go without food, to see if she would hunt something on her own?" Brynja asked.

Ursula shook her head. "She'd try to eat me in my sleep if I didn't give her dinner." She smiled at Mouse-Hunter, who looked up at her with bright green eyes as if seeking an answer to some question. "You know what I'm saying, don't you?" Ursula patted Mouse-Hunter on the head, eliciting a strong purr from the furry creature.

Brynja thought the elderly thrall was much nicer to her cat than she was to her, but she said nothing. Aside from the simple dress and apron she wore, Mouse-Hunter was the only thing that truly belonged to Ursula. Thralls did not own many personal items. And while Brynja didn't believe Mouse-Hunter would like to think *anyone* owned her, she smiled to see how the cat brought out the elderly woman's maternal instincts. Ursula had never married or had children of her own. But since adopting Mouse-Hunter as a kitten just a couple of years ago, she had started sharing bites of roasted meat with the cat and cooing sweet words to her when she thought no one could hear.

"What's the point of having that cat in the longhouse?" came a man's voice from across the room. "It watched a mouse run right past it this morning and didn't even budge. Worthless thing."

Ulrik and Helga appeared from the back of the longhouse then. Seeing them emerge together—Ulrik's hand on her mother's lower back—made Brynja's stomach turn.

"Let's close that damn door before we all catch cold," Ulrik said. "From the look of your thrall there, a strong breeze will blow her right into Hel."

Brynja noticed her mother's glare at the words. Ulrik could change his mind about Ursula working here any day. And unlike the younger servants who found farms and homes in town where they could labor, Ursula's advanced age made her less likely to find another home.

"That's beautiful fabric," Mother said, approaching them. She ran her fingers over the wool in Brynja's hands. "You have made a fine seamstress, daughter, thanks to Urulsa's teachings."

Ursula let out a tiny grunt, as though disapproving.

"She doesn't think I have the talent to make a truly great seamstress," Brynja explained.

Helga looked like she was hiding a smile. "Well, no one has her skill. The gods blessed you with a gift, Ursula." She put a hand on the woman's bony shoulder. "And you have been a gift to our house."

"A gift that's not aging so well," Ulrik grumbled.

Brynja saw her mother's eyes flash again, but she neutralized her expression before turning back to Ulrik. Brynja was surprised when Mother took his arm in hers. What game was she playing?

"I have chores that need finishing," Helga said, "but would you like to take a walk through the village first? I can introduce you to our shipbuilder Skarde."

Ulrik agreed to the plan, but not before casting a judgmental glance at Ursula. Brynja wanted to argue with him, to explain to him Ursula's worth. Yet just the idea of arguing with the new jarl made her shrink like a flower in frost. Since he had scolded her a few days ago for sneaking out of the longhouse, she preferred to stay out of his sight.

Before Ulrik and Helga could leave the hall, the front doors burst open and two of Ulrik's warriors entered. They looked heavy in their fur cloaks, and after a moment Brynja saw they dragged a third man between them. Though the man was hunched over as though in pain or drowsiness, his red hair was unmistakable.

"Alf," she whispered.

Ursula stopped her needlework, too. Alf had always treated the thralls well, commanding them with a gentle touch. With the other servants and slaves cast out from the hall, Ursula must have been glad to see a familiar face—but not like this.

Helga lurched toward him, then caught herself. Brynja could see the tension in her mother's jaw as she forced herself to remain at Ulrik's side, her arm still linked with his.

"We found this man three days' ride from here," one of the guards said, tossing Alf onto the floor in front of Ulrik.

Brynja winced at the way Alf crumpled like brittle bark. If

it were anyone else, she would suspect the man drunk—but not Alf. He was clearly injured. When he lifted his head to look at Ulrik, she noticed bruises on his face and dried blood caked into the hair at his temples.

Ulrik dropped Helga's arm and strode to stand over Alf, so close he could have kicked him. "I recognize you," he said. He cocked his head to one side, studying Alf for a moment. "Tove's favorite, weren't you? I recall you fought alongside him, though you let go of your sword as soon as he was dead."

Alf coughed as though trying to speak, but no words came out.

Ulrik squatted then, his face leering closer to Alf's. "Can barely keep your eyes on me, can you?" He glanced up at his guards. "What did you do to him?"

"He tried to escape, so we had to subdue him," said the guard who had spoken before. "Gave him some herbs after the tussle to make sure he stayed quiet."

Ulrik nodded his approval. Turning back to Alf, he said, "You seem like more of a messenger than a warrior, am I right?"

Brynja's breath seized in her throat. How could he guess?

Alf managed to spit out a few words then, but his phrases came out in gasps. "You cannot... blame... the people here... for wanting... to find... a new home."

Ulrik chuckled. "A new home, is it?"

The talkative guard laughed too. "He wasn't looking for a new home. He was on his way to Uppsala with a message for Tove's brother. Told us everything, once we'd given him enough of a beating."

Brynja swallowed. What had he told the guards? If she or her family were named in his plans, they would be next.

Alf's blue gaze drifted to Brynja, and she read the regret

in his eyes. Then his chin sank, his gaze fluttering to the ground like a bird whose wings have given out.

She wanted to cry. If only she could tell him she forgave him, that it wasn't his fault he told the guards the truth... If it had been her in such a situation, she would have confessed everything too.

Her eyes traveled to her mother then. Helga's mouth was tight, her eyes moist. Brynja read in her expression everything she herself felt: sadness for Alf, regret at what they had asked him to do, and fear of the new jarl.

"Well," said Ulrik, rising to his feet, "I'm not surprised someone wanted to start an uprising. I wonder, though..." His eyes locked on Helga. "Would a housecarl contrive such a daring plan all by himself?"

Helga froze for a moment, then narrowed her eyes at him. "Are you accusing me of something?"

Brynja winced. She registered the pain in her mother's eyes as she bit through her words. Denial now, after Alf's confession, only made their former housecarl more of a traitor. But he wasn't—he was only doing their bidding. If Helga admitted that it had been their plan, who knows what Ulrik would do to them all? Her mother was choosing their family, putting her daughters before all, being a devoted mother—no matter how much the betrayal of Alf hurt her.

"Servants are not, by nature, brave men," Ulrik said. "But they will always do their masters' bidding, so long as they love them." He looked down at Alf. "Do you love Helga still? Do you love your dead jarl?"

Alf's chin was resting on his chest. Brynja couldn't tell if he was even conscious anymore.

"Very well." Ulrik sighed. Taking Helga's arm again and yanking her toward the door, he said, "Keep playing your games, wife of Tove. I have enough weapons for many more traitors, and eyes enough to spot them from here all the way to Uppsala." Meeting his guards' eyes, he jerked his chin toward a rack of weapons against the far wall. "My axe."

One of the guards fetched Ulrik's axe from the rack and handed it to him. Ulrik took a step back from Alf, rolling his shoulders as though warming up for something.

Brynja stopped breathing. Time seemed to slow as Ulrik lifted the axe, lunged forward, and swung the weapon straight down onto Alf's head.

Alf did not move. Not even a flinch. Brynja hoped he was unconscious, prayed he felt nothing, as his head split in two.

CHAPTER 13

HALDIS

The smell of smoke and pine filled the evening air as the funeral procession made its way into the forest. The crowd had already gathered at the burial site. The wailing of mourners echoed through the trees, and many people staggered on their feet after the traditional day of drinking, sex, and feasting.

As a völva—or at least a seer in training—Haldis had the duty and honor of walking alongside their priest Gorm. He had prepared her, streaking dark kohl across her eyes and clothing her in a simple hooded robe. Helga had then brushed her hair until it shone like a waterfall of ice. She gave Haldis a neck ring to wear, with raven heads on the ends. These silver birds now rested on her collarbone, their weight a reminder of her family's importance despite everything that had happened to them.

If Ulrik noticed the neck ring, he said nothing. This was a day for the people to mourn her father, and by giving them this day, Ulrik publicly showed the passing of leadership from Tove to himself. It was a smart move.

Behind Haldis trailed her family and Ulrik's. A host of servants and thralls carried her father's body on a bed of wood cushioned with pine boughs. As the body passed them, those gathered lifted their ale horns in toast, cried out in grief, or reached to touch the hem of his garments in a final farewell. Nine goats, tied together with rope, made up the tail of the procession, ambling along on thin legs, their bleating mixing with the sobs of the crowd.

In the forest behind the longhouse, they came to a clearing scattered with stones: their family graveyard. The stones were arranged into shapes around the burial sites of several of their ancestors. For their father, like the jarls before him, the stones would form the curved oval shape of a ship. But not yet.

They stopped in the center of the large clearing. A pyre had been prepared here; now, the servants carrying her father's body set it atop the platform. In death, Jarl Tove wore new clothes, including a rich red tunic, sewn by Brynja and their family's seamstress Ursula for this special occasion. His wounds had been covered, but Haldis stared at his face in fascination, for it was almost blue and drooped in a strange way. This was not the face she remembered.

You must be on your way to Valhalla now, she thought.

The memory of her father's rejection—of that day when he left her by the lake, when she was only a few days old— brought stinging tears to her eyes. He had left her to the elements, a sacrifice to the gods.

And now here she was, leaving him.

Gorm had already placed several objects on the pyre around Tove, which the slain jarl would take with him into his new life. Haldis recognized many of the items, including clothing, jewelry, and weapons. Some of these would burn with him; others would be spared for his burial room in the earth, where he would find all the comforts of home.

Once the two honored families had found a place around the pyre, Gorm handed his torch to Haldis. Though it was heavy, she held it steady with both hands, her face flushing in the heat.

Gorm bent to scoop up one of the goats. The creature bleated in confusion, its legs dangling from Gorm's arms. He set the goat on the pyre beside Tove's body, then produced a bowl and a small knife from his robes. Calling for the gods to bless the scene, Gorm drew the knife across the goat's throat. Instantly, the bleating stopped, and the goat went still.

Across the pyre, Brynja buried her head in Helga's shoulder.

Gorm let the goat's blood run into the bowl. Once it was filled, he took a small branch from the ground and dipped it in the blood. Then he moved around the circle, starting with Helga, flicking blood from the branch onto their faces. Helga had to nudge Brynja to face the gothi so he could perform this for her; her face scrunched as the blood splattered across her skin. Svanhild, on the other hand, barely blinked as she accepted the sacrificial blood, her eyes drifting toward the sky. Haldis could almost imagine her saying a silent prayer to Odin in that moment, probably full of revenge.

Ulrik and his family surprised her with their silence as they, too, received the sacrificial blood. Haldis noticed Ulrik's son Andor glancing at Svanhild several times; eventually, her sister returned his gaze, and they exchanged sad smiles. Haldis was impressed. Whether or not Ulrik and his family wanted to be at the funeral of this man they had bested, at least they had enough honor in them to show Tove the respect such a beloved jarl deserved.

When Gorm arrived at Haldis, he helped move the torch aside enough that he could splatter her with the goat's blood.

She kept her back straight and her jaw tight, but as the blood rushed toward her, she shut her eyes out of reflex. When she opened them again, Gorm had already released the torch back to her and was moving to the next person.

She stared at her father's body on the pyre, willing him to hear her now. You did not want me, she said to him silently. You rejected me for my markings. You must have thought I was cursed. But I am still here, and you are gone.

She expected the thought to bring her some satisfaction, but it only left her heart aching. She had witnessed her father's love of Svanhild and Brynja, seen his devotion to their mother, even admired his wisdom and kindness as a leader. Though her first memories of him brought her nothing but pain, she knew he was also a good man. Yet how could a man have honor, when he could also be so cruel?

She sighed to herself, blinking away her tears. If only things had been different for her, she might have loved Tove the way her sisters did. If only...

Go in peace, Jarl Tove. They were the only words she could muster for him right now.

After the sacrifices were finished, Gorm took the torch from Haldis and approached the pyre. The full moon lit the scene from overhead.

Were the gods watching?

Haldis looked up at the moon as the shadow of a raven passed over it. She followed the raven's flight as it circled overhead. It seemed to be there for the funeral, though the way it moved in the sky was almost aggressive. Perhaps it was guarding Tove—or angry at his death.

Haldis returned her attention to the pyre as Gorm threw his torch onto it. It took several moments for the fire to spread. Though most of Kaldvik's people could not fit in the clearing to see the funeral clearly, gasps and wails resounded from the forest as the flames flew toward the sky, big enough to be visible even from where people watched through the trees.

The heat washed over Haldis as she watched her father's body burn. She heard someone choke with tears as the skull cracked open. The sound of logs splitting filled the night air. Flesh peeled away from Tove's bones. Another gasp. Haldis glanced over to see Ulrik's daughter Kindra breathing hard as she watched the scene. Perhaps this was the first funeral she had attended, the first cremation she had watched. Haldis could not blame her for being shocked at the sight.

"Odin, tonight we send your raven king to Valhalla," Gorm said. Usually a soft-spoken man, tonight his voice carried an eerie power. It was clear the gods spoke through him. "He has served you loyally all the years he lived. He has died valiantly in battle, protecting his family from conquering swords."

Haldis kept her face forward, her chin lifted, playing the role of the völva—yet still she cast a quick glance at Ulrik when the priest said this, trying to gauge his reaction. But the great bear remained stone-faced. Haldis got the impression he was not happy to be here, and likely he would not tolerate anyone speaking against him. Yet still he was here, honoring Tove as was appropriate for a jarl of Tove's status.

Gorm spoke a few more words, then flicked something into the fire. The orange flames burst upwards, and a rainbow of sparks danced on their edges as they made their way to the sky. The colors reminded Haldis of the rainbow bridge that connected the realm of mortals with the realm of the gods. She closed her eyes for a moment, praying to the gods, wanting to feel them in this moment.

Odin, do you hear me? Freyja, are you here with us now? Which of you will take my father to your hall?

She listened for an answer, but nothing came. Opening her eyes, she saw the raven that had been circling overhead.

It swooped down and landed on a tree branch opposite her. Through the flames, it seemed to come and go, like an apparition.

She felt someone take her hand then: Brynja. On the other side of her younger sister, Svanhild must have felt Brynja's hand too, for she cleared her throat and then began to sing.

Haldis recognized the song. It was a partial saga, composed by their skald, telling the story of their own family line.

According to legend, Odin's ravens led their ancestors to this place, a cold cove that seemed to have no special features other than its beauty. But the people trusted Odin, and so they settled and started their farms.

The soil surprised them, for it was more fertile than any they had known in the past. This was how they became such skilled farmers—not only because of their own talents, but because the gods had blessed this place. In the song, this is where Thor impregnated the earth goddess Sif; bountiful harvests then sprung up from their seed.

And since then, every year in winter, Odin himself visited their hall, disguised as a wanderer in need of food and shelter for the night. And each year, the jarl fed and housed the wanderer, offering his generosity without even realizing the man was Odin. Only before leaving in the morning would Odin finally remove his hood and reveal the patch over his eye.

Svanhild's voice wavered gently like a breeze passing over them, lulling everyone into a sort of trance. They all stared into the fire as though they could see the events unfolding in the flames. When the song ended, the last haunting notes seemed to continue in the distance, as though some goddess picked up where Svanhild left off to continue the saga.

What does our future hold? Haldis asked. She watched the

raven flickering beyond the flames. Directing her question there, in case the raven acted as Odin's eyes here tonight, she tried again. *What is the fate of my family?*

A wind picked up then, and Haldis felt words flow through her mind to her mouth, as though the breeze itself had entered her with the thoughts. Were they a gift from the gods? An answer? Before she could assess their meaning, she heard herself speaking them, her reed-like voice wavering in the wind.

"Odin is here tonight. The Norns weave their plans for our family. Our story is not over. Tove watches us now from the great feast in Valhalla, where he dines with gods and heroes. But his eyes will always be on this place, on our family, watching over us."

Haldis heard a sniffle from Brynja. She squeezed her sister's hand to comfort her. Words continued to spill from her lips.

"Odin sends his ravens to guide us on our path," she continued, "wherever that may lead. Let us trust in the gods now." Her gaze shot to Ulrik as she realized what she was about to say. He stared back at her with dark eyes. "And trust that this was all part of the gods' plan."

Ulrik's eyes narrowed, but just as quickly he nodded as though agreeing with her. If he had sensed a threat there, he must have realized it could just as easily be interpreted as him being the intended for this throne.

She stared into the flames again, imagining her father's spirit lifting from his body and floating across the rainbow bridge to Valhalla.

Go in peace, Father, she thought.

It was not quite forgiveness, but it was enough.

PART II

CHAPTER 14

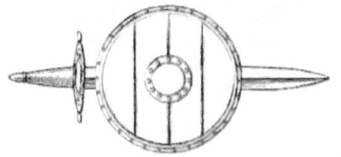

Sleep would not come to Svanhild that night. Her eyes burned from the funeral smoke and her own tears, yet she had no moisture left to shed. Her chest ached and her stomach turned. Even her nose was swollen, as was Brynja's, so they barely looked like themselves. She had never known grief could make her feel physically ill.

She lay on her straw sleep pellet as long as she could, curled up under the furs. At least Ulrik had given them a more comfortable place to sleep. She had her mother to thank for that. Or was it Andor?

Lying now on her sleep pellet, she whispered a prayer to Odin for guidance. The All-Father always looked out for their family. Her father had said he favored them. It was why they painted their shields with Odin's two ravens, their necks intertwined so they were looking over one another's shoulders. And just the same as those ravens, their family watched each other's backs. Her sisters would help her.

She glanced over at them now. Brynja was sprawled across her sleep pellet, limbs askew, dark hair strewn over the straw. The sight made Svanhild smile. No doubt Brynja, the fairest of them and the most ladylike, would wake up with straw in her hair. She still slept with the abandon of a child who felt safe knowing others would care for her.

Haldis, on the other hand, slept on her side, her hands pressed neatly together as though she held some token for the gods between them. She had wrapped her long white-blonde hair in a knot atop her head, probably to avoid fuss. Besides her head and her hands, her entire body was covered by her fur blanket, as though she were hiding from the world. Perhaps she was.

Svanhild threw off her own furs now, sighing to herself. If she could not sleep, she would take some fresh air. Like the rest of her family, she preferred to be out of doors, bathing in the light of the sun or moon.

As she stood, a flash of light caught her attention. Across the room, her mother sat up and looked at her. Apparently she could not sleep either. Svanhild understood why. As the eldest daughter, she imagined her own burden was the same her mother carried. They needed to take care of their family, to save them from this mess. Whatever duty Svanhild felt around this, she could only imagine Helga, as the new head of their family, suffered the same tenfold.

Helga rose with Svanhild, which is when Svanhild noticed something in her hand: a sword. Helga tied the sheath around her waist, then motioned for Svanhild to follow her outside.

They quickly put on boots and wool capes. As they tiptoed out the door, Svanhild scanned the corridor for any guards, but no one was about. Did Ulrik trust them enough not to worry they would leave in the night?

Helga put a finger to her lips. Though Svanhild thought

they would take the back door out of the longhouse—it was only a few meters away—Mother led her in the opposite direction, toward the main hall. They passed their old bed chambers, then sneaked past the small meeting room just behind the hall.

Svanhild held her breath as she followed her mother into the main hall. The large hearth sputtered its last embers; a whale oil lamp lit a table on the far side of the room. Here, two men with axes on their hips sat playing a game of hnefatafl. They spoke in low voices as they rolled the dice, which clattered on the tabletop. One of them chuckled.

Svanhild and her mother ducked behind the head table, staying low as they moved.

Their family's raven swiftness was with them tonight. In just a few blinks of the eye, they passed through the side door near the table.

The warriors did not even look up from their game.

Once outside in the crisp night air, Svanhild breathed again. She inhaled the scent of fresh pine, feeling free. Helga put a finger to her lips again to remind her they were not clear just yet. Then, she led Svanhild across the training yard, down the slope, and into the woods behind the village.

They hurried through the trees in silence. Svanhild tried to tread softly, but her boots crunched a few leaves and dead pine needles beneath her feet. Was autumn already here? She noticed Mother moved noiselessly through the same foliage, like a wildcat.

They ascended the hill into the pine forest. Here, Helga began whispering, though still they moved like they were hiding and running from something at the same time.

"Ulrik may have men outside the village," she told Svanhild. "We are not quite prisoners, but he does not want us meeting with our people or escaping in the night."

"Where are we going?"

Helga seemed not to hear her. "I fear he will treat us cruelly if he finds us gone. We have only a short time. As soon as the sky turns purple, we must return."

"What are we doing?" Svanhild tried again.

Her mother did not answer.

Soon they came to the clearing around the lake. It was peaceful here tonight, the only sound a gentle lapping where the water met the shore. The lake's silky surface reflected the moon and the surrounding trees as though someone had painted it.

Svanhild stopped beside her mother, taking in the view as her heartbeat slowed. It seemed nobody had followed them. She sent a silent thanks to Odin for keeping them safe on their short journey here.

"It is no wonder Haldis treats this place as sacred," she said, keeping her voice low so as not to disturb the spirit of the place. "This lake is too beautiful for men alone. I sense the gods here."

Helga looked at her with dark eyes. Svanhild could tell a memory lingered there, but her mother said nothing.

Instead, she unsheathed the sword that hung at her hip. The blade flashed in the moonlight. Now Svanhild recognized the runes etched into the blade.

"Father's sword," she breathed. "How did you get it?"

"I took it from our old bedroom," Helga replied. "Ulrik's chamber, now. He has not gone through all of our belongings yet. If the gods are on our side, he will never notice it is gone."

Svanhild wanted to ask how Helga managed to get inside Ulrik's chamber without him knowing, but her mother thrust the sword into her hands before she could speak.

"It is time for you to learn to wield this," she said.

Svanhild had to hold it with both hands at first. Her

father had taught her well with light training weapons, but this sword was twice the weight of any weapon she had held before—a blade truly made for blood-spilling.

Hrafnblód. Raven blood.

Some said the sword was crafted by Ulfberht, the most famous of weaponsmiths across their land. This blade was surely strong enough, yet it did not carry Ulfberht's famous stamp. This led others to believe the sword was dwarven-forged and blessed by the gods. The fact that it was covered in runes seemed to support this story.

Svanhild studied the silver blade. Though many important warriors carried swords, Hrafnblód was truly special. Whether or not the gods actually *made* the weapon, Svanhild was sure it had come to their family by their will.

"Did someone gift this weapon to our family?" she asked, though she knew the answer.

Helga shook her head. "We may never know the origin of this blade. Its story has been lost."

"Someone should have composed a saga about it."

"I believe *you* are meant to create the story of this sword, Svanhild. Your father wanted you to have it one day, when you were ready. Now that he is gone, it is my intention to make you ready."

"I've trained with Father. I can wield a weapon."

"Not that one," Helga said.

Svanhild laughed. In the cool night air, her breath formed a cloud before her lips. "Of course you are right. This sword is too heavy."

"That is how you know it is special. Strong." Helga reached out and rubbed her thumb across Svanhild's cheek. "Like you."

Memories of her fight against Thorbjorn clouded Svanhild's mind then, and she blushed as the shame of the lost battle washed over her anew. She was glad for the cool wind that swept the heat from her cheeks. She only hoped her mother could not see the hue, for she had yet to tell her about her public defeat.

Trying to think of something else, she asked, "Is it true you were a shieldmaiden, before you were a mother?"

Helga smiled sadly. "It is true. I loved the rush of battle, the companionship with the other warriors…" She chuckled. "We were like a pack of wolves. We fought together, were willing to die for each other."

"You fought in battles, then?"

"I went raiding once, but I did not care for such greedy bloodshed. Your father didn't either. I suppose that is what bonded us."

Svanhild's eyes widened. "You and Father fought together?"

"That is how he took notice of me. I was one of only two shieldmaidens in our clan." She smiled, her eyes dancing. "And I was the prettier one."

"And the humblest too, no doubt," Svanhild teased.

"But I also fought to protect our land. Before your father became jarl, his father before him suffered greatly from attacks. There was a ruthless jarl at that time, who made alliances with other raiders and tried to conquer anyone who refused to join him. He had his eyes set on our farmlands."

Svanhild thought of Ulrik then, of his greed for their farms. "It seems that has not changed much."

"Fighting to protect our home felt like my true purpose in this life. It is why the gods put me here." Helga looked out at the lake, her gaze far away. "That is what I thought for many years." After studying the water for a moment, she turned back to Svanhild. "Until I had you."

Svanhild imagined it for a moment. Her mother, a shield-maiden, fighting alongside her father in battles to protect

Kaldvik. It was a life blessed by the gods—the sort of life she herself longed to have. She pictured her mother discovering her pregnancy. There were ways to end such a thing, if a child was unwanted…

"Why did you have me?" Svanhild asked. "I will not hold it against you if you didn't want me. I would not want a child now."

"I admit I had not yet wed your father," Helga said. "But I loved him, and I loved you. The moment I knew you were inside me, I sensed *this* was the true path woven for me. I was meant to have you, to raise you. I was meant to be a mother."

Svanhild tried to imagine herself as a mother, but the idea of a family did not appeal to her. Yet as soon as she thought of battle, her heart raced, a jolt like lightning running through her veins.

She tightened her grip on Hrafnblód's hilt. Already she felt a tiny tremor in her arms from holding it upright for so long. And after her defeat in the battle against Thorbjorn…

Her mother was right. She needed new training.

Helga seemed to follow her thoughts, for she reached out and took Hrafnblód from Svanhild. "Think of your family now," she said. "What you did to protect them, promising yourself to Andor? That was love for your family."

Svanhild nodded. She could understand such loyalty. And as soon as she imagined her sisters and her mother, she knew she would give up everything—even the sword—to keep them safe.

"But you do not have to make such a sacrifice for your family," Mother continued. "We will find a way out of your marriage, without angering the gods by breaking an oath."

"Loki gave me the words," Svanhild said. "I'm sure of it."

Helga frowned. "Loki is a hard one to trust. But everything that happens is fated by the Norns."

"Even Father's death?"

Svanhild felt something inside her darken, thinking of the moment Ulrik licked her father's blood from his axe. Her father's body on the floor, blood spilling out. *Life* spilling out. And Ulrik would have killed them, if she had not agreed to marry his son. He had killed their housecarl Alf, and now their plans to seek their uncle in Uppsala were dashed.

So this is what hatred felt like.

"What good is wielding this blade," she asked, "now that we have no support? Ulrik is courting the warriors who want to raid, winning over the town little by little."

"Yes, Ulrik has supporters here." Helga's eyes flashed in the darkness, knife blades catching moonlight.

"Are we training to fight them? What about Asmund?"

"We can't risk anyone else's life to take the message to him," said Helga.

Svanhild had not seen Alf's death, but the way Brynja told the tale, it had been horrific. "Why go all the way to Uppsala for him? Why not seek our revenge here, once we are ready?"

Helga did not answer for a long moment. Svanhild shivered as the idea blew through her like a cold wind. Was this the fate the Norns had woven for her?

There was no doubt her uncle Asmund would be a strong rival to Ulrik, for he was Tove's blood *and* a man. But could he be trusted to give them the high-seat after Ulrik's defeat? Was it not better to kill Ulrik on their own, with support from the people of Kaldvik?

Her defeat in battle flashed through her mind again, and her mouth went dry.

"Mother, I have to tell you something." She took a deep breath, then told the tale of her failed battle against Thorbjorn. When she had finished, she felt how her body slumped in defeat as if she were feeling it fresh. "I wanted to win the people's favor, but I fear I've done the opposite."

Helga reached out to brush a strand of loose hair from Svanhild's face. "You acted on impulse. A mistake of youth. Now, we will make you a warrior."

Svanhild nodded. Her mother's words did not make her less embarrassed about her failure, but the way she brushed it off made her think she could recover from it, at least.

"I will train you with this sword," Helga said, touching Hrafnblód's blade, "but the rest is up to you. Skill in battle will only take you so far. To win the people's favor, you will need more than a blade."

"So you think I can lead the people against Ulrik?"

Helga narrowed her eyes, a dark expression crossing her face. "You are brave, daughter. I can't pretend to know the gods' plan yet, but as Tove's wife and the mother of three beautiful daughters?" She smiled, but Svanhild was surprised to see the merciless glint to it. "If you wish to kill Ulrik, I hope you succeed."

Svanhild's heart beat faster. She had never seen this side of her mother, but she admired it. Her mother had a warrior's heart, just like she did.

Helga took Hrafnblód from her then. Stepping back to put distance between them, she sliced the weapon in the air. It made a sound, like a strong wind whipping a sail. Svanhild was mesmerized by the runes glittering in the moonlight.

"For a woman to become a shieldmaiden," said Helga, "requires more skill, strength, and resolve than is required for a man to become a warrior. But take heart in that, for such challenges will make you the sharpest blade on any battlefield, and the respect you earn will be all the greater for it."

"I am ready," Svanhild said.

Mother looked at the sky, which was already shifting from black to a deep purple. "We don't have much time.

Every night when the guards are distracted, we will come here to train."

Svanhild lifted her chin, accepting the challenge and the responsibility.

"Just don't be too excited yet," her mother said. "We have much work to do."

CHAPTER 15

BRYNJA

*A*fter her father's funeral, the days grew shorter. Green leaves turned to orange fire in the trees before dropping from their posts. Nights turned colder than Skadi's breath. And still, Brynja did not see her friend Erik.

Ulrik would not allow her to leave the longhouse unaccompanied. Though they privately complained, Brynja knew her sisters suffered more than she did. Haldis longed to visit the lake, her favorite place to escape and commune with the gods. And though Svanhild's fingers itched for a blade, Ulrik did not allow her to practice in the training yard.

After tucking into bed at night, their family whispered in the dark. This was the only private time they had. Brynja was surprised to hear that their mother took Svanhild to train with Hrafnblód at night, when the guards were distracted. But what did her sister intend to do with their training? The idea of Svanhild battling Ulrik made Brynja shudder.

During the day, while Haldis sat in the main hall's loft and

Svanhild paced the corridors, Brynja made herself useful. When she was not weaving clothes and tapestries, she was working the loom with Ursula. When she was not helping servants cook in the kitchen, she was helping her mother oversee preparations for Ulrik's frequent feasts. Keeping her hands busy kept her mind busy—and that left little room for bad memories.

It was on a busy morning of work in the hall that Ulrik's housecarl burst through the front doors, motioning for several men to carry in crates behind him.

"What's all this?" Helga asked. She still wore the long-house's keys around her waist, a signal to all that she ran the place. Ulrik's wife Gertrud had never asked for them, for as far as Brynja could tell, she preferred feasting and gossipping to any sort of labor. "We are in the middle of preparing for nattmal."

"So are we," said the housecarl Olaf. A short man with broad shoulders, he had a brown beard oddly twisted into dozens of knots, reminding Brynja of a bird's nest. "These men bring fresh food from Kaldvik's farms, the last of summer's harvest."

Brynja did not recognize the men who entered the hall, all of whom wore the simple brown garb of servants and thralls. These were not farmers bringing tribute to their jarl, as was the custom in Kaldvik. No, Olaf had led these servants to collect food, no doubt on Jarl Ulrik's orders. From the look of the hefty wooden crates—some of them overflowing with cabbage, root vegetables, and many other crops—this was far more food than most people would willingly part with.

"Who sent this food?" Mother asked, frowning. She stood beside Brynja, concern etched across her face.

"Several farms," Olaf replied, waving his hand dismissively. He barked at the servants to take the crates to the kitchens and food storage rooms within the longhouse.

"We should not keep all the food here," Helga said. "We need to store some for winter."

Olaf chuckled. "The jarl says we can collect more food when we need it. The soil here is rich." His eyes lighted on Brynja, and he cast her a leering smile. "We will not go hungry."

As the servants carried the crates of food to the back of the longhouse, Brynja whispered to her mother, "*We* may not, but what about the farmers and their families?"

Helga gave her a dark look, nodding agreement. It was not right for all of this food to be here, instead of with the people who had labored for months to grow it.

"This is not what your father would have done," her mother said quietly. "When the servants are finished, we will take some food to the storehouses for winter. Nobody else needs to know."

"Because we cannot anger Ulrik?"

"Yes, it is better to be careful for now. With our actions, we are winning the jarl's trust. I can feel it."

Brynja did not know if she wanted to win Ulrik's favor, for she preferred being out of his sight. But she understood her mother's plan. The work Helga did around the longhouse made her indispensable, and Ulrik would be a fool not to value her.

Mother smiled at her then, running a hand over her long brown braid. "You are a great help to me, Brynja. In moments like these, I thank the gods you are here with me."

Brynja smiled as her mother's words filled her heart. She knew how her mother sacrificed for their family. It was not easy to play nice with Ulrik, to run the house while it was under his control, to keep her tears to herself after the death of her husband—all in the hopes her actions would keep their family safe.

"I am glad," was all Brynja could reply before Olaf strode over to join them. He stepped so close to her, she inhaled a musty scent clinging to his hair and beard, like wet foliage and unwashed scalp. It was stifling, but she forced herself not to step away.

"Tove's littlest warrior. *Brynja*." He said her name a few more times, as though tasting the word on his tongue. His small eyes, the gray-blue color of wet stones, looked distant for a moment as he savored the sound. "I have heard that word used for coats of armor." He turned to Helga. "Why did you choose the name for her?"

"We named her for her dark hair," Helga replied with narrowed eyes.

Olaf did not pry further. "Well, I have always admired your beautiful brown hair, Brynja. So many girls in Mosfell dye their hair yellow to match the fashion. Boys, too." He chuckled. "The women of Kaldvik are much more practical than that, aren't they? Less vain, more hardy." His eyes ran over her body with the same look a man might give a horse he were measuring for purchase.

Brynja swallowed, her skin itching under his gaze.

"You should wear it loose," he said at last. "Your hair. You are still a young maiden, after all."

As he walked away, Brynja shivered. Something about Olaf's attention made her want to dive into a steam bath and scrub herself clean.

Her mother watched him disappear through a doorway, leaving them alone again in the hall. "Stay away from that one," she said.

. . .

LATER THAT MORNING, Ulrik ordered Brynja and her family to join him on a walk through the village. "You see," he said with a dangerous chuckle, "I do not keep you prisoner here."

Svanhild glared at his words, but no one dared respond.

Brynja was glad to escape the longhouse and enjoy the crisp autumn air. But she knew better than to be grateful to Ulrik for such a treat, for he did not take them out for their enjoyment.

No, he wanted to show them off to the people of Kaldvik.

They donned their thickest cloaks and left the longhouse. Ulrik led the way, flanked by his wife Gertrud on one side and Helga on the other. Brynja and her sisters trailed behind with Andor and Kindra. After the strange encounter this morning, Brynja was relieved that Olaf was too busy to join them.

She wondered what people thought when they saw Ulrik's family walking with Tove's. Did they think their families had merged, that they were all happy together? The idea made her stomach roil, but what choice did they have? This was what Ulrik wanted people to think. This was the performance she had to be a part of, no matter how ill it made her feel.

As they came to the village marketplace in front of the fjord, Brynja's heart skipped in her chest. There, sitting on a tall table in the square, his legs dangling off the side, was Erik.

She had to force herself not to run over and hug him. He was usually secluded to his parents' farm on the outskirts of town, but today he sat selling several hefty baskets of fresh vegetables.

Erik met her gaze as their family approached. Brynja gave him a small smile, ducking her head in the hopes it would signal not to appear too excited. Though Ulrik's back was to her, he would notice a boy grinning at them, and she feared that calling too much attention to her friendship with Erik would only turn Ulrik's heart against the two of them.

Smarter to be sly about it.

Erik's green eyes flashed in understanding. Brynja sighed softly in relief.

Then, clearing her throat to give herself courage, she said, "May we stop and look at this boy's vegetables? His parents own one of the best farms in town."

Ulrik stopped and looked at her over his shoulder, without bothering to actually face her. "That boy?" he said, pointing at Erik.

Brynja swallowed, forcing herself to nod yes. Under the new jarl's gaze, she always felt like a withering flower.

Ulrik shrugged. "If you like, I see no harm in it." As they strode over to Erik, he even added, "These vegetables would make excellent additions to my table."

Brynja frowned. Had he not received vegetables from Erik's farm already? She wondered if the shipment this morning had anything from Torven and Ragnilde's farm. If not, Ulrik would likely seek them out now. She hoped she had not just volunteered them for more tribute to the jarl, for they would need to keep their own kitchen well-stocked to survive the winter.

Now, Erik jumped off the table and inclined his head to Ulrik. He did not meet Brynja's eye. She could almost feel how deliberately he was avoiding looking at her in front of the jarl.

"Good day, Jarl Ulrik," he said, then gestured to the baskets on the table. Each was filled with a different vegetable; together, they created a rainbow of colors that made Brynja's mouth water. "My sisters and I have brought our best vegetables from the farm," he explained. His voice was animated, drawing listeners to his wares. "Here we have cabbage, turnips, onions, beans, leeks, and…" He glanced at Brynja for the first time now. "… fresh peas."

She stifled a giggle. Peas were her favorite vegetable, and Erik's parents always dumped lots of them into their stews when she visited.

Ulrik leaned forward to survey the vegetables. Nodding his approval, he said to Erik, "Tell your parents they are the reason I have come to this beautiful land. Tales are told far and wide of the skill of Kaldvik's farmers. Now I see even more proof that the tales are true."

Brynja glanced at her sisters, who stood a pace behind her. Haldis's eyebrows shot up, and Brynja returned the look. Who would have guessed Ulrik could be so generous with compliments? But Svanhild's mouth remained a firm line as she glared at Ulrik's back. Lately, Brynja had felt the hate boiling off Svanhild like steam from a hot bath. She was not sure if anything had happened between Ulrik and her sister, or if Svanhild's emotion simply grew over time. Perhaps her weapons training was readying her spirit for revenge as much as her body.

Erik grinned. "Thank you, Jarl Ulrik. Please, take any vegetable you would like, and I will have my parents send a fresh basket to you for tonight's feast."

Ulrik frowned. "You know of tonight's feast?"

"You always have a feast," Erik said, still smiling.

"Is that what people say about me?" Ulrik shook his head and stepped back from the table. "Send the food, boy, but do not expect to stay long," he said, waving at Erik to dismiss him.

"Oh, I did not think I would be invited to a feast with a jarl," Erik said humbly, bowing his head. Brynja could hear the apology in his voice. Catching his eye, she gave him a small smile of encouragement, but he only shifted his gaze to the ground.

"I serve meals to those who are loyal to me. It is that simple," Ulrik said.

Helga put a hand on Ulrik's arm. His wife watched with hawk-like eyes but said nothing.

"Jarl," said Helga, "don't trouble yourself with young Erik. Brynja can bring the vegetables to you later."

"Olaf can take care of that," Ulrik grunted.

"We saw him bringing in fresh shipments of vegetables this morning," Mother went on. "He may be too busy to make another trip. This is a simple errand, and Brynja is accustomed to helping with such tasks."

A chill ran down Brynja's spine as she realized what her mother was arranging. It was hard to keep from grinning, especially when Ulrik grumbled his agreement.

The meeting was set between Brynja and Erik for the afternoon.

As they set off down the road again, Brynja dared to glance back at Erik. He shook his head at her, stretching his mouth into a comedic grimace over the whole exchange. Brynja laughed softly to herself.

"What was that?" Ulrik growled, looking over his shoulder at her again.

Brynja transformed her laugh into a small cough. "Nothing, jarl."

Though Ulrik would not allow Brynja to leave the longhouse without a guard, she walked to the village square late that afternoon swinging her arms and holding her face to the sky. She breathed in the cool air, smelling pine from the forest, fish from the fjord, and the fires of the forge. All the smells of home.

She met Erik in the village marketplace where she had

run into him this morning. His baskets were now gone, replaced by a single crate filled with assorted vegetables. It looked heavy.

She glanced at the thrall Ulrik had sent to accompany her, a young Englishman with dark hair tied back in a leather strap. Though he was skinny, his arms had some muscle from his work around the longhouse.

"I'm glad you are here to help me carry these back," she said to him, smiling.

"I can help you," Erik jumped in.

"You don't want to go near the hall. The jarl is…" She glanced at the thrall, wondering if it was safe to continue. "What is your name?"

"They call me Birger," the English thrall replied. His voice was high-pitched but beautiful, reminding Brynja of morning birdsong.

"Is that your true name?"

After a wary pause, he shook his head. "My birth name is Baldwyn."

Brynja offered a smile. "I have seen you assisting my mother around the hall. I am sure she is glad for the help, especially as it benefits all of the jarl's household and this village."

"It is common sense to store food for winter," replied Baldwyn. "And…" He hesitated, glancing at Erik. "And I like your mother. I am not used to such kindness."

Brynja thanked him for the words of appreciation for her mother, smiling to herself. If he admitted he was not used to kindness, he must not be happy serving Jarl Ulrik. Given his accent and foreign name, she guessed he was captured in a raid and sold into slavery. She shuddered to think the Norns could weave someone such a terrible path.

Still, she felt more free to speak with Erik now, knowing

Baldwyn may not be happy with Ulrik. "The jarl's moods shift like clouds during a thunderstorm," she explained to Erik. "It's best if you keep clear of him, and your parents too."

"Why was he so offended when I mentioned his feasts?" Erik asked.

"This is what I mean, Erik. Don't even try to make sense of his moods."

Baldwyn's voice jumped in, surprising Brynja. "The jarl is concerned about people's opinion of him. He wants you to see him as powerful but not frivolous."

"That explains why he was insulted when you said he feasts every night," Brynja said. "But how can he be so worried about what people think of him, when he takes so much from them? Does he not see how his greed affects people?"

Baldwyn looked at her intensely but said nothing more. Perhaps Brynja could learn more about Ulrik's leadership from him—if it could even be called leadership.

After a pause, Erik said, "Well, when does the jarl expect you back?"

Brynja glanced at Baldwyn, who shifted his weight from one foot to the other. Erik looked at the thrall too.

Seeing the attention on himself, Baldwyn said, "I am in no rush to return to the hall."

This made all three of them laugh.

Brynja looked out at the fjord's still waters. Before Ulrik, before her father's death, before all of this madness that had changed their lives so completely, she and Erik used to sit there at night, watching the waves and whispering together. Life was peaceful then. Her heart ached to remember those times.

"How long has it been since we sat out there?" she wondered aloud.

Erik whistled softly. "Longer than Odin hung from the sacred tree, and it feels just as painful."

Brynja jabbed him in the arm. "Should we go, then?"

"What, now? Won't Ulrik notice you're gone?"

"We won't stay too long. Just come." Brynja gestured to the water, which gleamed like liquid gold beneath the setting sun. "We have to enjoy this view while we can."

Baldwyn agreed to wait with the crate of vegetables while they went to the waterfront. It was only a few meters from the town square, so they were still within sight of one another.

Brynja and Erik made their way onto the wooden dock, which stretched several meters over the fjord. Longships bobbed in the water here—a few still bearing her father's red and white shields, but most boasting Ulrik's green dragon shields. A sign of the changing times.

When she and Erik reached the end of the dock, they sat and let their legs dangle over the edge, their feet nearly skimming the water. Brynja wished she had time to take off her shoes, but she didn't want to tempt Ulrik's wrath by taking too long.

She would need to savor these few minutes with her friend, for she did not know when they might come again.

"How have you been?" she asked.

Erik shrugged. "We are harvesting the last of our crops before winter. My parents are healthy. My sisters spend all day talking about who they will marry."

"So nothing has changed." Brynja meant it as a joke, but as soon as the words escaped her lips, they made her sad. While the rest of the town continued their lives much like before, her own had been turned upside down.

Erik reached over and took her hand. Giving it a squeeze, he said, "Much has changed, because I never see you anymore."

At his words, tears stung Brynja's eyes. Though she still had her sisters for company, she had no other friend like Erik. They had grown up playing together, ever since they first spotted each other in the village and instantly decided, in that silent oath children make, to be best friends for life. While other men in town had begun to look at her with a strange light in their eyes, flirting with her at feasts and nudging each other when she passed, Erik never treated her differently. With him, she felt truly safe.

"We all mourn your father," Erik added, his voice quieter now. "He was valiant in defending your family. I wanted to help, but…"

"I saw you with an axe that night. Where did you get it?"

"I found it in the hall, but I was too afraid to use it."

Erik said nothing more but swung his legs harder. Brynja could usually read his thoughts, but this time the silence was like a shut door. She didn't like the feeling of not knowing. Too much time had passed since they saw each other. This was one new way the threads of her life were unraveling.

Finally, Erik plucked at her dress. "I see you still favor red, like your mother and sisters."

"It is the color of our house. I will always wear it when I can."

Erik reached into a small pouch tied around his waist. From it, he plucked a piece of wood the size of a man's thumb, carved into the shape of a raven. He handed it to Brynja.

"Oh, it's beautiful," she breathed. "Did you carve this?"

"I did. It's for you. Share it with your mother and your sisters." He paused, until she looked him in the eyes. "Tell them it's a sign that some people in this village still follow them."

Brynja tucked the wooden raven into her dress. She heard

the cawing of real ravens overhead and saw their reflection in the water as they flew over the fjord. Her hairs stood on end, for despite all her practicality, she felt the presence of Odin with them.

And he had a plan.

CHAPTER 16

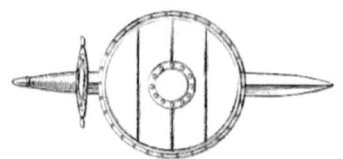

SVANHILD

*E*ven as snow began to fall in Kaldvik, Svanhild's training continued.

So many nights she followed her mother through the shadows, past her sleeping sisters, past the incompetent guards, and through the dark forest to the lake. Some nights, the moon lit their path, and she learned to wield Hrafnblód in the silvery light. Other nights, she saw the rainbow bridge to Asgard in the vivid greens, blues, and purples of the winter sky. And on nights when the moon hid from them, Svanhild felt she was battling a silhouette as she and her mother moved in almost pitch blackness.

As the weeks passed, her eyes grew accustomed to the darkness. Even on the blackest nights, she memorized the movements of her mother's shadow. A flick here meant her mother was thrusting forward. A swipe there meant she was lifting her sword overhead. Svanhild's eyes did not always confirm what she thought was happening, but her instincts taught her to read the battle almost as if she could feel it in her skin. She blocked, dodged, and wove away from her mother's training sword, Hrafnblóð heavy in her hands.

Though the nights grew colder, still Svanhild worked up a sweat during every training session. Helga was relentless. Svanhild had no idea her mother had so much stamina.

"Have you always been practicing while we slept?" she asked Mother one night, panting from their latest tussle.

"Once a shieldmaiden..." Helga lunged toward her, training sword outstretched. Svanhild jumped to the side just in time to avoid getting nicked. "Always a shieldmaiden," her mother finished, and swung her sword around to tap Svanhild on the hip. Though it was only a training sword, the thick blade still stung.

"Ouch," Svanhild said.

Helga sheathed the sword. Svanhild let out a gasp of breath, relieved for the break, even though she knew from experience it would not be long before her mother was ready to continue. In fact, she had a feeling Helga only took these breaks for her benefit.

"Where is the raven today?" Mother asked. "You need to be quicker."

"I'm sorry. I'm tired."

"War always makes one weary, but in battle there would be no rest."

Svanhild dropped to her knees beside the lake. The water's surface reflected the stars and magical green lights of the aurora borealis overhead. As winter approached, the sky showed its colors more and more. Whenever Svanhild saw the aurora, she liked to think Thor was crossing the rainbow bridge to join them in their training.

Now, she dipped her hands into the ice-cold water. The feel of it sent a welcome chill down her spine. She splashed water onto her face, then took some more in her palms and drank as best she could.

"You're right," she said, rising to her feet with a sigh. During their early training sessions, she had woken with aching muscles. Now that she had more strength, it was her bones that hurt. Only recently had she finally stopped waking up to fresh bruises. "But even in war, there would not be a battle almost every night."

Helga laughed, a friendly sound like clinking glasses. It was a noise that had always made her father smile. "You are lucky your mother is your trainer, or you would not get away with such complaints."

Svanhild grinned. Turning Hrafnblód in the moonlight, she studied the unique blade. "Have you ever read these runes? Divine... journey... gift... destiny." Looking up at Helga, she asked, "Do you think it means whoever wields this blade goes on a divine journey?"

"And enjoys the gift of their destiny."

"No wonder this sword has a special power."

Helga unsheathed her sword and tapped Hrafnblód with it. "A weapon may have power, but it is up to the one who wields it to bring it out."

Helga sliced the air with her sword, bending her knees to assume a fighting stance. Svanhild mimicked her, ignoring the pain in her back, the tightness in her hips, the trembling of her arms. Her mother was right: in a true battle, there would be no rest. She needed to get used to this feeling and fight through it.

Svanhild forced her weary bones to stand, preparing Hrafnblód for another round. As she approached her mother, she spotted a raven in a nearby tree, watching them from its perch. She pretended it was her father watching over them, if only because the feeling gave her strength.

Inhaling the fresh air into her weary lungs, Svanhild

focused her attention on her mother's movements. The sky was bright enough that she could clearly make out Helga's features, every gesture clear against the backdrop of lake and trees. Though Helga grimaced, her eyes were wide to take in every aspect of the battle—another trick Svanhild learned. And after training with Mother for weeks, she knew which blows were coming almost before Helga initiated them.

She practiced her footwork, spinning away from her mother and aiming her own sword in counterattacks. Then she swung Hrafnblód overhead, sideways, in quick undercuts that almost hit their mark. The two of them danced like this, taking turns slicing and thrusting their weapons, taking turns dodging and blocking each other's blows. They both began panting. Helga let out a grunt as she attacked; Svanhild roared as she charged.

Only a few moments passed before Svanhild felt herself sink into a sort of trance, moving almost without thinking. Soon, the only sound she could hear was her own heart beating like a drum in her ears. Her blood ran fast and hot through her veins.

The blunt side of her mother's sword struck her in the shin, nearly knocking her to her knees. She stumbled. Hrafnblód nearly dropped from her hands, but somehow she managed to tighten her grip on the heavy weapon just in time.

"Careful," Helga said, steadying her daughter. "That's a simple trick many warriors will use against you, especially when they see you tired. You weren't paying attention."

"I go into an extreme focus when I'm fighting," Svanhild explained. "But then, at some point... the trance just ends."

"The trance is good. That's the war god Tyr on your side. But as tempting as it is, you must keep your mind engaged in every battle." Helga tapped her temple. "Remember Odin's ravens. That is how our family wins our fights."

"Thought and Memory," Svanhild said, naming Odin's birds.

"Right now, we are working on the memory, for you will learn the best moves and strategies for any battle while you train with me." Helga smiled in encouragement, patting Svanhild on the shoulder. "But the *thought* is always up to you."

Svanhild sighed. Each time she thought she was improving—mastering a new move, defending herself against several attacks in a row, fighting for a little longer before tiring—she found some fresh wound to lick or new attack sequence to untangle.

"The battle happens so fast," she said. "How can I think my way through it?"

"You can't think too hard, but you also cannot completely abandon thought. You will learn the right balance."

A wave of weariness washing over her, Svanhild sat in the sand beside the lake, laying Hrafnblód across her lap. She almost expected her mother to begin a fresh attack—there was little rest with her during these sessions—but instead, Helga sat facing her, crossing her legs at the ankles.

"Why don't you attack Ulrik?" Svanhild asked. The question had been dancing in her mind for weeks. "I see you spending time with him. You must have earned his trust by now. When you are alone with him, why don't you strike him down?"

"I have wanted to," Helga admitted. "Just as I did the night Ulrik suggested you marry Andor. But you saved us all when you agreed to that betrothal, for Ulrik would have killed us all."

"Sometimes I wish I hadn't agreed."

"No, Svanhild. You were right to save us the only way you could. *That* was thought."

Svanhild tightened her jaw, saying nothing. She knew

that agreeing to marry Andor was the only way to save her family in that moment, yet still she wondered if she had made the right choice. Was there a way out of the wedding? Would she be ready for revenge before that day came?

"If I were to kill Ulrik now," Mother went on, "I fear the repercussions for you girls. The jarl has men on his side who might kill you. Not only his warriors from Mosfell, but men here in Kaldvik who believe Ulrik will lead them on raids where they can steal their fortunes." She sighed. "Protecting my family is my duty now."

Svanhild leaned forward. "But some people here still support us, perhaps more than we know. Frode the fisherman was going to look out for men still loyal to our family. Perhaps with those supporters on our side–"

"Be careful, Svanhild," her mother interrupted, surprising her. "I know you are eager for revenge, but if our numbers are not strong enough, we will fail. And to fail publicly would only make it clear to all that Ulrik is meant to be in the high-seat here. If he were to defeat us in true battle, it would be clear to all that Thor guided his axe, for the gods wanted him to win." Her eyes grew wet as she looked at Svanhild. "If he were to kill you…"

Svanhild reached out to clasp her mother's hands in her own. Her mother was right. Images of her defeat against Thorbjorn filled her mind. She could not risk such a defeat against Ulrik.

They would only have one chance at revenge.

"To be a shieldmaiden, you must learn to wield a weapon and shield," said Helga. "But to be a leader, you must learn to seek out wisdom in the wider world. Remember why your father went on his travels? Do you remember why he called on advice from elders and other jarls he respected?"

Svanhild nodded. "Learning wisdom seems the harder part of this training," she said with a small smile.

Mother smiled back.

Svanhild considered then. Her father had traveled to neighboring lands to seek advice from other rulers. Being so far north, the journeys took him longer than most, yet still he sought new perspectives. She recalled how he specifically looked to great warriors when he needed tactical advice and beloved leaders when he had a difficult decision to make. Though he did not always admit his needs, he made clever inquiries to learn how other great men thought and acted.

And he discussed matters with trusted advisors at home, too. Growing up, Svanhild would accompany him to her uncle's farm, where Father and Asmund talked late into the night over beer and fish stew. As a girl, she had been too energetic to listen to their conversations—it was more fun to play with wooden swords outside—but now she realized the two men must have been discussing important things like trade, disputes, and raiding.

Tove had trusted his brother, then. There was unity in shared blood. Strength, too. Perhaps Asmund could advise her as he had once advised her father.

"What if I seek out Asmund in Uppsala?" she asked, thinking aloud. "I remember how Father talked with him. He must have trusted his advice." She shrugged. "I could learn from him. We should have him on our side."

"You will have to leave soon, if you will make it back before the assembly."

"Not for the assembly," Svanhild said. "I will bring him back to aid our revenge. Right here at this lake, during our first training session, you told me you hoped I would kill Ulrik if that was my goal." She lifted her chin. "It is the gods' will for me. I feel it."

"It is true Tove trusted your uncle for advice," Helga said slowly, as though thinking it through. After a pause, she nodded. "Yes, I believe your father would like this plan."

Svanhild could not contain her smile. "Then I will need to prepare for the journey. I could try to make the trip on my own, perhaps on horseback…"

Helga shook her head. "When Alf tried that, Ulrik's guards caught up to him within days."

"Then I should take a ship." Svanhild's smile widened at the idea. In recent years, songs of sea-kings drifted through the lands; now she might have a chance to make her own voyage, one of the first sea-queens. "I can bring men to accompany me, who can help row the ship and join me in battle when I return."

"That will make your journey swifter," Mother agreed.

"When we reach Uppsala, I will ask Asmund for his support. Do you think he will know more warriors who would join us?"

"Yes, I think he will." Helga looked up at the night sky, splattered with stars, as though searching for the gods there. "Your uncle was a great raider, experienced in war. He will have a band of warriors at his side now, too. And he will help you strategize. With him, we will lay better plans than we could on our own."

A chill danced over Svanhild's skin. "I think the gods like this plan."

They were silent for a moment, thinking it through. Svanhild pictured herself leading a band of warriors in a longship—perhaps two or three, if she was able to amass such support—and storming the shores of Kaldvik to take back her home. It was almost like Haldis's vision. Did she not wield Hrafnblóð then?

"I will ask Skarde to prepare a ship for the spring," she said, thinking aloud. "I will find supporters through Balder and Frode, and when my training with you feels complete, I will escape and journey to Uppsala."

Helga patted her on the leg. "That is a good plan. You

should wait until the coldest nights of winter have passed, when the days grow warm again. That will ensure safer travels."

"But before my wedding in the spring."

Helga smiled gently. "How is your time with Andor? I see you taking walks with him."

"Only because Ulrik commands it," Svanhild said. The walks felt like performances, and though Andor sometimes struck up a conversation, Svanhild tried not to say too much. Better *not* to befriend the son of her enemy. "In truth, he is much calmer than his father, but I fear that is how he wins people over. I don't trust him any more than Ulrik."

"As long as you feel safe with him, we will make it through the winter." Helga's eyes misted for a moment, and then she said, "I worry more for Brynja around Ulrik's housecarl. He has noticed her."

Svanhild's stomach lurched at the idea of any man bothering her little sister. "If he tries anything, he'll be the first to taste Hrafnblód's metal."

"Let's not go that far yet," Mother replied. "But I see my old spirit in you, Svanhild. Go seek out Asmund and bring more warriors back with you. With our numbers stronger, there will be some here in Kaldvik who will take up arms to join you when you return. Let them see your father in you."

Svanhild smiled. A raven sang overhead, a sign of Odin blessing their plans. This was her true path. She felt it in every muscle.

There was a rustling in the trees then, and both hushed. Something crunched inside the forest, not too far from them. The raven let out a caw, as though in warning. Svanhild and Helga both rose to their feet slowly, trying not to make any noise. The raven spread its wings and disappeared toward the sound.

Svanhild held her breath. Had someone heard their battle

cries as they trained? They tried to be quiet while they worked, but it was hard not to let out *some* noises as they fought. Perhaps they had been too loud tonight, and Ulrik's guards had come seeking the source.

Or worse, had someone come and eavesdropped as they plotted their revenge?

A figure, cloaked in pale gray fur, emerged from the trees.

"Andor," she breathed. "What are you doing here?"

Andor's gaze moved from her to Helga and back again, his lips parting in a look of surprise. "Ulrik is looking for you," he said at last.

Svanhild's stomach coiled. What was Ulrik doing awake at this hour? And how did he know they were missing, unless he had peeked into their chamber in the dead of night?

Andor took a step back as though to retreat into the trees, then cocked his head to listen for something. That's when Svanhild heard the crunching of more footsteps. Her eyes met Andor's, and in that look she saw his regret as two of Ulrik's guards appeared behind him. Had he hoped *not* to find them, to guide the guards on a path away from them, to protect their secret? Her heart fluttered at the idea.

"You found them," said one of the guards, slapping Andor on the back. He chuckled when he saw Svanhild and her mother at the edge of the lake. "What are you two doing with swords and shields?"

Svanhild's muscles tensed as she realized both she and her mother were armed. If her mother made a move to fight, she would too.

Leering at them, the guard moved his hand to the handle of a battle axe that hung from his waist.

Svanhild tightened her grip on Hrafnblód. She sank her knees into a battle stance, tilting the sword up and to the side, poised for battle.

"Svanhild," Helga whispered. A warning. "Your sisters are asleep in the longhouse, remember?"

Svanhild cursed under her breath as she understood. Even if the two of them won this fight now, there would be repercussions.

Andor placed a hand on the guard's back before he could grab his axe. "Let's get them back to the hall," he said. "My father will decide what to do with them."

Svanhild glared at him. Perhaps she had misread him before. He was his father's son to the bone.

Helga sheathed her blade and touched Svanhild's arm, a small gesture of encouragement to do the same. Sighing, Svanhild sheathed Hrafnblód.

They strode to Andor and the guards, who grabbed their arms to jerk them into place beside them. Andor eyed the guards darkly until they lightened their grips. Then he led them back into the forest.

As they walked back to the longhouse, Svanhild and Helga glanced at one another nervously. This was no time to speak, though Svanhild could almost read her mother's mind. *What will Andor tell Ulrik?*

The guards joked about the two of them with weapons, as though women could not possibly know how to wield them. It made Svanhild regret not showing them her skill with a blade, but she understood her mother's caution. She had to keep her sisters safe.

When they arrived at the longhouse, Svanhild felt somehow naked as she walked into the hall where Ulrik watched them. Her sword felt conspicuous where it hung from her waist.

Ulrik stood near the jarl's chair. His eyes sparked like a forgefire when he saw them.

"Well, Andor, when you said you were going into the forest, I did not think you would be the first one back," he said. Then he turned his gaze to Svanhild and Helga as they stopped a few paces before him. "I see you were playing shieldmaiden together in the woods."

Andor moved to stand beside Svanhild. "We did not ask what they were doing," he said. "They should be the ones to explain."

Though he did not look at Svanhild in that moment, she felt his attention on her, an unspoken nudge. Perhaps he had not asked questions because he wanted to give them time to concoct their own story, one he would not interfere with.

Helga spoke first. "My daughter could not sleep. She has always been a troubled sleeper. So I took her to the lake, where we often go to talk. We brought swords to defend ourselves should we encounter a bear. Here in Kaldvik, our family has always looked after ourselves." She lifted her chin, a rare show of pride to Ulrik.

The jarl rolled his neck, then sat back in his chair with a sigh.

Svanhild could not help but ask the question that made her stomach clench. "Why were you looking for us in the middle of the night?"

Her mother tensed beside her but said nothing.

"Why should a jarl not call on his women?" Ulrik said, his gaze on Helga. "A man wants what he wants, and a jarl usually gets it."

Svanhild looked at her mother, not caring who saw her expression. Had Ulrik called on her before? The way he implied Helga was one of his women... Was she a concubine to him now?

No, her mother would never agree to such a thing. Helga, the only wife of Jarl Tove, would never degrade herself by entering another man's bed, especially not this usurper's.

But as Svanhild watched her mother hang her head, she understood the truth.

Turning to glare at Ulrik, Svanhild said, "You have no right to make a concubine of my mother. She was the wife of the great Jarl Tove. She's a leader to our people–"

Ulrik stood, his face reddening. "Enough!" he roared. "Your mother is a leader to no one. *You* are a leader to no one. You are a girl who plays with her father's sword."

He stepped toward her then. Though her instinct was to back away from him, she forced herself to hold her ground, lifting her chin as her mother had a moment ago. She would not be intimidated by this beast.

"That is Hrafnblód, isn't it?" Ulrik said, his voice soft with wonder now.

He reached toward her and brushed his fingertips against the hilt of the sword where it hung at her waist. His huge hand brushed against her hip—too close, too intimate. She wanted to cringe and pull away, but she set her jaw and stared at the wall somewhere behind him, trying to think about something other than his presence. His smell of sour ale and damp wool was overpowering. She tried not to breathe.

A movement out of the corner of her eye caught her attention. She looked over to see Andor watching her, his gray eyes full of sympathy. She was surprised at the expression, but what was the point of it if he refused to defend them now?

Ulrik pulled Hrafnblód from its hook, stepping back to hold it erect between them. He studied the handle first, clucking his tongue at the metalwork. Then his eyes traveled to the runes etched on the blade. He whistled his approval.

Lowering the sword to his side, he looked at Svanhild again. "How did you come by this weapon, girl?"

"You know it is my father's sword."

"Indeed," he said, "which is why, as jarl of this land, it should be in my care." He chuckled. "I see you carry it on your right hip so you can wield it with your left hand. Some would say Loki played a trick on you there, but I don't put much faith in the gods. What glory I have..." He made a fist with his free hand. "... I earned through my own decisions and my own deeds."

Svanhild swallowed.

"Remove the sheathe."

At least he allowed her to do that herself, for she didn't want him to draw near her again. She removed the sheathe and extended it toward him.

Ulrik snatched it from her. "I hope you know playing with weapons is not the life I intend for the women under my care."

Heat boiled in Svanhild's chest. "Under your care? Is that what you call the way you treat us?"

Ulrik raised a hand and lunged toward her. Svanhild braced herself for the blow, for it looked as though he would slap her back-handed across the face.

Instead, the blow landed on Helga's cheek. The harsh clap of it echoed through the hall.

"That is for training your daughter without my permission." Ulrik looked back at Svanhild. "Perhaps you should think before asking your mother to train you again."

Svanhild's blood chilled. For a man to hit a woman, especially of Helga's status, was a punishable offense—provided someone brought the issue forward to the jarl. The trouble was that Ulrik *was* the jarl, and there were no outside witnesses present other than his son and guards.

"Father," Andor said, stepping forward. Svanhild was surprised to feel the anger radiating off of him like heat from a fire. "There is no need for violence in our hall. Their family has been nothing but obedient to you since the day you took Kaldvik."

Chuckling, Ulrik placed a hand on Andor's shoulder.

"You are still young, my son. What would you do if someone came and killed me to take your land from you?" Though it sounded like he would go on, he waited for an answer.

Realizing this, Andor finally said, "I would seek revenge."

Ulrik patted Andor's shoulder in agreement. "Someday you will see more clearly the way people plot behind our backs. Then, you will do anything to protect what is yours." He waved his hand at Svanhild and her mother. "Go back to bed. I expect to see you there every night from now on."

As he turned and left the hall, Andor cast a dark glance Svanhild's way. Though its meaning was unclear, she sensed he did not agree with his father's words.

Strange though it was to realize, she did agree with Ulrik, for she *would* do anything to protect her family and gain back her home. Now more than ever.

CHAPTER 17

HALDIS

*H*aldis awoke to the sound of voices in the hall. She had been tossing all night, her dreams filled with scenes from Ragnarok, the final war of the gods that would end the world. And as soon as her eyes opened, her hair stood on end. Something was wrong.

The chamber was still dark, so she knew it must be the middle of the night. Who would be out of bed now?

That's when she noticed two of the room's beds were empty: Svanhild's and her mother's.

Footsteps grew louder as someone approached the hall. As the door of the chamber swung open, a flicker of lamplight filled part of the room. It was just enough light for Haldis to see her mother and older sister shoved into the chamber. The door slammed shut behind them.

"Are you all right?" Haldis whispered. "What happened?"

Though it was too dark to make out the forms of her family around her, Haldis recognized Svanhild's strong whisper. "Ulrik found us training by the lake." A bitter laugh escaped her. "No, that's not right. *Andor* found us training by the lake, and he brought us back for punishment."

Haldis's heart sank. The thought of her mother training Svanhild at night had worried her before, but she prayed to the gods they would never be discovered. Apparently the gods had other plans.

"I am sorry your training has come to an end," Haldis whispered back. "What did Ulrik do?"

"He hit Mother," said Svanhild. "And I sensed a threat in his words."

Brynja shifted on her bed then. "Are you all right, Mother?" Her voice was barely louder than a mouse's squeak.

"I am fine," Helga replied. Though she kept her voice down too, her tone was low and strong. "I have been wounded far worse in battles. I barely felt the slap."

Haldis knew that was a lie, but she appreciated Mother's strength. As always, Helga was the backbone of their family.

"He stole Hrafnblód," Svanhild said.

"Let us not focus on what we lost tonight," said Helga. "Tell your sisters about your plan."

There was the rustling of straw as Svanhild settled on her pellet. Though the room was almost pitch black, Haldis suspected the outline against the far wall was her sister's shadow as she sat up to tell this tale.

"I will go to Uppsala to seek our uncle," Svanhild whispered, her voice quickening in a rush of excitement. "Because he is a raider, he is likely to have more warriors who will join us, and he can help us strategize our attack."

"What if he is no longer a raider?" Haldis asked.

"And what if he doesn't want to leave his new wife?" Brynja added.

There was a pause as their older sister considered. Haldis wondered why their mother did not answer. Perhaps allowing Svanhild to tell this story instilled confidence in her. Svanhild would be the one to escape to Uppsala, after all. She needed to own this plan.

Finally Svanhild said, "I still believe he will help us. When Mother and I made our plans tonight, I sensed the gods listening. Haldis, can you ask them for their favor now?"

Haldis tensed. "Right now? In the dark?"

A round of giggles erupted from everyone else. Haldis shook her head, unable to avoid a smile. She realized how she sounded.

"Fine," she said, relaxing. "But I cannot promise the gods will show me anything."

"The gods listen more than you know," Svanhild whispered. "You should trust your abilities."

But Haldis was not so sure.

Biting back an argument, she closed her eyes—not that it made much difference in the dark—and reached her mind upwards to Asgard.

"Odin, Thor, and Freyja," she prayed softly, "show me Svanhild's path. Show me what will happen to my sister. Will she find our uncle? Will he help her seek revenge?"

Haldis waited, holding her breath. For a moment, it was so silent she could hear the beating of her own heart.

Just as she thought to give up on an answer, a light flared in her left eye—the eye that was supposed to connect her to the gods. At first, she saw only shadows playing against the light. But soon the shadows grew into shapes, and the shapes took on forms she recognized.

There was Svanhild, her long hair braided but wild. In her left hand she lifted Hrafnblóð, and in her right was a shield depicting their family's sigil: a pair of ravens looking over one another's shoulders. Several runes of war and protection were painted in blue across her forehead.

Behind Svanhild was a pack of warriors, including their

uncle Asmund. That's when Haldis saw they were on a longship, with other ships trailing behind them.

Her heart beat faster, the rhythm growing louder and steadier until she realized it was a war drum. The warriors on the longships pounded the rhythm with their boots against the floor and their weapon hilts against their shields.

They were preparing to attack.

A war horn sounded from the shore.

And then everything vanished like smoke.

Haldis blinked, trying to find the vision again, but it was gone. Her breathing came hard and ragged, as though she were trying to catch her breath after running.

"Are you all right?" The voice was Brynja's, full of worry.

"Was that a vision? What did you see?" That was Svanhild.

Haldis inhaled deeply to calm her racing heart. "I saw you on a ship, Svanhild. And you were with Asmund." She described the details of her vision, from her sister's wild braid to the horn that sounded at the end.

When she was done, she felt exhausted. Yet from the tingling in her skin, she knew her vision was true.

Was this what it felt like to trust her visions, to trust her connection to the gods? There was a thrill in seeing the future, but what she noticed more was the calm that flooded her body afterwards. She could fall into a dreamless sleep now, her duty done.

The gods had spoken through her.

"I will find Asmund," Svanhild breathed. "I will bring back warriors. And I will wield Hrafnblóð again."

"Then we must prepare," said Helga. "You should leave before your wedding. You must find supporters by then."

Brynja sat up. "I have something to show you. Or to let you feel."

Haldis startled when Brynja's fingers brushed her wrist. She smelled the soap in her sister's hair as she drew close.

Then she felt Brynja press something into her palm. It was a wooden trinket. Running her fingers along its edges, Haldis made out a point on one end and a swoop on the other. Could it be a beak and a tail?

"It is a raven," she guessed.

"Erik gave it to me," said Brynja. "It is a sign of his loyalty to our family, and he says he is not the only one."

Haldis passed the raven to Svanhild who slept on the other side of her. After a moment, she heard her mother's gasp as she, too, felt the carving.

"This is good, for it means the gods are with us," said Helga. "But we have much work to do."

CHAPTER 18

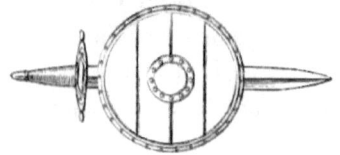

SVANHILD

*a*fter Ulrik's discovery of her training, Svanhild felt like a caged wolf inside the longhouse. Everywhere she went, guards stood at the doors, either barring her passage or keeping watch on where she went. And never did they allow her to leave the house.

Svanhild did not want to spend time with Andor, but in her confinement it was hard to avoid him. They took meals together, and on afternoons when they both sat around the hearthfire in the hall, she felt Andor gazing at her. Though she returned his stares with a defiant glower, she got the impression he wasn't just sitting and admiring her. No, his thoughts were elsewhere. Part of her wanted to ask him what was on his mind, but she refused to befriend him now—not after he had failed to defend her against Ulrik.

Still, she wondered about that night. When he had discovered her training with her mother—as the guards moved in behind him, and he had to play along with them—had she truly seen regret flash across his face? If the guards had not caught up to him, would he have led them away from the scene? Did he want to help Svanhild and her mother?

She told herself it did not matter. In the end, he had led them to Ulrik and watched as his father punished them. Any sympathy she saw in his eyes, any small protest at Ulrik's treatment—it was too little, too late.

Svanhild thanked the gods whenever Andor was out of the longhouse, for at least it meant she did not have to spend time with him. Many days, he went out hunting with Ulrik's warriors or oversaw repairs to his father's longships at the docks. Part of her longed to go with him just to get out of the house, but it was better to avoid him.

She just needed some way to contact Frode Fish-Nose about supporters. And she itched to get her hands on a weapon for more training...

One cold winter morning, as she sat by the fire awkwardly re-stitching the torn hem of one of her oldest dresses, Andor breezed into the hall in his usual fur cloak, looking ready to go out. But as he passed her, he stopped and raised an eyebrow.

"Svanhild," he said, "would you like to accompany me on an outing today?"

Her sisters sat across the fire from her, busy with their own stitchwork. They both cast her curious glances to see how she would react to the question.

She could refuse, but the idea of being outside in the fresh snow made her heart race. The only other way to enjoy fresh air today would be to clean out the pig stall behind the long-house. Whatever Andor had in mind must be better than that.

Casting aside her stitchwork, she rose from her stool. "Fine," she said, trying to keep some iron in her voice. "Let me fetch my cloak."

She went to retrieve her warmest wool cloak from the small room she shared with her family. As she tossed it on and tied it around her neck, she let her fingers brush the soft rabbit fur at the shoulders. This was a luxurious cape, finer than most people could afford. One last token to remind her that whatever her circumstances now, she had been born a jarl's daughter.

As she made her way back to the hall, she found Andor laughing with her sisters. The happy scene made her blood go cold.

"What is so funny?" she asked.

Haldis looked at her, a small smile still playing on her lips. "Your future husband just showed us where he stitched his own tunic. His hand is almost as clumsy as yours."

Andor chuckled. "It sounds like neither of us were born to sew clothes," he said to Svanhild.

She held onto her frown. It would be nice to feel happy again, to laugh with her family—even to jest with Andor, if she could forget for a moment that he was Ulrik's son. But she still didn't trust him. He had a more amiable nature than his father, but she feared that was his weapon. How quickly her sisters had lowered their shields.

"Where are we going?" she said, to change the subject.

Andor straightened his face and led her to the front doors of the hall. "I have a meeting with the blacksmith today."

Since when did Andor start making appointments with Balder? Svanhild had been wondering for weeks whether the blacksmith still favored her family over Ulrik. At least visiting him now gave her a chance to gauge his loyalty again.

As they exited the hall, the wind hit Svanhild's face like a whip, stealing the breath from her lungs. She froze a moment on the longhouse steps, hugging her cloak around her. Only when she finally found her breath again did she feel her blood flowing through her veins at last.

She inhaled the fresh scent of snow, smiling. The village looked covered in a heavy white blanket, bumps here and there revealing the positions of homes and shops beneath the piled snow. With everyone indoors, roads were empty. The only signs of life were the trails of smoke drifting from rooftops. The peace of winter was here, and the whole world felt cleansed.

She breathed in again. *Home.*

Because the snow was deep—nearly reaching her knees—she had to lift her legs high to move forward. After a few crunching footsteps, she realized she was alone.

She glanced over her shoulder. Andor stood like an ice sculpture on the longhouse steps.

"Are you coming?" she called. Her breath clouded before her lips.

Andor inhaled loudly, like a draugr becoming flesh again and breathing for the first time in centuries. Then he took a few steps forward to join her, his steps slow, weaving a careful path through the snow.

"You don't have to be scared of it," she said. "It's just snow."

They walked side by side then, Svanhild slowing her steps so she would not outpace him too much.

"I thought I knew cold in Mosfell," Andor said through chattering teeth. "I was wrong."

Svanhild let herself admire the view again. Though part of her wished to remain sullen, she felt her spirits lifting. "Isn't it beautiful, though?" she said. "I love days like this, frozen in time. It's like walking through a tapestry hanging in Freyja's hall."

Andor merely puffed air through his lips. The sight of his grimace, his lips turning blue, almost made her laugh.

Being away from Ulrik and his guards made her feel free for the first time in weeks. And despite not fully trusting Andor, she had to admit that he was far less of a nuisance than his father. Less intimidating, too.

She felt a question slip from her mouth before she could catch it. "Were you going to defend us?" Though she bit her tongue, the question was already catching in the wind like a lost snowflake. When Andor looked at her curiously, she explained, "That night you found my mother and me training by the lake. For a moment, it looked like you wanted to protect us, but the guards came too quickly. Were you going to lie for us?"

"So you *were* training," Andor said, raising an eyebrow.

She scowled at what she had just admitted, but Andor just chuckled.

After considering for a moment, he said, "You are right. I was going to lead the guards away from you. I knew my father would be angry to find out you had escaped the long-house with weapons. He fears you are against him."

"My mother does nothing but help him," Svanhild complained. "She runs the longhouse, sits by him at meals, stands with him at feasts... Why would he fear us?"

"Let me correct myself," Andor said. "He fears *you*."

Svanhild's heart thumped hard in her chest. Did Ulrik suspect something? Perhaps her mother was right to be so careful around him...

"You don't hide your anger at him," Andor continued. "I admire you for that."

Svanhild was surprised at the compliment. Did that mean he shared her anger at Ulrik? She thought not. Perhaps he only complimented her now to play the diplomat, to win her over, to please his future wife.

She did not trust him yet.

"Why did you want to protect us, then?" she asked.

"Unlike my father, I have nothing against you. Besides, you are free women. I'm sorry my father does not treat you that way."

Svanhild wanted to protest that if he was sorry for it, he should help them more.

But too quickly he said, "One day my father will treat you better. You just need to earn his trust."

The same thing her mother wanted, and what Ulrik had warned her to do just after he took the high-seat.

Svanhild forced herself to remain silent now. If she started an argument now, Andor might take her back to the longhouse and never invite her outside again.

She wished her mother were here to see how well she was behaving herself, for it was not easy.

Eventually they came to Balder's workshop, a stout building of wooden slats, smoke puffing out the roof. The familiar sound of hammering echoed from within.

They only had to knock once before Balder was at the door. His rugged face was flushed from his labor, coal smudged across his forehead. He nodded to Svanhild, but she was surprised when his brown eyes lit up at the sight of Andor.

"You look like Skadi's got you by the balls today," he chuckled, slapping Andor on the back. "Come in before they drop off."

Svanhild watched the scene, her eyes widening with wonder, as Andor strode into Balder's workshop as easily as if this were his own home. Clearly he had visited before.

Balder turned to her then. "Forgive the language, little one," he said. "Come in and sit by the fire. I have stew for you both."

She said nothing about his nickname for her, which made her feel foolish. How was a *little one* supposed to lead him and an entire band of warriors against Ulrik?

Inside, Balder closed the door behind them, shutting out the cold. Instantly the room was quieter, the only sound the crackling fire. Balder motioned for her and Andor to sit at stools by the fire where they could warm themselves. Svanhild was happy to oblige.

"I've thought about the design," Andor told the blacksmith as he sat. "I'll go with Yggdrasil, woven in knotwork like yours, with the eagle in the branches."

"Did you have a drink before you came?"

Andor shook his head. "I wish I had, if only to survive the cold. How do you make it through the winter here?"

"It's no wonder you're cold after sitting in the longhouse all day. It's best to keep your body active." Balder poured Andor a cup of beer and passed it to him. "That's why so many babies in Kaldvik are born at the end of summer."

He winked at Svanhild before shooting Andor a knowing look. Svanhild blushed. She was rarely alone around men like this; though she had overheard such bawdy conversation, nobody had ever brought her into the discussion before.

Ignoring the comment, Andor downed his beer in three consecutive gulps, then shoved the cup back at the blacksmith. "Another."

Svanhild watched in awe as Andor drank two more cups in quick succession. She wondered how he stayed upright on his stool. Balder slapped him on the back again, as though approving of his speed. Svanhild continued staring, trying to work out why they were here and when these two men—who she had never seen together in the same room—were as comfortable with each other as brothers.

Finally, she said, "Are you two friends?"

The two men exchanged glances, silent for a moment. Then Balder roared out a laugh at the same time Andor chuckled. That confirmed it, then.

"Well, I give up," Svanhild said, throwing up her hands. "What are we doing here?"

Balder passed her a steaming bowl of stew. She breathed in the savory smell of roast duck. Then he said, "Did your betrothed not tell you why he braved the cold today?"

Svanhild shook her head. That word "betrothed" sounded so casual when the blacksmith said it, as if he didn't mind, as if the two of them joining in marriage were as natural as snowfall in winter. This, from a man who had claimed to want revenge against Ulrik, who should hate Ulrik's family. Did he not realize *she* hated Ulrik and his family?

She would have to right this false impression today, without Andor sensing it. She needed to test Balder's loyalty.

The blacksmith passed another bowl of stew to Andor, who thanked him. Then he rummaged in a wooden box on a nearby table, pulling out tools she had not seen before: a bone needle and a fist-sized jar filled with a deep blue liquid. When Andor's eyes lit on the objects, he grimaced. This only made the blacksmith chuckle.

"You'll be fine," he said. "The first poke is always the sharpest, but think of it as battle training."

Svanhild recognized the tools then: a needle and paint.

She raised an eyebrow at Andor. "You are being tattooed?"

He nodded, tapping the left side of his head, where his russet-colored hair was shaved clean. "Here, above my ear. That way everyone can see it, but if I grow tired of it, I can just grow my hair out again."

"A clever plan," she admitted.

The blacksmith prepared his tools by the flickering firelight. "I will paint interlocking knots that will become tree branches, with the eagle in the uppermost branches. Does that suit?"

Andor nodded. He took a slurping sip of his stew, then set

193

the bowl aside. Straightening his back and smacking his hands on his knees, he said, "I am ready." His voice was louder than before—probably from the drink doing its work.

Svanhild hid a smile. He looked like a warrior steeling himself for someone to close a wound with a fire-edged blade. She could almost picture the boy he once was, a little rounder in the face, with a dash of uncertainty in his eyes. He must have been a quiet child, and today he was the same, going silent and still as he braced himself, only clenching his jaw a little tighter and gripping his knees a little harder.

Balder dipped his needle in the paint pot, and the work began.

"I WOULD SAY it's my finest work," Balder boasted later that afternoon, "if you don't count my own." He held up his muscular left arm where the sleeve was rolled up, revealing knotwork tattoos starting at his wrists and running all the way up into his shirtsleeve.

"You did that work yourself?" Andor said incredulously. His face was flushed, though Svanhild could not tell if it was from the beer, the fire, or the pain of the needle—likely all three.

The blacksmith nodded as he put away his tools. "I endured far worse pain than that in my life, believe me." When he turned back to them, a shadow passed through his eyes, and Svanhild remembered he had a wife once, years ago.

"We need someone neutral to decide this." Andor turned the left side of his head towards Svanhild. "I will trust her judgment. How does it look, Svanhild?"

Her name was like warmed honey when it issued from his mouth, and she weakened at the sound. The beer Balder had given her to sip was working too well. She had to admit that

Andor was handsome, with his bronze hair, wide gray eyes, and full mouth. But in the crackling firelight of Balder's forge, the blue tattoos added edges to his fine features. He looked like someone new now. Fiercer. Stronger. Someone she would fear in battle, and someone she might reach for in bed.

Blushing, she shook the thought from her mind.

"Well?" Andor asked. His eyes danced as he looked sideways at her.

She could not draw her eyes away from his tattoo. Unlike the rough knots drawn on the blacksmith's skin, Andor's tattoo was an elegant pattern of sworls that curved up and over his ear. As the pattern stretched up toward the top of his skull, the lines thinned and evaporated like smoke.

"Come," Andor said, motioning her nearer.

She rose from her stool and drew close to study the pattern. Andor radiated heat almost as much as the hearthfire; he had flung away his cloak a long time ago. The pain of the tattooing must have made him sweat.

"I see the branches of the sacred tree," she said, then noticed a sloping figure tangled in the top branches. "And there is the eagle, with the hawk Vedrfolnir perched on top."

"I know what it is," Andor teased, "but do you like it?"

She scraped her gaze over his profile, feeling the warmth in her face. She hoped he would only blame it on her beer. "It looks good," she said simply, then moved away from him and tried to change the subject. "Why did you choose that design? Why Yggdrasil?"

"It is my favorite story, Odin sacrificing himself for knowledge. I wanted to remind myself of it, and show others what I value."

Svanhild's heart ached at how much the words sounded like her father's. She almost asked Andor if he had seen her father's tapestry of Odin and Yggdrasil in the meeting room behind the main hall. But she bit her tongue before the words escaped her. For all she knew, Ulrik's family would replace that tapestry soon with something more suited to them. A war scene, perhaps.

"My father might not have chosen it," Andor admitted, "but when I become jarl someday, I want people to know who *I* am."

Listening to him speak about being jarl made Svanhild's mouth go dry. He truly believed they would marry, that he would rule here someday, that she would be his wife and all would be well with the world.

She glanced over at the blacksmith then, wondering what he thought of this. But his back was to them as he polished freshly-forged swords and wrapped them in linen.

"Those weapons are beautiful," she commented. "Did you just make them?"

"An order for Jarl Ulrik," Balder replied.

Svanhild raised her eyebrows. "Why is he in need of so many new weapons?"

Andor was the one to answer. "My father is sending for warriors from Mosfell. They will leave their safe homes with my grandfather to live here, in a much colder climate, even though it will sever them from my grandfather. It is a big sacrifice, but the ones who will come have raided with my father for years. They believe he will bring them greater riches than my grandfather ever did. For their loyalty, they will be rewarded with new swords."

So Ulrik was calling for reinforcements. Svanhild frowned. She was preparing to go to Uppsala, but the trip would take weeks—perhaps months—and it was dangerous to leave in the dead of winter. Besides, she only had a few weeks of battle training with her mother, and that time had been cut short. Was she ready to lead people in battle already? She needed more time, but with a fresh batch of warriors behind him, Ulrik would be far more formidable than he already was.

She cursed under her breath. She had lost herself in the day, feeling free just for being away from the longhouse. She had watched in fascination as Andor and Balder laughed together—often after the blacksmith's coarse ribbing, a sure sign he liked Andor—and listened as they swapped stories of smithing and fighting and family. Svanhild was surprised to feel at home with them both.

But in her comfort, she had forgotten her purpose.

She needed to see if Balder's friendship with Andor extended all the way to loyalty. If he was friends with Andor, perhaps he would not mind seeing Andor in the jarl's high-seat. But did that mean he supported Ulrik now? The idea made her skin go clammy. She could not let her plans slip away so easily…

Choosing her words carefully, she said to Balder, "My father would have appreciated your hospitality to Andor, after everything that has happened."

The blacksmith's motions flickered for a heartbeat—barely enough for anyone to notice, but Svanhild caught it—before he continued packing the swords in cloth. Over his shoulder, he said, "I make it a habit to judge each man by his own merit. Andor, I respect." He cast Svanhild a quick look, and she understood the meaning.

It was enough. Her heart raced. He specified Andor because he did not respect Ulrik, and that was all she needed to know for now.

As she rose to retrieve her cloak and take her leave of the shop, Andor said, "Wait, there is one other reason we are here." When he looked at Balder, the blacksmith turned to pull an axe from a weapons rack on the wall.

Svanhild gasped when he extended the blade to her. "What is this?"

"For you," Balder said.

She took the axe by the handle and held it up to the firelight. It had the sheen of a virgin blade, newly forged and yet to draw blood, but instead of the usual silver it was almost gold. The grip was comfortable in her hand, molded with inward curves to fit her fingers. On one side of the blade, the blacksmith had carved interlocking runes—symbols for the gods, wealth, and luck—to offer protection to the wielder of the weapon; on the other side was a swirling pattern depicting a warrior on horseback.

"It is beautiful craftsmanship," she said. "How did you get it this color?

Balder chuckled. "Every smith has his secrets, little one."

Svanhild tossed the axe from hand to hand, testing its weight. It felt swift and easy to carry, yet the blade itself had a satisfying heft. This was a weapon meant to draw blood and steal lives.

She admired the runes and picture again; such elaborate work must have taken the blacksmith weeks.

"Is this truly for me?" she asked.

"It is a gift for you," Andor explained. "I know you have always dreamed of being a shieldmaiden. It was unfair of my father to stop your training and take your father's weapon from you. With this new blade, I hope your training may continue."

Svanhild glanced from Andor to Balder and back again. How long had these two men been planning this?

Her gaze landed on Andor then. "This was your idea?"

He nodded, a small smile touching the corners of his mouth.

Now she understood why the blacksmith respected Andor, for it took a brave man with a good heart to prepare such a gift for his future wife, knowing it could anger his own father.

Andor's gray eyes were warm in the firelight as he watched her, waiting for a reaction. Although he had not protected her against his father, he had cared enough to spend weeks forging such a weapon for her.

"It's true, my training is important to me," she said. "I suppose you know me better than I thought."

"It is one of the few secrets I've learned about you," he said. "That, and how you favor napping during the day, and you wish to be outside in the fresh air more, and you are a terrible seamstress…"

This time, she let herself laugh.

"You pray to the gods all the time, and you love your family more than anything." He grinned. "Besides wielding a weapon, of course."

Svanhild admitted that was true.

Andor grew more serious then. "In time, my father will start to trust you again. Until then, I will do my best to find times for you to train with your mother, if that would make you happy."

"It would," Svanhild said. "Thank you, Andor."

"You look more bewildered about this weapon than you were my tattoo," he teased.

"I suppose you surprised me." She shrugged. "A little."

He chuckled, a sound that warmed her more than the fire. "I like surprising you."

They donned their cloaks and took their leave then, Svanhild thanking Balder once more for forging such a beautiful axe for her. As they traded the warmth of the shop for the icy wind outside, she was grateful that the wind howled too loudly for them to speak.

She needed time to process the surprises of the day.

CHAPTER 19

BRYNJA

*A*s winter snow blanketed Kaldvik, Brynja sat in the main hall of the longhouse, working at a loom that stood in front of an open door.

Ulrik and his wife Gertrud had already escaped to the back rooms after complaining of the cold. But Brynja didn't mind the icy chill that swept in through the side door. Even as it numbed her lips and made her nose tingle, the clean scent of snow reminded her of her father. Her family always loved winter's embrace. They were creatures of the snow, ravens who flew faster on the winter wind.

And the fresh air was a novelty these days. Brynja was too scared to ask Ulrik if she could take a walk or run an errand. Ulrik had been furious at their family for weeks now—ever since he learned that Mother and Svanhild were sneaking out to the lake at night—and nobody wanted to poke the bear.

And so Brynja was glad of the opportunity just to sit by

the open door, weaving wool, letting the cold air numb her skin as it warmed her soul.

Today, Ursula worked beside her. Two people at the loom made the weaving much easier. Ursula, shorter than Brynja, struggled in her old age to lift her arms to reach the highest threads on the loom, so Brynja took care of the weaving while Ursula handed her what she needed. All the while, the old thrall's cat meowed and rubbed her head against their ankles.

"Is it too cold for you here?" Brynja asked, realizing the freezing air from the open door might chill the poor woman's skin.

Ursula grunted, which was answer enough. Brynja left the door open for light and air, continuing her work in silence.

Since Alf's death, the seamstress had spoken even less than she had before. Brynja tried to talk to her about it, but Ursula waved away her words like she was brushing out dirt with a broom. Still, Brynja sensed that her silence was her grief. More than once, she had spied Ursula hidden in the shadows of the main hall, hugging Mouse-Hunter fiercely when she must have thought no one was looking.

The image of Ulrik licking her father's blood from his axe stormed through Brynja's mind, and she shivered. She forced her attention to the loom so Alf wouldn't spring to mind next. She hated that such memories clouded her head now.

Suddenly a man's gruff voice interrupted the quiet rhythm of their work. "Your skin must be made of jewels to withstand such cold."

Brynja tensed as she recognized the man. She refused to turn and greet him, but it was hard to focus on her weaving as she heard his footsteps draw near. She wrinkled her nose as the musty smell of dirty hair and wet forest leaves announced he was right behind her.

"It certainly shines like polished jewels," he said in her ear, making her shudder.

Trying her best not to squirm away from him, she finally bit out a greeting. "Hello, Olaf. What does the jarl have you doing in the hall today?"

"I am preparing for the arrival of his warriors soon. Several families from Mosfell have decided to follow him here, for they know the gods are with him."

Brynja wanted to laugh at that. If the gods were with Ulrik, why did he keep guards at every door so her family could not leave? She and her sisters barely found time to talk anymore, other than whispers in the night. Ulrik's men were always watching.

She said none of this. Instead, she returned her attention to her weaving with a small breath of impatience. She hoped the sound was enough to dissuade him from staying.

"Is that annoyance I hear?" Olaf chuckled, coming around to stand where she could see him. "Such feelings are attractive in a young woman like yourself, but they will grow stale by the time you're her age." He gestured at Ursula.

"You are blocking the light," Ursula complained.

Brynja hid a laugh. Olaf was nowhere near the doorway, but it was a good lie to express frustration at the intruder.

"And you are speaking out of turn," Olaf shot back. "What are you still doing in this house?"

In reply, Ursula leveled him with a glare that could freeze a waterfall in place. Brynja tensed when she saw Olaf's face reddening in anger, but fortunately another member of Ulrik's household staff arrived to call him away.

As he left, Olaf gave Ursula one last glower, then bent to whisper in Brynja's ear. "If you should like to venture outside sometime, I can arrange it with the jarl." Then he walked away.

As much as Brynja longed to be outdoors, she would rather Ulrik lock her in a cell than take a walk with Olaf.

Though she tried to continue her work, Brynja pricked her finger with her needle and winced. She was surprised when she felt Ursula touch her arm. She looked down at the old woman's hand, knotted with veins and covered in age spots, the markings of a long life. When she lifted her gaze to Ursula's face, she chilled to see the seamstress's eyes had gone almost milk-white as she stared out the door.

"Take care of Mouse-Hunter for me," she said. Though her voice sounded like she was dreaming, Brynja knew the words were meant for her. "This little warrior will survive longer than I will in this house."

As Brynja finished at the loom later that day, a group of Ulrik's warriors and their families arrived in Kaldvik. Brynja watched as they flooded the great hall like mites invading a fresh apple. Ulrik had asked for these reinforcements, but he had not had the foresight to properly prepare for them. Helga enlisted Brynja's help in finding them shelter.

"There will be families willing to take them in for the winter," Helga said. Brynja sensed a sigh of frustration lodged in her mother's throat, but she would not complain while Ulrik was seated on his throne just a meter away. "Find them storerooms and servants' quarters on farms if you must."

"Are you sure anyone will house them?" Brynja asked quietly. If Erik had been right about their supporters, few people in Kaldvik would want to give shelter to the enemy.

Helga gave her a stern look, warning her away from such conversation. "The people of Kaldvik have long been known for their hospitality," she said, her voice a little louder than before.

Ulrik overhead. "Take Birger with you, girl," he said, waving toward the thralls who were serving ale to the raucous gathering of men and women.

Brynja scanned the group. Some warriors sat with one another, their faces unlined but scarred. These were men who had seen battle, but they did not have any women attached to them yet. Other men sat with their wives and concubines, wrinkles around their eyes, their beards adorned with jewelry from years of raiding. All around the hall, children squealed as they ran around like pigs who had just been let loose from a pen. A few mothers called for their offspring to sit on their laps, but most of the women looked too tired from the journey to bother with mothering. Several were already through a couple of horns of ale. Brynja couldn't blame them.

Helga rested a hand on Brynja's shoulder, following her gaze to a pair of boys wrestling near Ulrik's feet. They seemed completely unaware that their jarl was watching them. Or perhaps they were showing off what good warriors they would become.

"You will have a family one day, daughter," Helga said.

Brynja blanched. "Let us hope they are not like those boys."

Mother laughed. The thrall Baldwyn approached then, inclining his head to Helga and Brynja in turn.

"I am to accompany you on your journey through town?" he asked, confirming the jarl's command.

Brynja smiled at him. Though it had been many weeks since he accompanied her to the market to meet with Erik, she had never forgotten the thrall's discretion. He had kept her stolen time with Erik that day a secret. Though she had suspected then she could trust Baldwyn, now she knew just how right she had been.

Now she would have a walk with him in the fresh air,

with no other guards—and no Olaf—to bother her. And she had an excuse to meet with anyone and everyone in Kaldvik. Brynja could not wait to be among her people again.

After saying goodbye to her mother and Jarl Ulrik, Brynja led Baldwyn through the crowded hall. They wove around the feasting warriors and their wives, dodging an old man who drunkenly stumbled toward a post before catching himself on it. As they neared the entrance, Baldwyn grabbed her arm and jerked her away from a young warrior as he leaned over and vomited on the floor. A few shouts from nearby men cheered him on.

"Thank you," Brynja said. "They are certainly making themselves at home."

"This reminds me too well of the raiding party when they found me," Baldwyn replied.

Brynja looked at him curiously. But when his mouth tightened, she decided it best not to pry further right now.

She led him into the fresh air outside. The cold washed over her all at once, sending a chill down her spine. She breathed in deeply, smiling. Winter in Kaldvik, though brutal, was always beautiful. The air smelled clean and moist, as though the snow were cleansing the town. She watched the snowflakes drifting from the sky, lazy in their descent. A sign that it was time to slow down and enjoy domestic life—that was what winter and its quiet snowfalls meant to her.

"Isn't it pretty today?" she asked Baldwyn.

He smiled shyly. "Where are we going, my lady?"

"We need to find homes for those families. Or at least shelter for a few nights, until we can figure out what to do with them. Let's make our way through the village first, and then we can try the outer farms."

Baldwyn looked up into the sky. "Will the snow grow heavier?"

Brynja shook her head. There was no wind today, which

meant the weather would not shift. "This is all we can expect for now. Let's enjoy the day, shall we?"

They took their time strolling through the town, stopping regularly to check in with the local craftsmen who made their homes here in the village. Everyone greeted Brynja with a smile. At times, she could almost pretend she was on one of her strolls with Father, for the two of them used to make these trips all the time.

She sighed wistfully at the memory. *That* was what had made her father so beloved here. He was not as strong a warrior as some jarls, nor as ruthless. He preferred Svanhild to sing songs of the sacred tree and the gods who sought wisdom—perhaps a tale of Loki's trickery, too—rather than songs of war and death. Brynja knew her father would fight to defend his people, but violence was not his usual way. Instead, he shook hands. He invited everyone to feast with him, when the time was right. He visited farmers to learn their techniques. He checked on the sick and elderly as if they were his family. He smiled at everyone, told jokes, remembered names and special events. Brynja had felt honored to accompany him on his rounds, and she saw first-hand the joy he brought to his people. The joy they brought him, too.

To her surprise, several people in town agreed to house Ulrik's warriors and their families. Though their compassionate spirit warmed her heart, something inside her darkened as they made their way to the farms. The gods may practice some hospitality, but would Odin or Thor have housed the enemy? Or had Jarl Ulrik begun to win some loyalty in town, even among the disgruntled farmers?

After finding rooms for most of the warriors, they made their way to Erik's farm. His was the last on their route, for it was the farthest from the longhouse and village. Brynja waved as she and Baldwyn approached the house. Out front,

Erik was slicing the air with an axe, stepping forward and then leaping back as though engaged with some invisible attacker.

"What are you doing?" Brynja laughed. "Pretending to be a warrior instead of a farmer?"

Erik smiled at her, but his jaw was tight. "I am training."

"I won't ask what you are training for, then," Brynja replied.

She and Erik used to play with wooden swords as children, one of them a Norse invader and the other an English king defending his home. It was a fun game, but she had to giggle, seeing that Erik still played it by himself.

Erik's mother emerged from the front door of their house then, a humble wooden building with smoke drifting from the roof. The smells of woodsmoke and fresh bread wafted from inside. Brynja's stomach rumbled at the memory of Ragnilde and Torven's cooking. She looked up at the sky, which was darkening to a deep blue as night approached. Winter nights always came on suddenly and sooner than expected. She would need to return to Jarl Ulrik's house soon —no time for eating here.

"Good day, Brynja!" Ragnilde called, waving to her. Her red hair was loose today, a nest of wild curls. "And who is this with you?"

"This is Baldwyn," Brynja said. "He is part of Ulrik's household, but I think it's safe to admit among friends that he is far more amiable than the rest of Ulrik's staff."

Though he said nothing, Baldwyn's blue eyes twinkled with humor.

"Then it is good to meet you," said Ragnilde with a smile. "Would you like to come in for a pastry? We are making good use of our dried cloudberries this winter."

Brynja smiled to see Ragnilde so cheerful. She wanted to offer her help, for before Father's death, she had spent many hours in Ragnilde's kitchen, baking bread, folding pastries, and sprinkling herbs into stew to taste what flavors worked best together. Though she did not consider herself a skilled cook, it gave her a sense of normalcy. Often she had pictured herself living on a farm like theirs, milking cows in the morning, sheering sheep in the afternoon, tending to the vegetables growing on the farmland, and then retreating inside to weave wool and cook dinner for her family.

She almost laughed now, imagining it. Though she could picture herself doing all those things, she could not picture a husband. Once, her parents had teased her about marrying Erik someday, but they had read the friendship wrong. There was love there, but it was not romantic. Brynja had never had any romantic feelings for any of the men in Kaldvik. Try as she might, she simply could not envision that part of her future.

Brynja smiled sadly at Ragnilde. "That sounds delicious. I wish I could stay and cook with you, but I'm afraid I am in a hurry to return home before dark. I came to ask a favor of you."

Erik stopped his axe play to listen. His mother wiped her hands on her skirts to clean them, walking down the short path to where Brynja and Baldwyn stood.

"Jarl Ulrik has invited a band of warriors and their families to Kaldvik," Brynja explained, "but they have no housing yet. Several families have agreed to take them in until they can build their own houses. Winter is not the ideal time for building, but they should get started on the project very soon. In the meantime, there are still a few families from Mosfell who need housing."

Ragnilde lifted a hand to let Brynja know she understood the rest. Brynja went quiet. She didn't expect Erik's mother to agree—not after Ulrik had taken so much from the local farms, theirs included.

There was a long pause as Ragnilde pursed her lips in thought. Brynja glanced at Erik where he stood several paces behind his mother. He simply shrugged, for no one could predict what would come out of Ragnilde Aricsdotter's mouth. Once, while cooking with Brynja, she had announced that Helga should have continued to raid with Jarl Tove, for the wife was fiercer than the husband; that had made Brynja laugh.

"I am surprised," she said at last, "that the new jarl dares to ask us for hospitality, when he has shared so little of his with us."

Brynja glanced nervously at Baldwyn, who clasped his hands behind his back and looked down at the ground as though to give them space to talk. She knew she could trust the thrall, yet she had never spoken so openly against Ulrik in front of a member of his household.

After considering, Brynja said, "I understand your frustration. I heard he sent his housecarl to visit farms and take crops for his hall. *Our* hall, I suppose." She sighed. "I fear he took too much."

"We have little left. Torven is awake at night with worry for our family. He has always taken great pride in providing food for us, in taking care of us. Now, he's not sure he can anymore."

Brynja nodded in understanding. It was not like Ragnilde to share such vulnerabilities. That meant things here must be bad.

"His men can sleep in the stables," she said finally. "One family only."

Brynja forced a smile. "Part of me hoped you would say no," she admitted.

"Part of me wanted to say no, for the jarl should have made accommodations for them before they arrived. They are his problem, not ours."

"Then why did you say yes?"

"Did I say yes, or did I say one family will sleep in my stables?" Ragnilde raised her eyebrows. "My stable thralls have first choice of beds there, though. And if anyone steals my cow's milk in the morning, I will kick them right back to Ulrik."

Brynja laughed. "They may not know how to milk a cow. The people of Mosfell are not known for their farming."

Ragnilde laughed, though the sound rang hollow. "I suppose that is one thing in our favor."

Brynja alighted with an idea then. "The jarl will hold an assembly in a few weeks. Perhaps you can bring your grievances to him then." She knew it was dangerous to complain to Ulrik, but he would never care unless enough people brought issues to him. "Tell other farmers to do the same. Ulrik may be greedy, but that extends to the favor of Kaldvik's people."

Ragnilde nodded. "I will consider it."

Brynja noticed Erik swinging his axe again in the background. His movements were clumsy, but he waved the weapon with warrior-like roars.

"He is really trying to use that axe," Brynja remarked.

Ragnilde turned slightly to look at her son. In a low voice, she said, "Ever since Jarl Tove was killed. He hasn't been sleeping much, either."

Brynja watched her friend for a moment. A chill ran down her spine. Whatever anger Erik felt about Ulrik taking control of Kaldvik, she hoped he would let it out in this yard and sleep well soon.

CHAPTER 20

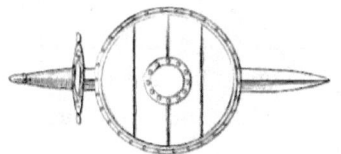

SVANHILD

Svanhild slept with her new axe tucked under her bed pellet. And each time she closed her eyes, the same dream swept behind her eyelids.

She stood on a battlefield, Hrafnblód in one hand and her family's raven shield in the other. She felt the presence of Huginn and Muninn with her as she flew into battle.

That's when she realized she *was* flying, for she was on horseback, and the horse rode on the wind, sweeping the tops of trees. Odin's ravens cawed as they flew on either side of her.

So this was how the Valkyries flew.

Her battlefield was the sky now, and with each swipe of her sword, her legs gripped the sides of her steed tighter. She feared she would slip off her horse any moment...

And then she did. She was falling.

She awoke with a start. Sweat dampened her forehead.

It took her a moment to realize she was in the bed

chamber she shared with her mother and sisters. The sounds of their breathing filled the room.

She was safe. Or as safe as she could be, in Ulrik's household.

Sitting up, she reached beneath her bed pellet to check that her axe was still there. A sigh of relief escaped her when she felt the cool metal against her fingertips.

Since Andor had given her the axe nearly two weeks ago, he had led her and Helga into the forest for two training sessions, both in broad daylight, with no one else around to watch them. Andor even allowed them privacy, though the occasional snap of twigs told her he was always nearby. His presence, even unseen, prohibited personal conversation between her and her mother, but it was still better than being stuck in the longhouse all day.

She touched her upper arms now, smiling to feel their strength. The training was working.

When she tried to sleep again, her mind reeled with images from her dream. Would she fight like a Valkyrie someday? Or would those women of Asgard one day find her on a battlefield and lead her to Fólkvangr or Valhalla?

She tossed on her sleep pellet, attempting to find a comfortable position. Try as she might, she could not quiet her racing mind.

Deciding sleep was hopeless now, she rose from bed to pace the halls. As long as they knew where she was at all times, the guards did not mind if she was out of bed. Perhaps she could sneak to the kitchen to snack on leftover pastries.

She tip-toed to the door. The guard standing outside glanced her way, then inclined his head to her. She was surprised at his deference.

"I need water," she said.

"The kitchens are that way," he whispered back, as though

she had not lived there her whole life. "There are guards everywhere, so don't try sneaking away."

She nodded as she slipped out the door. Keeping her steps light, she scurried down the corridor, past the jarl's quarters and into the main hall.

The man was right. Ulrik had two guards stationed at the front doors of the hall and another at the side door to the training yard. There would be no escaping the longhouse anymore.

Noticing the side door was wide open, she shivered at the strong breeze that blew in. Spotting a pile of cloaks on a bench by the door, she grabbed one to throw over her shoulders, then hugged herself against the chill.

Movement outside drew her attention. In the training yard, a figure swung a blade, barely more than a shadow in the pale light of the half-moon. Straining to see who it was, she realized the man was shirtless. His broad back was tight with muscle and gleamed with sweat. His hair, braided back in a single line running from the top of his head, looked slick with sweat too. She admired the way the muscles knotted and rippled beneath the surface of his skin.

If she didn't know better, she might have thought she was watching a battle of Freyr, most handsome of the gods. There was a reason Freyr so often gave young girls their first sweet pangs when they began dreaming of men.

Heat flushed her skin as she watched the man battle alone. She stood silently in the doorway, trying to avoid notice, enjoying the fantasies that danced through her mind as she admired his powerful movements.

Then she recognized the blue tattoos on the side of his head. *Andor.*

She stood in silence for a moment, unable to take her eyes off the scene. She hadn't realized Andor was such a strong warrior. Wielding a spear, he did more than just stab training pells with it. Instead, he brandished it as though a flag flew at the end of it, generating a strong breeze with each quick move. The spear whirred and snapped in the night air.

Though she knew she should leave him alone, she was frozen in place. Watching him battle was too mesmerizing to leave, a spell she did not want to break.

He stopped suddenly, breathing hard, and glanced over his shoulder to meet her gaze. When had he noticed her there?

She blushed, feeling caught in a trap. "I should let you train."

He turned to her, a smile spreading across his face. He was still panting as he said, "I like company. Come join me."

She bit her lip. She had to admit that staying to watch Andor wield a spear sent a thrill through her.

"I should try to sleep," she argued, more to herself than Andor.

But his next words sealed her position. "Come train with me."

She smiled. If her mind had been too restless to sleep before, now it was impossible.

She stepped outside, glad to be away from the watchful gazes of the guards in the longhouse. If Ulrik had stationed someone in the training yard, Andor had already sent him away.

Testing the scenario, she closed the side door of the long-house behind her. Rather than stopping her, Andor grinned. Now they had privacy.

"How long have you been training with that spear?" she asked.

Andor tossed the weapon from one hand to the other, looking at it the same way her father had once admired Hrafnblód. "This is Thor's Lightning," he said. "A gift from my father when I was twelve years old. I've been learning to wield it ever since."

Svanhild raised an eyebrow. "Are you sure you're still learning? That was many years ago, and you look accomplished."

"Does anyone ever stop learning to fight with a weapon? It's an evolving relationship."

"It sounds like you are in love with that spear."

Andor chuckled. "No need to be jealous." Because he was panting from exertion, his expression gave him the appearance of a puppy. Svanhild had never seen him look so free. She had almost forgotten the feeling herself.

"Well, if we are training, I should have brought my new axe," she said.

"Here." Andor pulled a blunted training sword from a weapons bin and carried it to her. Up close, his body radiated heat. She breathed in the cedar-like musk of his sweat, surprised at the way her own skin heated and flushed in response.

Once she held the training sword in hand, Andor went back to retrieve another for himself. Sword against sword—a fair fight.

"Let's play a game now," he said. "For each hit, the attacker may make one inquiry of his opponent."

"Or *her* opponent," Svanhild corrected with a laugh.

Andor raised his eyebrows. "So you agree to the game?"

Saying nothing, she flung her cloak from her shoulders and dropped into her battle stance, knees bent and sword held at the waist.

That was answer enough. Andor mimicked her. Svanhild gripped the hilt of her sword, trying to focus on the battle and not the plush muscles in her opponent's chest. She wondered how they would feel beneath her fingertips.

Suddenly he lunged toward her. She reacted on instinct,

blocking with her sword at the last moment. The clang of blunted steel startled some birds in the nearby trees, who screeched and flew away.

Svanhild's heart pounded in her chest as she took position again. The battle was on.

"It is fine to feel distracted," Andor teased.

Sensing the flirtation in his words, she replied, "Well, it's true I've never seen quite this much of you. You're usually bundled in that fur cloak of yours."

She leapt at him. Her sword thumped against his shield.

"I would pretend that I like the mystery," he replied, "but in truth this place is colder than a frost giant's…" He stopped, too polite to finish, but the smirk on his face told her he knew that *she* knew how that ended.

She clucked her tongue at him, as though shocked as his boldness. "You shed your inhibitions with your clothes, I see."

He chuckled. She liked seeing the pleasure on his face. "Before I came here, I heard rumors that you had a clever tongue. Even before the betrothal, I hoped to meet you, just so I could hear for myself."

She sliced her blade low, nicking him in the calf. "And you say *I* am distracted."

Andor lowered his sword and shield. "You have won your first inquiry, then."

Svanhild considered what to ask him. She could make serious inquiries—like what Andor imagined their future would be like, or about his father's true nature, or what work he did around the village now—but she was tired of being serious. She had been far too serious for far too long.

So she asked, "What is your favorite thing to do when you are alone?"

Andor raised his eyebrows at her, making her flush again.

SONG OF THE SHIELDMAIDEN

She had never seen him like this before. And why did everything inside her flutter in his presence?

"I enjoy riding my horse," he said. "His name is Rikki. My uncle gave him to me when I was ten."

Svanhild smiled at his honesty. "Why have you never taken me riding, then?"

He raised a scolding finger at her. "You already had your first question. Let's go again."

He lifted his sword and shield, and they battled once more.

Andor did not take it easy on her. She struggled to block his blows or land her own. Though she called on the swiftness of the raven, the sight of Andor across from her—his bare skin still slick with sweat—truly was a distraction. Just the sound of his breath in the night air made her feel weak.

When he landed a hit against her arm, she cursed out loud. Andor chuckled in surprise.

"I apologize," she said then, straightening. "I can't focus tonight."

She knew her mother would reprimand her for that. In a real battle, she could not throw up her hands and walk away just because she was distracted. And surely she would come across handsome warriors during her fights...

But none she would know like Andor.

"One inquiry for me," Andor said with a triumphant grin. "What is *your* favorite thing to do when you are alone?"

"I would say fighting, or at least training with my sword..."

"Or axe?"

She smiled at the memory of his gift. "But when I am alone, I prefer singing."

Andor looked surprised at first. Then he said gently, "I heard you sing at your father's funeral. You have a beautiful voice."

"I will pass that compliment to Valí, my father's skald. He taught me many songs." She looked up. The half-moon peered down at them through the trees that surrounded the training yard. "There is something about singing that makes me feel connected to the gods."

Andor strode to the nearest patch of fence and leaned against it. He stuck his sword in the ground and propped his shield against it. Sensing his change in mood, Svanhild joined him. She was surprised when he drew closer to her, his arm brushing against hers.

"You fight as well as you sing," he said.

She stuck her tongue out at him, knowing she didn't fight her best tonight. "Do you always compliment people so they lower their shields?"

"Only if the compliment is true," he insisted. "Now it's your turn for a question."

She considered for a moment. When the sound of wings in the trees brought her mind to the gods, she asked, "Who is your favorite god?"

"I hope I don't upset the others too much, but Thor. The meaning of my name is Thor's eagle, and he has always called to me."

She blew a stray strand of hair from her eyes. "I like your honest answers."

Andor laughed. "Did you think I would lie to you?"

She shrugged. "When I first met you, I wasn't sure I could trust you. I thought your good nature was a mask."

She was surprised at how comfortable she felt sharing this with him. He did not seem bothered by her honesty.

"My turn," he said, then shot her a wicked grin. "Who is your favorite sister?"

She gasped at the scandalous inquiry. "That is such a mean question!"

Her reaction made Andor chuckle. "If you can't answer, then at least tell me what you like about each of your sisters."

"That is easy, for Haldis is wise and brilliant, and Brynja is sweet and loving."

"Hmmm," Andor said, looking her up and down. "Are you the one who is tough and clever?"

"I am many more things than that," Svanhild said slyly.

Her heart skipped in her chest as she realized the tone in her voice. It was the same one her mother used with her father, the one many women used with their husbands and handsome warriors—and if those women were lucky, they were one and the same.

Was this what it felt like, to flirt with someone she actually desired? But when had she started to desire Andor?

Trying to clear her thoughts, she said, "My sister Haldis is blessed by the gods, and Brynja is the most beautiful. I suppose I always feel lacking, until I pick up a sword."

"I don't think that's true. Haldis is not more blessed than you, and Brynja is not more beautiful." Andor turned to face her. His gray gaze studied her with an intensity that made her blush. "Your hair…" His voice was distracted. Gently, he reached out and tucked a loose strand of her hair behind her ear. His thumb was warm where it grazed her scalp. "You have hair like Sif," he said, referring to Thor's wife, famed for her golden tresses.

Svanhild's heart raced at his touch, for he kept his thumb behind her ear, partially tangled in her hair. Her skin vibrated as her blood rushed through her.

This was not right. She was not supposed to have feelings for Andor, and he was not supposed to feel anything for her. Theirs was an arranged marriage, and she would not go through with it.

She needed to change the subject, to back away from him, to do *something* before his gaze fell to her lips…

Struggling to find her voice, she whispered, "My turn."

The reminder of their game seemed to snap Andor from his reverie. His hand dropped from her ear. Once more he leaned against the fence, looking at the empty training yard instead of her. But his arm was still warm against her shoulder.

"If you could have a moniker," she said, "like Tove the Wise or Ulrik the Bear, what would you wish it to be?"

"Did you invent those examples yourself?"

"Maybe."

Eyes dancing, Andor mulled it over for a long time, scanning the yard as though the training pell or trampled grass might have an answer for him. Perhaps he was picturing himself as jarl, imagining the decisions he would make and how people would revere him. Though Svanhild wanted to hate the picture, she couldn't. As far as she could see, Andor would make a good leader someday.

She just didn't want him to be a leader *here*.

Finally he said, "Andor Mind-Reader."

She stifled a laugh. She had expected him to choose something like *Andor the Brave*, but *Mind-Reader* just sounded like he wished to do magic.

"Before you laugh, let me explain," he said, giving her a mock look of warning. "A good ruler knows the needs and wills of his people. If they bring me complaints, I will address them. I will seek wisdom and employ it in all of my affairs. But if I can, I will go further than that. I hope to anticipate problems, for that's the only way to prevent them. If I can read the minds of the people..." His voice trailed off, and he shrugged.

"Then you can give them a specially-crafted axe," Svanhild finished for him, smiling.

Andor studied her for a moment. She held her breath, holding his gaze. She wanted to draw closer to him. The heat of his body after the fight was like bait to her. But she knew better than to give in. The gods had other plans for her.

Finally his voice came in a cool rasp, a secret between them. "Did I read your mind accurately, then?"

She nodded. He *had* read her mind when he gave her the axe, a gift that provided meaning and purpose during this difficult year. He knew her better than she liked to admit.

She scolded herself then. What games were the gods playing, to give her feelings for this son of her enemy? Andor might think this a courtship, but in her heart she kept her secret: she would not marry him. She would flee this place before then, a band of loyal supporters at her side, to seek out her uncle Asmund in Uppsala.

In the meantime, she needed to keep herself locked like a cairn.

The way her heart raced and her skin flushed at Andor's presence tonight, it was dangerous to spend any more time with him.

"I should go back to bed," she said, pushing herself off the fence.

"Are you sure you don't want to train some more?"

She shook her head. "I am tired." She opened the longhouse door.

"Good night, then."

"Good night." Without looking back, she slipped into the hall, leaving him alone again.

As she rushed back to her room—ignoring the smirks of the guards who had seen her go—laughter echoed in her head. She scowled as she recognized who it was.

Loki, what games are you playing?

CHAPTER 21

HALDIS

*I*n the darkest part of winter, Ulrik held his first assembly to address the grievances of the people. The main hall was decorated with just a few benches pushed up against the walls, so people like Haldis and her sisters could sit and watch the proceedings. Other than the two oak high-seats and the crackling hearthfire, the rest of the hall was empty, leaving room for people to gather for the proceedings.

The place filled with quiet chatter as the people assembled. Haldis scanned the crowd, recognizing so many faces. She had not seen the people in several moons. And now they gathered not to celebrate, but to complain.

She sighed. As troubled as her relationship had been with her father, she had to admit he was always a wise and caring ruler. She wished he were still here now.

Svanhild's whisper snapped her from her thoughts.

"There are many of them here to complain today. More than with Father."

Brynja nodded. "That's because Father always checked on them in their homes. He took care of them."

"I'll bet Ulrik has only met five or six people so far," Svanhild said, laughing bitterly. "He only invites his own friends and warriors who came from Mosfell to his feasts. He probably doesn't recognize anyone here today."

Though Haldis agreed, she kept quiet. Her skin prickled with nerves today. She could not tell whether it was the presence of the gods or some premonition of trouble—only that the feeling reminded her too much of her unease when she read runes for her father the night he died. The memory made her shiver.

Olaf, standing at the front of the hall, called for the assembly to begin. Haldis frowned to see Ulrik and his wife Gertrud sit in the high-seats at the front of the hall, where her parents sat just a few months ago. The chairs were stained to a dark brown and polished until they gleamed like glass, their backs carved in elaborate knotwork patterns, the ends of their arms shaped like the heads of ravens. Ulrik and Gertrud did not belong in such seats. What did they know of Odin's ravens, the symbols of Tove's family?

She lifted her eyebrows when she saw the first person to face Ulrik was not a man but a woman: Erik's mother Ragnilde.

"Do you know what she wants?" Svanhild whispered.

Brynja nodded. "She has complaints. I encouraged her to bring them here."

Though Haldis was glad to see Ragnilde here, she feared what Ulrik's reaction would be.

"I am Ragnilde Aricsdotter, and I come with a complaint." Her voice rang like sharpened steel. Her deep red hair hung in a long braid behind her back, with several loose strands that gave her a wild look. As she glared at Ulrik, her eyes flashed as though she dared him to answer her.

"Where is your husband?" Ulrik replied. "He should be the one to bring his issue to me today."

"It is not only his issue, but mine as well," said Ragnilde.

She did not offer any other explanation as to why he was at home and she was here, but Haldis was not surprised that was the way of it. According to Brynja, Erik's father Torven was never one for people, preferring the company of animals and the solace of the fields.

"My family has farmed this land for more than six generations, since Kaldvik was first founded," Ragnilde went on. "Every year as far back as we can remember, our harvest has been sufficient to feed our family and share with the rest of the town." She took a deep breath. Haldis sensed the nerves vibrating beneath her iron exterior. "Sadly, that is not true this year. We do not have enough to feed ourselves through the winter, and it is no fault of ours."

Ulrik cracked his knuckles as he studied her. Perhaps he knew what would come next, for it took him a long time to ask, "Whose fault is it?" He growled the words like a threat.

But Ragnilde merely threw back her shoulders at the challenge. "Everything we grew on our farm is now right here, in this very house. We always shared food with our former jarl and his family, but I fear you have demanded too much from us."

Feeling Brynja tense beside her, Haldis reached out to give her sister's hand a reassuring squeeze. Brynja was close to their family, and anything that happened to the parents would affect her friend Erik, too.

Haldis caught sight of her mother, seated across the hall at a bench near the front—a position of honor. But now her mother's face was lined with worry. Standing beside her bench was Andor, his back straight and his jaw set tight. She wondered what he was thinking about all this, for he was hard to read.

Ulrik surprised them all with a booming laugh. Others in the hall stiffened at the sound of Ulrik's guffaw, but no one joined in.

When the jarl did not explain his reaction, Ragnilde finally gave in and asked, "What is funny, Jarl?"

"Why, you seem to be confused," Ulrik said, still beaming like a wolf fresh from feasting. "A jarl shares food with his people, not the other way around. Or did you forget who here is the jarl and who the farmer?"

Ragnilde frowned. "I forget nothing. In Kaldvik, we share our food with our leaders as a sign of respect. Without generosity, we would all perish. Perhaps you are just unprepared for Kaldvik's winter."

Ulrik's smile turned to a snarl. "Be careful what you say next."

Haldis held her breath.

Just then, Andor stepped out of the shadows to stand nearer to his father. He looked commanding in his fur cloak, which covered one shoulder but was swept back behind the other to display the weapon at his waist, a traditional style.

Svanhild shifted beside her. Glancing over, Haldis saw her older sister's eyes were set on him, her cheeks strangely flushed.

"Father," Andor said, "perhaps I should visit their home to discuss how we might prevent this next winter. After surveying their farm, we might come up with an appropriate solution to this matter."

His words were like a cool breeze through a roaring fire, and Haldis sensed people shifting in their seats, relaxing a bit. Svanhild's fingers fidgeted in her lap. Only when Haldis placed her own hand over Svanhild's did her eldest sister finally sit still.

Haldis eyed Andor curiously then. Had something transpired between him and her sister? Svanhild seemed to be avoiding him, and she never wanted to talk about him. She acted like his name was a curse word on her tongue. But today, she looked mesmerized by him.

Ulrik grumbled something to his wife, who gave a curt nod. Then the jarl said, "That will suit." To Ragnilde, he added, "Just keep in mind that if your farm cannot produce enough crops for you to feed your own family, that is your own problem to solve."

Ragnilde's eyes flashed again, but she lowered her chin and stepped back, accepting the decision. Andor nodded to her, a look of understanding in his eyes. Haldis sensed Ragnilde must trust him over his father, even without knowing him. Andor would be fair.

They watched several more people air their issues to the jarl next. There was a feud between neighbors over a fence line, and another man claimed his brother had killed one of his thralls. Ulrik made quick judgments, but Haldis noticed nothing out of the ordinary. He had probably been watching his own father rule his whole life; such decisions came easily to him.

"Ragnilde got the worst treatment," Brynja commented at the end of the day. "I wish more farmers had come forward about the loss of their food. There is strength in numbers."

"Ulrik thinks less of women," said Haldis, "and Ragnilde was bold to blame him directly for her complaint."

"I'm glad Andor spoke up," Brynja said. "I think your future husband will be a good jarl someday, Svanhild." When Svanhild bit her lip, she added, "I am sorry. I should not have made a jest about that."

Svanhild merely shook her head.

Haldis tried to bring the conversation back to the assembly. "Ragnilde was not the only one to complain of less food than usual, though. No one else dared to blame Ulrik, but we clearly have a problem with supplies this winter."

Suddenly Ulrik's voice roared through the hall. "It's time to prepare for the feast." Turning to the sisters, he added, "Wear something prettier, or people will think I'm mistreating you." And he chuckled, his wife joining in.

Svanhild glared at his back as he lumbered from the main hall. "And now he will waste all the food on another feast."

"At least he is inviting everyone in town to this one," Haldis remarked. "This would be a good time to see if we have any supporters in our midst."

CHAPTER 22

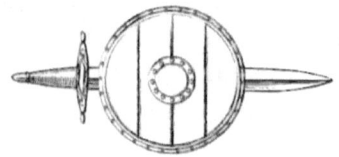

SVANHILD

*a*fter the assembly, Ulrik invited the people of Kaldvik into the longhouse for a feast, as was tradition. As the chamber once again filled with people, Svanhild remembered the last time so many had gathered in this hall: the night her father died.

The memories made her stomach churn. She took a sip of mead to clear her head, then another. The taste tonight was dry and laced with spices.

Tonight she would forget.

Sitting at the jarl's table, she glanced at the nearby door to the training yard. It had only been a few nights since she had sparred there with Andor. Since then, she had avoided him— but how long could she do that, especially with him sitting right beside her tonight?

Ulrik's musician strummed a lyre and sang battle songs as thralls emerged from the kitchens bearing trays of fresh-baked bread, fish, and vegetables seasoned with herbs.

Though at first people's eyes widened at the sight of so much food in one place—something they had likely not enjoyed for many moons—they soon gave in to their appetites, and the hall filled with the sound of chatter and laughter.

Svanhild watched from the jarl's table in dismay. It was smart for Ulrik to share with the people tonight, of all nights. With full bellies, a warm fire, and good company, people easily forgot the troubles they had aired before their new jarl earlier in the day.

She looked over at Mother, seated a few seats down at Ulrik's side. Svanhild and Helga were the only ones still afforded seats at the jarl's table, as both were game pieces for Ulrik to play. If the people of Kaldvik wondered which family to follow now, seeing them together must make it seem like they did not have to choose—just as Ulrik wanted it.

Tonight, Mother was dressed in a green gown that perfectly matched the dragon shields hanging on the wall behind the table. Gone was the red of their family's banners; now Ulrik's green decorated the hall. Svanhild hated seeing her mother decorated in the same way, as though she were just another object for him to claim and display.

Spotting her sisters at a table near the front of the hall, she lifted her horn of mead in toast to them. Haldis, who had thrown off her hood for once, inclined her head, her pale blonde hair shimmering in the firelight. But Brynja was the one who surprised her when she took a long drink of her mead. Her youngest sister did not usually handle strong drink well, but perhaps she needed it tonight.

Svanhild understood. Even with all of their people gathered here, this hall no longer felt like home. She took a swig from her own cup.

"Should I have someone bring more mead?" Andor asked, raising an eyebrow at her.

"Not yet." Lifting the cup to her lips once more, she drained it in several large gulps. She only hoped Mother was not watching her unladylike behavior. Then, slamming the cup on the table, she said, "I'll take more now."

Andor studied her with a frown.

Sensing his judgment, she sighed. "It's a feast. And the mead is good."

Andor raised a hand for a thrall to refill her cup. Then, leaning in close to keep the words just between them, he said, "This would be a good night to train. Everyone will sleep well after the feast. We could meet in the training yard again, if you'd like."

The idea of training with Andor again sent a thrill through her. She had enjoyed her time with him that night, perhaps too much. Ever since, her insides felt full of moths, always fluttering, never settled. The sensation was new to her. And she always felt it most when Andor was nearby.

But then the memory of the night her father died charged into her mind. That night, people had feasted and drunk to excess and slept well too—so well that Ulrik had swept in, killed her father, and stolen the high-seat.

"That reminds me of another night your family took advantage of mine," she commented.

Andor sat up straight as though struck. Svanhild regretted the words immediately, but she would not take them back. Andor may be trying to help her now, but was she not right to remember the attack on her father's house, tonight of all nights?

As kind as Andor was to her, he was still Ulrik's son. Svanhild needed to remind herself of that. Though he may think they would wed one day, she knew he was *not* her future husband. No matter how amiable he was, he was her enemy.

After a few more moments had passed, Ulrik stood and

lifted his ale horn for a toast. "Welcome, people of Kaldvik," he shouted, making Svanhild jump. Unlike Tove, who did not have to raise his voice to be heard throughout the hall, Ulrik's voice crashed like trees being toppled in a forest. The unsettling sound making people stiffen where they stood. "It is good to see the faces of my people as we warm ourselves on this cold winter's night. Let us enjoy the food from your summer harvests and fresh meat from your farms."

Everyone else at the jarl's table lifted their horns and cups to toast—even Helga. Svanhild forced herself to join in, ignoring the irony. After listening all day to the people's concerns about dwindling food supplies, here he stated outright that all of this food came from them. While Ulrik took from farms and normally feasted with only his own family and warriors, he left the people to make meals from whatever was leftover.

Tonight, he bribed them with their own food. Another bit of trickery.

"We are prepared for the winter ahead," Ulrik continued, "thanks to the hard work of my wife Gertrud and the lovely Helga. I am grateful for the continued support of Tove's family, who still lives in this house with us."

Svanhild exchanged looks with her sisters. Lies—all of it. Gertrud had done almost nothing to help Helga run the longhouse, and none of their family supported Ulrik.

The jarl turned his gaze to Svanhild then, lifting his horn once more. "Once winter is over, we shall truly join our houses with the wedding of my son Andor and Tove's daughter Svanhild."

A few people cheered, the only appropriate response to this announcement. Beside her, Andor stirred a breeze through her hair as he stood.

This was her chance to show some dissent—just enough

for the people gathered here to understand that her family did *not* support Ulrik.

Instead of rising to join the toast, she stayed seated. Ulrik's eyes narrowed at her, and Andor turned to see what she was doing. Though a few people drank to toast them as a couple, many others waited on her, their cups hanging in the air. As if adding to the tension, the fire snapped in the hearth as logs broke into smaller pieces, the flame leaping toward the rafters.

Svanhild caught her mother's forehead wrinkling in worry. Perhaps she was pausing too long.

Andor's hand appeared near her shoulder, an offer to help her up. Ignoring it, she kept her face in a tight frown as she stood on her own. Andor's hand hung there for a moment before falling to his side, unused. She didn't look at him, fearing any confusion or disappointment on his face would only make her feel guilty.

Once she was standing, Svanhild lifted her chin and took a long swig from her cup—another show of her anger. She felt Ulrik glaring at her now. Andor shifted from one foot to the other, clearly uncomfortable. The only sound in the hall was the pop of the fire as everyone froze to watch her.

Suddenly, Andor's voice filled the hall. "This winter, Svanhild and I look forward to meeting with all of you in the village and in your homes, to learn how we can all work to make our community stronger. I know many of you are concerned about preserving our resources, balancing trade activities, and preparing for next summer's raiding. We look forward to discussions about this." Raising his ale horn, he added, "I am especially excited to learn how you manage to survive such cold winters here, for I have been living in this fur cape since summer."

A few people chuckled, the tension dissipating.

As they sat again, Svanhild whispered to him, "You are quite the diplomat."

"And you are trying to anger my father, which will not serve your family well," he snapped back.

"Let us enjoy our food and company," Ulrik said, casting Svanhild a warning look as he sat in his chair again.

Svanhild chewed her food in silence for a moment, pretending at an appetite. When she glanced at her mother, she found Ulrik whispering in her ear. Her stomach twisted at the idea of him asking Helga to his chamber later. She wanted him dead—the sooner, the better.

Andor took Svanhild's hand for a moment, surprising her. His grip was warm and firm as he whispered, "This will end soon. I will talk to my father."

Svanhild nodded without words. She would not thank him. She wanted to get away from him, to forget her feelings for him just as she would cast out memories of her father, of her happy family, of her life before Ulrik came.

For now, all she could do was take another gulp of mead.

AFTER EVERYONE HAD FINISHED EATING, servants dismantled tables or pushed them aside to make room for dancing around the central hearth. Svanhild jumped at the opportunity to escape the jarl's table. She found her sisters on a bench at the far end of the hall, half-hidden behind a pillar.

"Good evening, sisters," she said, lifting her cup to toast them again. "Skol."

"What is the toast for?" Brynja asked.

"For mead." Svanhild laughed. "We drink mead to toast mead, and we toast mead to drink mead."

Haldis narrowed her eyes. "How many cups have you had tonight?"

"You are just like Andor, always watching, always

observing. This is a feast. We should have a good time for once. It might be the last chance we have to be happy for months."

Brynja grabbed her wrist and gently pulled her onto the bench beside her. Keeping her voice low, she said, "What about your plans? This is the perfect time to ask Frode if he has found you any supporters."

Svanhild knew her sister was right. When had little Brynja grown so wise?

She scanned the crowd for Fish-Nose. She spotted the warrior Thorbjorn first. He waved at her before sneaking out of the hall with a young woman, whose auburn hair was cropped short to indicate her status as a slave. Svanhild's mouth went dry at the memory of her defeat against him, but there was no point in thinking about that now. She could not take it back.

Besides, she had more training now. In a few weeks, she would be ready to lead warriors on the road to Uppsala. She would just have to prove herself first...

"There's Frode," Brynja said, jerking her chin toward a nearby pillar.

Svanhild followed her gaze to where Fish-Nose stood with Balder. "They make an odd pair, don't they? Balder is muscular and covered in tattoos, while Frode is so skinny. Look at his skin from all that time in the sun. It's like leather."

Svanhild sensed her sisters exchanging some hidden message in their looks.

"Are you sure this is a good time for her to make plans with them?" Haldis said softly, her voice light as smoke.

"This is the only time," Brynja replied. "When will we all be in the hall like this again? And she can't very well talk to Frode when she's out on a walk with Andor."

Svanhild glared at them. "I am sitting right here."

Brynja snatched the cup out of her hands. "No more mead."

Though Svanhild tried to protest, Haldis nodded her approval.

"Be careful what you say, and keep your voice down so no one overhears," said Brynja.

"I can't believe I am taking orders from my littlest sister," Svanhild complained, yet still she smiled.

Brynja just shook her head. "I mean it, Svanhild. Be careful."

Haldis looked up into the rafters. "Odin is with us. He will watch over you now." Then she turned to Svanhild. "But Brynja is right. Take care with what you say tonight, sister."

Svanhild waved off their warnings with a laugh. She knew her sisters meant well, but she was fine.

When she stood, the floor seemed to tilt beneath her, as though she were standing inside a longship on a stormy sea. Her sisters gripped her arms to steady her. Once she was fully on her feet, she felt better.

As she approached Fish-Nose and Balder, they stopped talking and looked at her in surprise.

"Good evening, little one," said Balder. "How are you enjoying the feast tonight?"

"I came to ask you about the mood of the town," she said, drawing nearer and keeping her voice low. "What color do you think people favor for their banners?"

The two men exchanged glances before Frode said, "Some prefer red and some prefer green."

Svanhild bit back a sigh. Could they be any less helpful? "And in a battle between a raven and a dragon, who do you think would win?"

Balder placed a hand on her shoulder. "You are brave, little one, but let's not pretend a raven could kill a dragon."

"But a raven could *outsmart* a dragon," she said. "And why

do you always call me *little one*? I am not so little anymore, am I?"

Balder chuckled. "I suppose not." But the way he said it only made Svanhild suspicious that he was humoring her. Perhaps he could tell she was a little drunk. "There are many here who would prefer your father to what we have now…" Balder cast a dark look toward Ulrik, who was helping himself to a third helping of fish at the head table. "But they are all farmers. It is warriors we need, and many of them want to raid next summer."

Svanhild frowned. "Don't they also farm in the spring and pull crops in the autumn?"

"They do," said Balder, "but they also earn silver through trading. Now, they will spend their summers raiding. They have enough wealth not to rely on farming the way others here do."

"One bad winter, blame the weather," said Frode, staring out at the crowd of dancers. "Two bad winters, blame the gods."

Svanhild knew where he was going. Only with three bad winters would people truly lay the blame with their jarl—or so went the saying.

"I do not wish to fight against my own people," she said.

Balder patted her shoulder. "You may have no choice."

Shaking the thought from her head, she explained her plan to find her uncle in Uppsala. Balder and Fish-Nose nodded along, for they remembered Asmund as a raider. She did not have to work hard to convince them he would be invaluable to their revenge.

"Asmund has a strong mind for battle," Balder agreed.

"Then we only need enough men to form a traveling party," Svanhild went on. "Whether or not my uncle still raids, he will surely have men behind him. Then we will return in greater numbers to fight the usurper. With luck and the gods on our side, others here may join us when they see our strength."

Fish-Nose's gaze was somewhere beyond Svanhild. She could not tell if he was thinking things through or if he had stopped listening altogether. He had a distant way about him that made her want to shake him until he paid attention.

Balder, however, gave her shoulder another pat. "Does Andor know of your plans?"

She shook her head. She tried her best to keep thoughts of Andor far from her plans for revenge, for the two did not mix. In her mind, they were tucked in two separate chests, locked away from each other.

Balder's jaw twitched. "When do you wish to leave?"

That was it, then. Whatever friendship had been forged between the blacksmith and Andor Ulrikson, it was not strong enough to survive this. Svanhild was glad to have the blacksmith on her side—and grateful he did not press the issue.

Still, her gaze darted to Andor where he sat on a bench with his sister Kindra. They whispered together, laughing as they observed the drunken festivities. What were they gossiping about? She smiled to imagine it, for she knew Andor must be a caring older brother, just as he was kind to her, kind to Balder, kind to everyone...

"Svanhild?" Balder prompted, raising his eyebrows.

She turned her attention back to him. "So you will follow me, then?"

"You will need strong warriors," Balder replied.

She sensed in his words an unwillingness to admit he would follow her. Immediately her mind shot to her fight with Thorbjorn, and she blushed. Who else had heard about her failed battle? Or perhaps it was even simpler than that. Maybe they failed to believe in her only because she was a woman. But there was no time to argue that now.

She glanced around to make sure nobody else was nearby. The sound of music, voices, and laughter drowned out their conversation.

"Before my wedding in the spring," she whispered.

Balder and Frode exchanged glances again, but neither commented on that. Perhaps she had surprised them, for that would only be a few weeks from now, at most. At least old Fish-Nose was listening.

"I will tell our shipbuilder Skarde," said Balder. "He can prepare a boat for us."

"Thank you." Her gaze drifted back to Andor. Some part of her wanted to speak with him now, as if she could balance this betrayal with kindness toward him. But she knew she owed him nothing. It was safest to avoid him.

Suddenly Andor's gaze met hers, and he grinned. She felt a blush creep up her neck as she returned the smile. Then she cursed to herself.

Being around Andor was too dangerous. She didn't trust herself anymore.

Balder's voice brought her back. "You are going to break his heart, you know."

She looked at him. "Who, Andor?"

"Who else? Will you really not tell him anything?"

She wanted to laugh. "He is Ulrik's son." She said nothing more, for that fact should be enough.

"This plan will work," Frode commented. He sounded like he hadn't followed their exchange at all and was only thinking aloud. "We will make ready to leave as soon as the snow starts to melt."

Svanhild nodded. A strange glow filled her at the idea of rowing away in a boat with the likes of Balder, Frode, and Skarde—strong men who had once followed her father, men she had always admired for their skills and loyalty. Would they truly follow her now? A chill ran through her as she imagined it.

Fish-Nose was right. This might actually work.

"If you can, talk to Thorbjorn and Hafdan," she said, remembering how Thorbjorn mentioned her father on the day they battled. "They are skilled warriors, and I believe they may prefer red to green."

Balder nodded at her, while Frode merely gazed into the crowd again. Svanhild took her leave of the men. Her blood rushed faster now. Seeing the people smiling and dancing, she finally wanted to join in.

All she needed was one more drink.

CHAPTER 23

BRYNJA

*B*rynja watched her oldest sister speak with Balder and Frode from a bench behind a pillar, her stomach in knots. But it was not only their scheming that made her nervous tonight. Across the hall, seated beside Ulrik at his table, she caught Olaf looking her way.

Trying to focus on Svanhild's mission, she asked Haldis, "Do you think she is making a fool of herself?"

Her sister shook her head. "The gods are here. I believe they will bring her success."

"You always say the gods are here."

Haldis laughed. "I almost forgot you do not pray the way Svanhild does." She shrugged, gesturing toward a raven in the rafters. "Then perhaps the gods are not here, but that raven is."

Brynja joined in her sister's laughter. It felt good to sit with her family tonight, free to talk without Ulrik's guards eavesdropping.

Still, she wished her mother could join them. Helga sat beside the jarl at the head table, quietly sipping from her ale horn as she watched the festivities. Though Ulrik had been upset with Svanhild for training in the forest, Brynja now saw how he kept Mother closest. Perhaps she was the one he did not trust. After all, Helga was the experienced shield-maiden in their family, wife of the man Ulrik had killed, a mother who would always protect her cubs.

Ulrik leaned over to say something then, making Mother laugh. Brynja frowned. Her mother's performance was convincing.

Suddenly Svanhild turned to them, her face flushed pink from mead and the heat of the hearthfire. She smiled as she approached them. When she sat, she brought with her the scent of flowers, mead spice, and sweat.

"They will find us more supporters," she whispered. "Now can I have my drink back?"

Pretending a sigh, Brynja handed her the cup she had been saving for her. Svanhild drank a large gulp before issuing a quiet burp into her fist. That was something her mother would never allow her daughters to do. Though Brynja wrinkled her nose at first, when Svanhild and Haldis began laughing, she had to join in.

"I'm sorry," Svanhild said. She pinched Brynja's cheek. "I will never be quite the lady you are, Brynja. I admire you for that." She smiled as she surveyed the room, where people danced to the beat of the skald's song. "I am glad we can be together tonight. It is so rare we are able to talk freely."

Haldis pretended to cough into her hand, making Brynja laugh. If only they could play their old game of taking fresh air.

But tonight, just being together was enough.

· · ·

As the evening grew late, Ulrik called for attention, banging his cup on the head table and raising his voice again. "Before this night ends, I have one more announcement to share." As people stopped dancing to listen, he continued, "During these cold and dark winter days, let us picture our future. With the gods on our side, summer will one day grace Kaldvik again, and it will be time to go raiding. I know many of you are great warriors." He chuckled. "In fact, I may have fought alongside a few of you in years past. Now, I call for the warriors of Kaldvik to step forward and swear their oath to join me on next summer's raids."

Brynja's stomach dropped. Svanhild tensed beside her.

Ulrik swept his gaze around the room, his expression hungry as he looked for supporters. "If you have the courage to come with me, you will be sitting here next winter as very rich men."

Several people lifted their ale horns or cheered, "Skol," at Ulrik's words.

Brynja and her sisters exchanged dark glances.

"Who here will swear their oath tonight?" Ulrik shouted, lifting his own horn. His form, already huge, loomed even more bear-like as he spread his arms, his fur cloak growing at the sides.

Brynja shuddered. In the rafters overhead, the raven Haldis had spotted earlier fluttered its wings.

Ulrik looked up at the noise. His broad face split into a rare smile. "The gods are with us!" he said, motioning to the bird. "Under the watchful gaze of Odin, Thor, and Tyr, who will swear their oath?"

This was the prompting they needed. Several men stepped forward, their upper arms bare since they had removed the silver arm bands from Jarl Tove. Ulrik moved in front of his table then and unsheathed a sword from his belt.

It looked old, but it had been polished to shine. Brynja noticed the ring on its hilt, marking it as a sword for pledging oaths. Ulrik stood with the tip of the sword planted in the ground before him, both hands on the hilt. He motioned for the first man to step forward.

Brynja recognized the dark-haired warrior who knelt before the sword: Hafdan, one of her father's favorites. He placed a few fingers on the ring of the hilt. His voice was loud and firm when he swore his oath, as though to make sure his voice carried all the way to Asgard. Then he stood, and as he turned back to the crowd, everyone lifted their cups and ale horns to salute him.

"Look at how they betray us," Svanhild said. "How can the gods bless this?" She glanced up at the raven as though pleading to the gods for an answer.

"These men do not think of this as betrayal," Haldis replied. "They swear their oath to the man who sits in the high-seat, as they have done all their lives. That is all."

"Don't be naive, Haldis. They pledged to our father first, and now they swear loyalty to his killer when they should be seeking revenge." Svanhild glared at them all. "If I succeed in returning to fight Ulrik, they will have to lift their blades against me."

Brynja shuddered at the thought, for Svanhild was right. No warrior who broke an oath would ever feast with the gods in Valhalla. Now that they had pledged to Ulrik, these men would not hesitate to slay their family to protect him, if it meant they would die with honor. She hated the idea of Svanhild fighting against Hafdan. Even with her sister's training, could she truly best such a strong and experienced warrior?

Several more men swore their oaths to Ulrik, until he had a large band of warriors ready for the raids.

"Thorbjorn is absent," Svanhild whispered. "He was Father's best warrior. Perhaps he will still be loyal to us."

When the oath-taking was done, Ulrik turned to Andor, who sat at the head table just behind him. The young man had watched the procession with a serious expression. Brynja always found him unreadable, except when he looked at Svanhild. Several times tonight he had glanced at her, his gaze softening, but he quickly turned his attention back to his father whenever Svanhild looked back.

Now, Ulrik said, "There is one warrior who has yet to swear his oath before the gods and this gathering tonight. Andor, my son, will you pledge your sword to me now?"

Svanhild grabbed Brynja's hand and squeezed. So there *was* something between them.

Andor hesitated, his gaze darting to Svanhild. Then he stood, inclining his head to his father. He strode around the table to kneel before Ulrik, placing his fingers on the hilt of the sword.

"I swear my allegiance to you, Father. My blade is yours." The words were simply spoken, but his voice echoed like steel through the hall.

Slumping on the bench, Svanhild took another long drink of mead. Brynja put her arm around Svanhild's shoulders, wishing she had words to comfort her.

Ulrik placed his hand on the top of Andor's bowed head. "You honor me, son." As Andor stood, he said to the crowd, "I am glad to hear my son is with me still, for we have raided together for..." He glanced at Andor. "How many summers now?"

"Five summers," Andor said.

"That's right," Ulrik said. "And given your love of raiding, I have a gift for you." To the people, he said, "For those of you willing to brave the cold, follow me!"

The people parted for Ulrik and Andor to pass down the middle of the hall. Carrying their cups and horns with them, nearly half the people followed them.

Svanhild swallowed, her eyes on the departing crowd. "He swore an oath to Ulrik." Her voice sounded hollow.

"What else could he do?" Haldis said.

Svanhild narrowed her eyes. "Let's see this gift then." Her voice was now edged with poison, more like she usually sounded. Brynja wasn't sure which was worse: her sister's anger or its lack.

Brynja stood with her sisters, and together they followed the crowd out of the longhouse. The night air froze her face as soon as she stepped outside. Instead of walking down the main path toward the village, Ulrik led the crowd into a patch of forest that ran along the left side of the fjord.

A breeze stirred her hair, and she turned to find Erik joining them.

She smiled. "Where have you been?"

He gave her a half-hug as they continued walking, almost making Brynja stumble. They both laughed as they caught their footing.

"My mother returned to the farm to be with Father. She was not happy about the way the jarl treated her today."

"I do not blame her."

"So with her gone, it's my job to keep an eye on my sisters tonight."

Erik jerked his chin toward two girls walking arm in arm a few paces away. With curly blonde hair, wide-set blue eyes, and freckles splashed across their pale skin, they were identical in every way—except how they acted. One stumbled and giggled from too much drink, while the other cast demure glances at nearby warriors. Brynja recognized the giggling one as Asa; the quieter one was Estrid.

"I see they are enjoying the festivities tonight," she commented. "Have they already picked out new husbands?"

Erik groaned. "Estrid can never choose, but Asa has been flirting with that warrior Thorbjorn half the night. At least he knows she is far too young for him, so he's shrugged her off as best he can."

"Thirteen years old is not too young to marry, or at least make an engagement."

"Then why are we unmarried at fifteen?" Erik asked.

Haldis looked at Erik from beneath her hood. "You are growing a beard now."

Erik ran a hand over his chin, where auburn stubble poked his skin. "I know my hair is blond, but this beard is coming in red as my mother's hair," he laughed.

Svanhild piped up then. "I thought I saw Thorbjorn sneak out with a thrall earlier. Is he back?"

Erik eyed her with curiosity. "Why do you want to find him?"

"He would make an excellent ally," Svanhild said, raising an eyebrow.

Erik's eyes lit up. "You are looking for allies?" He cast his gaze around at the people walking near them. Although others in the crowd were chatting as they wove a path through the forest, it was hard to speak freely with everyone so close. Lowering his voice, he asked, "Are you planning something?"

Svanhild nodded but said nothing more.

"I have an axe," Erik said simply.

Brynja hit him on the arm. "You cannot join my sister! You are a farmer."

Erik opened his mouth to say something, but his gaze latched onto his sisters first. He sighed. "Estrid!" he called. "Don't let Asa wriggle away!"

Brynja looked over to see Asa twirling in a circle, her face lifted to the sky. As she flung her arms out wide, she smacked several people who cursed at her or jumped away.

"You should put water in their mead," Brynja recommended.

Erik nodded. "Good idea. It's too late for that one, though." He gave Brynja's shoulder a squeeze of farewell, then jogged over to grab Asa's hand and guide her back to her sister Estrid.

Brynja walked with her sisters in silence for a moment. Her mind fought the idea that Erik wanted to join Svanhild. For months before he died, her father had asked Erik if he would join his band of summer warriors—but every time, Erik refused. Just like his parents, Erik loved working the farm. Surely this axe training was just a game, something to occupy his mind for a short time.

Ulrik led them down a path into the forest that ran alongside the fjord. People muttered in wonder, trying to figure out where they were headed.

"I hope he doesn't mean to bring us into the woods to kill us," Svanhild muttered.

The idea of cutting away from the others to sneak into the forest flickered in Brynja's mind, but she snuffed it out before it caught fire. They would not get far without food, and Ulrik was sure to send out a search party as soon as he noticed they were missing.

She looked around to find Olaf watching her from across the crowd. His gaze made her shiver. If anyone was going to notice the raven sisters trying to escape, it was him.

"We are still being watched," she whispered.

Svanhild and Haldis followed her gaze to Olaf. Seeing their attention, the housecarl waved at them.

"Stay away from him, Brynja," said Svanhild. "He is nothing but trouble."

"I want nothing to do with him," Brynja assured her.

Haldis, striding in between her two sisters, linked arms with them both. Brynja felt safer when joined with them.

They soon stopped behind the crowd at a small dock beside a house. This was where the shipbuilder lived, for he could gather wood from the forest here and build near his home, where he kept all his tools. The inlet was hidden from the rest of the village, which was just beyond a bend in the river. The thick cover of pine trees all around the shore here made it feel like a secret place.

In the water beside the dock, a longship bobbed in the waters. Though small, it likely seated at least 20 men—a decent warship, then. Brynja admired the carving at the prow: an eagle with folded wings. Even in the darkness, she thought she saw a gleam in the wooden eyes, as though the creature were watching them all now.

At the front of the gathering, Ulrik stood beside Andor, sweeping his arms toward the longship. "I had this made for you, my son. She is a sturdy ship, built by Kaldvik's shipbuilder Skarde."

The shipbuilder, standing near the front of the crowd, waved a hand shyly. Several people shouted, "Skol," and slapped him on the back.

"For the past five years, you have proven your skill at sea," Ulrik continued. "Next summer, you will captain this ship and lead your own band of warriors on our raids. May the gods guide you."

The people toasted, and Andor took a gulp from his own horn to thank his father for the gift. Several people drew closer to admire the ship, while Ulrik put an arm over Andor's shoulder and spoke to him quietly.

"A grand gift," said Svanhild darkly. "He must be ready to follow his father into Hel for that one."

"What is going on between you two?" Brynja asked. "You two have been looking at each other all night."

"Nothing," said Svanhild too quickly.

Haldis said, "The gods are not with them, sister. Trust me, they are with *you*. And we have found supporters tonight. Take heart in that."

Svanhild nodded, but her eyes were still dark.

CHAPTER 24

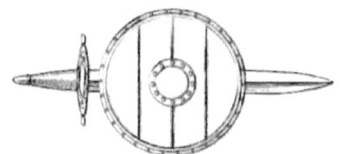

SVANHILD

*a*s the night wore on, Svanhild drank more mead.
Haldis shoved water at her to temper the strong drink, and Brynja danced with her by the fire to sweat it out. Though she appreciated the way her sisters cared for her, Svanhild was even more grateful for the way the drink stole her memories and left only the present moment.

As she danced, the hearth's flames seemed to grow and whip around her, until she was like a torch spinning in the night. She could not tell if this was happiness or just numbness, but it was all she had for now.

After a dance around the hearth that left her dizzy, she stumbled to a bench where Brynja sat with her friend Erik.

"I don't think I have ever seen you drunk before," Erik laughed.

Svanhild shrugged. "I like the mead tonight. It's one thing the new jarl does well." She raised a hand for a servant to bring her a fresh cup. After taking a swig, she said, "Not that the jarl actually does *anything* around here."

"Be careful what you say," Brynja snapped. "Anybody can overhear now."

Svanhild pretended to sew her lips shut, a common jest in their family.

"He's looking at you again," Brynja said then.

Svanhild turned to see who she was looking at. *Andor.* She sighed. He had been looking over all night.

"Andor likes you," Erik remarked. "Is the feeling mutual, or is he another suitor you intend to scare away?"

Svanhild shook her head. If only she *could* scare him away like every other suitor. There was a reason she was still unmarried at 18, when so many girls in the village were wed by Brynja's age—and she was a jarl's daughter. Half the young men in the village had tried to woo her over the years, but their attentions had faded as they received rejection after rejection. Svanhild knew how to bat a man away from her. But she could not do that with Andor.

Before she could answer, Brynja said, "You just admire him because he's so handsome. I bet you like his new tattoos."

Svanhild nudged her sister in the ribs. "Why don't *you* marry him, if you like him so much?"

Brynja stuck out her tongue, making Erik chuckle. The two friends rose to dance again, but first Brynja put a hand on Svanhild's shoulder.

"Let this be your last cup," she said.

Svanhild laughed at the motherly sound in her little sister's voice. "I swear it. If I could pledge on a sword, I would."

"That did not take away your victory tonight," Brynja reminded her.

Svanhild waved the pair away. As she watched them dance, she knew Brynja's words were true. Just because several warriors had pledged an oath to Ulrik did not mean they had lost all hope. Frode and Balder were still seeking supporters for her. Soon, Skarde would have a longship ready for them too.

And Haldis had promised the gods were on their side.

Her heart lifted as she took another sip of mead. This *would* be her last, or she would be sick in the morning. She savored the rich flavor of spices as she watched the dancing, feeling a sense of peace at last. There was nothing left to do tonight but enjoy this, as much as she could.

Across the fire, her gaze met Andor's again. He lifted his horn to acknowledge her, making her smile. She knew she was supposed to be avoiding him, but he was hard to ignore when he kept staring at her, his eyes more watchful than Heimdall's.

In the orange glow of the fire, she let herself study him. His short, ring-adorned beard and blue tattoos made him look like a young raider prince. She admired his cool gray eyes, the strength of his jaw, the rich curve of his mouth. Every girl had her own fantasy of what the handsome god Freyr looked like. How much Andor reminded her of her own private fantasy now.

She bit her lip, considering a new idea. Would it be so wrong to enjoy time with Andor while she was still in Kaldvik? Even if she had no intention of marrying him, *he* didn't know that. And he liked her, she could tell.

She did not know if it was the goddess Freyja urging her toward pleasure or just the mead flushing her body now, but the idea of playing games with Andor made her heart race.

Finally, she could sit no longer. If nothing else, she would find out why he kept looking her way.

As soon as she stood, Andor followed suit. He met her in the shadows behind a pillar, away from the other benches, where they could speak without being overheard. Though she noticed people eyeing them out of curiosity, nobody dared draw near.

"What do you want with me?" she asked. "You've been watching me all night like an eagle watching a mouse."

"I have no intention of making you my prey, if that's what concerns you," Andor said.

Svanhild narrowed her eyes. Was he teasing her? With his serious jaw, sometimes it was hard to tell.

"How did you know I was looking your way?" Andor added. "Unless you were watching me too?"

"Only because you were watching me first."

Andor released a soft chuckle, like the stirring of leaves in the trees. Though Svanhild wanted to keep interrogating him, she had to smile at the sound, now becoming familiar to her.

Lifting her chin, she said, "I need air."

"Now? In this snow?"

"Did you not just brave it for your father's gift?" She lifted her chin, sensing his desire to stay by the fire. "Don't worry, I like time alone. Enjoy the evening."

"I can accompany you," Andor said.

Svanhild was already turning to leave, but his words made her stop. She bit back a smile, for despite all of her time avoiding him in recent days, she craved his company now. "I don't need a man's protection. This is my village," she said, testing him.

Andor touched her arm to stop her. But rather than grabbing her, he simply placed his fingers on the sleeve of her dress. A request, not a demand.

"I would benefit from fresh air too," he said. "Would you have my company tonight?"

The words were not what she had expected, but she refused to admit he had surprised her again. "Fine," she said, feigning disinterest. His fingers slipped from her arm, sending a chill through her. "If it pleases you."

Her heart beat faster and her stomach fluttered as she led him out the front doors of the hall. She threw a cloak over her shoulders as she left, feeling his movements mimic hers, feeling his closeness.

Outside, the icy air hit her skin like a thousand tiny blades. She hugged her cape around her as they set off toward the village. The smoke of hearthfires from people's homes added a comforting scent to the frozen air.

Svanhild looked at Andor, admiring his profile. Away from Ulrik, away from bad memories, away from the noise of the hall, she felt free. And she had a strong man at her side, a man who might care for her. Though she knew it was dangerous to let herself feel anything around him, she could not control the way her body reacted to his presence. Just being alone with him now sent a warm flush over her skin.

They passed the fjord, where lights from the aurora over-head made the still water sparkle in a thousand shades of green and purple. They paused to admire the view.

"It's as though the rainbow bridge is stretched out before us," Svanhild breathed. "Can you imagine stepping onto that colored water and crossing the bifrost?"

Andor smiled. "I should like to meet the gods one day, but not yet."

Svanhild laughed. She imagined the gods just across the water, watching them. After the success of the night's plan-ning, she sensed magic in the air.

"Somewhere over there is Valhalla, where my father is feasting with the All-Father," she said. "But you're right. We should not rush to meet the gods. I just…"

"You miss him."

Svanhild nodded. Somehow she knew Tove saw her now,

standing here on the fjord with Andor. And he was smiling in that soft way of his, when what he saw was good.

"You seem to be your father's favorite," Svanhild commented, changing the subject. "I didn't realize you had raided with him for so many years. No wonder he favors you."

"I am his only son and heir, and he trusts me." Andor shrugged. "I am not fond of raiding, but every man in Mosfell learns to fight. And my father is the jarl's youngest son. Instead of learning to lead, he made raiding his specialty, something that could bring him honor."

"So before you both came here, you were going to follow his path as a raider?"

"At least that is how I was trained," Andor replied.

Though it was easy to picture Ulrik charging the shores of foreign lands, a band of warriors at his back, Svanhild did not picture the same for Andor. Yet when she had caught him training with his spear, shirtless and steaming in the cold night air, she had found new respect for him.

Such was the power of physical prowess. It was why she needed to show everyone she could wield a blade, too. Only then would they follow her.

Looking up into the night sky, painted in the rainbow colors of the bifrost bridge, she sent a silent prayer to Asgard. *Guide my heart. I know you are with me tonight.*

They continued walking then, silent for a while. Svanhild was surprised at how peaceful it was just to walk beside him, saying nothing. They shared the comfort of two people who knew each other well, compatibility Svanhild had not expected. And the contrast between Ulrik's booming shouts and Andor's quietness was striking.

"You are not your father," she said. She felt as if she were admitting it to herself as much as to him.

Andor breathed a cloud into the air. "I admire my father's

strength. He commands respect from his warriors. He fights for those he loves. But I hope to find other ways to lead, without the sword."

"Yet you fight so well," she said, remembering his movements in the training yard.

Andor thanked her, then asked, "Do you remember the meaning of my name?"

"Thor's eagle. How could I forget?"

He nodded. "In the stories, Odin's eagle sits atop Yggradsil to watch over the nine realms. I try to live by that. I may wield a spear when I go raiding with my father, but my nature is to observe, to watch over, to see things others cannot. At least, that's what I hope to do." He looked at her. "Your father inspired that in me."

Svanhild looked at him in surprise. In all their time together, Andor had never spoken about her father like this before. "Did you know him?"

"He came to my grandfather's hall once, to discuss their accord. Right away, your father gave me a knot of bread in the shape of a raven."

Svanhild laughed. "Oh, he loved those."

"Your father was kind to me. And when my grandfather invited him raiding, he agreed but said he was not interested in killing. He saw himself as an explorer. He said the gods had seeded the world with knowledge, and he traveled to reap the harvest."

Svanhild smiled to herself. She had heard those same thoughts from her father, almost to the word.

"That is something I've always remembered." Andor chuckled then. "And when I returned home, I learned how to bake bread in the shape of an eagle."

"Did the eagle look so different than the raven?"

"It was much bigger," Andor explained, making Svanhild laugh again.

"Well, it sounds like you belong in the sky just as much as I do," she said.

"The eagle and the raven. We should have something with those images made for our wedding."

Svanhild turned from the waterfront, not wanting to look at him in that moment lest her eyes betray her. They sounded so much like any other young couple about to be wed, she could almost forget she would have to leave him soon.

She did not want to think on that tonight.

They began walking down the main road of the village again, their steps slow. Tonight, there was no rush and no one outside to observe them. The town was peaceful in the falling snow. Their only task now was to enjoy the bracing air on this beautiful night.

Brushing away any thoughts of the wedding, she breathed in the scents of sea water and pine trees. She was glad the cold cleared her head after the excess of mead she had drunk, for she wanted to enjoy this moment just as it was.

"I've always longed to travel," Andor said, breaking their silence, "not as a raider, but as an explorer. These waterways connect us, and we can benefit from one another's knowledge and goods. We can form alliances, help each other. My father seeks only to conquer, but I see other ways to flourish."

"With your new longship, I suppose you can travel anywhere you want." Svanhild glanced sideways at him. "So long as you have men to follow you, that is."

He chuckled. "Do you resent the gift?"

Svanhild shook her head. "It was a fine gift. It suits you." She smiled. "You sound like my father, really. This past summer, he took his warriors to beautiful ruins, where they found treasures from the Romans. In the end, they had to fight another clan who sought to take everything for themselves." She shrugged. "Such is greed. That is why my people trained to be strong warriors, even without raiding."

"Because they are greedy?"

Svanhild hit him playfully for the jest. "Because we must protect ourselves from *others'* greed."

"You speak of your people as though you truly belong to them."

Svanhild glanced up at him. The moonlight cast strange shadows on his face, making him resemble a draugr just emerged from a tomb. Still, he was handsome even in his bones.

"Do you not belong to your people?" she asked.

Andor shrugged. "My father never taught me that. It is something I must learn on my own."

They came to a shrine at the edge of the village, where several large wooden carvings of the gods were lined up. Some were painted, but in the moonlight they all took on shades of gray and pearl. Odin, the tallest of the effigies, stood in the middle of the row. Offerings of flowers and berries rested at the base of the statue.

Andor knelt in the thin layer of snow before the carving of Thor, god of thunder. He reached into his cloak to produce a small leather pouch, which hung around his neck. From the pouch he plucked a small piece of metal. He turned it over in his hands a few times.

"What is it?" Svanhild asked, leaning over his shoulder to see the object.

The metal gleamed in the moonlight, as though it had been polished. Though it was only the size of a fingernail, intricate runes were etched everywhere, overlapping and forming patterns that looked like trees and wolves.

"Is that a trick of the moonlight, or are those images?" she said.

"They are images. I do a bit of metalwork when I have spare time, to honor Thor."

Svanhild recalled Thor was the god of metalwork as well as thunder. "It's impressive," she said. "Is that also why you became friends with Balder?"

"He has the best tools."

Andor smiled at her over his shoulder. A heat crawled up her neck at the intensity of his gaze. The way she leaned close to see the metal, their faces were only a breath away from each other. He smelled rich and warm, an intoxicating mix of cedar and honey. It was a scent that belonged only to him, and she was growing too familiar with it.

Standing to back away from him, Svanhild breathed in the cold air to cool her face and calm herself. Still, her heart raced.

Turning back to the shrine, Andor set the metal piece at the base of Thor's statue. He whispered a prayer under his breath, so soft that even in the silence of the night Svanhild could not make out the words. Then, he stood and gazed at the shrine, taking in all of the gods represented, one by one.

"And who is your god, Svanhild?" he asked her.

She stepped up to Odin's carving.

"Of course," Andor said. "The All-Father has the place of honor in this shrine."

"My family has always been connected with Odin's ravens. We think of ourselves as creatures of the sky and sea. It's why my father's name was 'dove' and mine is 'swan.'"

"Your name means more than that," Andor said, passing her a small smile. "I would be glad to spar with you again, if you'd like to test your new axe."

Svanhild remembered her cutting words earlier that night, when Andor had suggested she train later. Now she cursed herself for them. Part of her wanted to apologize, but the words did not make it to her tongue. Instead, she thanked him, then repeated, "You truly are different than your father."

From the glimmer in his gray eyes, she knew he drank in her words. "All is forgiven," he said, a small smile flashing across his mouth.

She shook her head, laughing. "You read me too well."

"I don't think that," Andor replied. Then, studying her, he said, "I have always wondered something about you. Why did you choose the path of a shieldmaiden, when your father does not like to fight?"

Svanhild thought on it for a moment. She remembered the long hours Tove spent training her with a wooden sword. There was a reason Hrafnblóð had been passed from generation to generation of their family. They did not need to be raiders for passion to run in their veins.

"Every family needs a protector," she said. "My father taught me to wield a sword, and my mother was a shieldmaiden before she wed." She looked up at Andor, who joined her now in front of Odin's carving. "Perhaps it is my mother's blood that runs through me when I'm in my battle trance."

Andor raised his eyebrows at her. "Then I should like to see you fight in a true battle someday, if you love it so much." He chuckled. "As long as I am not on the other end of your blade."

She felt a cold clutch in her heart then as she envisioned her sword scraping against Thor's hammer.

No, not Thor's hammer. Andor's spear.

Was this a vision from the gods—a warning? Or was it simply the realization that, if she did not marry Andor but instead led a rebellion against Ulrik to regain her family's throne, she may have to cross blades with him someday?

The idea made her go cold.

"We should return to the hall," she said quickly. "Get out of this icy air."

Andor observed her, a dark look in his eyes. Svanhild swallowed under his scrutiny. She felt he could read her more than she liked. And now, she had sparked his suspicion.

"Stop," she said. "You look at me as though you can read my mind."

"I wish I could," he replied.

They stood there for a long moment, watching each other. She wished she could read him, too.

"I should visit my father's burial mound," she said at last. "I need to speak with him, in private."

Andor nodded. "I will return to the hall, then."

"If your father asks—"

"I know what to say," Andor said.

Svanhild thanked him. She appreciated that he asked no questions and offered no arguments. The thought crossed her mind that, if they were to wed, he would make a good husband for someone as willful as she was. But she brushed the thought away. It did her no good now.

"Good night," Andor said.

He started turning to leave, then stopped himself. When he faced her again, his pale skin subtly reflected the colors of the bifrost. She found herself staring at his mouth, tinged purple. His eyes drifted downwards too.

Then, like an arrow to a target, he kissed her. He moved so quickly, her breath escaped her all at once.

Everything inside of her melted.

It had been a long time since she kissed anyone, and not someone she wanted like this. She kissed him back. His mouth was pleasantly warm in the frozen air. When they parted, she felt like molten metal, glowing all over.

Andor's smile was quick. "Good night, Svanhild."

The sound of her name on his tongue made her limbs weaken.

And then he was off, disappearing into the forest before she could even find her voice to respond.

As WINTER PASSED, Svanhild's dreams were filled with Andor.

She tried to think of other things before she closed her eyes—practicing battle moves in her head, recounting conversations with her sisters, praying to the gods—but by the time her mind drifted into dreams, all she could think of was Andor.

She grew restless as she tried to sleep, knowing what was coming. Try as she might, she could not avoid the memory of his lips finding hers in the chilled winter air. In her dreams she relived that kiss again and again, each night some new sense awakening in her. One night, she felt the warmth of his touch; the next, the strength of his body against hers; then the taste of his skin beneath her lips; finally his voice, rough and ragged as she coiled so tightly the only thing left to do was burst. And when she did it woke her, and she shuddered to find herself alone on her sleep pellet, flushed and breathless.

She was grateful that Andor kept his promise to find her training time with her mother, for taking up sword and shield was the only thing that kept her mind occupied. Training with her new axe gave her arm fresh strength. Svanhild felt readier for revenge every day, her body growing taut as a lyre string.

Yet each time she thanked Andor for this time he had stolen for them to train, guilt lurched in her stomach. He thought he was humoring her, giving her something to do that excited her. Perhaps he imagined they would one day marry and go traveling together on his new longship, far from Ulrik's gaze, away from bad memories, to places where they would feel free together.

Little did he know he was giving her practice for her betrayal.

Andor kept true to another promise, too: visiting the families of Kaldvik to hear grievances and find solutions. He took Svanhild with him, both of them bundled in their thickest cloaks as shields against winter's ice and wind.

Though they talked sometimes—when the wind was not too strong—Andor did not try to kiss her again. Perhaps he was waiting for her to return the gesture. After a while, it almost felt like the kiss had never happened, and Svanhild began to wonder if she had dreamed the whole thing.

But then he would glance her way with a secret smile on his face, or reach over to squeeze her hand when no one was looking. Those were the moments her heart fluttered at the memory, and she knew he remembered too.

On their outings, Svanhild tried her best to concentrate on the needs of her people. Farmland frosted over in winter, and many families complained of low supplies to get through the season after sending so much food to the great hall. If this had happened under her father, Tove would have shared from the town's stores, giving back if he had taken too much. Ulrik only took, without restraint.

Svanhild admired the way Andor handled the conversations with people. He listened patiently, and from the way he leaned forward she knew he was interested in every word. The families seemed to feel that too, for if anyone was hesitant at first to speak, they soon shared their stories freely, tears sometimes forming in their eyes.

Andor then turned to Svanhild, and together with the families they discussed ideas until a fair solution emerged. Without bothering to consult Ulrik, Andor kept his promises to everyone. He commanded servants to carry goods to hungry homes or invited people to share with each other so everyone had what they needed. Watching him take over like this, Svanhild was learning Andor was a man of his word.

As long as she was out of Ulrik's sight, Svanhild enjoyed her life like this. She could picture herself leading the people with Andor, the pair of them making rounds just like this, as jarl and wife.

Yet she could not be only a wife. And she could not rest while her father's killer led her people. Even if she forgave Andor his bloodline, he would come to the high-seat inherited from his father's bloodshed, cowardice, and trickery. The gods would not favor their family.

No, the gods were on *her* side. Haldis had promised it, and she felt it in every breath.

If only her heart could catch up.

PART III

CHAPTER 25

HALDIS

"The first spring flower."

Haldis looked up to find her mother standing in the open doorway of the small chamber, a purple blossom in her hand—Svanhild's favorite flower. Though the words should have been happy ones, Helga's voice was dark.

Winter was coming to an end. Outside, snow melted on the ground, and the sun lingered longer in the sky each day. It wouldn't be long before Ulrik would begin planning Svanhild's wedding to Andor.

They were running out of time.

Today Haldis and her family clustered in a back room of the longhouse, preparing for the spring blót. This day was usually a time for celebration, as people made sacrifices to the gods for a good harvest, for fair weather, for love and babies and safe summer travels. As everyone emerged from their winter hibernation, the goddesses Frigg and Freyja put romance in everyone's mind. Unwed women dressed in their finest gowns, hoping to attract the attention of farmers and warriors who would make good husbands. Men, meanwhile, engaged in physical contests to show their mastery of weapons, doing their best to woo their future wives.

Already thralls had helped the sisters into beautiful new gowns, woven by the seamstress Ursula and her helpers. Any other year, Haldis might tease her sisters about their dresses —especially Svanhild, who always shirked her suitors. Today Svanhild wore a purple gown with an intricate tablet border stitched in yellow thread along the neckline and hem. A pair of large gold brooches held the dress in place on either side of her neck, a string of polished yellow beads draped between them. Tucked behind the beads, her amber pendant —the one their father had given her on the night he died— flashed like lightning when it caught the firelight.

But Haldis would not tease her this year. Everything was different this year.

She shifted on her stool, adjusting her red gown at the waist. The heady scent of incense wafted in through the open doorway, for the priest Gorm had already started burning herbs for the sacred day. Combined with the stench from the animal pens across the corridor, the intense smells were giving Haldis a headache—the last thing she wanted to endure during a festival that would last all day and night. She tried not to sneeze.

Mother crossed the small chamber to where Brynja sat combing her hair. "I am wearing your dress today, daughter," she said, running her fingers over a sleeve. The dress was a rich blue color, with a swirling pattern stitched along the neckline in gold thread, ending in a raven on each side. "I hope Ulrik doesn't mind the ravens," she said, touching the border.

"I hope he does," Svanhild shot back, yet still she smiled as she took in Mother's gown. "You made this, Brynja? It's lovely. Clearly you have much more patience than I do."

Brynja smiled, her cheeks pink from the compliments. "I started making the dress last summer, when Father returned from his travels. Since then, it's been good to have a project."

Helga crossed the room to place a kiss on Brynja's forehead.

"Well," she said, "I would say you all look beautiful, but I know this is not the year for that."

Haldis frowned at the words, but she was right.

"Well, this is not the first year I've gone to the blót armed," Svanhild said, twirling a small silver folding knife in one hand, "but it is the first time I have to hide the fact."

She closed her pocket knife, which folded in half to protect the blade, before tucking it into the waist of her skirts. Haldis was surprised at how the blade disappeared into the fabric, completely hidden.

Svanhild caught her eye and smiled wickedly. "I had this slot in my dress specially-made," she explained.

Haldis raised an eyebrow. "That is clever, but I pray you don't have reason to use it today. This is a time to honor the gods."

"And a time when everyone is gathered together, which makes it ideal for setting our plans," said Svanhild.

Helga crossed to where Svanhild sat perched on a stool like a bird on a branch. "We must be careful today. Ulrik will have his eyes on us, so anyone we speak to may become a target for his suspicions." She picked up a comb from a nearby table and ran it through Svanhild's dark blonde hair. "What sort of braids would you like today?"

"Something that will keep all of the hair pulled back off my face," said Svanhild. "I have plans."

Helga froze for a moment before beginning to braid her

hair. "What sort of plans require your hair to be pulled back?"

Haldis and Brynja exchanged concerned glances. Because their oldest sister was stubborn, Haldis worried that if she had an idea in her head, it would be difficult for anyone to shake her of it. She just prayed it was a wise one.

Svanhild explained, "This is my last chance to prove myself publicly to the warriors of Kaldvik, to gain supporters to our cause. And now that the first flowers have bloomed, my wedding day will be set, which means we have no more time." Her eyes darted to where Haldis sat across the room. "I would like to challenge Thorbjorn to another fight, now that I have more training."

Haldis frowned. She knew her sister looked to her for approval now—especially after her first fight with Thorbjorn, when Haldis had reprimanded her for her vanity and recklessness. But Haldis had not witnessed Svanhild's training or even seen her wield a blade in months.

"You are prepared to fight him already?" she asked.

"If not now, then when?" Svanhild said, her eyes flashing. She looked poised to lunge from her stool.

Haldis glanced at her mother then, for Helga was the one who would know if Svanhild was ready. Her mother's mouth was tight, but she gave Haldis a subtle nod. It was enough.

"You are right, sister," Haldis accepted. "Challenge Thorbjorn if you must, but pray first that the gods are on your side, and listen for their guidance today. They will watch over you."

Svanhild's eyes—a light brown in the firelight, with flashes of green where the lamplight hit them—were wide as she drank in her sister's words. Haldis shuddered as she realized how her sister looked to her for the gods' guidance. How was Svanhild able to put such faith in her, when she had such little faith in herself? But then, Haldis's sisters did not know the story of her birth, of how she was almost left to the elements, of how her father had preferred to let her die than take her in as a member of their family.

She glanced at her mother, the only other person alive who knew this story. The woman who had saved her.

"Thank you, Haldis," Svanhild said, recapturing Haldis's attention. "We should make an offering to the gods today, to pray that he watches over his ravens as we make our plans."

Helga smiled. "A good idea." She had woven two small braids on each side of Svanhild's head, close to the scalp. Now, she joined them in the back and began braiding one thicker braid to hang down her back. "Who will you seek out today for your plans?" she asked.

"Balder and Frode have been my eyes and ears in the village these past few months," Svanhild said. "I trust they have found followers by now. Skarde is preparing a ship for my departure. I would have liked to have my father's warrior Hafdan on our side, but he has pledged himself to Ulrik. He will be a fierce opponent when I return for my revenge." She bit her lip then, considering. "I would like to test Thorbjorn's loyalty today, for he would make a strong ally if he still favors our family. And if I fight him in public, I may win others to our cause. Even if they do not join me on my way to Uppsala, perhaps they will raise arms with me when I return."

Haldis felt a warm chill run through her at the wisdom of her sister's plan. Svanhild had clearly been preparing for this. Though Haldis worried about her sister's fight with Thorbjorn, if their mother believed she was ready, that was enough for her. Svanhild would have to take such risks at some point. She would have to prove herself. And though Haldis now saw her sister's knee bouncing with nerves, she trusted the gods were with them.

For a time, they were all quiet, the only sound the crackling fire and the soft voices of thralls at work in the kitchen down the hall. It had been a long time since Haldis felt at peace like this, with nothing to do and nowhere to go—for the moment, at least. Her body and mind were weary from months of confinement, but she knew they had grown stronger, too. Such was the way of hardships: the pain was what strengthened a person.

"Do not be nervous, sister," she said at last, breaking the silence. She knew nerves would not do Svanhild any good today. "The gods are with you."

As Helga finished braiding Svanhild's hair, she moved to stand in front of her, placing her hands on her daughter's shoulders. "You are ready, daughter," she said. "You have been training for many moons now. Just remember..." She tapped her temple, then her chest.

Though Haldis didn't know what their mother meant, Svanhild nodded and lifted her chin. "I am ready," she said.

Haldis felt a flutter in her hair, though nothing was nearby to cause the breeze. Perhaps it was the spirit of the gods, telling her everything was all right. She closed her eyes a moment, issuing a silent prayer to the All-Father.

Guide Svanhild's choices today. Guide her sword hand and her heart. Watch over your raven family today.

As she opened her eyes, a wave of calm passed through her. The gods were with them today—she could feel it. Though it was hard for her to let go of reason, she was beginning to trust these sensations as small signs from the gods.

On a nearby stool, Brynja made an odd hiccuping sound that drew their attention. She had been quiet all morning. Haldis expected it was just excitement at being able to spend time with Erik, but now Brynja's eyes grew dewy with tears.

"What is the matter?" their mother said, crossing the

room to put an arm around Brynja's shoulders. "You look beautiful, my dear."

Instead of looking comforted by the words, Brynja covered her face with her hands, a sob escaping her lips. "I am afraid, Mother," she said, her voice muffled.

Helga gently drew Brynja's hands from her face and peered at her. "What are you afraid of?"

"I have a bad feeling about this day."

"Do you think I will lose my battle again?" Svanhild asked, looking worried.

Brynja shot her a furious look. "It's not about you, Svanhild."

Haldis bit back a laugh. She liked seeing Brynja put their older sister in her place. Brynja even looked the part today, the tiara from Father atop her head. She wore a rich green dress that brought out the green in her eyes, the shoulders layered with rabbit fur. With her brown hair cascading down her back, she looked like a princess of the forest. Haldis had always known her youngest sister was beautiful, but this was the first time she no longer looked like a girl, but a woman.

"I fear being out today," Brynja went on. She had collected herself enough to speak clearly now, but she kept her voice low, as though afraid someone might overhear. "Ulrik's housecarl has been pestering me for months. I feel his eyes on me all the time when I'm in the hall." She visibly shuddered. "I dread his attention today."

Helga gave her shoulders a squeeze. "We will look out for you, Brynja. Stay close to one of us at all times, and you will be safe."

Svanhild nodded. "There will be many women craving attention today," she said. "Perhaps one of them will catch the eye of Ulrik's righthand man. Surely many women desire him for his status, even if he is a brute. That makes this the perfect day for him to forget about you."

Brynja gave her a weak smile and nodded. She said nothing more. Haldis hoped her family's reassurances had been enough for her.

Gorm entered then, a jar of kohl in his hands. "It is time to prepare you," he said to Haldis.

"Let me," said Helga, gesturing for him to hand her the kohl. When he had, she sat on the stool in front of Haldis to apply the cosmetics to her face. Gorm stood behind her to watch. "You will command respect today," Mother said, smiling.

Haldis blanched at the idea. She wondered if her face looked as pale as it felt.

Gorm must have noticed, for he said, "I can speak the words and toast the gods," as though to make her feel better.

But Helga shook her head. "It would be better if Haldis performed the toasts. The people of Kaldvik will appreciate hearing from our family, and this is a good time to present her to Ulrik's new warriors."

Haldis clutched at the raven pendant around her neck, willing Odin to bring her luck. Her parents had always intended for her to preside over the sacrifices with Gorm, but every year, she shirked from the idea. She didn't want two hundred pairs of eyes watching her. And this year was worse, for she would have the additional stares of Ulrik's warriors to contend with. At least the people of Kaldvik were accustomed to her, knew about her markings and her unseeing eye. Even the ones who gave her a wide berth in the village respected that she would one day be their völva. But what would the new villagers think when they saw her leading rites for the first time?

Part of her wanted to escape her duties. She could plead the truth: she was afraid. Surely her mother would understand her reticence to stand in front of so many people, especially after the trauma of these past months.

But she shook the idea away. If this would help their family, she would do it. She needed the respect of the town's new people, and she needed Ulrik to accept her along with the rest of the family if they were to keep their positions here.

Gorm nodded his approval. Aside from the seamstress Ursula, he was the only one of their family's household to remain in the longhouse with Ulrik. Haldis suspected he was accepted only because Ulrik did not have any gothar of his own. As much as Ulrik liked to call on the gods when giving a speech to the people of Kaldvik, in private he was a man of little faith—perhaps none.

"The more she presides over the ceremony, the more she will become indispensable to Ulrik and his rule here," Gorm said. His voice was slow and quavering, as though he had grown weary and wise after long travels to other realms.

As Mother finished applying the kohl to her eyes and a berry stain to her lips, Haldis studied her. Today, Helga's green eyes were like still water under a canopy of trees. It was the same expression she'd had seventeen years before, when she scooped Haldis from the lakeshore to bring her back to the hall. Haldis had never thanked her mother for saving her life. Instead, she had spent her years tormented that she had no special connection to the gods, believing everything her mother said about her powers was a lie.

But surely such torment was better than being dead.

When she was finished with her work, Helga sat back and gave Haldis a long look, then smiled. "You look radiant, daughter. Freyja has granted you true beauty." She brushed her thumb across Haldis's left cheek, where the red mark was. Haldis felt tears well in her eyes at the gentle acceptance in that touch.

"Thank you, Mother." She did not explain all the ways she

was thankful—not in front of Gorm and her sisters—but she hoped it was clear on her face.

"Now, let us take these last few moments to make our offering to the gods," Helga said. Turning to Gorm, she asked, "Will you help us?"

Gorm inclined his head. Without a word, he moved to check the corridor for guards. When all was clear, he motioned for them to hurry to the back door out of the long-house. He closed the door of the chamber behind them and stood guard outside of it. Though Haldis wondered what he would say if Ulrik or one of his men came to call on their family, she trusted the gods were with him.

STANDING in a ring of pine trees in the middle of the forest, Haldis took the pocket knife from Svanhild's hand—the one she had earlier tucked into her dress—and lifted it toward the sky.

"Odin, we come to you today with an offering to ask that you watch over our family," she said.

Though she and her family had woven deep into the forest, Ulrik's guards could be anywhere, so she kept her voice low. Still, the pitch of it wavered in the air like a plucked lyre string on a high note.

"Accept this sacrifice. With this blood, we honor you."

She knelt on one knee in front of the sheep, which they had led here for the sacrifice. The creature's dark eyes stared into hers. For a moment, she could have sworn the ewe knew what was coming, but the creature was quiet and refused to look away, as though she accepted her fate.

"Thank you," Haldis whispered to the ewe. Then, knowing hesitation would only make this harder, she quickly plunged the knife into the creature's throat and slid the blade through the flesh. The feel of the skin tearing made her shiver. Soon the ewe collapsed in a heap on the ground, the life flickering from her eyes.

Helga passed Haldis a small bowl to collect the blood. Normally she would dip a twig into the blood and splatter it on each of them, but returning to the longhouse with blood on their finest clothes would only arouse suspicion.

Instead, she waited until she had collected enough blood, then rose and carefully dipped her fingers into the bowl. Facing her mother first, she drew a rune of protection on her forehead. Then she did the same for Svanhild and Brynja. Helga dipped her fingers in next and drew the same rune on Haldis's forehead.

Haldis lifted her eyes to the sky. An eagle flew from a nearby tree branch, his majestic wings flapping loudly as he passed just over their heads. The breeze he generated stirred their hair and sent a cool chill through Haldis's skin. But she knew it was a sign from the gods.

"Odin's eagle is here," she said, smiling at her sisters. "The All-Father hears our prayers."

"How long do you womenfolk take to get ready?" came a booming voice from down the corridor.

Haldis and her family had only just slipped back into the chamber, their foreheads still traced with runes. Gorm quickly closed the door, remaining outside, so Ulrik would not see them.

"You can do your own," Mother said, passing wet rags to Svanhild and Brynja, who immediately began scrubbing the blood from their foreheads. Turning to Haldis, Helga said, "Let me do yours so we don't ruin your kohl."

The banging of fists at the door made them all jump.

Gorm's voice was quiet in the hall as he calmly explained, "They are still preparing themselves for the blót."

"They've had half the morning," Ulrik complained, his voice much louder than the priest's. "My women are ready and waiting. They've already had two helpings of fish for dagmal while they wait. What's taking these girls so long?"

Haldis closed her eyes as her mother rubbed the scratchy rag across her forehead.

"Hurry, Mother," Brynja whispered, her eyes wide with fear.

"This is my house," grumbled Ulrik just outside the door. "Let me through."

The door burst open. Helga spun to face away from the door, rubbing at her forehead with small motions so as not to attract attention. Haldis and Svanhild moved to stand in between her and Ulrik, hiding her at least a bit.

Ulrik's body nearly filled the frame of the doorway as he stood glaring at them. "I've never seen ladies take so long to get ready. Olaf says people are already gathering in the grove. They are waiting to see me, and I can't show up without my lucky tokens."

"Is that what we are to you?" Svanhild muttered.

Ulrik lunged toward her and slapped her. The snap of it rang through the air. But Svanhild remained facing forward, lifting her chin in defiance. Haldis saw a red imprint blossom across her struck cheek. She could only imagine how it must sting, yet her sister's eyes were all fire as she glared back at Ulrik.

"Watch what you say to me, or I might change my mind about our deal," Ulrik said. "What is that on your forehead?" He peered at each of them in turn, frowning in confusion. "You all look pink there."

"We have just washed our faces," Brynja said softly.

Haldis was surprised she was the one to answer, but her soft voice seemed to calm Ulrik. He stroked Brynja's cheek.

"Aren't you pretty," he said. "It's time we found you a husband. That will be one of you out of this house, at least."

"Where is Andor?" Svanhild asked.

Ulrik glared at her. "You will stay close to him today," he commanded. "Expect punishment if I see you parted from his side for even a moment." Then he whipped his gaze to their mother. "You will stay close to me, of course." To Haldis, he said, "And you remain with the gothi for the sacrifices. Otherwise, stay out of my sight."

Haldis straightened her back without answering. As much as she dreaded being in front of everyone at the ceremony, she relished the look of surprise on Ulrik's face now as he took in her attire. She had chosen a red dress to remind people of her family's sigil. But instead of a traditional dress, her gown had a black hood trimmed in gold thread and sweeping white sleeves that fluttered like wings when she raised her arms. Around her neck was a string of glass beads, and she let her white-blonde hair hang like a curtain in front of her shoulders. Dressed like this, she realized she must finally look the part of a völva.

She hoped that stirred at least a small feeling of fear in Ulrik. It took him a moment to stop staring and snarl at her. And in that moment of hesitation, she believed she had succeeded.

Perhaps being a völva *did* give her a special power. She just needed to learn how to wield it.

"Let's go," said Ulrik, turning to lead them from the room.

Haldis glanced at her mother and sisters. Though they all wore different expressions at first—Brynja wide-eyed, Helga's mouth grim, and Svanhild's eyes flashing—when they looked at each other, they became one. They shared the same purpose, and today they would make ready for their plans.

It would not be easy, but the gods were with them.

CHAPTER 26

BRYNJA

*A*s the spring blót began, Brynja followed the jarl and her mother into the sacred grove.

As Brynja passed from the forest into the clearing, a strange heat hit her, a combination of body heat and fires roaring in several small pits. The way the warmth was contained, it almost felt like walking into a building, yet they were still outside, under the clear blue sky, the trees forming a protective ring around the site.

Brynja's eyes widened as she took in the lively sight. Already people had pitched tents, where they gathered to play games of dice and drink mead, no matter the early hour. Children played at battle with wooden swords, and a few people even danced and drank the cold from their limbs.

With the coming of spring, the first touch of warmth seemed to cheer people. Being so far north, Kaldvik's winters were long and dark, a time for hibernation—and this year had been harder than most. Now, Brynja felt the joy people shared at being out of doors again, closer to the gods and reunited with each other.

She had not seen such celebration since her father's feast the night he died.

They walked past a row of archers practicing shots at targets set up along the perimeter of the grove. One of the men glanced at Brynja as she passed behind him, winking before shooting his arrow with hardly a glance. There was a satisfying *thwack* as the arrow hit the target. His friends whooped in celebration, but the archer's eyes were intent on Brynja's reaction. She inclined her head to honor his good aim, then hurried to catch up with Ulrik and her mother.

At the center of the clearing was the sacred elm tree. As they passed it, Helga touched Ulrik's arm to stop him.

"May we take a moment for prayers?" she asked.

Ulrik grunted his approval. "Meet me at the tent when you're done, and don't take too long."

Brynja watched as he continued on to the largest tent in the clearing, where his wife Gertrud sat with their daughter Kindra. Both women sipped from wooden cups, chatting together like a pair of cooing doves. She wondered at their happiness, when they had to live with Ulrik. But then, they were never on the sharp end of Ulrik's anger.

Mother took her hand then, drawing her attention from the scene to the tree. Legend had it this tree was borne from a seed of Yggdrasil, planted here by Odin to guide his ravens as they led the first settlers of Kaldvik to this spot. All winter, the tree had been bare, but now a few green leaves sprouted on the branches, the first signs of life and a promise of harvest ahead.

Brynja sighed as she joined her mother to kneel before it. All around the tree were offerings people had made—trinkets like wooden carvings, animal pelts, and flowers—all in the hopes the gods would hear them. But Brynja had never made such an offering before.

Yes, she had joined her sisters in their sacrifice this morning, and she saw the way it lifted her mother's spirits and gave Svanhild confidence. Her whole life, Brynja had participated in blóts and joined others in prayers to Odin, Thor, and Freyja. But she had no special words for the gods, and she did not feel their presence the way others did. She only went through the motions to make others happy.

Helga muttered a few prayers, barely audible, before taking the purple flower she had been carrying all morning and setting it in front of the tree. "For you, Freyja," she whispered. "Bring my daughters the fate they deserve, the fate you will for them." She turned to Brynja, her eyes damp with tears. "Are you ready for the blót?"

Brynja's stomach knotted at the question, but she nodded. She didn't know why she felt nervous. She wanted to seek out Erik, to say hello to the people from town she had not seen in so many moons. Yet she dreaded spending the day in Ulrik's company—especially if Olaf was nearby.

As they rose, a familiar voice called her name. She could not contain her smile as she turned to find her friend Erik jogging over to them.

"I was hoping I would find you today," Erik said. He was panting.

"You sound tired. Staying indoors all winter has made you weak," Brynja teased.

"I'm not tired from the running," Erik said.

He spun to show off a battle axe slung across his back. It was much larger than any of the training weapons Brynja had seen him playing with before, a true weapon of war. She was surprised his back was now broad enough to carry it well.

"I've been involved in some axe-throwing competitions, among other things," he said, facing her again.

"Did you win any of them?"

He grinned. That was answer enough.

"Good morning, Erik," said Helga, placing a hand on his shoulder in greeting. "You have grown taller than me."

"I am sixteen now," Erik said. "It's my time to join in battles, so I had Balder craft me a new weapon."

"It is a fine blade," Helga remarked.

Erik smiled shyly. "Balder did not ask for as much payment as this weapon is worth. But we have much in common."

Brynja frowned. "I thought you loved farming. What use is a battle axe to a farmer?"

"Yes, I thought you favored Freyr," Helga added, referring to the god of harvest.

"I am a farmer," Erik replied, "but I will also be a warrior. With my weapon, I hope to honor Tyr, Thor, and Odin."

Brynja's mind reeled at the dangers of battle, something she never imagined Erik would seek out. She pictured him bent over his crops and caring for his animals—not fighting on a bloody battlefield.

"Why would you do that?" she asked.

"That night your father died, I did nothing to help," Erik explained, his voice lowered now so they would not be overheard. "I had an axe at the time, but it was little more than a toy to me. I could not defend your family. I could not defend my jarl. I was weak, a coward. And I failed." He ran a hand over his face. Brynja's heart ached for him, for she had never seen her friend in such a state before. Then, straightening, he said, "I will not fail your family again."

Brynja was speechless. She remembered his mother Ragnilde's words about the change in him since Tove's death, but she had not seen it so clearly before. It was not merely grief that tormented him. He was changed for life.

"Thank you for your courage and loyalty," Helga said softly. "I just ask you to take care. My husband would not have wanted you to put yourself in danger for him."

"I do it for all of you," Erik said. "And for our home."

Brynja clasped his hands in hers. "Erik, you are like a brother to me. Promise me you won't do anything foolish."

Erik's forehead wrinkled—just for a moment—before he forced a grin to his face. But in that quick expression, Brynja caught his disappointment. He wanted her to believe in him, yet she could not help worrying. She was already scared for Svanhild; now Erik was another person she had to fear losing.

"I'll always be a little foolish, but I promise it's for a good cause," he joked. Then, growing more serious, he gave her hands a squeeze. "I swear I will be careful."

"You know you owe our family nothing, Erik," said Mother.

Erik released Brynja's hands. "I appreciate that, but it's not true. Since Jarl Tove's death, I've barely seen you, and our family's farm suffers. It's clear now that I owe your family everything." He gave them each a hug, then said, "I should find some more competitions now."

"Find me later for a game of dice," Brynja said.

He put a hand to his heart to swear the oath, making her laugh.

If she had her freedom, she would follow him now to watch him throw his axe and wrestle with the other men, to share mead with him, to take a walk to the fjord like they used to. She missed the days his company was as constant as the sun rising in the sky each day.

But she could not follow him now. She wasn't even sure if Ulrik would allow him to play a game of dice with her later.

For so many months now, she had felt so alone.

As she and her mother began their walk back to the jarl's tent, Brynja felt a breeze stir her hair as someone ran to join them. Suddenly Olaf was striding in step with her, so close to her his shoulder rubbed against hers. When she moved away from him, toward her mother, he closed the gap so they were touching again. The unwanted contact made her shiver.

"It's a beautiful day to honor the gods," he said in his gruff voice. "But it does not do justice to how you look today, my lady."

Brynja forced a smile. "Thank you." She kept her attention ahead, though the odor of damp leaves and unwashed hair, along with the gravelly voice, made it clear who was beside her.

"How are you today, Olaf?" Mother asked.

"I've been busy setting up the jarl's tent and keeping everyone in order," he said. "Jarl Ulrik wants no trouble today, no matter how drunk everyone gets."

"I thought his warriors were the ones who enjoy getting needlessly drunk," Brynja commented, then tensed for his reply. Ulrik would get upset at any hint of an insult.

But Olaf surprised her by chuckling. "Perhaps, but his warriors are not the ones he is worried about, are they?"

They stopped at the entrance to the tent, where Ulrik now sat between his wife and daughter, a cup of mead in hand. He waved for a thrall to fetch more drink for the newcomers, then motioned to empty chairs nearby.

"Olaf, I am glad you found them," he said. "We can't have them wandering off today. Perhaps you can help keep an eye on these two if they try to get away again."

Brynja glanced at her mother, surprised at Ulrik's words. They had only been gone a few moments, and only after he had given them permission. And the only person worse than Ulrik to have around all day was Olaf. She caught the tightening in her mother's jaw, but otherwise Helga remained calm and composed as she took a seat beside Gertrud.

"You look fine today," Ulrik said to her. "Don't sit so far. Come sit here." He tapped his lap.

Brynja felt sick at the idea of her mother sitting in Ulrik's lap. But hadn't Svanhild said her mother now acted as his concubine? How far did things go between them, when Ulrik forced her to be alone with him? Brynja didn't want to think about it.

Helga laughed lightly, a sound like flowers catching in the wind. Brynja sensed it was fake, but she admired how convincing her mother was as she said, "You always know how to make me laugh, Jarl. I am glad to keep you and your wife company today."

Mentioning his wife was the trick. Ulrik gave a satisfied grunt as he reached over to take his wife's hand in his. Gertrud smiled at him. Brynja wondered why she wasn't more upset at Helga's presence and Ulrik's desire for her. Did she not care that Ulrik had his eyes set on another woman? Perhaps she was glad his attention flitted elsewhere. If Brynja had to marry such a brute, she would be grateful any time he favored someone else, if only to have him away from her.

"Go on, sit," Ulrik said to Brynja, waving to a pair of chairs on the other side of his daughter Kindra. "You're blocking the view of the party."

As Brynja took the seat nearest Kindra, the girl passed her a small smile. Brynja returned it.

Though she and Kindra had shared some duties over the past several months, they had not taken much time to talk together. Brynja would rather be with her own sisters and keep their confidence. But if Svanhild was going to Uppsala for reinforcements, perhaps it was time to make the best of her situation, for as long as it lasted.

Kindra seemed sweet, saying little to anyone but her brother Andor, often working the loom and sneaking berry bread from the kitchens. She might make a good friend for Brynja, once Svanhild was gone...

As Olaf sat in the chair beside her, he pulled it closer to her, so their legs were touching. She tried to move away, but he invaded her space like a warrior charging into battle.

"Keeping an eye on you will be a pleasant task today," he said to her, keeping his voice low.

Brynja felt Kindra watching for a heartbeat, but the girl quickly turned her head away as though too shy to watch the scene unfold. Brynja hoped Kindra didn't get the wrong impression that she and Olaf were engaged in some sort of tryst. Just the thought of it made her feel sick.

The thralls brought out fresh cups of mead. Brynja took her wooden cup gratefully, burying herself in the drink to avoid meeting Olaf's gaze. She glanced at her mother for aid, but Helga was engaged in a conversation with Gertrud.

"We should toast something," Olaf said. "Something for just the two of us. With those rosy cheeks, I sense the presence of Freyja in you today."

Brynja felt her face go hot at his words. Among other things, Freyja was the goddess of lovemaking.

"I am here to honor the gods," she lied, hoping it would be enough to make Olaf more serious. "This is a sacred day."

"There are many ways to honor the gods," Olaf said. He placed his hand on her knee then, tugging just a bit at the skirt as though to pull it up.

Brynja's skin went cold at the suggestion.

"Frigg and Freyja are goddesses of spring, aren't they?" he said with a shrug.

Brynja forced down another swallow of mead, trying to think of a way to respond. His hand was still hot on her leg, and she wanted it gone.

Ulrik's voice interrupted her thoughts. "I see your intentions with that one now, Olaf," he said with a chuckle. "She looks lovely today, doesn't she?"

Olaf quickly withdrew his hand from her knee. "What's that, Jarl?" he said, feigning ignorance.

"Don't be shy about it," Ulrik continued. "She is the prettiest of the three by far, matched only by the beauty of her mother." He nodded to Helga before returning his attention to Olaf and Brynja. "You should have come to me about this, you know. I've been wanting to marry this one off, get her out of the longhouse. And you are my most trusted advisor and a strong warrior. I am lucky to have you by my side." His eyes flashed as he looked at Brynja. "A gift for your loyalty would not be out of the question."

Brynja felt her skin going clammy with sweat, her heart pounding a rhythm in her chest. She felt like a fish caught on a hook.

Olaf put his hand on Brynja's knee again, giving it a squeeze. He seemed emboldened by the permission the jarl granted him. "Thank you, Jarl Ulrik. Let's just say my task to keep her close today is the best job I've had since we arrived in Kaldvik."

Ulrik let out a roaring guffaw at his joke, nearly spilling his mead onto the ground. He lifted his cup to toast his right hand; Olaf joined in. The men exchanged a hearty, "Skol!" before draining their cups.

Brynja met her mother's gaze, feeling miserable. Helga gave her a small smile, as though to pass her courage, but Brynja saw the anger flashing in her mother's eyes and the concern etched across her forehead.

And Olaf's hand was still planted on her knee.

CHAPTER 27

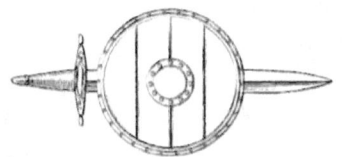

SVANHILD

"What do you wager?"

Several people standing nearby whooped and whistled at the challenge. Svanhild stood in the center of the gathering, a throwing knife in her hand. After taking leave of Andor while he visited with Balder, she had sought out a dagger-throwing contest at the edge of the clearing.

Her challenger was the warrior Thorbjorn, who gave her a smirk that would have melted another woman. But she stood strong, ignoring the strange energy that flashed like lightning in his blue eyes.

"This," Svanhild said, lifting the delicate amber amulet that hung around her neck. If she invoked her father now, she might spark all of them to remember him. "I have never been fond of jewelry, but this is significant to me. You all saw me choose this gift from my father, Jarl Tove, the night that he died. Freyja's teardrop. Wear it on the battlefield, and it will draw the eyes of the Valkyries should you fall."

Thorbjorn grinned his approval.

"And what will you wager?" she challenged back.

His tongue played at the corner of his lips as he considered. Then he lifted his axe, a sturdy weapon with a polished blade. He had clearly taken good care of it, and for a common warrior, it looked expensive. Was this the weapon Brynja had called Blood-Drinker?

Svanhild tried not to stare at Thorbjorn's muscular arms as he tossed the axe back and forth between his hands, showing off its light weight as well as his own dexterity. Rather than imagining him on the battlefield, she imagined him in a more private place.

Then she cursed under her breath at her own foolishness. The goddesses toyed with her today, as they did so many during the spring blót. A blush crept up her neck, but she kept her chin raised in defiance as Thorbjorn continued to show off.

"After a great battle, this was gifted to me by your father," he said, nodding to Svanhild, "and so it means something to me too."

She smiled. Her plan had worked as expected. By bringing up her father, she hoped to inspire other memories of him—and expressions of loyalty, too.

"To my father, then," she said, glancing around at the crowd. Several people lifted their ale horns to toast him.

Thorbjorn raised a fist to honor Jarl Tove, too. If she could convince him to join her on her trip to Uppsala, he would make a strong ally—not only for his physical strength, but for the heart and courage it took to express his love of her father while another man ruled.

She only hoped Ulrik was not nearby to overhear.

"So you think you can beat me at dagger-throwing?" she went on, raising her eyebrows. "My father would have loved to see you try."

Several people laughed. This was the Svanhild they had known, the one who played with swords and scared away men with her wit. She had almost forgotten how fun it was to truly live.

"Let's hope it goes better than last time," Thorbjorn teased her.

Svanhild glanced around, fearing the reactions of anyone who might have seen or heard about her defeat so many months ago. Instead, she was surprised to see people smiling —a few chuckling, too—all with good cheer. They were happy today, and they seemed glad to see her. Perhaps they remembered who she had once been too, daughter of a great jarl, someone they cared for, from a family they loved and respected.

Casting aside any doubts about her abilities, Svanhild replied, "A defeat only makes the next victory sweeter. Perhaps a dagger-throwing contest is not enough for this fine day. What would you say to a rematch of our last battle?"

A few people whistled at her challenge, eager to see another fight between Svanhild and Thorbjorn, Jarl Tove's shieldmaiden daughter and his wildest warrior. She could tell, despite his brazen attitude, that he wasn't as drunk as the other men watching. He would give her a fair battle, a second chance to prove her prowess before her people.

She looked up at the bright sky overhead. The gods were with her today. She sensed them in every breeze that blew through her hair and every bird that called from the trees. Every person was born with some measured amount of luck, and today she felt it. Her skin tingled with its power.

"I accept your challenge," said Thorbjorn. "Does someone have fresh axes for us?"

A nearby warrior plucked a pair of axes from his waist, handing one each to Svanhild and Thorbjorn. Two others shared the wooden shields off their backs.

Svanhild gripped her gear, ignoring the tightness in her stomach. Her mother had taught her that nerves were the body's way of readying the muscles for battle. If she was smart, they would sharpen her mind, too.

"Until first blood again?" Thorbjorn asked, sweeping past her. He winked at her as his shoulder brushed against hers, then took position in the middle of the gathering.

Svanhild glanced around at the people. First blood would ensure a quick fight with no major wounds, but would it be enough to show her true skill with a blade? After her months of training, she knew she could do more. This was her chance to prove herself in front of a crowd. Afterwards, with the gods on her side, she would inquire who would be courageous enough to follow her to Uppsala, to retrieve her uncle Asmund and to seek their revenge.

No, first blood was not enough today.

"We fight until one of us yields," she said. "A true test in personal combat."

As the crowd cheered, Thorbjorn grinned. "If you say so, shieldmaiden," he said.

She shot him a gritty smile back. Though she sensed an irreverent playfulness in his nicknames for her, she would rather be called shieldmaiden than princess any day.

A man nearby, who oversaw the dagger contest, announced that the fight would begin at his call.

Svanhild nodded her readiness to him. Then she sank into her battle stance, knees bent, shield in her right hand and axe in her left. She took a few deep breaths to steady her nerves.

Thorbjorn circled her, his eyes flashing like lightning. He wore a light tunic today with dark trousers, but she spotted the same silver pendant depicting Thor's hammer hanging from his neck. Perhaps it was his token of luck.

He would need it today.

The man overseeing the fight let out a shout, and the battle began.

Before she could draw another breath, Thorbjorn lunged at her. She raised her shield to deflect his blow. Pushing his axe away with her shield, she swung her own axe at his waist. He jumped backwards, avoiding the blow.

Several in the crowd clapped or cheered, but Svanhild did her best to block out the sounds. In this moment, there could be nothing but her and Thorbjorn. Shield against shield. Her blade against his.

Thorbjorn let out a wolfish howl and leaped toward her again. As she lifted her shield to deflect the hit, he danced to the side and nicked her leg. She winced at the pain in her calf. She felt a tickle of blood there, but it was only a small cut.

Thorbjorn grinned again. He was playing with her.

She scowled. Letting out a cry, she jumped at him, axe raised. When she brought it down, the blade grazed his shoulder.

She shuddered at the contact. If she was not careful, she could truly kill him.

And that meant he could kill her, too.

Refocusing her attention, she called on the gods for their aid.

Odin, you know my path is true. Guide my blade.

It was all she had time to pray before Thorbjorn swung at her again. She dodged out of the way, then dropped easily to her knees and rolled sideways to avoid his subsequent slashes.

They danced like this—him attacking, her retreating—for several more breaths.

Her attention narrowed, like a wolf seeing prey.

The sounds of the crowd vanished, and the rest of the forest peeled away.

She began to sense Thorbjorn's movements before she saw them. Even the slightest flick of his wrist or the whir of his blade told her which direction he would aim next.

She wove away from him, feeling light on her feet, swift as a raven.

If only her father could have seen her now.

She waited until Thorbjorn tired of the chase. She waited until the sweat gleamed on his forehead and his gestures grew heavy. He slowed, panting like a dog. He circled her, eyes wide and wild. And for a moment, while he caught his breath, his attacks ceased.

This was her chance.

Unleashing a savage yelp, she rushed at him. She called on all the gods she had ever prayed to as she tore across the clearing to meet him with her axe.

Her blade crashed against his shield, hard.

He stumbled backwards.

She hit again.

This time he fell, his axe flying from his grip. He held his shield overhead as protection.

Though part of her felt bad going after him now, when he looked so much like a cowering rabbit, she had to finish the fight. This is what warriors did.

She just needed to find an opening. She sidestepped around his shield and swung her axe toward his unprotected side. Though he tried to block, his movement was too slow, his arm too weary.

She halted her axe, holding it at his shoulder. The blade pressed against the beating in his throat.

"Do you yield?" she said.

The cheers of the crowd grew louder in her ears as she came back to her senses, the world filling in around her again. There was the forest, and the blue sky overhead, and the people of Kaldvik gathered to watch.

And there, in the branches of the sacred elm tree across the grove, was a pair of ravens.

Odin's eyes, watching.

She hoped her father, if he saw the battle from Valhalla, would be proud.

A clucking sound below drew her attention back to Thorbjorn. He was smirking up at her. In her battle rage, she wished she could slap the smile from his face.

Then she felt the sharp touch of a blade against her abdomen. Looking down, she saw Thorbjorn held a knife to her side, just above her waist, tearing a small hole in her purple dress.

She gasped. If this were a true battle, he could slide the blade right into her stomach and watch her bleed out. They would have died together, then.

A few people in the crowd chuckled when they noticed the small blade too. Thorbjorn had been quick to draw it after losing his axe.

"I'll yield," said Thorbjorn, "if you do."

Several people laughed in surprise, then whooped their approval at the even match between the two warriors.

Though Svanhild scowled, she withdrew her axe from his neck. Tossing it aside, she reached down to help her opponent to his feet. He tossed his blade as well, then gripped her forearm with his.

"The shieldmaiden has been practicing!" he shouted to the crowd. When she pulled him up, he drew close to her, his lips almost brushing her ear as he whispered, "But every warrior knows the real fun happens off the battlefield."

Her blood rushed as his breath warmed her neck. She glanced at him, smelling a masculine mix of grass and ale on him, along with his own musk. Without thinking, she bit her lip, making him grin again.

Only when she looked past him into the crowd did she

spot Andor standing near the front, frowning. Had he witnessed the entire battle? Had he noticed Thorbjorn whispering in her ear just now?

As Thorbjorn backed away from her to stand near Andor, she saw the two men as different as day and night. Where Thorbjorn wore only a fur vest, exposing his powerful arms, Andor was clad in a dark cloak trimmed in gray wolf fur. Thorbjorn had the wild eyes of a warrior just home from battle, and he grinned broadly when he caught Svanhild's eye; but Andor stood still as a tree, giving her the smallest of smiles, one only she could catch. She let her mouth twitch in response, giving him the same secret gift back.

Then Thorbjorn grabbed her around the waist, pulling her close to stand at his side. "Today you have all witnessed the strength of Tove's warrior daughter," he said to the crowd.

She flushed at Thorbjorn's nearness, at his compliments, at the adoration from the gathering. Yet her gaze was locked on Andor.

His was set on Thorbjorn.

In the rush of competition, she had almost forgotten Andor was not just a man she took walks with, a man who sometimes intrigued her, a man she had kissed and dreamed about in secret. He was her future husband. And everyone in the village knew it.

Thorbjorn was bold. Perhaps *too* bold.

Andor glanced at her, his jaw clenching as she had seen it do before when he was angry.

She writhed out of Thorbjorn's grasp and lifted her hands to quiet the people's cheers. "I have heard that Thorbjorn was once my father's fiercest warrior," she said. "Today, I hope I have proved myself just as fierce." Smiling, she added, "The alternative would be that Thorbjorn has spent his winter getting soft with mead."

A few people laughed. Thorbjorn shook his head like a dog shaking off water. Even now that she had taken a few steps away from him, she felt the heat steaming off his body.

"Don't worry, shieldmaiden, you proved yourself today," he said. "Besides, everyone knows I don't drink mead."

Before Svanhild could respond, several people parted to make way for someone entering the clearing. She froze when she saw who it was.

Ulrik. He barreled into the arena like a bear into a wolf den. "What is going on here?" he bellowed.

Stopping at the front of the crowd, he looked at Svanhild, Thorbjorn, and Andor. Though his face was red with anger, he said nothing else. Clearly he was waiting for someone to answer him.

Thorbjorn stepped forward first, surprising Svanhild. "You have given your son a rare prize in this shieldmaiden," he said. "We have just had a battle, and she fought well. The gods favor her. I would even say she is blessed by Thor."

He glanced around at the people for confirmation. A few nodded or clapped their agreement.

Svanhild bit her lip, unsure of where Thorbjorn was going with this. Though she appreciated his compliments, she could hear the snarl in his voice as he faced their new jarl.

"It must take a powerful alchemy to turn a shieldmaiden into a bride," Thorbjorn continued, louder now, the anger seeping out of him like a leaking ship. Turning back to Ulrik, he sneered, "What a special treasure you have polished for your highest shelf."

A few people gasped at his words. Svanhild felt a rush of warmth at his defense of her, for it felt like no one had defended her in nearly a year. At least not like that—not with an anger fueled by a desire for justice.

It was the same anger she felt every time she looked at Ulrik.

But she did not need a man to say such things for her.

Stepping forward to join Thorbjorn, she said, "Ulrik knows I am no prize." She purposely left out his title as jarl, for he would never be the true ruler of Kaldvik in her mind and heart.

Ulrik glared at her, his face growing redder. She wondered if he would have liked to slap her as he had this morning, if only they were not in front of such a crowd. "You have no right to disrespect me, not after all these months I have kept you and your family alive. I have fed you. I have given you beds to sleep in. I have provided you and your sisters with everything you need. Your mother lives like a queen, side by side with my own beloved wife."

Svanhild's stomach turned at his tricks. He made it sound like he did them favors; only her family knew how he mistreated them.

"Interesting," she said. "Somehow every word you speak is both truth and lie at the same time."

She caught Andor's eye then. He watched his father with a stormy expression on his face. Knowing Andor, Svanhild guessed he was judging the best thing to say or do in this moment, seeking wisdom from past experience, perhaps issuing a prayer to the gods. She could almost see the thoughts flashing behind his gray eyes.

"I could have killed you the night I killed your father," Ulrik said to her. "I *should* have. Instead, I gave you a great honor."

Svanhild laughed bitterly. "What was that, to live like prisoners in our own home?"

Ulrik spat on the ground before answering. "You know what honor, *bikkja*," he said. *Bitch.* "What greater honor is there than for you to be the wife of my only son!"

She wanted to lunge at him, to pick up her axe and swing it at him, to tear at him until he bled. Maybe it was her blood still ringing from her battle with Thorbjorn, but she could not remember a time she had felt such hatred.

Before she could move, Andor's voice stopped her. "Marrying me was her choice," he said. Compared to the raging of his father, his voice was lower, controlled. Some might call it calm, but Svanhild knew him well enough to hear the knife's edge in every word. "It is *still* her choice whether to marry into our family or not, just as it is every woman's choice to accept a marriage proposal or decline it."

Svanhild frowned, uncertain of how to respond. Did Andor truly believe these things, or were they merely tricks of diplomacy? Perhaps a lifetime of living with his father had made him a bear tamer, skilled at diffusing conflicts. But she did not want any part of that.

As Ulrik continued to glare at her, Andor took a few paces to stand beside her. "Svanhild has fought a brave battle today," he said.

When his eyes swept to Thorbjorn, he put a hand around her waist just as Thorbjorn had done a moment ago. Another time, Svanhild would have enjoyed the feeling of Andor's hands on her, but now she just felt claimed.

Thorbjorn's eyes flashed as he stared at Andor. Svanhild winced in anticipation of the two men exchanging insults, but instead, Thorbjorn just grinned. Everything was a game to him.

Svanhild looked around at the crowd still gathered around them. What did they think of this scene? Did they see Ulrik's cruelty, or did they think this a minor argument? Did they have any idea of his true nature?

She had hoped to win the people's favor today, but her time was cut short—again. She only hoped people saw the truth of who Ulrik was, if only for a heartbeat. If the gods were truly on her side, these people might lift their weapons with her when she returned from Uppsala, her uncle and his warriors at her back, ready to kill this pretend jarl and reclaim the high-seat of Kaldvik.

"It is almost time for the rites of sacrifice," Andor continued, tearing his gaze from Thorbjorn, who continued grinning at him. Andor took a moment to study his father then, as though to judge whether or not the bear had been tamed. "Let us rest and gather our families as we prepare to honor the gods tonight."

A few people shifted and muttered, but nobody left. Ulrik seemed frozen in place, breathing hard but evenly. Svanhild thought at least his face was not as red as before.

After an odd pause, Thorbjorn clapped his hands over his head. "That is why we are all here, isn't it? To honor the gods?" He swept his wild gaze around the crowd. When they still didn't budge, he leapt towards them, yelping like a dog nipping at ankles, until they startled and backed away. Gradually they trickled away from the scene, casting curious glances over their shoulders as they left.

After a moment, only Svanhild, Andor, Ulrik, and Thorbjorn remained. Andor removed his arm from around Svanhild's waist, then shot a look at Thorbjorn she had never witnessed before. Though she could not read what was in his eyes, Thorbjorn responded with a laugh before stalking off, leaving them alone.

Ulrik grabbed Svanhild's arm, squeezing so tight she winced in pain. "You will not fight like that again," he snarled, his voice low now. "You may belong to my son, but don't underestimate the torment I can unleash on your family if you misbehave like this again."

"What are you doing?" Andor snapped, pulling his father's hand from Svanhild's arm. Now that they no longer had an audience, the anger escaped. "Remember, Svanhild will soon be my wife. And you are a jarl."

"You are lucky you were even allowed at this blót," Ulrik growled to Svanhild. Then, to Andor, he asked, "Why did you let her out of your sight?"

"She is a free woman," Andor scoffed. He turned to Svanhild. "We should speak."

Ulrik's eyes clouded in a way Svanhild had never seen before. "You don't keep secrets from me, do you, son?" he asked. Far from being threatening, his tone was almost sad.

"Of course not, Father. Let me take Svanhild for a walk. I think we all need to cool down right now. We will be back in time for the feast."

Ulrik grunted his agreement before storming away. Svanhild wondered at how her betrothal must rankle him, even though it was his idea. He may have longed to punish her, but he could not abuse his son's future wife. He hadn't been afraid to hit her in private and shout at her in public, though.

Although she would not admit it out loud, his threat against her family did worry her. When she left for Uppsala, what would happen to her mother and sisters?

She shook the thoughts from her head. She needed to focus on her plans today.

"You are good at handling your father," she said to Andor. "How long does it usually take to remove his teeth?"

He glared at her. Where she had expected to see warmth, all she saw was ice. "No more games, Svanhild. Let's walk."

CHAPTER 28

BRYNJA

*T*he sacrifices began at dusk.

Brynja clutched her cape around her as the wind picked up, the moon rising in the night sky overhead. Although the days grew longer now, the hour of dusk still brought back winter's chill. The sacrifices this evening would honor the gods and awaken the sun, bringing the first breath of spring.

She was relieved Olaf was no longer here, for Ulrik had called him to stand as one of his guards during the rites. He had pestered her all day, following her around and making sure she didn't stray far from Ulrik's tent. More than once, he had grabbed her around the waist to pull her close when she tried to wander a few paces away from him, laughing as though she were a cat he was trying to catch. She was thankful her mother was always nearby to give him a warning look, which made him stop.

But in the end, she had never had time for that dice game with Erik.

Now the people of Kaldvik gathered around a large fire pit roaring in front of the sacred elm tree. Its twisted branches were just beginning to green with fresh leaves, stretched towards the sky like fingers scraping at the doors of Asgard, beckoning the gods to come out. A pair of ravens perched in the upper branches to watch the ceremony. Though Brynja had never paid much attention to the gods, even she knew these were Odin's ravens, Huginn and Muninn.

Thought and memory. Her mind was filled with them.

At the last blót, her father had presided over the rituals alongside Gorm, sacrificing nine goats before making toasts to the gods Odin, Njörd, and Freyr. Brynja had stood in this same spot at the front of the crowd, her view of the sacrifices all too clear. She hated to see the animals killed. But she knew their deaths were honorable, for they were offerings to the gods, their blood blessing the people and their meat providing food for tonight's sacred feast.

Haldis stood in front of the fire, the priest Gorm on one side and Jarl Ulrik on the other. Brynja shuddered at how powerful her sister looked as she presided over the sacrifices, her black hood casting shadows over her opposite-colored eyes. She had never seen Haldis in this position as a leader of the ceremony before.

As much as Brynja tried to ignore the presence of the gods, she felt them here tonight. And Haldis had brought them. The power of the völva was with her now.

"Tonight, we make offerings to the gods to bless our people and our home," Haldis said. Though her voice was high-pitched, it carried on the wind like a song. "In this tree, Odin's ravens have come to witness our sacrifice. The gods are with us."

Several people lifted their ale horns in agreement. In response, the wind howled in the trees, a call from the gods. It blew Brynja's cloak around her legs and whipped her hair across her face. She clutched the cape tighter around her, trying to keep all of the skin below her neck covered from the cold. Already her nose and lips had gone numb.

Yet even half frozen, she was glad to be outside. *Free.*

She closed her eyes for a moment, letting the breeze chill her. If she allowed herself, she could imagine everything was as it had been last year—her mother standing on one side, Svanhild on the other. Her father and Haldis at the front, looking out at their people. Alf, Ursula, and all the other thralls and servants who made up their household were there with mead in their horns, enjoying the celebrations and taking time for prayer. Every life was sacred. Everyone was glad to be there.

Everything was as it should be.

When she opened her eyes, the memory was gone. Nothing was the same.

Tears burned her eyes, but the wind whisked them away as soon as they dropped. She felt her mother's arm around her, squeezing her in a show of support. Whatever Brynja felt, her mother must feel it too. The memories tonight were almost too strong to bear, but perhaps that was the gods' will too. If they were truly here, maybe they wanted the people of Kaldvik to remember her father and the way things used to be.

Brynja wanted it all back so badly, her heart ached.

Servants brought a queue of nine goats to the place where Haldis, Gorm, and Ulrik stood before the gathering. Haldis took the smallest one, still a baby, in her arms. It kicked and squealed as Ulrik stepped closer. Haldis's lips moved near the goat's ears. Brynja wondered what she was saying—probably offering prayers to the gods and soothing words to the poor creature.

Then Ulrik drew his sacred knife and sliced the goat's throat. The gesture was quick and harsh, much more violent than the way her father used to slide his blade during sacrifices.

The goat went limp in Haldis's arms.

The gothi Gorm held a bowl beneath the goat to collect the blood that flowed from its throat. Another goat, larger, was brought before Ulrik then. This one was too large to fit in Haldis's arms, so she kept cradling the first while Ulrik killed the second, then the next, until all nine goats were sacrificed. A servant then took the goats' bodies to be cut and roasted for their meal tonight.

Meanwhile, Haldis took the bowl of blood from Gorm. She dipped a twig into the bowl, then walked through the crowd, gently splattering the blood onto people's skin. Many closed their eyes as they received the gods' blessings. Some moved their mouths in silent prayers.

While Haldis was still weaving her way through the congregation, Ulrik stepped forward and lifted his hands for attention. "We have another sacrifice tonight, someone who has been chosen to give her life as offering to the gods."

Brynja glanced at her mother, whose arm was still tight around her. Helga simply shook her head, her brow knit with the same confusion Brynja felt. Her father had never performed human sacrifice, believing such acts to be beyond his faith. *They perform such sacrifices in great blóts,* he had once told her, *but not here. Not in Kaldvik. The gods hear us even without such bloodshed.*

Ulrik waved his hand to a servant nearby, who yanked on a rope. Brynja gasped when she saw who was tied to the other end.

"Ursula," she breathed.

Her mother's body tensed, her grip on Brynja's shoulder so tight it frightened her. Brynja almost expected her to protest, but as the servant brought Ursula forward, Helga was still as a stone.

Ursula did not look like herself. Her eyes were blackened with kohl, her face smeared with paint that made it impossible to make out her expression. She staggered with more than just her age; someone had given her too much drink, or perhaps a potion to quiet her fear. As she passed, Brynja heard tiny wails issuing from her lips, like the whimper of an injured animal. Her hands were clasped in front of her where the rope tied her wrists together, the servant yanking her forward every few steps.

"Ursula," Brynja said again, a little louder once the woman was near her.

Ursula's eyes rolled toward the sky and beyond Brynja, into the crowd, as though she were trying to find the source of the noise but could not focus on anything.

"Are you all right, Ursula?" Brynja said.

It was a ridiculous question. How could she be all right? She had been driven out of her mind and prepared as a human sacrifice. The very idea of it made Brynja's blood turn to ice.

Helga's grip on Brynja's shoulder loosened, but she kept her arm around her. "It is too late," she whispered. "Ulrik will kill her anyway. This way, the gods will see her sacrifice."

Brynja stared at her mother in shock. "You will let her die?"

Helga's voice was still hushed so no one else would hear. "I have seen such sacrifices before. One day, you will too." She shook her head, watching Ursula as she was laid out on a wooden slab before Ulrik. "Some would call this cruel, but even your father knew this is how our people honor the gods."

"Do you really think this was her choice?"

"I don't know. But Ursula is a woman with faith, and she knew her days with Ulrik were numbered..."

Brynja shook herself free of her mother's grip. She couldn't watch this. Nothing her mother said could justify this. Ulrik was killing another one of their household, someone who had been nothing but loyal to them her entire life, someone they loved. Ulrik could have chosen anyone for this sacrifice—could have asked for volunteers, even—but he chose an innocent, harmless woman whose death would be like a knife in their hearts.

Tears flooded from her eyes, and she did nothing to brush them away. Turning from the spectacle, she caught sight of Haldis standing off to the side of the crowd, staring at Ursula in horror, her skin pale as bones. Even Gorm's lips were parted in surprise.

So Ulrik had not told any of them this was happening. He wanted the shock to hit them like a wall of fire, before the flames of grief engulfed them and left them no better than ashes in his hall.

She ran around the people gathered, brushing past Haldis on her way into the forest. Her sister called something to her as she left, but she didn't stop to hear it.

She could not be here. She could not watch this. Ursula had been like an aunt to her, a grandmother. Who would she weave with now?

Once Brynja was deep enough into the forest, too far to hear anything happening at the blót, she sank to her knees. A pile of pine boughs cushioned the fall, but the ground was damp where snow had melted earlier. She wanted it to freeze her, wanted to go numb to all of this.

"You care nothing for our family," she spat, looking up at the darkening sky in search of the gods. "My family believes you have plans for us, but I see the truth. You *hate* us. And I will never forget your cruelty."

She sank onto the forest floor then, sobbing. Part of her hoped her mother, Haldis—someone, *anyone*—would come to comfort her, but she remained alone. Maybe they couldn't get away. Maybe they tried to find her but got lost in the woods.

Maybe they didn't care in the same way she did.

She had always been the one in their family to cry most easily, and now her emotions threatened to crush her.

As she wiped the hot tears from her face, she heard the snap of pine boughs behind her. She sensed his presence before she glanced over her shoulder and saw him, a shadow emerging from the clearing.

She knew who it was even before she saw his face.

Olaf.

CHAPTER 29

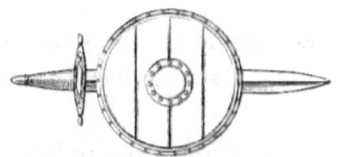

SVANHILD

The silence was unbearable.

Svanhild could have taken Andor's questions, his anger, his jealousy, even mockery—but the silence was too much. They had traversed the forest from the sacred grove all the way to the main road of the village, and neither had said a word.

Gods help her, she would *not* be the first to speak. He had warned her against playing games, but what did that mean? She prayed to the gods he didn't know of her plans to slip away to Uppsala. If he knew them, he would surely inform his father, ever the loyal son.

She kicked at a pebble with her boots. Andor watched her, his expression unreadable. She glared at him, hoping her look would taunt him into speaking. But he said nothing.

Finally, she cracked like an old vase. "What do you want?" When he didn't immediately respond, she lifted her chin. "Andor, answer me."

Instead of answering or chuckling or releasing any of the responses she expected, he simply groaned. She had never heard him groan before. Was he actually expressing anger? It would be the first time she had seen such evidence of such feeling, beyond the clench of his jaw and the storm in his eyes.

"And what does that mean?" she said, trying to bait him into saying something. "I am not well-versed in interpreting animal noises."

He stopped walking, turned toward her, and sighed. "You know, I have met many daughters of jarls over the years. One or two intended to marry me, but I refused. Do you know why?"

Svanhild stopped, her mouth opening in surprise.

He went on without waiting for her response. "They thought too highly of themselves." He paused for a moment, a small grimace on his face as though he had just realized the strength of his words. "I mean no offense to their families, and wishing them all the best in their futures..."

Svanhild waved him past his politeness. "Just say it."

"I thought they were the most spoiled, selfish creatures I had ever met." His eyes darkened. "And then I met you."

Svanhild scoffed. "After everything I have been through, you think me selfish? Haven't you seen what my family has endured–"

"I am trying to help you!" he cried, then laughed in frustration. "Why do you think I take you on these walks to get out of the longhouse? Why do you think you have a warm bed to sleep in? Why do you think you have escaped my father's punishment tonight?" He sighed, running a hand over his head. "I asked Balder to forge you an axe, for I know how important your battle training is to you. I know it's not much, but I am doing everything I can to bring you small moments of peace, Svanhild. You are to be my wife. I want to make you happy."

He drew nearer to her then and took her hands in his, his skin warm, his grip strong. She had not expected this. She could handle arguing, but this made her heartbeat quicken and her stomach flutter. Somehow his presence made her react, like a dead forest tree struck by lightning. He made something in her catch fire.

When he spoke again, his voice was softer. "I'll admit I didn't like seeing you with that warrior today. You are a free woman, and it's not my right to forbid you anything, but..." He let his voice disappear into the wind, his eyes finishing the thought.

Her breath caught in her throat, for she understood his jealousy. She would have felt the same, had she spotted Andor with another woman.

"All this time, I've wanted to hate you," she admitted. "Your father killed mine. How could I not?"

For a moment, the truth of her words made the light in his eyes flicker, like a cold wind snuffing out a candle. She saw what must be running through his mind—their long walks, their conversations, their kiss—and now he must worry it was all in his mind, none of it real because she hated him.

He had to know how her heart betrayed her. She wanted to curse Loki for playing these games with her. But she was grateful to him, too. Andor *had* made her life better these past months. Andor had helped her survive.

She looked up at the full moon in the sky, feeling the presence of Freyja and Frigg, the goddesses of lust and love. Spring was the time they came and breathed new life into people's hearts, inspiring romances. They had made her flush for Thorbjorn earlier, but this was where she was meant to be.

She cursed under her breath, for there was no more denying it.

She was in love with Andor.

His forehead knit as he tried to decipher her reaction, but she didn't give him time. Casting aside any rational thought, she kissed him.

She felt him tense at first, startled. Then his cloak wrapped around her, enveloping her as he returned the kiss. She smiled a bit at the remembered warmth of his mouth, his lips soft as he drew her in. His taste made the blood rush to her stomach, until she wanted to explore every part of him.

Beneath his own cloak, his hands slid beneath her cape, caressing her waist, holding her tighter. She felt the strength of his hands where they roamed and his arms where they held her. Her body melted against him.

Without breaking the kiss, she reached up and around his head, feeling where the sides were shaved, until she caught the hair braided behind his neck. Grasping it, she tugged gently, snapping his head back just enough that she was able to bite his lower lip. He groaned in pleasure.

Happy to have surprised him, she broke away to laugh lightly at his response.

"Do you want to find shelter?" he asked, a strange rasp in his voice.

She raised an eyebrow at the question. Was it not clear from the look in her eyes and the heat of their kiss that she wanted him now? She almost expected him to grab her, but instead he went completely still, waiting for her answer. She felt the tension in his muscles, the pain of having to wait, yet he did it for her.

She took this moment to study him. Their breath, warm between them, made clouds that cast his face in an ethereal fog. His eyes were like smoke as they watched her. His mouth was pink in the moonlight, a tiny bite mark on the lower lip. She admired his handsomeness, the strong jaw and clever gray eyes.

And right now, on this night, he was hers.

She swore to herself she would never forget this moment.

AFTER THEIR JOINING, Svanhild and Andor sat at the edge of the docks, their legs dangling over the fjord's waters. Svanhild was glad for the night breeze that cooled her flushed skin. Her whole body glowed in the wake of their actions, yet she also felt utterly spent.

They were silent for a long time. Svanhild thought she had never felt more at peace. Yet as the moon moved through the sky overhead, the reality of their situation began to sink in. As wonderful as the night was, she could not live here with Andor under Ulrik's rule. The gods had other plans for her. *She* had other plans.

As if sensing her thoughts, Andor reached over and took one of her hands in his. "Why is your mother so intent to train you?" he asked.

She looked at him in surprise. Did he suspect?

Forcing herself not to overreact, she explained, "Before she had me, my mother was a shieldmaiden. And my father trained me before her." She kicked her legs where they dangled, smiling. "Did you know, the night your father came, my father announced I would join him in battle next summer?"

"He must have respected your skill with a blade. I did, when I saw you fight today."

Svanhild frowned then. Her heart ached as she realized that, were her father still alive, they would be making preparations for their travels now. "Summer is almost here, but my father is gone."

"I am sorry to hear your grief," Andor said.

She withdrew her hand from his. "I don't want your sympathy. I want your help." She turned to look at him. "Don't you see how my people suffer under your father's rule?"

"Of course I see it." Andor sighed, gazing out at the fjord's waters as though searching for answers within their depths. "My father is a third son. He never got along with my grandfather, for he takes after my grandmother's passion. Years ago, in a raid, a Saxon warrior killed his oldest brother, the future jarl. That act sparked a bloodlust in my father. And for some reason, he wanted to rule. My grandfather never gave him much responsibility, other than raiding. In time, with enough warriors to follow him, my father saw he could take what he was not given. So he set his sights on Kaldvik. He always admired the fertile soil here."

"Is that the only reason he chose this place to attack?" Svanhild shook her head. "If only he had gone somewhere else..."

"It wasn't just the fertile soil. It was also..." Andor hesitated, as though weighing his words, before saying, "He did not respect your father the way I do."

Svanhild's blood heated at the affront, but Andor went on before she could speak.

"He did not see your father's wisdom. Or if he did, he was too foolish to respect it. He is a raider at heart, and he believed your father was weak." Andor's gray eyes sought hers then. "I am sorry for it. You know I don't agree with my father."

Svanhild glared at him. "If your father didn't respect him, why did he sneak in to murder my father in the middle of the night? He should have brought his ships during the day and battled all of my father's warriors. Or he should have challenged my father to holmgang..."

"I agree. But I had no say in it. Olaf is his advisor, and he thinks trickery is a smart tactic in war."

"Your father is a coward," she spat.

Andor stiffened at the insult, but his voice was calm when he spoke again. "I am sorry for what happened to your father, Svanhild. But this is what jarls do. They kill and conquer. It's ugly, and I don't agree with my father's actions, but..." He sighed again, running a hand over his head. "He spared your family afterwards."

Svanhild couldn't believe it. Did he really think keeping their family alive was an act of mercy? "Of course he keeps us alive," she said, "so the people of Kaldvik think we are with him. The people who put their trust in *our* family." In the moonlight, she caught Andor's jaw tightening, but he said nothing in response. She went on, "I was supposed to rule after my father. There may be some people who still believe my family is meant to lead here. That is why your father keeps us close. Or are you so blind you don't see that?"

"So you would have been jarl after your father," Andor said, as though thinking it over.

Svanhild nodded. If her father were alive now, she would be learning to rule. Perhaps she had preferred sharpening her sword to sharpening her mind, but she knew that being jarl was her fate.

"I thought I had more time to learn," she said. "I trained to be a shieldmaiden. Proving myself in battle was the first step in leading the people."

"Then we will lead together, Svanhild. You and me in the high-seats. I know your people are suffering, but look at how much we have accomplished already when the two of us are united. I believe this is the gods' destiny for us."

Svanhild pictured it then, ruling with Andor, traveling with him, helping the people. It was not an unhappy image—

except that she was marrying into the family that killed her father.

"In the meantime," Andor continued, "we can travel together. Seek out new places."

"In the meantime?" she asked.

"Until my father's rule ends."

She swallowed in a dry throat. Andor had a pretty idea of their future, but he would never overthrow his father. She admired his loyalty, but she could never forgive Ulrik the way he did.

Her mind drifted as Andor's voice filled the night air with stories about their life together. It was a fantasy. As long as Ulrik drew breath, her family would suffer. Even if they eventually garnered his trust, they would never feel truly free with Ulrik in charge. Her mother would likely be forced to remain his concubine, unless she managed to escape Kaldvik altogether. Brynja would suffer in whatever marriage Ulrik forced on her. And what would happen to Haldis in such a godless house?

Perhaps things would get better once she and Andor ruled, but that would be many years from now. Too many.

And if she stayed, she would become a daughter by marriage to her father's murderer.

She shuddered at the thought.

"I can't marry you." The words spilled out of her before she had a chance to bite them back. As soon as she said them, they felt right.

From the sky, she thought she heard a laugh. *Loki.* The trickster god had anticipated this day.

"I agreed to marry you to save my family," she explained. "But I don't know if I can be wife to the son of my father's killer."

Part of her wanted to spill everything, to tell Andor of her plans, to see if she could win him to her side. But it was too dangerous. She knew he would remain loyal to his father until the end—and even if Ulrik were dead, he would never escape his father's shadow.

Still, admitting she did not want to marry him was a lot to accept.

Andor did not answer for a long time. She tried to read his expression, but in profile it was even harder to make out his feelings than when he was facing her. She studied the Yggdrasil tattoo curving above his ear, that symbol of wisdom he wished the world to see. She had witnessed it too many times to count.

"I have grown to respect you," she said softly, reaching out to take his hand again. "You are not your father."

Andor yanked his hand away, a harsh chuckle escaping his lips. "And yet you judge me by my father's actions." He shook his head. "I cannot pretend your stubbornness surprises me, but the confession that you do not wish to marry me still stings."

"I'm telling you because I respect you. And you were the one to tell me I am still free to choose. You do not hold me prisoner like your father does."

Andor climbed to his feet, his gaze directed at the water rather than at her. "I need time to think, Svanhild." He looked at the longhouse then, lit from within on the other end of the long road. A few people were beginning to enter from the forest. "Let's not speak any more of this tonight."

When he offered his hand to help her up, she took it.

Once they were standing together, he finally looked at her. "Svanhild, you know I love you, right?"

The words brought stinging tears to her eyes. She blinked them away, wanting to answer but unable to find the words.

She needed to decide what to do now. She couldn't think

clearly with him staring at her, making her heart ache like this.

"I'd like to visit my father's burial mound," she said. "I'll be back at the hall soon."

Andor blinked in surprise. Had he expected her to say the words back to him? But just as quickly his jaw set and he was back to his stoic self. "My father will be upset to see me return without you."

"Hold him for me?"

Andor nodded. After casting her a last warning look, he turned and began the walk back to the longhouse.

So this is what it felt like to be alone.

JARL TOVE'S burial mound was in the forest clearing where the funeral had been held. A grassy mound here, just big enough to cover his body in its burial chamber, rested among others belonging to their family's ancestors.

Svanhild knelt in the grass before the mound. A ring of stones encircled it, forming a sharp oval with the largest stones on either end. The arrangement of stones was meant to look like a ship, in honor of her father's love of travel. If anyone were to happen upon this burial, they might think the man inside a raider, but Svanhild and the people of Kaldvik knew who Jarl Tove truly was.

That, she realized, was what she wanted for her life. She would be a shieldmaiden, but she could not be a mindless killer. If the gods wanted her to fight, it was for her family. She would protect her sisters. She would keep her mother safe from Ulrik's greedy gaze. She would liberate them and make Kaldvik the land of the ravens again.

And now she had more time.

With her wedding to Andor off, she was free to gather supporters on her own timeline. Summer would be the best season to leave for Uppsala, when Ulrik was away raiding with the warriors who had pledged to him. That would help her target people who preferred her family to his, for they would be the ones left behind in Kaldvik. It would be easier to escape in the summer, too.

A pair of ravens cawed from the trees overhead. She took it as a sign that Odin heard her and blessed her plan.

Thank you, All-Father, she thought.

Her mind whipped around to Andor then. She touched her lips, the memories of tonight warming her again. He'd said he loved her, and she had not returned the words.

She closed her eyes, squeezing them tight to banish the feelings from her body and heart. She did not want to love Andor Ulrikson.

But she did.

She did not want to understand his loyalty to his father, either—but she did. Ulrik and Andor were like fire and ice, and yet she knew Andor would never lift his sword against his father. Like her, Andor was loyal to those he loved. And for some reason, he loved his father. Family bonds were hard to break.

As Svanhild contemplated what to do about Andor, she heard a muffled yelp from somewhere in the trees. Though the sound was smothered in the wind, she sensed it was nearby. At first, she thought it was a cry of passion from a pair who were honoring the goddesses tonight.

Then she heard a man's voice, rough and angry. "Quiet!"

Svanhild jumped to her feet and followed the noise into the forest. The tussle of leaves and snapping of pine boughs guided her steps.

Then she saw them. Olaf's broad back was unmistakable even in the darkness, for he had a bear-like figure similar to Ulrik's.

And beneath him was Brynja, struggling to break free.

Svanhild registered what was happening in her body more than her mind. Everything inside her sparked, and she acted without having to think.

Grabbing the pocket knife from her dress, she crept around Olaf's back.

As she drew near, she caught Brynja's eye. Just in time, she put a finger to her lips. Any recognition on Brynja's face disappeared as she continued to squirm.

Olaf grunted as he tried to pin her limbs to the ground, oblivious that anyone was behind him.

Svanhild leaned close to Olaf. Taking a deep breath to steady her hand, she thrust the knife into his throat.

The blade caught—just for a breath—as it fought against his skin. Then it sank into his throat.

Brynja cried out as blood splashed across her face.

Olaf hollered too, but the action was too final for him to fight back. Air wheezed from his lungs and blood spurted from his neck.

Svanhild yanked the knife free and stood behind Brynja, looking down at Olaf's final struggle.

His eyes went wide when he saw her. His mouth opened, but no words came out.

Issuing a final gasp, he crumpled on top of Brynja.

Svanhild stood motionless for a moment, her heart pounding. As she looked down at her knife, still slick with blood, her hand began to shake.

Then she saw her sister's eyes filling with tears. She sprang into action again.

Taking hold of her Brynja's shoulders, she used all her strength to pull her out from under Olaf's body.

As soon as she was liberated, Brynja scurried backwards across the forest floor, distancing herself as much as she could from his body. She never took her eyes off him.

Finally Brynja's back hit a tree trunk. Only then did she

stop and hug her knees to her chest, as though she wished to fold into herself and disappear. Tears streamed down her face.

Kneeling beside her, Svanhild put an arm around her shoulders. "Are you all right?"

Brynja nodded wordlessly.

Svanhild wanted to ask what had happened, but she already knew. Olaf had been eyeing Brynja for months. It was only a matter of time before he tried something like this.

She had failed her sister. She was the oldest, the protector, the one who was supposed to right wrongs and keep her younger sisters safe. With her father gone and Helga forced to play at Ulrik's side, her duty was more important than ever.

She should have seen this coming.

"I'm sorry," Svanhild whispered, kissing the side of Brynja's head in hopes it would comfort her. "I should have protected you better. I should have watched over you. I knew how he looked at you, and yet I did nothing. I am so sorry."

Brynja leaned her head against Svanhild's shoulder as sobs shook her body. Svanhild continued to hold onto her, letting her cry.

They sat like that for what felt like a long time, the wind howling around them. Both of them stared at Olaf's body where it lay face down in the dirt.

Svanhild tried to think of what to do next, but her mind was blank, her hands shaking, her body numb with cold. All she could do now was stay here with Brynja, her brave little sister who had watched her father killed, then poor Alf, and now *this*... It was too much.

Finally Brynja's voice broke the silence. "You can't stay here anymore."

Svanhild leaned away to look at her. "What do you mean?"

"When they find Olaf here, they'll come after you. Ulrik will not forgive you for this. If he finds out the whole story, he might kill us all." She looked down at her dress and cloak; they were drenched in Olaf's blood. "I can't go to the hall like this. He will know as soon as he sees me."

Svanhild removed her own cloak, which was untouched by the blood. "Take mine." After Brynja had removed her cloak too, Svanhild draped hers over her sister's shoulders. "Hold it around you to cover your dress. Get back to the longhouse before anyone sees and change into a new dress."

Brynja nodded, her gaze on Olaf again. "Yes. Everyone else is still at the blót." Her voice sounded distant, like someone speaking far away, the sound only drifting over on the wind.

Svanhild gave her shoulder a squeeze. "You are brave, Brynja. You have seen too much bloodshed in one year."

"Ulrik killed Ursula," she blurted then. "He sacrificed her to the gods."

Svanhild shut her eyes, shuddering at the thought. Ursula had taught them all how to work the loom and sew, and Brynja had spent many hours at her side this winter. Her death was now one more thing the poor girl had to witness.

"I am sorry," Svanhild said. "Ulrik is a monster."

The heat of rage filled her then, pumping the blood through her body faster than before. She clutched the amber pendant around her neck, the one her father had given her the night he died, drawing strength from it.

Brynja was right. Once Ulrik found out she had killed Olaf, he would never allow her to live.

She needed to leave tonight.

The crunch of footsteps in the forest made Svanhild's mouth go dry.

"Is someone there?" came a man's voice from the nearby trees.

Someone must have heard Brynja's cry when she killed Olaf. It would not be long before people crossed this path and found his body...

She jumped to her feet, then reached down to help Brynja up too.

"We need to get away from here," she whispered. "Fast."

CHAPTER 30

HALDIS

*I*n the warmth of the hall, Haldis felt dizzy. The smoke choked her lungs until it was difficult to breathe. Everywhere she looked, revelers were toasting, drinking, talking, and laughing. The buzz of activity and noise so great she could barely choose where to look first. The world rushed around her like a spinning wheel, and she was the spoke.

She stumbled toward the central hearth, where a great cauldron hung from the ceiling. Gorm, along with a few of Ulrik's servants, were stirring the pot, preparing the goat meat from the sacrifices. The smell of roasting meat, mixed with the spices they added for flavor, was overpowering.

But she had to do this. No matter how her mind reeled with memories of Ursula's death, she had to carry out this one final task to show the people of Kaldvik that she was, and would continue to be, their völva. Chosen by the gods. Friend of Odin.

The idea of it made her want to laugh, then cry.

Gorm motioned her to the cauldron. "It is time for the toasts," he said.

As if cued for the performance, a thrall handed her an ale horn filled with mead. She closed her eyes briefly to remember the traditional toasts to the gods, which Gorm usually performed before the feasts. Now, it was her turn to take over such duties.

When she opened her eyes, she glanced at Gorm and forced a smile of gratitude. He could have been jealous of her rise today, but instead, he had guided her hand, taken over when she felt overwhelmed, read her every emotion and acted as her mentor, never stealing the attention from her. When Ursula had been brought out for the sacrifice, she was afraid to watch, worried she might faint at the sight. Gorm had given her a single look—eyes narrowing, then a nod— and she had known he would handle everything for her. She remained watching from the crowd, safely away from any duties she would have otherwise been forced to perform, while Gorm held Ursula's hands against the slab and Ulrik sliced her throat.

Catching her expression now, Gorm gave her a nod of understanding. She wasn't sure she had ever seen him smile, but it was enough that he accepted her thanks.

Gorm hit a spoon against the side of the cauldron to call for attention. The din of chatter and laughter died down as all eyes turned to them.

Haldis lifted her ale horn for the toasts. "Tonight, we thank the gods for all the abundance they have provided us," she said.

Though she trembled with nerves, her voice was steady, as if the gods were truly speaking through her tonight. She did not have to think hard about the words, memorized from past ceremonies, as they spilled from her lips.

"A toast to Odin the All-Father. May he share his wisdom with us and guide us to victory in battle. And to Njörd and Freyr, that they bless our harvests and gift us a peaceful future."

Everyone lifted their horns and cups to toast, and a round of, "Skol," erupted.

Haldis poured her cup of mead onto the floor of the hall then, leading everyone else to do so too. The drink splattered on the floor like heavy rainfall as offering to the gods.

One man stepped forward then, a red-haired warrior who had flirted with Svanhild the night of Ulrik's attack. His hair and beard were better combed now, though his face was pink from drinking all day.

Lifting his cup in the air, he shouted for everyone in the hall to hear. "I pledge to honor the gods with my axe, should Jarl Ulrik choose me to join him in his raids. I will do all I can to bring honor to our new leader and our land, even if it means giving up my life one day in battle."

In the periphery of her vision, Haldis spotted Brynja slipping from the back of the longhouse into the main hall. Her younger sister kept to the shadows, sliding behind a pillar before finding her mother in the crowd.

Something about her seemed different.

That's when Haldis noticed she was no longer wearing the beautiful green gown she had donned for the blót, but a rough-spun brown dress, more fitting for a day of chores than a ceremony. Why had she changed clothes?

Haldis glanced at Ulrik then. He was too busy beaming at the warrior's pledge of loyalty to notice Brynja's stealthy entrance from the back of the longhouse.

Around the room, several men joined in the warrior's pledge. As one they poured their mead onto the floor as offering, marking their intentions. Jarl Ulrik clapped his hands for them.

"It is good to hear your desire to raid with me," he said. "I will be glad to have your blades join mine when we leave to make war this summer."

There was a roar of approval as other men lifted their cups and horns, signaling they, too, wished to raid with their new jarl.

Haldis smelled Ulrik's approach, a stench of damp wool and ale, before she felt his heavy fur cloak brush against her shoulder. She stepped aside as he cast a shadow over her, wanting to give him as much berth as she could.

She had always thought him a beast, but tonight he proved himself capable of more manipulation and cruelty than she had thought possible. Having him next to her now—leading their people, smiling as though all was well—made her skin itch and her stomach churn.

And these people were ready to follow him into battle.

She looked around for Svanhild to judge her reaction, but her sister was nowhere to be seen.

A darkness passed over her then, like a shadow that was felt rather than seen. Something was not right here. A strange fear gripped her heart as she scanned the crowd, hoping to spot strong men who refused to offer their support of Ulrik, men who remained loyal to her family...

All the breath flew from Haldis then, and in a haze of smoke she collapsed to her knees. Everything went dark. She heard a few concerned voices around her, but soon they dimmed to nothing.

And then she was by the lake. The moon shone overhead. All was still, except a gentle breeze on her skin and the call of a raven overhead.

It took a moment for her to notice she was moving, and then all at once she felt her wings outstretched, the wind rushing under them to keep her in flight. The lake passed below her as she soared higher.

The raven called again, but this time, she recognized the source.

She was the raven.

She flew over the village, moonlight guiding her way. Soon, she was over the fjord. As she followed the water south, the sky changed from night to the bright pink of dawn in an instant, shifting then to sunlight, as if time were moving more quickly than normal.

She continued flying south. Day turned to night, and then night became day again. She journeyed to a fork in the river and, by instinct, took the path to the left. A few more days, and she spotted a boat reaching the shores of a great city.

Uppsala. She recognized it from the great blót she had attended so many years before. Grand wooden structures—many bigger than their own longhouse in Kaldvik—lined the wide roads where people had set up stalls to sell their wares. The streets were packed with people.

She slowed, wings flapping to keep her in place above the commotion.

On one of the roads that ran through town was Svanhild, leading a pack of warriors through the streets. She must be on her way to find Asmund. She had made it.

A blond man walked at her side, his disheveled hair strangely familiar to Haldis. She tried to catch a glimpse of his face, but all she felt was a strange dread in her stomach, the same feeling she had the night her father died.

Though this seemed a promise from the gods, could it be a warning, too?

The scene below her grew foggy, then vanished like smoke.

She blinked. The smell of roasting meat brought her back to the hall, where several sets of eyes peered down at her. Helga, Brynja, and Gorm hovered over her. But the face she wanted to see was Svanhild's. She needed to tell her of her vision.

"Where is Svanhild?" The words came out of her like a cough.

"She is not here," Helga said in a hushed voice.

Brynja handed her a wooden cup of water. Haldis forced herself to sit up and drink it. She realized now that she had been carried off to the side of the main hall, sheltered by a pillar. Brynja cast nervous glances over her shoulder.

"Why are you wearing that dress?" Haldis whispered. "What is going on?"

"I will tell you later," Brynja replied.

A few paces away, Ulrik stood leading more toasts as thralls wove through the gathering bearing plates of roasted meat. Vaguely she remembered she was suppose to drop the sacrificial blood into their ale horns…

But that was not important now. She needed to find Svanhild and tell her what she saw.

The doors of the longhouse suddenly blew open as a man and woman rushed inside. They were hand-in-hand, clearly just come from a tryst in the woods. But they stood panting as the doors slammed shut behind them, as though they had just been running from a bear.

The man looked wild-eyed as he shouted, "Jarl Ulrik!"

Ulrik stopped the toasts to look at the man. "Why do you interrupt our celebration?"

"Your housecarl Olaf!" the man continued, rushing forward through the parting crowd until he fell at Ulrik's feet. "I saw him in the forest. Someone stabbed him in the throat!"

Haldis's blood went cold at his words.

"What do you mean, someone stabbed him?" Ulrik said.

"He's dead."

The longhouse grew quiet in the wake of the man's news.

Brynja turned pale. The wooden cup she held fell from her hands and clattered on the floor.

Helga looked at Brynja. "My daughter," she said slowly, keeping her voice just above a whisper, "where is Svanhild?"

"She saved me," was all Brynja said.

Haldis's heart thundered in her chest.

Helga held her hand to her mouth in sudden realization. Svanhild was behind this.

Behind them, Ulrik motioned to his guards. "Search for the killer," he ordered. Then, louder to the crowd, he added, "To anyone here who wishes to help in this matter, may the gods reward your loyalty. Tonight, we feast to honor the gods, but this crime will not go unpunished."

Several men in the hall left with the guards to search for Olaf's murderer. The rest of the gathering remained, their voices lifting as they gradually began talking with one another about what had just transpired.

Ulrik's gaze swiveled to Haldis, and he snapped his fingers at them all. "Where is your sister?" he growled.

Haldis merely shook her head. She could not find her voice.

Before anyone could respond, Ulrik barked at a nearby guard, "Tell the others to find Svanhild and bring her back to the hall. I can't have these women out of my sight tonight."

The guard nodded his agreement before leaving out the side door.

Haldis glanced at her mother and sister then. Ulrik didn't know yet. Perhaps if Svanhild was found and brought back without a fight, Ulrik would never suspect she was the one to kill Olaf...

But that was not the will of the gods, and she knew it.

Once Ulrik had returned to the feast, Brynja whispered, "She is leaving tonight."

Haldis wanted to tell her the vision, but there was no way now. They had finally run out of time.

She clasped hands with her mother and sister, the three of them forming a circle. They had woven their plans for months. They had made their offering to the gods just this morning. Now, it was time for action.

Haldis only wished she had the chance to say good bye.

"It is the gods' will," she said. "May Odin watch over her."

CHAPTER 31

BRYNJA

*B*rynja felt more herself once she was in a clean dress, but the events of the night still tormented her.

She had snatched the first dress she found in her chest, not caring what it looked like, barely able to think. Then, she had waited until everyone returned to the longhouse for the feast. Though she was ready to slip into the crowd as soon as they arrived, the sound of her sister's voice leading everyone in toasts to the gods made her stop.

She would not toast the gods again. Not after tonight.

When she finally slipped into the main hall, she could have sworn she spotted Haldis looking at her. Was it so obvious she was in a different dress? She hoped no one else noticed.

There was no way to tell her mother what had happened to her. But when Helga saw the tears in her eyes, she hugged her, probably assuming they were tears for Ursula.

They *were* for Ursula. They were for everything.

The gods had truly forsaken them. That much, she knew.

Now, the hall was abuzz with the news that Ulrik's housecarl was killed. Guards were already out looking for Svanhild. How long until they realized the truth?

Shaking off memories of Ursula and Olaf, Brynja forced down a bite of goat meat. She sat beside her sister near the front of the feast, close to the jarl's table. She hoped Ulrik would not look at her and wonder about Olaf. Had he seen his housecarl chase her into the forest during the sacrifices? Surely he was too distracted to catch that. But Olaf had been after her all day, and if Ulrik noticed her new dress, what would he think?

She forced another bite of food. The soft meat melted on her tongue, and she devoured a few more bites, surprising herself. She didn't think she could feel hunger after everything she had been through tonight, but perhaps the turmoil left her body weak and needy for sustenance.

"Is anyone standing yet?" she whispered to Haldis.

Her sister nodded toward a pair of warriors striding from one table to another. A few others were rising now too, finding friends in the crowd and sharing quiet toasts.

It was time, then. Brynja had one task tonight: to find Balder and tell him to meet Svanhild at Skarde's house. That was the one promise she had made to her sister, the shieldmaiden who had saved her life.

She wondered when she would see Svanhild again.

She would not let her down now.

Ignoring her growling stomach, she rose and found the blacksmith seated at a table near the front doors of the hall. That was good, for he was far away from Ulrik who sat across the hall at the jarl's table.

Remaining in the shade of the nearest pillar, she waved her hand to draw his attention. A man next to him saw her first and winked. She ignored him, pointing her eyes toward Balder. Realizing, the man made a disappointed face, then nudged the blacksmith in the ribs and motioned to Brynja.

Balder stood and joined her in the shadows then. Thankfully, a few others were standing and chatting, ale horns in hand, which made Bryna and Balder less conspicuous. And from her position behind the pillar, she couldn't quite see Ulrik—which meant he could not see her, either.

"Brynja," said the blacksmith, his rumbling voice full of surprise. "What news do you bring me?"

"My sister Svanhild wishes to meet you and other supporters at Skarde's house. We have run out of time."

Balder frowned. "Has something happened?"

Brynja nodded. "I can't go into details here, but it's important that you leave tonight. Ulrik cannot see Svanhild again."

The blacksmith's jaw twitched, and in his eyes Brynja saw the understanding. He knew what had happened.

That meant it would not be hard for others to figure it out too.

Svanhild did not have much time.

He gave her one curt nod of agreement. There was no need to discuss more. Brynja was grateful at how ready he was.

"Do you know how many men my sister can expect?" she asked.

Balder's eyes scanned the room for a moment, pausing here and there as they alighted on possible allies. Then he said, "At least four or five. Fish-Nose found more, but it's difficult to call on men in the midst of a feast. Some will not be prepared, and the jarl will notice too much commotion."

Brynja didn't answer. Four or five did not sound like enough warriors, but she understood the challenge of gathering men with such unexpected haste. There was no point in discussing it more. Just as there was no point in admitting she had no use for the gods anymore, that they had brought her nothing but pain of late. If Balder needed them to feel courageous, let him have his gods.

She would rely only on herself.

As Balder strode away to find Svanhild's supporters, she felt a tap on her shoulder. Spinning around, she found herself face to face with Erik, who grinned at her in greeting.

She smiled in surprise. Though she opened her mouth to say hello, no sound came out. Instead, a lump formed in her throat, and she bit her tongue as hard as she could to hold back the avalanche of tears that threatened to burst from her eyes.

Erik's smile faded. Then, seeing what was happening on her face, he enveloped her in a hug.

"It's all right," he whisperered into her hair. "Whatever happened, it's going to be okay."

A small sob escaped her, and she felt the hot tears wet his shoulder. Her fingers on his back slid against the handle of his axe. It was still so strange to her that he carried a weapon, but she was grateful of his presence now. She felt safe with him—perhaps moreso now than ever.

"Thank you," she whispered back.

When they finally parted, Erik asked, "Do you want to tell me what happened?"

She shook her head. "We can't. Not now."

"I understand. What were you discussing with Balder just now? Is it what I think?"

She let out a shaky breath, drying the last of her tears. She didn't want to draw anyone's attention with her crying. Glancing over at Ulrik, she was relieved to find him engaged in conversation with his wife, oblivious of her across the room.

Still, she froze when she noticed a pair of sharp blue eyes

watching her. It was the warrior Thorbjorn, leaning against a nearby pillar with an ale horn in his hands. When a thrall approached him to refill his horn with more mead, he waved her away.

Seeing Brynja looking back at him, he grinned and lifted his horn as though to toast her.

"My sister is leaving tonight," she said to Erik, keeping her voice quiet. She noticed Thorbjorn shifting in the shadows, drawing a little closer. She hoped he would not start pestering her for a dance later. For now, she ignored him. "Balder is collecting supporters."

Erik frowned. "I didn't realize it would be tonight."

"Neither did we," Brynja replied. Glancing around to make sure no one would overhear, she then whispered, "They are searching for Olaf's killer. They cannot find her. That's why she needs to leave tonight."

Erik's green eyes narrowed for a moment, then lit in understanding. "It was *her*?"

Brynja just nodded. She did not dare tell him what happened to her in the forest, what Olaf tried to do to her, why Svanhild had killed him. Not with so many people around to overhear. Not when it was still so fresh that she could barely keep the tears from her eyes. Perhaps when he returned, they could finally sit together by the fjord again and share everything. But not tonight.

"What will happen he finds out?" Erik asked.

Brynja looked at where Ulrik sat with his family across the hall. "I hope he doesn't."

"It will be good, if he thinks she is only escaping because of Olaf," said Erik. "Let him suspect nothing else of her plans, right?"

Brynja had not thought of that. "That's a good point. I just wish she had Father's sword with her."

Erik gave her a sad smile. "I'm sorry for all that you have

been through. And about Ursula. I know how much she meant to you."

She bit back more tears, nodding to him. "Thank you."

"I wish I could stay and protect you, but I have a feeling you can do that yourself. Stay strong while I'm gone."

She gave him another quick hug, knowing it might be the last time she saw him for months. "I expect you back here with all your limbs," she said.

"Don't worry, I'm very attached to them," he joked back.

She stuck her tongue out at him, feeling a small flicker of happiness at his presence. Despite the fear that gripped her heart and the grief over all that had happened, she believed now that he had what he needed to be a strong fighter.

"You know what my father used to say about warriors?" she said.

He shook his head.

"The greatest warriors are the ones strongest of heart." She smiled at him. "You have always been strong of heart. That's how I know you will be great."

Erik's back straightened at her words, a fresh smile flickering on his face. She had not seen this expression on him before, but she sensed it was a warrior's confidence. Her heart warmed to see him there, clad in armor with an axe on his back, ready to fight for the honor of her family.

"I am lucky to have you as a friend," she said.

"Indeed you are," he replied with a wink.

She laughed.

The front doors of the longhouse suddenly opened, bringing a gust of cold air from outside. Andor strode in with heavy footsteps, flanked by two of Ulrik's cloaked guards. With the swirling tattoos curving around his ear and his fur cloak billowing behind him, he reminded her now of a raider. She wondered if his father's cruelty ran like iron in his veins.

Many pairs of eyes watched him as he made his way to Ulrik's table at the far end of the hall. Though his voice was not loud when he spoke, enough people had hushed in the hall for Brynja to make out his words.

"We cannot find Svanhild," he said.

Ulrik's face reddened. "How can you not find her?"

"There are still men searching, but so far we have only discovered two couples who were clearly engaged in some harmless activities tonight. They knew nothing of Olaf's murder."

The two men bent their foreheads closer together to speak more privately. Voices picked up around the hall, making it impossible for Brynja to make out more of their conversation. But she didn't like the look of growing rage on Ulrik's face, like a blood stain blossoming across a cloth.

Erik placed a hand on her shoulder. "It sounds like we need to hurry, and Balder is already leaving the hall," he said. "When I see you again…"

She swallowed, nodding. When they saw each other again, it would be the time for war.

"Tell my sister I expect the same from her," she said. "All your limbs."

CHAPTER 32

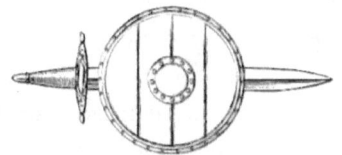

SVANHILD

Svanhild's hands shook as she waited by the fjord, pacing back and forth over the dock beside Skarde's house. She had been trembling ever since she left Brynja in the forest.

So she was a killer now. Was this what it felt like to be a warrior? She always knew being a shieldmaiden would require bloodshed, but the way she killed Olaf—sneaking up behind him and stabbing him in the throat with a knife— would not win her a seat in Valhalla.

Perhaps she should have fought Olaf face to face, but how could she? In the surprise of seeing her sister struggling beneath him, she had reacted on instinct, her body working while her mind barely processed what was happening.

She told herself Olaf was not honorable. She told herself he deserved the death she gave him. She had saved her sister —and that part, she would never regret.

Yet still her hands trembled as she paced, unable to stop moving, barely able to breathe.

The wind sliced at her skin. When her teeth began to chatter, she knew it was more than the cold that made her feel so shaky.

Someone must be looking for her by now. Skarde's house sat perched on the shore, surrounded by trees, with only this small dock leading into the fjord. The wooden boards creaked beneath her boots as she treaded back and forth, her sister's blood-stained cape billowing behind her in the breeze. If anyone came to this small clearing now, she would be easy to spot, a silhouette against the water.

Yet she needed to keep moving. She needed to get away from this place. She could not hold still.

She wondered what would happen when Ulrik discovered Olaf's body in the forest. Would he suspect her, when people found her missing from the blót?

Her mind flitted to her family, and she tensed. When Ulrik realized she had run away, the bear would awaken. And he would have nowhere to unleash his anger except at her mother and sisters.

He had always worried they might plot against him—it is why he kept them so close all these months—and now she gave him more reason to.

How would he punish her family while she was away? Without her marriage to Andor, would he even care to keep them alive?

Shutting her eyes, she prayed to the gods to keep them safe from his wrath. Yet in her heart, she knew it was too late for that. For her actions, her family would suffer. It was just a matter of how much they could endure before she returned.

The only thing she could do for them now was hurry. The longer she was away, the more time Ulrik had to torment her family. And the people of Kaldvik suffered, too. She needed to find her uncle quickly, rush back to these shores, and free them. The sooner that happened, the better for all.

The caw of a raven drew her attention. She watched it swoop down and dip its legs into the water, sending ripples across the glassy surface of the fjord. They were a reminder that every action had consequences—some she would never even see with her own eyes.

Taking a deep breath to calm herself, she clutched the amber pendant around her neck. *Freyja, Odin, make me ready for your halls.*

But she was not ready for the Valkyries to find her yet. Tonight, she needed to escape.

A sharp whistle like a birdcall made the hairs on her arms stand on end. Crunching footsteps from the forest told her someone was coming. She froze, clearly exposed on the dock.

A shadowed figure emerged from the treeline. She recognized the broad shoulders and strong stride.

"Balder," she said with a relieved smile. "You came."

The blacksmith led five others behind him. As they stepped into the moonlight, she recognized some of their faces: Skarde the shipbuilder, Frode the fisherman, and Brynja's young friend Erik. With them was a red-haired shieldmaiden and a skinny young man with a sword sheathed at his waist.

"Welcome," she said. "Thank you for coming so quickly. I hoped we would have more time to lay our plans, but time has run out. " She turned to Erik. "I see you were serious when you said you had an axe."

Erik nodded, his eyes flashing in the moonlight. She had never seen signs of battle in him before, but tonight he wore thick leather over his torso, a battle axe strapped to his back. "I failed to fight that night Ulrik killed your father. I will never fail again."

She placed a hand on his shoulder. "I should have lifted my sword that night too. But my father will see our actions now, from Valhalla."

Balder introduced the rest of the party then. "This is the shieldmaiden Dagmar. She fought for several summers alongside your father."

Up close, Svahild noticed a scar trailing across the shield-maiden's left cheek, clipping the side of her lips as it ran down to her chin. Clearly she was experienced in battle, and the gods had seen fit to spare her from death for some purpose.

"It's good to have another woman here," she said.

"I saw you fight Thorbjorn," Dagmar replied. Her voice was a low rasp, like hot coals shifting in a fire. "Both times."

Svanhild winced. "That means you have yet to see me win."

"You fought bravely. I can see the improvement in your skill."

"Perhaps you can teach me more."

Dagmar inclined her head. Her hair shone like orange embers in the moonlight.

"And this is Sten, another loyal warrior from your father's band," Balder continued, gesturing to the skinny warrior. He could not be much older than Erik.

"That's a fine sword," Svanhild commented.

Sten grinned, revealing uneven teeth that made him look even more boyish. "A gift from my father, who earned it from his father before him. Someday, I will pass it on to my son."

"You must come from a great line of warriors."

He turned pink in the moonlight, saying nothing.

"He is," Balder jumped in for him, "but that's a story for another time. You already know Skarde and Frode."

Svanhild nodded her thanks to them. She wasn't sure how

well a shipbuilder and fisherman fought, but she would take all the blades she could.

Still, six warriors was not many. She had hoped for a war band—even a small one, perhaps eight or twelve fighters—but this was barely enough to paddle the ship.

Balder must have noticed the tension in her jaw, for he said, "We had to hurry from Ulrik's hall. We hoped to rally more warriors, but this was all we could collect so quickly, especially with Ulrik watching everyone at the feast."

"Do you think we have more supporters in town?" Svanhild asked hopefully.

Balder nodded. "I believe many more will join us when we return."

Svanhild sighed. If only they had more time. If only Olaf had not attacked her sister. If only...

But there was no point in wishing for another path. This was what the Norns had woven for her.

Now, she would put her trust in the gods.

Taking a deep breath, she looked around at the six who now stood facing her, waiting for her command. Though few in number, they were loyal and armed. For now, that would have to be enough.

A rustling in the trees nearby sent all of their hands to their weapons. Svanhild froze as she waited to see what might emerge from the shadows. She prayed it was just a bear.

"You are forgetting something," came a familiar voice.

Svanhild's breath hitched when Thorbjorn stepped out of the forest and into the moonlight, waving a sword in the air. A wave of relief flooded through her, for with him she would have at least one proven warrior on her side. And after the way he had defended her today, she knew he was loyal.

"Thorbjorn," she said, smiling.

Then, noticing the sword in his hands, she gasped. She would recognize the runes on that blade anywhere.

"Hrafnblóð," she breathed in surprise. "My father's sword. How did you take it?"

"You seem much happier to see the sword than me," Thorbjorn complained, then winked at her. "Found it in some little treasure chest in an old man's chamber. I heard you might like to have it."

Svanhild took the weapon, admiring the runes in the moonlight. She felt the gazes of the others as they studied the weapon up close too, probably for the first time.

A wind blew through the trees, and a dove skittered over the water nearby. Just as she was named for the swan, her father was named for the dove.

Father, I know you are here.

Shivering in the breeze that answered, she inhaled the scent of saltwater and pine trees, the smells of home. A sense of peace washed over her as she recognized her father's presence. He watched over her now.

"I can't believe you thought you would leave me behind," Thorbjorn said, bringing her back to the present. "I brought a few others, too." He gestured to a group of warriors emerging from the trees behind him. Svanhild counted nine in all. "I had to leave one out, or we wouldn't have the sacred number," said Thorbjorn with a grin.

Svanhild laughed. Nine was the number of the gods. "You could have left yourself out."

Thorbjorn put a hand to his heart, feigning a wound at her jest.

Svanhild's hands steadied as she gripped her father's sword, surveying the group before her now. They all wore some sort of armor, with swords at their hips or axes strapped to their backs. Some were fresh of face, others scarred from old battles, but all had powerful builds. These were strong warriors to have at her side. Her heart filled to see them.

Balder's voice interrupted her thoughts. "We need to leave now, little one. Ulrik has noticed you are missing. A search party is out now looking for Olaf's killer."

From the dark look in his eyes, Svanhild sensed he knew she was the killer.

She looked at the others, her heart pounding. Though they may not know the truth, there was no point in keeping secrets from them. This was her band of warriors now. They risked everything to leave with her, to travel to Uppsala, and to one day return for their revenge against Ulrik. Honesty was the least she could offer them now.

"I killed Olaf," she said.

In the hush that followed, her words rang like sharpened steel in the night air. A few of the men's eyes widened in surprise.

"Olaf threatened my sister," she explained. "I did it to save her. I would do it again. I would do anything to protect my sister, my family, and my home. And the same is true of Kaldvik."

She strapped Hrafnblód's sheath around her waist, then placed a hand on the sword's hilt. It was a reminder that she was the daughter of a respected jarl, a man of wisdom who led with his head as well as his heart. She would follow his path now.

"I know I am not the strongest warrior among you," she admitted, "and I have yet to see real battle. Many of you have been fighting far longer, and I admire your skill and strength." She inclined her head to them, a small sign of respect. "More than that, I admire your loyalty. Through these hard winter months, you have stayed true to my family. I know it has not been easy. Ulrik is a poor leader who does not care for the people of Kaldvik. He may be brave, but he is also greedy."

A few of the men nodded in agreement.

"Ulrik is a raider, and raiders are driven more by their greed than their courage. Some of you have suffered this winter from that greed, and I believe Kaldvik will continue to suffer under his leadership."

"If you can even call it leadership," Thorbjorn smirked.

Svanhild nodded. "You all know that my father was quite different than that. I hope to be more like him."

Balder nodded at her in encouragement. She was glad to have him here.

Gazing up at the stars that marked a path through the sky, she prayed aloud, "Odin, watch over your ravens now. Tonight we sail from this land, from our home that we love, from this place that was stolen from us. When we return, we will seek our revenge against this faithless man whose heart is hard as stone. Guide us in our plans, All-Father. Guide your ravens safely to Uppsala, and when we return, bring us the vengeance we so crave."

A horn sounded in the distance. That could only mean one thing: *they knew.*

Svanhild's heart hammered in her chest. "You are all ravens now."

She whipped her gaze around the group to meet each of theirs. She smiled to see the glint in their eyes as they nodded to her, some placing fists over their hearts in silent pledge.

Her ravens were ready.

"That's the ship," Skarde said, pointing to the longship bobbing by the dock.

Svanhild frowned when she recognized the eagle design at the prow. "Andor's ship?"

But there was no time to discuss it. In the distance, the horn sounded again. Skarde's house and private dock were only a short walk from the longhouse. Ulrik and his men could appear at any moment.

Heart pounding, Svanhild jumped aboard Andor's ship. She would have to give it a name to make it her own. The others leapt aboard after her.

Once they were all there, she turned to find Frode Fish-Nose at the prow, watching the horizon. Because this inlet was just around a bend in the river, it wasn't possible to see the village from here. She wondered what he was looking for.

"Are you ready?" she asked him.

Instead of answering, he jumped off the ship. "I am not made for battle. Go without me. I will keep an eye on things while you're gone."

"Are you sure?" she said. "You could fish for us. That alone would be a great help."

He shook his head, his eyes still on the horizon. "I should get back before they notice me gone."

Though Svanhild had always found something unsettling in the fisherman's manner—always looking into the distance, as though lost in his own thoughts—she was sad to see him go. In her plans for revenge, he had been her first ally. "Thank you for everything, Frode," she said.

Watching him walk back into the forest, Svanhild grabbed the prow of the ship. Her fingers brushed the carvings of ruffled feathers at the eagle's neck.

"I wonder what Andor will think when he sees his ship gone," she said aloud. He would know she had taken it.

"Don't feel bad," Skarde said, standing behind her. "I always intended for you to take this ship. Why else would I make it so fast and good-looking?"

Thorbjorn laughed, overhearing. "I can tell I'm going to like you, ship-man," he said.

A third horn sounded in the distance. Svanhild's heart

raced as she pictured Ulrik and his men boarding another longship in the harbor, preparing to give chase.

They needed to hurry.

She looked at the longship then, counting the seats. The people joining her had taken positions on either side. The ship was built to seat twenty men, ten on each side at the oars.

They were fifteen. Thanks to Thorbjorn and his warriors, it was enough.

Svanhild commanded everyone to take an oar. She sat across from Skarde at the back, her knees bent in front of her, the wooden oar hot in her hands as though the gods had dipped it in fire for her.

"We need to row quickly to outpace Ulrik's ships," she shouted. "He will be giving chase now."

Skarde's voice called back over the splashing of oars. "Don't worry, Svanhild. I have destroyed the oars of all the other ships. They will not catch us yet."

She laughed. "I am glad to have you on my side."

"The day I first saw you after your father died, I thought the sun in the sky was a good sign," he admitted. "I always respected your father, but I thought perhaps the gods blessed this new jarl. But I was wrong there." He smiled at her. "I believe I just knew, somewhere in me, that *this* night was coming."

Behind her, Thorbjorn let out a howl, and the others joined in the sound. Svanhild could not keep the smile from her face as they rowed away from the shore, Skarde counting the rhythm for them to move in unison.

Lifting her head, she howled too.

As the ship picked up speed, Skarde drew in his oar and jumped to the center of the ship. When he pulled a rope, a wooden mast shot up from the floor of the ship, soaring over their heads as it reached toward the sky.

Svanhild motioned for the others to stop rowing. Balder jumped up to help Skarde with the rope. Another tug, and a massive sail flew open overhead, ushering the boat faster as it picked up the breeze.

"The wind is with us tonight," Skarde said, securing the rope to a hook.

"Njörd is with us," Svanhild agreed.

The god of wind and sea would guide them now.

Standing at the back of the ship, she watched as another bend in the river brought Kaldvik into view, now little more than a distant light on the horizon.

It was too far for her to see who might be looking for oars, wielding weapons, or shouting commands. Still, she pictured the shadows on the shore were the figures of her mother and sisters, watching her depart. Once again, she prayed the gods would keep them safe until her return.

She felt someone behind her then, a shadow passing over the ship's tail. Turning, she found the blacksmith approaching.

"Your father would have been proud of you, little one," came Balder's voice behind her. "If you killed Olaf to protect your sister, he would call that courage."

"I hope so," she said. Her hands no longer shook, but her stomach twisted at the thought of Olaf's body on the forest floor…

"And you know Andor will forgive you," Balder added.

Svanhild swallowed the lump that formed in her throat. *Andor.* Their last exchange had ended with her refusal to marry him, and when he told her he loved her, she said nothing back. What must he think of her now?

Tears stung her eyes. Not wanting the blacksmith to see them, she kept her face turned away from him, watching the trees and hills rush by on the shore as their ship gathered speed.

If Andor suspected she had killed Olaf, he must think she was gone forever. In his mind, she must be a murderer. A *skogarmaor*—a woman of the forest—cast out for her crimes and forced to run or hide from Ulrik's punishment forever. If he truly loved her earlier tonight, he would not love her anymore.

And here she stood on his stolen ship.

"Do you think he knows why I'm leaving?" she asked at last.

Balder put a hand on her shoulder. "He will find out soon. But people may not realize your intentions to return. With the gods on our side, we might surprise the jarl when we come back to fight."

"And surprise Andor, too?"

Balder's hand left her shoulder. "Let us pray we don't have to fight against the people we love."

At the sound of Balder's retreating footsteps, she closed her eyes, letting the spray of saltwater cool her skin. Her heart ached at the thought of lifting her sword against the man she loved. Yet she knew Andor was not her destiny. This was.

A raven passed overhead, its wings silhouetted against the moon. It was just the sign she needed.

Clouds swept across the sky then, briefly shielding them from the moonlight. She listened to the raven sing overhead. A breeze fluttered her hair as the black bird drew close, then perched on the eagle's head at the prow of the ship.

Thank you, All-Father, she thought. The gods were here.

She glanced back at the people who had been brave enough to join her. Balder stared out at the water, his face pensive. Sten and Erik were asleep, heads on the edge of the boat. Thorbjorn, Skarde, and Dagmar sat in a small circle, knee to knee, playing a game of dice on the floor of the ship.

Other warriors sat in silence, watching the scenery pass by. All seemed content. At least for now.

She looked forward to meeting her uncle again, though she frowned when she realized she would have to deliver the news of her father's death. But Asmund would know what to do. And with the gods' favor, they would have time to make new allies in Uppsala.

The ravens would have their revenge.

She touched the hilt of her father's sword again. No, *her* sword. Her mother had passed it to her, and its story was now hers to weave.

Hrafnblóð. Raven's blood. She felt it coursing through her now.

She realized now she did not seek revenge only out of anger. No, she did this for her family. She sent a silent prayer of thanks for them now—for her mother who trained her to wield Hrafnblóð, for her sister Haldis who showed her the gods' path, for Brynja who had seen too much yet still showed courage.

As the sky brightened overhead, she began a song to commemorate their trip. It was the saga of a shieldmaiden, a woman who braved Hel to retrieve a legendary sword. Perhaps that weapon was not unlike the one she wielded now.

She clutched Hrafnblóð tighter. Was her father watching from Valhalla now? With their sword in her hands, she felt his presence.

She would make him proud. And someday, when the Norns fated it, she would see him again in Valhalla.

Gods, guide my path, she prayed.

A laugh sounded in response. She froze, for it could only be Loki, here to cause mischief again.

Hurry while you can, shieldmaiden, but you can never outrun your heart.

TOPICS AND QUESTIONS FOR DISCUSSION

1. Which of the three sisters—Svanhild, Haldis, or Brynja—did you relate to the most, and why?

2. Svanhild makes many sacrifices for her family. Do you think she made the right choice in agreeing to marry Andor? What would you have done in her place?

3. Andor is the son of the enemy, yet he shows unexpected gentleness. Did your opinion of him change throughout the book? Can a person truly stand apart from the sins of their father?

4. Haldis struggles to believe in her own power and connection to the gods. How do doubt and faith shape her journey?

5. Brynja is often protected by her family, yet she faces her own challenges. What role does innocence play in the story, and how does it evolve?

6. Helga, the girls' mother, was once a shieldmaiden. How does her past shape their future? What do you think of the way she navigates her role under Ulrik's rule?

7. The sisters each have very different relationships with their father. How do those relationships influence their decisions and identities throughout the book?

8. Secrets are a recurring theme—whether it's Svanhild's secret training or Haldis hiding her doubts. How does secrecy protect the sisters, and how does it isolate them?

9. The story is deeply inspired by Norse mythology and Viking culture. Did any mythological or cultural elements stand out to you or surprise you?

10. At the end of the book, Svanhild sails away to seek allies. What do you think awaits her next? What do you hope for each of the sisters in the next book?

AUTHOR'S NOTE

When I was in college, I studied both history and literature, because I couldn't choose between them. Fast forward 15 years, and I still enjoy both while writing historical fantasy books!

Writing a Viking story is an interesting challenge, because there's only so much we know about these people who lived 1,000 years ago. They used runes to scratch notes to each other and decorate monuments, but that's pretty much the extent of our firsthand written records. Vikings shared their stories orally rather than writing them down.

So what we know of Viking life comes from a.) the secondhand accounts of foreign visitors, b.) sagas written hundreds of years after the fact, and c.) archaeological evidence. How much can we glean from these sources? I like to think a lot... but we have to use educated guesswork and imagination to fill in the blanks.

Song of the Shieldmaiden is a work of fiction, but I did my best to root it in historical accuracy. I enjoy the research involved in writing historical fiction—in fact, it's one of the reasons I write this genre!

For example, I studied Norse mythology to get into the mindset of how Vikings thought about the world. What would they think if they saw a raven flying through the sky? They must have thought it was a sign from the gods—perhaps even one of Odin's twin ravens. I also learned the kinds of crops Vikings grew on their farms, the meals they probably cooked, the clothes they wore, and the weapons they wielded. When I came to a point in the story where I *didn't* know something, I left myself a note to research further. After researching, if I still had no answers—either because history is a mystery, or because I wasn't able to find a source—I used my imagination. That's just what I do as a fiction writer. And it's that balance between history and fiction that makes writing this genre so fascinating for me.

Now, I'll admit there *are* a few instances where I chose my story over historical accuracy. For instance, there is a scene where Andor gets a tattoo—but there is very little historical evidence that Vikings actually had tattoos. This might seem strange to fans of shows like *The Vikings;* modern-day Viking fiction is filled with tattooed characters, right? But it's more likely that foreign accounts of Vikings with tattoos were actually talking about paint. Yet I fancied that image of the tattooed Viking, and I also liked that bit of character development for Andor. So I gave him a tattoo.

That said, if you are interested in learning more about the *real* Vikings, I highly recommend *Children of Ash and Elm* by Neil Price as a starting point. I also share other book recommendations as I read them in my newsletter.

There are also wonderful online resources, such as FollowtheVikings.com and Viking Valley, where I spent hours exploring Viking life.

And Neil Gaimen's *Norse Mythology* is a wonderful introduction to, well, Norse mythology.

Finally, I often share fun facts from my Viking research on my blog if you'd like to learn a little there, too. Happy reading!

ACKNOWLEDGMENTS

This book has been in my head and my heart for many moons, and I am so grateful for all the opportunities that came together to allow me to share this book with readers. Publishing this novel has been a dream come true for me. And I could not have written *Song of the Shieldmaiden* without the help and support of many others.

First off, I must thank my mom Brenda, who encouraged me in my writing from a young age and still cheers me on today. Thank you for your unconditional support, and for being such a wonderful example of living a creative life.

Thanks also to my early readers, members of writing groups who offered advice, and especially my critique partner Christine, who has supported me as only a fellow writer can. I look forward to many more years of swapping chapters!

Thanks also to my good friend and fellow book-lover Megan, who read this story before release and encouraged me in my self-publishing journey. I am so grateful for our friendship.

I must also give a huge shout out to my friend Diane, who has not only read every book but supported my career in countless ways. She is the mastermind behind the *Daughters of Valhalla* wiki, my cheerleader whenever I have a new idea or book release, and my QA tester who always finds the bugs in my work! Thank you for going the extra mile to help me in my writing journey.

A huge thank you goes to my husband Roberto, who not

only paved the road for me to become a published author in every possible way, but also made this book so much better than it originally was. I am thankful for all the times you stayed up with me into the early hours of the morning, discussing the story and providing invaluable feedback. This book is what it is because of you.

Finally, thanks to my inspiring little sister Alyssa. You're still my best friend, and I write about sisters because of you.

SPECIAL THANKS

A very special thank you to my November 2022 Kickstarter backers, who made the physical editions of these books possible. You have made a significant impact on my author career, and I am grateful to each of you:

Cynthia M Coffman
Roberto Cataneo
Diane Martinez
Alex Strom
Jesikah Sundin
Dragondarium
Nicholas Kotar
Lyn Perry
Megan
Sarah
Hana Correa
Amanda
Alyssa Scheepers
Ty Patterson
Linda Rumsey
Melanie
Holly
Michael Brooker
Kthylla Rutherford
Brenda Hagood
BennyBunny
Nicole
Sabrina D
Jade Alters
Elza
Esapekka Eriksson

Scott Casey
Lindsay D
Brittnay King
Emily Prebich
Ernie Ridley
PunkARTchick *Ruthenia*
Chris Burkhart
Vicky S.
Jennifer P. Wick
Karen Bulgarelli
R. A. Morley
Tamara Hart Heiner
Ellen Pilcher
John Idlor
Gerald P. McDaniel
Megyn "Crimson" MacDougall
Lisa Ferland
Tessa
Jerome Anello
Kathy Brady
Elizabeth Van Doren
Jessica Cassidy
R.S. Johansen
Holly Colvin
Cassie Greutman
Richard Novak
Christina Phillips

Alicia Wanstall-Austin
Tom Gray
Anij Fallows
Kerry Chorvat
Katrina Gilles
Eric Vilbert
Heather Tingl
Alyssa Lucero
Seamus
Sara
Yves Heim
Katherine Shipman
Lavonne Bjelland Chin
Jonathan Veguilla
Elio Garcia
Kristy, The Sleeper
Dani'el Norman
James Manion
Christian Roessiger
Laura Nelson
Birgitte
Jonah Pavlicek
Erik S
Remy Don
Mary McKenna
Luis Andrés

SPECIAL NOTE

ABOUT THE AUTHOR

Ashley Hagood crafts mythic fantasy brimming with action, magic, and heart. She especially loves writing fierce heroines and exploring deep family bonds in historical and fantastical settings. A history major turned web designer, she swapped a career in video games for the adventure of being a full-time author.

Off the page, Ashley embarks on imaginary quests with her son, levels up in role-playing games like *Dragon Age*, and devours books. She lives in California with her husband, son, and a cat who's convinced she's a Valkyrie.

www.ingramcontent.com/pod-product-compliance
Lightning Source LLC
Chambersburg PA
CBHW020927260626
47169CB00006B/1611